BY LINDSAY CAMERON

Biglaw

JUST ONE LOOK

JUST
one
LOOK

A Novel

LINDSAY
CAMERON

BALLANTINE BOOKS
NEW YORK

Published in the United States by Ballantine Books, an imprint of Random House, a division of Penguin Random House LLC, New York.

BALLANTINE and the HOUSE colophon are registered trademarks of Penguin Random House LLC.

Hardback ISBN 978-0-593-15905-7
Ebook ISBN 978-0-593-15906-4

Printed in Canada on acid-free paper

randomhousebooks.com

9 8 7 6 5 4 3 2 1

First Edition

Book design by Diane Hobbing

To my parents, Robin and Elizabeth, my biggest cheerleaders

JUST ONE LOOK

He has no idea that I have access to every corner of his life. Even the dusty ones. I can see the messages he's composed and the notes his loved ones have written him in response. There are photos, receipts, reminders, reservations. He has no secrets from me. I know where he's been, who he's met, and most important, all about his lovely wife. I might as well be living inside his head.

Eyes aren't the windows to the soul. Emails are.

Chapter One

As I STEPPED off the elevator on the second floor, I found myself silently begging for a calamity. A fire, a flash flood, even a tiny earthquake would suffice. Anything that would give me a legitimate reason to evacuate the area immediately. Or, better yet, I wouldn't make it out in time and the somber voice of Brian Williams would detail my demise on the nightly news. *Cassie Woodson entered the midtown office building on the first day of her new job mere seconds before the entire skyscraper was reduced to rubble by the powerful explosion.*

Calling this a "new job" would be generous, though. That implied some degree of longevity. But hopefully Brian Williams would throw me a bone.

I smoothed my hands over my wrinkled pants and scanned for a floor directory, feeling disoriented. It had been six months since I stepped foot inside an office building—or almost anywhere outside of my apartment for that matter—and there was something about the buzz from the overhead lights that was making me dizzy. Or maybe it was just being in the upright position for longer than the time it took to walk from my couch to the bathroom.

"There will be a temporary employee badge waiting for you at the reception desk in the lobby. From there, you need to take the elevator to the second floor and head to Room 241," the man from the temp agency had painstakingly explained on my voicemail last night, as if he was giving directions to a confused toddler.

He was obviously in need of the fee he received for placing me. There was a note of foreboding in his tone when he finished with, "I told them you were coming, so *don't* go AWOL." I wondered how many of his clients accepted a job and promptly went AWOL. If it was more than zero, it wasn't a good sign.

A petite woman with an armload of accordion files and a no-nonsense expression emerged from one of the numbered doors and walked briskly toward the elevator bank. I stood up straighter and threw my shoulders back, trying to force my body to emit a sense of composure I wasn't really feeling.

"Can I help you with something, hon?" she asked, arching a quizzical brow.

If only you could. I swallowed hard and said, "I'm just looking for Room 241."

"Second door on your right." She gestured with her head as she stepped onto the elevator.

"Thanks," I called out as the doors banged shut. The dread that had been accumulating since morning collected in my throat.

It's only temporary, I silently repeated to myself, wishing the Advil I'd chased with Pepto minutes ago would somehow help dull the thoughts ricocheting in my head. Clearly, I needed something stronger.

Room 241 was beside the emergency exit door, and as I chewed my lip, briefly considering which one to open, the voice of the *Let's Make a Deal* game show host ran through my mind. *Cassie Woodson, do you want door number one or door number two?* I was almost certainly going to pick the door that had a family of goats bleating behind it instead of the shiny new car, but what choice did I have? I couldn't go AWOL or I wouldn't get a paycheck. And I was fresh out of other options. It was bleating goats or be evicted from my apartment for not paying my rent.

I took a deep breath, cautiously put my hand on the chrome door handle, pushed it open, and stepped inside Room 241.

"Seriously? Another one?" A beaky-faced man called out when I entered the bunker-like room. "Shit," he huffed. "That must mean we're getting another data dump if the higher-ups are sending in more troops." He pushed his chair back from his spot on the long, industrial table of computers, stood up, and dusted his fingertips against his leg, spreading powdered sugar streaks all over his black pants.

"I'm Ricky." He stuck out his hand. "Staff attorney extraordinaire. I run the ship around here."

"I'm Cassie." I shook his clammy palm and forced a smile. My eyes darted around the windowless room which, judging from the piles of banker's boxes pushed into the corners, doubled as a storage area. I had the sudden feeling that the stained white walls were closing in on me, constricting around my lungs.

Deep breaths.

"Cassie." Ricky nodded, furrowing his brow, as if rolling the word around in his head. "Well, Cassie, I didn't know the temp agency was sending over a new girl today so your arrival is news to me." I cringed at both the word "girl" and "agency." It made me feel like Peggy Olson showing up for her first day at Sterling Cooper. Except Peggy was embarking on an upward career trajectory, but I most certainly was not.

"I was . . . I was given this at the reception desk." I held up my laminated ID card that read TEMP 021.

He took the card and studied it like a border guard inspecting a passport before handing it back to me and exhaling a frustrated sigh. "Well, one of the associates or partners up there must have called for you." He pointed at the ceiling when he said "up there," reminding me that we were, quite literally, at the bottom of the legal industry's totem pole. The real lawyers, the ones with titles and offices and steady paychecks, were thirty floors above us, while the temps were relegated down below, like steerage passengers on the *Titanic.*

"Okay, guys." Ricky whirled around, addressing the room. There were four rows of computers, each with a faceless person clicking robotically at the mouse. Ricky waved his arms around like he was hailing a rescue helicopter and waited as the robotic

mouse-clickers removed their earbuds, peered over their computers, and reluctantly gave Ricky their attention. They reminded me
of a family of moles peeking out of their dark holes.

"We've got a new girl from the temp agency," Ricky called out.
"So, I think this means we can expect more documents to be
dumped on the server today."

I gave an awkward wave, not sure if I should introduce myself
to the group by name. Considering my username was Temp 021
maybe they didn't really do names around here. The knots in my
stomach tightened. Four years of college, three years of law school,
and the hardest bar exam in the country and this is who I had become: the new girl from the temp agency.

"Follow me, Cassie." Ricky gestured to me, leading the way
down a row of chairs. "Your station is the one closest to the wall."

I sucked in my breath to squeeze behind the chairs, repeating
"excuse me" quietly, but everyone had already replaced their earbuds and turned their attention back to mouse-clicking. I blinked
back unexpected tears. I knew working as a temp would be a step
down from being a law firm associate—you can't take a sixty percent pay cut and not realize your career is moving in the wrong
direction—but this was even worse than I had envisioned. I
thought temps would be assigned cubicles, but the only walls in
this place were the ones holding up the building. No one had a
separate desk or even a phone—just a computer, a chair, and barely
enough personal space to blow your nose.

I felt the heavy weight of claustrophobia on the back of my
neck.

"So, did your last temp job wrap up recently?" Ricky asked.

My fingers curled tighter around my purse strap. *Careful now.
Careful.*

"Um . . . yes. About a week ago," I said, wiping my suddenly
damp palms against my leg. I've never been someone who could
lie without an instant physiological reaction. Landon once told me
he'd never met anyone who suffered as much anxiety as I did from
telling a white lie. *I can never take you to Vegas*, he'd joke. *You'll lose
all our money at the poker table with those tells of yours.* He'd smile that

crooked smile of his and wrap his arms around me, as if my tells were just one of the many ways he found me irresistible, while I would think of nothing other than how he'd used the word "our," like we were an inseparable unit.

Fuck Landon.

I had to resist the urge to pull out my phone and send him a text saying exactly that. *Fuck. You.*

And fuck me for tossing off that lie to Ricky for no good reason other than I wanted to nip the line of questioning in the bud. Now I was going to have to remember that I was supposed to have worked at another temp job a week ago in case Ricky brought it up later. I would have to come up with a few unverifiable details to substantiate the story.

More lies added to the pile.

"Here we are—workstation twenty-one." Ricky gestured grandly to the black pilled swivel chair and a computer that was likely acquired during the Bush administration. The first one. "Your new home." He smiled and I couldn't help but notice he had powdered sugar on the cracks of his lips. I looked away, feeling embarrassed for him.

"This project started about two weeks ago so everyone else in here is already up and running. I'll get you the binder with the information on the background of the case we're all working on, but the long and the short of it is our client, Falcon Healthcare, is being sued for Medicare fraud in a whistleblower complaint so we need to review both internal and external databases to weed through which documents or emails would be responsive. The alleged fraud goes back five years and Falcon is one of Levy & Strong's biggest clients, so it's a huge data set. The keyword search narrowed it down for us, but still spit out hundreds of thousands of documents and correspondence, so we've got a lot to sift through. As you know, all kinds of crap gets caught in a keyword search." He rolled his eyes as if a keyword search were a mischievous but lovable toddler.

I nodded, doing my best to appear engaged, as my eyes drifted to the man two rows back who bore a strong resemblance to the

Unabomber with his sunglasses and hood up. He appeared to be either asleep, passed out, or deceased. Thankfully, I noticed his chest rising and falling, which ruled out option number three.

"Our job is to do the first-pass review and weed out all the obvious crap. No need to worry about privileged versus non-privileged at this point. The higher-ups will take care of that after we narrow down the data set. Here . . ." Ricky continued, swiping the screensaver away with the mouse. "Your password is the same as your username," he explained as he tapped on the keyboard.

"Should I change the password once I get started?" I asked, noticing the Unabomber had now twitched himself awake and was back to mouse-clicking.

Ricky shot me a look as if I'd raised the possibility of setting fire to my computer.

"Why would you want to do that?" he asked incredulously.

I felt my face flush. "I just thought for . . . um . . . confidentiality reasons." My voice trailed up, sounding more like I was asking a question than answering one.

Ricky shook his head. "Just use the preset one. That's the way it is for all the temps. It makes it easier for the firm in the event that you stop showing up for work one day, which has been known to happen. Your password is always your username. No secrets around here." He eyed me for a beat longer than necessary before turning his attention back to the monitor.

"Okay, here's your home screen. Basically, what you need to do is open your 'unread' folder." He moved the mouse and clicked while he spoke. "The centralized database sorts documents to be reviewed into each temp's unread folder based on date range, so you'll have documents from both our server and our client's server to move through, but they'll all be clustered around the same date." He squinted at my screen. "Looks like you'll be working from the early 2019 section of the database. Once you've brought up a document from your folder you need to review to see if it's relevant. Then check the box for either responsive or nonresponsive, depending on your determination. Lather, rinse, repeat." He straightened up and folded his arms across his scrawny chest.

"Sounds simple enough." I forced a smile, as if I hadn't already learned the ins and outs of document review for e-discovery during my five-year legal career. *Monkey work*—that's what we called it when I was one of the "higher-ups." Except when we reviewed documents for e-discovery we did it in the comfort of our glass-walled offices with high-backed leather chairs and even higher paychecks. We had to endure our time doing monkey work during our first year as lawyers, but we knew it was a necessary evil in our inevitable ascent up the corporate ladder. Everyone had to pay her dues. I'd certainly paid mine. For five long years. But like a cruel game of Chutes and Ladders, I'd somehow landed on the wrong space and slid back down to the beginning.

"Well," Ricky huffed, looking slightly piqued. "It's not as simple as it sounds. You need to be focused and have a keen legal eye. There's no room for error on this."

"Of course," I answered, a little stiffly. God my head was aching. I wondered how soon I could excuse myself to go to the bathroom and crack open the mini-bottle of Don Julio in my purse. The Advil clearly wasn't up to the task today.

"This used to be work that first-year associates would do before clients decided they didn't want to foot the bill for their four-hundred-dollar-an-hour rate. That's when law firms realized it made more sense to have a dedicated team of temp lawyers whose sole focus is to review documents. That's where you come in—cheaper and more efficient for the client." He said this like he'd single-handedly solved the law firm's cost-inefficiency problem himself. *Just take twenty attorneys desperate for jobs and heavily laden with the burden of student loan debt and offer them twenty-five dollars an hour and no benefits—problem solved!*

"So, let me go over the rules around here then. One." He held up an index finger. "When you need to go to the bathroom you have to sign out on the clipboard by the door." He gestured to where a tattered clipboard hung from a hook on the wall. I narrowed my eyes and noticed the heading BATHROOM BREAKS had been crossed out, replaced with SHIT BREAKS with a sketch of a stick figure on a toilet, giving it a "frat house meets nerdy men's prison" vibe.

My stomach twisted. I shouldn't be here.

"Try to keep your bathroom breaks to under two per shift," Ricky cautioned.

I nodded, picturing the first day of law school when I'd crowded into the lecture hall along with three hundred of my peers at Penn State Law to hear the dean welcome the new 1Ls to the school. "You—the future of the legal profession—will have the skills to adapt to the new economy," he'd boomed, while we hung on every word like he was some kind of Wall Street prophet. I wondered now what he would think about one of his former students adjusting to the new economy by working in a bunker with monitored "shit breaks."

"Two." Ricky counted it off on his stubby fingers. "Meals. We have a lunch break and a dinner break. We get twenty dollars for dinner, but it must be used at the firm cafeteria on the thirty-fifth floor. The breaks last for thirty minutes each and you can't eat your food at your workstation because last month we had a major cockroach problem. Those suckers were everywhere. And three, make sure you have your ID badge on at all times." He held up the tattered laminated ID badge around his neck. "Capisce?"

I unclenched my jaw. "Capisce."

Ricky looked me up and down, seemingly evaluating my worth, gauging whether I was a suitable foot soldier, before giving a brusque nod.

"Oh, and some of the stuff you read is going to be . . ." He hesitated. "Sensitive."

"Sensitive," I echoed, nodding. "Right. Is there a separate folder where you want me to put the confidential or privileged documents?"

He shook his head and a dark blush crept across his neck. "No, I don't mean privileged or confidential. I mean . . ." He lowered his voice. "Well, the keyword search is supposed to weed out personal emails, but that isn't always successful if you know what I mean." He raised his eyebrows indicating we were both in on the same secret.

Out of the corner of my eye I saw the ruddy-faced guy at the computer next to mine smirk.

Ricky glared at him and cleared his throat, regaining his no-nonsense edge. "So, when you come across those emails you obviously don't read them, you mark them nonresponsive and move on to the next document."

I nodded, remembering that when I'd done document review in the past the paralegals would've already done a first-pass cursory review and culled any personal emails errantly caught in the search, leaving only work-related correspondence behind for the lawyers to review. The most sensitive email I'd ever seen in document review was an email between associates complaining about the number of hours they were working. Certainly nothing juicy enough to cause the red tide that had swept across Ricky's cheeks now.

Maybe this was going to be more interesting than I thought.

Later, when Ricky had returned to his workstation and I clicked open the first document to review, Ricky's parting line was still ringing in my ears.

You'd be surprised how much people are willing to reveal in an email.

Chapter Two

THERE WERE SIXTEEN warm bodies, other than mine, all crammed into Room 241 and, even after a few days on the job, that was all I could really tell you about them: They were warm bodies. At least I assumed so. I hadn't actually heard their voices and the only proof of life was the tiny tap of their index fingers on the mouse and the occasional trip to the bathroom. My coworkers could've communicated solely with clicks for all I knew. Which was why I was startled when my ruddy-faced seatmate plopped down at my table in the cafeteria during our dinner break on my fifth night on the job.

"There's no way that's good enough to eat every night," he said, gesturing to my plate of garlic stir-fry, the same meal I'd eaten for the past four dinners. It was the cheapest thing on the menu in the firm cafeteria that would still fill me up, leaving me thirteen dollars in my dinner stipend to spend on yogurt and granola bars I could stockpile for breakfast and lunch.

"It's not terrible," I said, startled by his boldness, as I shifted my tray closer to me to make room for his. It was the longest sentence I'd heard him utter since my first day of work when he'd given a perfunctory introduction (mumbling, "The name's Dalton—welcome to the jungle") before turning his attention back to his computer. He had dark hair, cut short in an attempt to hide the fact that it was thinning, patchy stubble, and the only thing I knew about him, other than his name, was that he smelled like a mix of maple syrup and shaving cream. Thankfully, given our close proximity, it wasn't a terrible combination.

"Well, you're violating the first rule of temping," Dalton said, arranging the food on his tray just so. "Rule number one." He planted his elbow on the table and held up an index finger. "Our days are mundane and repetitive; your meal should not be."

A smile twitched on my lips as I peered down at a wilted green pepper on the plate. It looked like a slimy worm slithering away from a bed of rice. "You make a good point. And I think I prefer that rule over any of the ones Ricky gave me," I ventured.

Dalton chuckled and shook his head. "Can you believe the shit that guy says? You'd think we were a group of preschoolers with some of those rules. Except preschoolers are at least allowed to go to the bathroom when they want." He dunked his French dip sandwich in the tiny bowl of gravy and took a bite.

"This has to be one of the worst gigs I've had in a while," he said between chews.

I nodded and poked at a piece of rice with my fork, struggling to think of what to say next. Spending six months holed up in your apartment tends to dull your social instincts. Not that I had a deep well to begin with.

"So . . . um . . . have you been doing this for a while?" I managed.

Dalton dabbed his mouth. "This gig? Or temping in general?" He didn't wait for a response before answering. "I've been working at this gig for three weeks and temping since I graduated law school four years ago."

I tried to keep my eyes from widening in horror. *Four* years of temping. I remembered an internal email I'd reviewed a few hours ago: *I've been working on the Falcon Health FDA issue all day and am STARVING. Let's hit the cafeteria before the hordes of temps get there! Those guys are like wild animals!* Before I clicked "nonresponsive" I'd checked the date on the email—March 3, 2019—and wondered what project that particular horde of temps had worked on and where they were now. Were any of them still here? The thought of still doing temp work four years from now made my stomach churn.

"What about you?" Dalton leaned in conspiratorially. "I heard you say you came over from another temp job, but I got the distinct feeling you were lying to little Ricky."

I felt my face flush as a stab of regret pierced through my body. It seemed to be my default state now: regretful. It was only the degrees of regret that varied.

"Don't worry, everyone lies to Ricky." Dalton smiled disarmingly. "Just the other day I told him I had to leave early because of the Jewish holiday. Well (a) I'm not Jewish and (b) it wasn't even a holiday. But he bought it hook, line, and sinker." He leaned back and crossed his arms over his chest, clearly pleased with himself. "So, what's your story? Are you fresh outta law school?"

I fidgeted with my napkin. "No, I worked at a firm before this," I replied vaguely, tucking a piece of hair behind my ear. "For a while."

"Oh yeah?" Dalton leaned forward, his interest piqued.

"Yeah, but things didn't really work out there." I shrugged one shoulder, as if it was all just too tiresome and uninteresting to explain any further. Intentional omissions were my specialty.

Dalton nodded, studying me as if he was trying to figure out what cards I was holding from across a poker table. I wondered if he was going to press on with questions, but after a minute he sucked his teeth and said, "That really sucks."

More than you know. I picked up my drink and took a long gulp from my straw to fill the suddenly heavy silence.

"Well, I figured this was your first temp gig because you don't look like a temp," he said after a moment.

I released a high, strangled laugh. "Thanks, I think."

"I just mean you don't look dead behind the eyes like the rest of us." He jerked his head in the direction of the table beside us where four of our colleagues sat, all staring vacantly at the screens of their phones while they shoveled food into their mouths. Their scruffy hair, hunched backs, and averted eyes were a sharp contrast to the group of four impeccably groomed twenty-something men with expensive haircuts and finely tailored suits strutting past our table like a group of alpha chimps with grins so wide you'd think they'd just successfully hunted the Cheshire cat. You could practically hear Jane Goodall's voice, *The alpha male attains his high-ranking position through intimidation and dominance displays.* They backslapped another alpha chimp before sliding into chairs around a table in the center of the room. The temp attorneys all congregated in the same block of tables night after night, while the lawyers who did not work in the bowels of the building all sat on the other side, like a law firm version of *West Side Story.* I knew which side of the tracks I belonged on now.

I bit my lip. Threads of anxiety twisted together, pressing on my insides and evoking a familiar feeling of injustice. I wondered what my old friends at Nolan & Wright would think if they could see me now. Of course, thinking of them as "friends" was a bit of a stretch. "Former colleagues" would be more accurate. I imagined telling them I couldn't even get an interview for anything other than a temporary position paying less than most partners paid their nannies, watching their jaws drop in shock, the uncomfortable silence as if I'd revealed I had started a career as a street corner prostitute.

It was a struggle for me too, reconciling what the truth used to be with what the truth was now.

Dalton followed my gaze. "What a group of entitled fucks, huh?"

I nodded, extremely grateful none of their faces looked familiar to me. They wouldn't know me. There was a small chance they would know *of* me thanks to the legal gossip blogs that detailed my swift exit from my former firm with Machiavellian glee, but they wouldn't connect the dots. They wouldn't glance in my direction with a delighted expression of recognition crossing their faces as it hit them. *Hey, aren't you that girl? The one from that firm? The one who . . .*

"You see that guy with the red power tie?" Dalton gestured with his chin.

I peered at the group. "You mean the one giving the other guy the finger?"

Dalton snorted. "I don't even have to look back in that direction to know that's the one." He rolled his eyes before continuing. "Well, I happen to know he's getting fired at his next review."

My ears perked up. "Really? How do you know that?"

He shrugged, a tiny smirk playing at his lips. "I have my ways."

I raised a curious eyebrow.

"Okay." He dropped his voice and I had to lean in farther to hear him. "I came across an email last night in the review from one of the corporate partners. This guy named Forest. I remember because I couldn't help thinking about how many times this guy must have heard 'Run, Forest, run!' in his life." He stopped to chuckle at his own joke. "Anyway, this Forest guy sent an email to another partner saying that Will Chambers's work wasn't up to snuff for a fourth-year associate and they should terminate him at the next review." He shook his head. "These guys just can't help themselves from using asshat words like 'terminate.'" Dalton scrunched up his face and, in his best Arnold Schwarzenegger voice, repeated the word "terminate" before launching into a full-blown Arnold Schwarzenegger impression. "I'll be back! Hasta la vista, baby!"

I cast another look over at Red Power Tie, who was gesticulating wildly about something while the others nodded in agreement. I was staring openly now, confident in the knowledge that guys like him never noticed what was happening beyond the two-foot radius around them.

"But how do you know that guy over there is Will Chambers?" I asked, cocking my head. "Do you know him?"

"Of course not. Do I look like a person that knows a guy like that?"

I shrugged, but I understood what he meant. Dalton had a lanky build and thick glasses—the kind worn by people who've destroyed their eyes by squinting at a computer screen all day. He was the type of guy who would've been shoved in lockers by the Red Power Ties of the world.

"I looked him up on the firm website," Dalton explained, a sly grin spreading across his face. "After I read that email I had to know which one of those fuckers was going down."

"Geez, poor guy."

"Poor guy, nothing." Dalton scoffed. "Do you have any idea how much those guys get paid?"

Dalton kept talking, but I found my gaze drawn back to Will Chambers. It was surprisingly enjoyable, this feeling of being privy to insider information. I couldn't help but feel a surge of power from the fact that I had this knowledge about his future while he remained foolishly unaware. *I know something you don't know,* I wanted to sing. My eyes scanned the other three satisfied faces at the table, suddenly wishing I had inside information about them too.

I returned my focus to Dalton, who had finished his rant about our working conditions and was now midchew. "Your folder must have emails that are more recent than mine," I said. "All of mine are from over six months ago."

He swallowed hard and ran his tongue over his teeth before answering. "Yeah, the date range for this project is crazy. It's going back, like, five years. Ricky said he thinks this gig could go on for *months* with the number of documents that still need to be reviewed." He said this like it was a good thing so I kept my expression neutral.

Months. I put my fork down, feeling nausea rise in the back of my throat. *Months from now I could still be doing this. Mindlessly clicking a fucking mouse.*

A loud laugh erupted from the table of Will Chambers. Dalton crossed his arms over his chest and glared in their direction. "God, I hope I come across another termination email. I want to see *all* of those guys annihilated like the termites they are."

He must have misinterpreted the discontent on my face for disapproval because he said, "Hey, you aren't one of those rule followers, are you? The ones who actually listen to Ricky and don't read all the juicy personal emails that show up in our review?"

I shook my head, hoping the heat on my cheeks didn't reveal exactly how often I was disregarding Ricky's instruction. The truth was that the only thing getting me through the days was the times I came across an email with a spark of humanity in it. It didn't even have to be salacious. My highlights so far:

I've been working all day on the Falcon Health case so haven't had the time to ask you about your date—how was it?

   Ugh the worst! The guy has two obsessions—credit scores and feet

I've billed 210 hours this month. If the Falcon case doesn't settle soon, I'm never going to get laid.

   Look on the bright side, working long hours means you don't have to pay for birth control!!

No wonder Ricky had blushed. These people didn't exactly follow the "don't put anything in an email that you don't want on the front page of *The New York Times*" rule. Their personal emails got caught up in the cache of emails that were part of our review because of the unwise decision to include the name of the client in the email. Falcon—*bing!* The keyword search flags the email as potentially relevant to our case and their personal correspondence becomes fodder for temp gossip.

I loved reading those emails. There was something about being privy to other people's private conversations that I treasured. It was as if someone pried open the door of my solitary confinement cell and invited me to join the group again. I pictured myself leaning up against a mahogany bookshelf with the women from that email exchange, my hands wrapped around a warm cup of coffee we'd picked up on our Starbucks run, joking with them about a horrible date, or commiserating over our mutual loathing of the long hours. And for a moment—a tiny one, but a moment nonetheless—I would forget.

"Good," Dalton said, interrupting my thoughts. "Because these people share their secrets like drunk reality show contestants. You would not believe some of the crazy shit I've read on this project." He smirked as he twirled his index finger. "I could probably tell you something personal about every person in this room."

I raised my eyebrows. I couldn't decide if I was intrigued or creeped out. Probably a bit of both.

"Knowledge is power, Cassie," he said with a degree of intensity that was unsettling.

I nodded, wondering how much Dalton already knew about *me* before he sat down. If he went out of his way to google the name of an associate in the corporate department simply because he wanted to know who was getting fired, he was certainly capable of googling the girl at the workstation beside him. But he probably wouldn't be sitting here talking to me if he had.

"Wait, why was there an email from a partner in the corporate department in your review folder?" I asked, my mind still stuck on Will Chambers. "I thought the only Falcon Health emails we're looking at are from the litigation department."

Dalton shrugged. "It's not my job to question the keyword searches. Those things are like the Amazon algorithm—no one knows how the hell it works. Besides, they don't pay us to think." The smirk returned to his face. "You'll learn, Temp 021. If that is your real name." He raised an eyebrow dramatically.

I exhaled a snort. "Why do you think they do that anyway? Can't they just give us a username that's our real name?"

He shrugged like the answer was obvious. "It's like how the U.S. Army makes everyone shave his head so they all look the same. They're trying to take away our identities in order to crush our spirit and make us follow orders blindly."

As if on cue, the group of temps beside us stood, trays in hands, like obedient foot soldiers.

"Well, I guess that's our signal. Thirty minutes on the nose." Dalton picked up his tray. "Come on—let's go see who else is getting teeeer-minated."

Chapter Three

MY GRANDMOTHER USED to say that "destiny" was a term coined for lazy people. "There isn't some hocus-pocus, mystical force guiding your life," she would say, rolling her eyes at the absurdity of the thought. "If you make bad choices, then you'll be stuck with them." Staring down the barrel of another demoralizing day clicking a mouse, I'd say I agreed with her. There was no mystical force steering my directionless ship. I certainly wouldn't have believed that this was where I would be sitting—in a pilled swivel chair, underneath an overhead light that flicked at strobe-like intervals, and squinting at a dusty computer screen—when Grandma's theory was proven wrong.

If Dalton hadn't been talking about him last night at dinner I wouldn't have thought twice before marking the email nonresponsive. One quick scan could tell me it was clearly a personal email and not even one Dalton would refer to as juicy. When I noticed his name, though, I thought about Red Power Tie getting terminated, which was enough to make me stop and give the email a closer read.

That was when my relationship with Forest Watts began.

To: Annabelle Watts
From: Forest Watts

Got your voicemail—love hearing your voice when I'm at work. That's great news about the sale! I'm so proud of you. I knew you could do it, my love. Let's celebrate tonight! I'm in a meeting now, but as soon as it's done I'll head out and come home early. I'll pick up dinner from Scalini on the way and we can open a bottle of Caymus. I love you and can't wait to see you. xo

I peered at the screen, rereading the words until my eyes blurred. Even though I'd come across an email an hour earlier with sexual details that would make Dr. Ruth blush, this message was somehow far more intimate. Special. These two people could not even make it through the *day* without connecting with each other. *Really* connecting. She couldn't keep herself from picking up the phone and calling her husband at work to share her joyful news and he couldn't help but express his sheer, generous pride in return. It was all so tender and private and completely unexpected.

I knew you could do it, my love.

I licked my lips as my eyes ran across his words, surprised by the fluttering sensation in my chest. The feeling was so foreign to me that it took me a second to realize what it was: excitement. I, Cassie Woodson, had been invited into this couple's inner circle. My fingertips began to tingle with the thrill of being chosen. It was as if a tiny fleck of gold from a giant, glittering sculpture had smudged off and affixed itself to me.

I love you and can't wait to see you.

Did relationships like this really exist? Certainly not in my world. My mom was never in the picture. That was how Dad always explained our situation: "Cassie's mom isn't in the picture." When I was old enough to question *why* she wasn't in the picture, Dad's standard response was "Your mom didn't want to live in Lancaster anymore," shrugging like the answer was as simple as that. He made it all sound so reasonable, as if a mother deciding to move and leave her daughter behind forever was the most natural thing in the world.

I hereby resign from my maternal responsibility.

It wasn't until I was thirteen that my grandmother finally filled in the blanks. I remember I was lying on my butterfly comforter crying about not being invited to my friend's sleepover. Needless to say, without a mother in my life helping me navigate my teenage years, I was especially ill equipped to deal with female friendships. In a page right out of the child-rearing playbook *Stop Crying or I'll Give You Something to Cry About,* Grandma sat down on the edge of my bed, let out a long, frustrated sigh, and said, "Cassandra." (Grandma didn't do nicknames.) "You need to stop this. You're acting like your mother." The mere mention of my mother from Grandma's lips was enough to shock the tears right out of me.

"How am I acting like my mother?" I held my breath for any shred of information about the mysterious vanishing woman who had given birth to me.

"She—" My grandmother stopped and pressed her lips together, as if pulling the rest of the thought back into her mouth before it could escape.

"She what?" I probed.

"Well . . ." She shot a look at the door before continuing in a lowered voice. "Your mother was not well *here,*" she said, tapping her temple with her sun-spotted finger. "And having a baby somehow made her problems even worse. She'd always had a short fuse, but after you were born, your mom was angry all the time. Anything could set her off. And god forbid someone ask her to look after her own baby. It was like she didn't even want to acknowledge there *was* a baby in the house." She clasped her hands on her lap and for a moment I thought she wasn't going to say any more.

I didn't *want* her to say any more. Until then, I could imagine any number of reasons my mom was gone—a once-in-a-lifetime job opportunity, or she was backpacking in Africa, feeding the poor in Venezuela. But Grandma had gone and crushed all that. Now I knew exactly what had caused my mother to leave—me.

That was the problem with the truth. It always destroyed my fantasies.

Oblivious to the nausea burning in my gut, Grandma let out a shuddering breath and continued. "So, when I came over and found you in your crib crying—this horrible, desperate cry—and your mother buried under a lump of covers with her headphones on, I told your father I thought she needed a break. We had to think about your *safety,* for heaven's sake. And he agreed. He told her to go visit her parents for a few weeks, to regroup and come back when she was ready. How was he supposed to know she would never come back?" Grandma gazed out the window, wringing her hands. "But I guess she never really wanted . . ." Her voice trailed off, but I could hear the word she had swallowed down.

You. She never really wanted you, Cassie.

Grandma turned her face back to me, her expression pleading. "You can't be like her, Cassie. You're all your father has left. You have to be strong here." She tapped her temple again before clasping my hand in hers and squeezing hard. "Promise me you won't be like her."

"I promise." The words clumped together like magnets in my throat, making me choke.

Of course, when I think about it now, I realize Grandma's worst fear came to fruition: I turned out exactly like my mother. I got out of Lancaster the first chance I had. In my defense, though, I did at least try to keep my father from ending up alone.

"Why would you think I would want you to do that?" Dad had groaned one night after he came into my bedroom and caught me setting up a dating profile for him on Match.com. Which, in retrospect, would've been a difficult task to complete considering how introverted and detached Dad was. *This emotionally incapacitated single dad enjoys a quiet night in front of the TV watching the History Channel with a plate of microwaved spaghetti on his lap, while allowing his daughter to be raised like a feral cat. His dislikes include human interaction and shoveling snow.*

"I just think it would be good for you to find someone, Dad,"

I'd mumbled, avoiding his eyes. I didn't tell him I was on a mission to find a replacement for the woman I'd so clearly driven away, like buying a new goldfish for someone when you've mistakenly killed the one in your care.

"Cassie." Dad put a stiff arm on my shoulders. "I'm never going to get remarried. Ever."

I looked into his red-rimmed eyes and anger flooded my body. Why didn't he ever think about me? Didn't he realize what a burden it was for an only child of a single parent? I pushed his hand away. "Is this really how you want to live, Dad? Alone? Because I'm not going to stick around here with you after high school," I fumed, enraged by his unrelenting apathy. I wanted to push his buttons. For once, shake him out of his corpse-like calm. "Don't you ever want to be *happy*? Like everyone else out there." I gestured out my bedroom window dramatically, like there was a whole world where everyone was living in harmonious marital bliss.

"Those people aren't happy, Cassie," Dad argued, sweeping his hand through his graying hair. "I've been in a relationship before and I can tell you it's the furthest thing from happiness. That—" His voice rose as he gestured out my window. "That isn't *real*. It's all just an act. A fucking act," he repeated, louder, before storming out of my bedroom and slamming the door so hard the glass on my bedside table shook.

I had never heard my father swear. I'd never even heard him raise his voice. It was more unrestrained emotion than I'd ever been able to provoke from him, and the whole experience was so foreign, so utterly confusing, that I decided it could only mean one thing: Dad had to be right. Relationships *are* a fucking act, a farce.

Of course, that didn't stop me from dating, but nothing in my anemic personal life had ever even poked a small hole in Dad's theory. Sure, I had boyfriends, but they always ended up disappointing me, only proving Dad's point. Happy couples don't exist. It's all pretend, like a scripted TV sitcom.

This loving message from Forest Watts to his wife, though, wasn't fake and it wasn't for show. Forest didn't think anybody other than Annabelle would ever lay eyes on it, and he sent it anyway. This email was hard evidence, a smoking gun that proved relationship happiness *does* exist.

Ladies and gentlemen of the jury, I present to you Forest Watts.

I made myself exhale and take another breath. If I closed my eyes I was there, in Forest's partner-sized office, seeing the grin spread across his face as he listened to his wife's jubilant voicemail, replaying it two more times before he laid his fingers on the keyboard to compose an adoring message to her. I could picture Annabelle, her flawlessly lipsticked mouth smiling as she read his words, goosebumps dotting her willowy arms, before she tossed her phone into the buttery leather purse Forest had given her for her birthday (*such a splurge, he really shouldn't have,* she'd said to her friends when she showed it off the next day), thoroughly content with her perfect husband and even more perfect life.

I could feel the corners of my mouth creep up. *A smile!* Instead of shining a light on the unfairness, the absurdity of two people being so lucky while the rest of us are left to fight it out for crumbs, Forest's email was doing something else entirely. Somehow, it had parted the gray clouds and showed me the beauty in the world. The possibility. I wasn't thinking about Landon, or my crappy temp job, or what a terrible daughter I turned out to be. For once, the nasty voice in my mind was silenced. I was a million miles away from my shithole life. Which is really the only explanation I can give for what I did next.

What I should have done, what I was being *paid* to do, was label the document nonresponsive and move on to the next document. Lather, rinse, repeat. But when I slid my cursor over the "nonresponsive" button, I couldn't bring myself to pull the trigger. Forest's email was a diamond I'd been lucky enough to unearth. It shouldn't have been part of our cache of emails—it didn't contain any information about the case, no keywords, and wasn't even from the correct department in the firm. It had to be a glitch. A lucky glitch. Clicking my mouse now would make the email disappear, only to be replaced by some mind-numbing document to review.

I removed my hand from the mouse, my breath quickening, and darted my eyes around the room. The moles were all firmly in their holes, completely oblivious to anything beyond the scope of their glowing screens. I rolled my chair backward and craned my neck so I could peer down the row of computers toward Ricky. His head was bobbing to whatever music was pumping through his noise-canceling headphones. I snuck a glance at Dalton, who was squinting down at his phone, his forehead creased into a frown.

I took a deep, practiced breath. *I shouldn't do this*, I told myself. *This is not what mentally stable people do.* I squeezed my eyes shut remembering the anxious expression on the face of the woman from human resources on my last day of work at Nolan & Wright. *Cassie, this is not what mentally stable people do.* She raised the end of the sentence like she was asking me a question, like I was supposed to nod and agree with her that what I'd done meant I was out of my mind, cuckoo for Cocoa Puffs. I still had the ridiculous hope of keeping my job in that moment, so I didn't tell her what I really thought: The only difference between a mentally stable person and me was better aim.

I stared at the email from Forest. *It's not like I'm hurting someone. No one will ever even have to know.*

With my heart pounding, I picked up my phone and swiped to the camera mode. There was only a tiny sliver of red left in the battery. I had to act fast. Angling it as surreptitiously as possible, I pressed the round white button with a shaky index finger, snapping a photo of my computer screen.

Click.

I laid my phone back down on the table, as tentatively as if it were a grenade, and took a deep breath. A joyful swell grew in my chest and I let it swish around inside me, like fine wine in a tall glass.

I felt like a hunter who'd successfully trapped an elusive snow leopard. Now, I just had to make sure I never let it go.

Chapter Four

I PICKED UP the bottle of wine from my kitchen counter and inspected the ornate yellow label: *Caymus Vineyards 2016 Cabernet Sauvignon Napa Valley.*

Is this the right year? I wondered as I tipped my wrist and watched the red liquid fill my cracked ceramic mug. Forest's email to Annabelle didn't specify the vintage and the clerk at the wine store had not been much help. "What's the occasion?" he'd called out as I'd wandered to the back of the store where the high-end bottles were housed. He recognized me, I realized, and was not used to seeing me venture past the cheap bottles by the register. "I'm looking for a bottle of Caymus," I'd replied carefully, trying to keep my expression dispassionate as I eyeballed a bright orange price tag that read $89.99. "Which one would you choose if you were celebrating something with your, um . . ." I faltered a moment before adding, "spouse." The clerk raised his eyebrows slightly. He hadn't expected me to have a partner. He'd assumed I was some kind of lonely recluse only capable of spending $9.99 on a bottle of crappy merlot. "My husband is bringing home pasta from my favorite restaurant," I added, taking pleasure in watching his whole demeanor change.

Now I was someone. Now I was worth his time.

I'd only planned on having a look out of curiosity, but the next thing I knew the clerk was wrapping the bottle in purple tissue paper and tying a silver ribbon around the neck, carefully curling each end with a scissors blade. I'd been frequenting that store for years and never once had any of my bottles been wrapped.

What was that lyric Grandma used to sing? *"You're nobody 'til somebody loves you."*

I hummed a few bars as I picked up my mug of ninety-dollar wine and swirled. Inhaling deeply through my nose, I brought it to my lips and took a long gulp. A warm, velvet feeling spread across my chest.

Good god this is good. I silently congratulated myself on the impulse purchase.

It's important to see how the other half lives.

I curled my fingers around the mug, hugging it to my chest like a comforting teddy bear, and tried to picture Forest and Annabelle Watts raising their crystal wineglasses, the sound of the sweet clink as they toasted their perfect life. *To us!* Annabelle would say. *To you,* Forest would respond.

"Cheers!" I said out loud in my empty apartment, lifting the mug into the air, my voice reverberating off the walls. I wished I could drink this out of a proper wineglass. I used to have some of those. Hell, I once had a set of eight matching Riedel glasses I'd purchased at the Williams Sonoma after-Christmas sale, in preparation for all the cozy dinner parties Landon and I would throw. But the fancy stemware hadn't survived any longer than our pathetic relationship.

It's amazing, really, how fragile some things are.

I pushed the pile of dirty laundry off the coffee table, set down my laptop and the bottle of wine, and sank into the couch. In the early days, after the breakup with Landon (if you could call it a breakup), this couch was like my coffin. I'd lie here motionless for days, un-showered and wrecked with insomnia. It probably wouldn't have mattered if it *was* a coffin, I still wouldn't have had any motivation to move off it. Why would I? It wasn't like there was anywhere I needed to be. Nobody I needed to see. Nobody who wanted to see me.

Landon had set fire to everything around me. Everything. Yet, I hadn't altered his course at all. I'd barely been a blip on the radar.

Not even a fucking blip.

The only thing that remained from my former life was this overpriced apartment I remained chained to for the next four months thanks to my lease. I remember the night I moved in, Landon and I sitting knee to knee on this couch toasting my good fortune in finding an apartment with both a washer-dryer and a balcony, while I silently wondered whether we would keep this place when we moved in together or whether we'd shop for something bigger. I spent a lot of time weighing my various options back then. But that was a lifetime ago. It was hard to remember ever feeling audacious enough to believe I had options, as if I got to choose how my life would turn out.

What a ridiculous tempting of fate it had been to think I had any say in the future at all.

I shoved my hands into my hair, gripping the roots as if I could somehow rip the thoughts from my head if I pulled hard enough. I hated it when Landon crept into my mind uninvited. He was like a prowler, lurking in the shadows ready to pounce the minute my guard was down. I took an irritated swig of wine. Then another. I drained the mug and leaned my head back against the cushion, savoring the feeling of alcohol sliding through my veins, dulling the sharp edges.

Licking my lips, I tried to imagine which dishes Forest and Annabelle ordered from Scalini. When they paired their dinner selections, did it bring out different characteristics in the wine?

I bet it did.

Even their taste buds were luckier than mine.

I swiped my phone awake, tapped open my photos, and reread the email despite already having committed it to memory. *I'm so proud of you. I knew you could do it, my love. Let's celebrate tonight!* The perpetual knots in my stomach loosened. Somewhere in this world, this man existed.

But what did he look like?

I pulled my legs into the lotus position, refilled my mug, and fired up my laptop, relishing the sudden burst of adrenaline that was pulsating underneath my skin now. For once, it wasn't coming from anxiety, or angst, or fear. It was anticipation.

God, I loved anticipation. I hadn't had anything to look forward to in . . . I couldn't remember. I wanted to bask in its velvety warmth, like a cat stretched out in a sunbeam. I swirled my mug, putting my nose to the rim and inhaling deeply as a memory of Dad crystalized in my mind. I closed my eyes for a moment, hoping to mentally capture it, like a butterfly in a net.

I was seven years old, standing in the hot summer sun, impatiently waiting for my chance to take a turn on the new half bungee–half trampoline attraction that had been set up in Parking Lot C of our local mall. There weren't a lot of entertainment options in our tiny town, so this one had drawn a throng of sweaty children who had managed to form themselves into more of a mosh pit than a line. "Okay, who's next?" the irritated operator called out after I'd managed to push my way to the front of the group. My hand flew up, but Dad put his weathered hand on my wrist, bringing it down gently. "I think he's next." Dad pointed to the boy beside me before dipping his head down to my level. "Don't rush it, Cass," he whispered in my ear. "The *best* feeling in the world is the feeling of being next."

Dad was right, of course. Every dangling carrot I've experienced in my twenty-nine years—my first kiss, first apartment, first bonus check—has never been as enjoyable, as wholly gratifying, as the feeling of anticipating the pleasure those things would bring.

You're a pleasure delayer, Cassie, I remember Landon growling in my ear after our third date when I was hesitating to invite him into my apartment. *You're killing me with your delayed gratification. But I like it.*

I slammed my mug down on the coffee table so hard the wine sloshed over the edges. *Fuck Landon.* I let out an annoyed sigh before grabbing the bottle and refilling my mug to the top.

There, that's better.

I navigated to Google and typed "Forest Watts" into the search bar. My pinky hesitated over the "return" key. There was a small part of me that didn't trust the sliver of happiness Forest's email was providing me, that worried he wouldn't look the way I pictured.

When I get to know people, they tend to disappoint me.

I closed my eyes and hit "return." When I opened them, tiny little pictures of Forest Watts bloomed across my screen, filling it like a mosaic. I moved closer to the screen until my nose was almost touching it.

My immediate thought was that I had been wrong. Forest Watts did not look how I'd imagined. Not at all.

He was so much better.

Strong jawed and classically handsome with a tiny bit of salt in his jet-black hair, he looked like he belonged on the set of an *Ocean's Eleven* movie rather than a law firm. A zip of happiness flew through me at the sheer perfection of him.

"Of course," I whispered, a wide smile spreading across my face. "Of course, you are flawless."

I double-clicked on his profile on the firm website. *Education: J.D. New York University School of Law, B.A. Dartmouth College (with honors); "Excellence in Pro Bono" Award for work with New Yorkers for Children.*

When I was finished reading, I hit the "back" button, zeroing in on the light gray number at the top of the page. The computer had spit out eleven thousand hits. Eleven thousand! My knee bounced with excitement. I was having so much fun I wanted to meter each one of them out like a tasty piece of chocolate cake. But patience is not a virtue I possess.

My fingers flew across the keys as I refined my search with each new nugget I unearthed. "Forest Watts NYU"; "Forest Watts pro bono"; "Forest Watts lawyer." More hits. A house in Bronxville. A board seat at the Frick. A photo of Forest from the NYU Law annual alumni luncheon. I reviewed the information like I was studying for a test, but it was getting harder to keep it all straight in my mind.

I pulled a notepad out of my purse, tore off the scuffed top page, and wrote *Forest Watts* at the top, underlining it twice. Staring down at the lined paper, I realized it was the same legal pad I'd tucked under my arm to bring to the fateful meeting with human resources on my last day of work at Nolan & Wright, and it suddenly struck me as the most ridiculous thing about that day—how I'd foolishly thought there would be something I would need to jot down during my meeting. *Screwed up royally. How to remedy?*

I shook my head, shaking off the thought, and began scribbling—Forest's alma mater, previous residences, political donations. All the little pixels that come together to form the complete picture of a person. *New York City Marathon,* I wrote, *two hours forty-seven minutes.*

Of course his marathon time was impressive. Everything about Forest Watts was impressive.

Run, Forest, run, I whispered.

A realization began to unfold in my mind, one inch at a time. With all of my excitement in reading Forest's words to Annabelle, I'd completely ignored an important fact: Dalton had been privy to one of Forest's emails too—the one where he said he was firing Red Power Tie. And if Dalton had a Forest email in his folder, and I had one in my folder, then this was not, in fact, a one-time glitch. There was a very good chance there would be more emails to review. Perhaps even more to Annabelle.

My heart rate kicked up. I refined my search. *"Forest and Annabelle Watts images"; "Forest and Annabelle Watts wedding."*

A wedding announcement in *The New York Times*! I picked up my pen and readied myself to record it all . . . *married in Vail . . . Roman Catholic priest performing the ceremony . . . the bride, a graduate of Wellesley College who received a doctorate in art history from Columbia is the daughter of Mr. and Mrs. . . .* The blurb practically included an entire family tree for each of them. It's amazing how much personal information these newspapers require for one little wedding announcement. Worrying, really, when you think about it.

I descended farther into the rabbit hole. My wrist ached from scribbling down all of the new information I unearthed.

Time passed. I don't know how much time, but the shrieks of the drunken revelers leaving the bars for the night had long since died out.

I felt high. I swallowed every new crumb about Forest and Annabelle down like a Valium. The legal blog Above the Law had profiled Forest and Annabelle's Bronxville home a few years ago in their "Lawyerly Lairs" feature, picturing the six-thousand-square-foot home with the headline A BIGLAW PARTNER AND HIS ART COLLECTOR WIFE'S NEW FIVE MILLION DOLLAR PERCH. I typed the address into the search bar and slid my cursor around on Google Earth, viewing every possible angle.

I had never seen a more beautiful home in all my life.

Does Annabelle breathe a sigh of relief every time she walks up those elegant pale-gray stone steps leading to the front door? I wondered, taking another gulp of wine. I would. I was certain I would.

Six thousand square feet, I scratched down in my notebook. *Five bedrooms.*

I twisted open the bottle of Tylenol PM on the coffee table and popped four in my mouth, washing them down with more wine.

I tried to imagine which of the four bay windows led to the bedroom where Forest and Annabelle slept at night, their bodies twisted together in cozy down and peaceful dreams. *Good night,* he'd whisper before kissing her. Always on the lips, never the forehead. He wasn't her father-surrogate. They were equals.

When I'd exhausted the details of their home, their wedding, their neighborhood, his job, and their charitable work, I went back and took another look at the eleven different pictures I'd discovered of Forest and Annabelle together.

Forest Watts with his wife, Annabelle, at the New Yorkers for Children Fall Gala, read one of the captions.

I examined the photos, stifling a dull ache, the same one I used to get every May when I would walk past the long row of Mother's Day cards in the Hallmark store.

Annabelle was beautiful, *of course,* but not in the way I thought she would be. She surprised me. I'd pictured a Sandra Bullock type of beauty, but she was more Kristen Stewart with cheekbones so sharp they could double as weapons. I would've killed for cheekbones like that. I touched a finger to Annabelle's face on the screen. How could I have ever thought there would be a single thing that would be average, girl-next-door-type about a woman lucky enough to be married to Forest?

I tapped to zoom in on the photo, examining all angles of her lithe form. She was tanned, whether from a recent holiday or simple genetic good fortune it was hard to tell, but she radiated. She had the posture of a woman who's stood in the spotlight of every room she's ever been in, with her hand propped on her hip and her weight shifted to her back leg just like all of the "How to Strike a Hollywood Pose" articles always advise.

But Annabelle didn't need to read those magazines. Social nuances came naturally to her. As did everything in life.

She was at ease in her own skin. Unlike me, who wanted to crawl out of mine.

She never lost her temper. Not her. Why would she? Nothing ever went wrong for her.

She would never be fired. She would never get left.

I tilted my head and pursed my lips, the same way she did in the photo. I let my hand drop onto the armrest of my couch, imagining it was Forest's forearm, and gave it a little squeeze.

At an event like that, Annabelle would squeeze Forest's arm three times. Her private way of telling him she loves him. *I. Love. You.* He would add a fourth squeeze in return. *I. Love. You. Too.* Definitely not I love you *more.* Their relationship wasn't a competition.

I picked up the bottle and poured the last dregs of "their" wine into my mug. Well, it was "our" wine now.

Draining my glass, I propped my laptop on the side table, double-clicked on his photo on the firm website, and lay back on my pillow. With my eyes fixed on the screen, I ran my hands down my stomach slowly, slowly down between my legs. *Forest. Forest. Forest.* I moved my fingers to the rhythm. I tried to stay fixed on his perfect face, but my eyes involuntarily squeezed shut. I gasped as my whole body convulsed with tiny bolts of pleasure washing over me. I sunk into the couch and exhaled a deep, satisfied breath.

My arm fell to the side and I curled into the pillow and closed my tired eyes. My last thought before I fell asleep was how I couldn't wait to go to work. Then, for the first time in months, I fell into a deep, peaceful sleep.

To: Cassandra Woodson
From: Mary Woodson

Cassandra,

I've been trying to get ahold of you for weeks. You aren't an-
swering your phone or returning your emails. I finally tried you
at work and they said you were no longer employed at the firm.
I'm getting worried. What is going on?
Love,
Grandma

Chapter Five

No ONE CAN eat just one chip.

The urge to read more of Forest Watts's emails washed through me like a physical substance. I woke up craving it, like a drug addict, counting the minutes until my next fix. Which was why, as I stood at the Starbucks counter the next morning waiting for my venti dirty chai and hoping the heavy dose of caffeine would work as an antidote to the bottle of expensive wine I'd polished off last night, I found myself feeling a tiny seed of gratitude. Gratitude! Sure, my temp job was akin to the migrant farmworker of the legal industry, but it had introduced me to Forest and Annabelle. They were like a beacon of light sweeping through the darkness.

It felt good to finally have a focus again.

I took a deep breath and surveyed the impatient faces around me, thankful that none of them looked familiar. I hated bumping into people out of their usual context. Especially now. The Starbucks I used to frequent was located at the base of the looming, dark building that housed Nolan & Wright, and every time I pushed through the glass doors for my morning latte, it was like stepping into a small-town hair salon with the number of familiar faces I would encounter. Just the thought of being anywhere in the vicinity of that neighborhood now was enough to send a shiver down my spine.

Of course, I wouldn't be greeted with the same friendly smiles I used to get if I saw anyone from my old firm today. They had long since tossed me in the trash like their empty coffee cups.

Assholes.

After I was escorted out of Nolan & Wright, I assumed my work friends would call or email with concern. *What happened? We were so worried about you! We miss you!* I mean, it wasn't like I'd done anything to *them*. But I'd sat on my couch for months and those calls and texts never came. The only email I ever received from an employee of Nolan & Wright came from the head of HR and that was only to provide a recommendation for a therapist. Which I assumed was the final step in the handbook of firing a disgraced employee. The colleagues I used to sit next to every day in the cafeteria and share Ubers with on the way home from firm events vanished into thin air. It was as if I'd been diagnosed with some extremely contagious flesh-eating virus and any form of contact with me would be deadly.

Maybe they were afraid of me.

"Venti dirty chai," the barista called, shaking me out of my thoughts. I unfurled my fists and slipped a sleeve around the cup. There was a tiny tremor in my hand, the same one I've experienced every morning since I tried my first sip of caffeine in middle school. Some might say this proves I have an addictive personality. I prefer to think of it as being focused. My body knows what it wants. And it simply will not rest until it gets it.

I took a greedy gulp of my latte and strode to the exit, anxious to kick off my workday.

"Cassie?" a disembodied voice called out as I reached for the handle on the door.

Shit.

I briefly wondered if I could pretend I hadn't heard. A quick mental calculation of proximity eliminated that option as a viable one. He was five feet away—six tops. If I ignored him now he would probably follow me out the door, calling my name at increasingly embarrassing volumes until I responded. Answering him now was the path of least resistance. I plastered on my game face and turned around.

"Hi, Ricky."

"Cassie! I thought that was you. Small world!" Ricky gave me a toothy grin. "Looks like we have the same taste in watering holes." He gestured with his chin to my cup, and I noticed the piece of toilet paper still affixed to the shaving nick on his neck.

"Looks like we do," I answered with as much cheeriness as I could muster.

There was a beat of awkward silence before Ricky spoke. "Well, I'm glad I bumped into you because there is something I forgot to get from you on your first day of work and it keeps slipping farther down my long to-do list." He blew a rogue piece of gelled hair off his face before continuing. "I need to get your phone number." I must've given him a dubious look, because he quickly added, "I get every temp's number and send them a text from my phone so they have my phone number too. That way if there's ever a problem, like you get sick or something, I can be your first call. Ricky Sandos, first responder." He puffed out his chest and his smile widened.

The headache I'd been ignoring all morning began pulsing in my temple. I really didn't have the energy for this.

I inhaled deeply. "Sure," I replied.

He pulled his ancient phone, ensconced in a case thick enough to be bulletproof, out of his pocket. If the world came to an end right here in this Starbucks, Ricky's phone would surely be the lone survivor. His forehead wrinkled with concentration as he tapped the glowing screen. "Here!" He held the phone up like an attorney entering an important piece of evidence in a trial. "See—here are the texts I've sent other temps." His eyes swiveled from me to his phone as he scrolled down. "As you can see I gather the phone numbers from every temp purely for management purposes. Not . . . not . . . personal purposes," he stuttered as two red patches bloomed on his cheeks.

"No problem. It would definitely be useful to exchange numbers." I forced a smile and held out my hand, trying to smother my impatience. "I can punch my number right into your phone. That will probably make it easier."

"Great!" He handed over his phone and wiped his palms on the sides of his pants. "Where it says 'company' feel free to put Levy &

Strong, but make sure you add the word 'temp' so I don't confuse it with my other Levy & Strong contacts."

I mentally rolled my eyes and began tapping in my name. Out of the corner of my eye I could see the bearded man in the bright yellow construction vest smirking at me from one of the stools by the window. He probably thought I was willing to hand out my number to any Joe Shmoe ballsy enough to ask for it. I shifted my shoulder to block him from view. It was too early in the morning for judgmental stares from complete strangers.

"So, are you getting the hang of our . . ." Ricky lowered his voice and leaned his head toward mine before adding "review," as if the mere word was meant only for those with the proper security clearance.

I hesitated for a moment. "It's a steep learning curve, but I think I'm getting the hang of it," I replied, seizing the opportunity to oil Ricky's fragile male ego. Keep your friends close and your enemies closer, as they say. It was too early for me to tell which category Ricky fell into.

I tapped the last digit of my number and handed back his phone. "There, all set. See you at—"

"I know what you mean," Ricky interrupted clumsily, clearly not ready for our conversation to end. "There are a lot of complicated aspects to this project. A lot of moving parts, ya know?"

I nodded. Clicking a mouse didn't seem too complicated to me, but who was I to judge Ricky's ability to multitask?

"Excuse me!" A woman in a red power suit huffed as she jostled past me, tossing a glare over her shoulder as if the mere fact that we had the audacity to have a conversation in a coffee shop had ruined her entire day.

I returned her glare. God, I was growing tired of this city and the impatient, mean-spirited people who infested it. Did New York attract that kind of person or did it turn you into that kind of person? It was the classic chicken-or-the-egg conundrum. I'd been enamored with New York City when I moved here bright-eyed and fresh out of law school. But back then I was escaping a small town in Pennsylvania and probably would've been thrilled to be moving to Siberia if it meant I never had to return. Perhaps I should've put more thought into where I was headed instead of only thinking about what I was fleeing. Maybe things would've turned out differently if I'd picked another city. Maybe then the script of my life wouldn't have been completely rewritten into a cautionary tale.

"It helps if you've taken an advanced civil procedure class in law school like I did," Ricky rambled. "It gives you the total picture. Remember if you have any questions about what you're reviewing you know who to come to." He pointed both thumbs at his chest the way people do when they say "this guy!" as the punch line to a joke.

His smile dropped and he furrowed his brow. "So, do you?"

I blinked at him, too cloudy-headed to follow.

"Have any questions, I mean. Have you come across anything in your review that you need to ask me about? Anything at all . . ." he trailed off.

For a fraction of a second I wondered if Ricky somehow knew about Forest. Maybe he'd witnessed me taking a picture of my computer screen and was trying to trap me. But that was absurd, of course. Ricky didn't know. How could he?

Ricky leaned his head closer to mine. "You can ask me back at the office if you're worried about confidentiality," he whispered, misinterpreting my hesitation.

"No, you gave me really good instructions so I haven't had any problems," I replied, choosing my words carefully. "But I'll definitely come to you if there's anything I need help with. Thanks, Ricky." I shifted my purse up on my shoulder, readying myself to leave, hoping he would take the hint.

"When in doubt, check it out. That's my motto. Maybe I should type that out and stick it on the wall as a reminder." Ricky gazed off into the distance as if considering the idea before snapping his attention back to me. "Anyway, where did you say you went to law school, Cassie?"

I stiffened. "Um . . ." He was looking at me intently now. "I don't think I *did* say . . ." My finger tapped on the cardboard sleeve around my cup as possible responses flickered through my mind. I could tell the truth. Or . . .

"Tulane." I took a gulp of my latte to mask the shake in my voice. "I went to Tulane Law School."

"Wow, New Orleans. Home of Mardi Gras," Ricky replied, oblivious to being thrown off the scent. "That must have been a really interesting experience. Lots of beads and stuff." Color flooded his cheeks once again. "I mean, I've never actually *been* during Mardi Gras, but I've heard they, uhhh . . . throw beads." His eyes darted to my chest, as if noticing it for the first time.

"Yeah, it was a great place to go to school," I replied, my voice shifting up an octave. I could already see the depth of the hole I was digging, but there was nothing to do but press on. "New Orleans is a really fun city. And everyone should go to Mardi Gras at least once in their life, right?"

He nodded vigorously.

The truth was I'd never even ventured south of Virginia and I knew nothing about New Orleans or Mardi Gras or Tulane Law School for that matter. But Ricky didn't need to know that.

"Anyway, I'll see you at the office?" I gestured to the door and gave a quick wave of my hand without waiting for a reply.

For the first time since I started temping, I couldn't wait to get to work. Forest Watts was waiting. And my body was craving a fix.

Chapter Six

IT WAS JUST after lunch when he finally made an appearance. I'd spent the morning anxiously clicking through document after tedious document, steeling myself, as hope seeped from my body like sweat. I was beginning to think I'd been too optimistic last night, that my newfound happiness really was the result of a one-time glitch. But then, like a glorious rain shower after a long drought, his name flashed on my screen again.

> To: Maryanne Hackett
> From: Forest Watts
>
> Maryanne,
>
> Please cancel my lunch with the folks at Blackwood Partners tomorrow and reschedule for either next Wed or Thurs at one. Four Seasons dining room. Thx

A delicious jolt of exhilaration zipped through my body. Just as unassumingly as the first time, Forest Watts was back. Whispering in my ear again.

I shot a cautious look over my shoulder before slipping my hand in my purse, retrieving my legal pad, and setting it on the table. I couldn't risk taking another photo of my computer, but I wasn't going to let the email slip away either. Carefully, I flipped to a clean page and transcribed it verbatim, right down to the date and time it was sent.

Tiny details should never be overlooked. Any good lawyer knows that.

After ensuring I'd recorded everything, I tapped the mouse and watched it disappear. But this time, to my utter delight, another email from Forest spread across my screen.

To: Brett Kruse
From: Forest Watts

Brett,

Annabelle and I are looking forward to having you and Elizabeth out at the house this weekend. Below is our address.
   19 Woodland Drive
   Bronxville, NY

An invitation to their five-bedroom house in Bronxville! I could barely contain my excitement. Breathing quickly now, I scribbled down *Brett and Elizabeth Kruse,* and the time the email was sent, before gripping my mouse and clicking again.

To: Forest Watts
From: Annabelle Watts

You are the sweetest. Scalini sounds perfect and a bottle of Caymus will be decanted when you get home. I'll be waiting . . . xoxo

My heart shuddered to a stop. There it was—Annabelle's reply to Forest's loving email. All at once, I was hit with a mixture of elation and affection, like a baby in one of those viral videos, hearing her mother's voice for the first time, and I had to look away from the screen for a moment to collect myself.

You are the sweetest. I'll be waiting . . .

What did that feel like? I wondered. To be so secure—so wholly self-assured—about your place in someone else's heart.

I studied the time stamp on the email and compared it to the two I'd just read. They were mere seconds apart. The only relevance I could see to the other documents we were reviewing was that they were within the same date range. No client names. Nothing to do with Falcon Health or Medicare fraud. I didn't know why, but somehow Forest's inbox had been caught up in the keyword search.

My eyes slid to Ricky's workstation. His brows were furrowed as he studied his computer screen with the intensity of a doctor performing critical, lifesaving surgery. *If there's anything that doesn't look right in your review folder you should bring it to my attention immediately,* he'd instructed me on day one. Having Forest's inbox in my cache of documents would surely fall into that category.

I chewed on a loose piece of skin on my lip, rereading Annabelle's words. *I'll be waiting . . . xoxo.* There was no reason this email should be in my folder. It was the kind of irregularity that should be flagged for Ricky. But I didn't do that. Instead, I pulled a long breath into my stomach, navigated the arrow to "nonresponsive," and clicked, eager to read what came next.

I filled three pages of notes over the next few hours. Like an amateur archeologist, I gathered every morsel systematically. *Children's Literacy Gala* (an event Annabelle asked Forest to be home by six to attend), *Hermitage Bay, Antigua* (where Forest and Annabelle were looking to vacation during the month of December), *Maison Thai* (restaurant in midtown Forest swore would convince Annabelle to move back into the city again). I wrote down names of friends, addresses, even the type of cookie Annabelle had asked Forest to pick up from Zaro's in Grand Central on his way home. Mini black and white cookies. Of course. Annabelle was naturally skinny, didn't need to count calories, but she also didn't require a full-size cookie to satisfy her sweet tooth.

When my wrist began to ache, I paused for a moment to assess my handiwork. Running my fingers over the smudged pages of my notepad, I marveled at the feeling of lightness in my lungs, as if the three-ton weight that had been sitting on them had been lifted. Forest and Annabelle were slowly helping me breathe again.

"Prison break time." A deep voice tore through my thoughts.

With the knee-jerk reaction of someone who's been caught surfing porn at work, I minimized my screen, bumping my water bottle with my elbow in my haste. "Shit!" I hissed, swiping the puddle of water off my notepad before swiftly turning it over as if it was evidence of a murder.

Dalton was standing over me, casting an inquisitive glance at the notepad. "Are you doing some super-secret temp work now, Cassie?" He smirked.

I stuffed my suddenly shaking hands in my pockets. "Oh, this is just . . . um . . . I'm just making a to-do list. I have a lot on my plate right now and I'll forget it all if I don't write it down right away."

"Okaaaaay." Dalton dragged out the word, nodding doubtfully. "Well, do you have room on that busy plate of yours for dinner?"

"Dinner?"

"Yeeees, dinner." He peered at me like my face had just sprouted another nose. "You know, dinner—the last meal of the day, the one they spring us out of here for exactly thirty minutes for? We eat it in the cafeteria?"

"Oh, right." I let out a nervous chuckle, casting a glance at the clock. How had five hours passed without me noticing? "I was just . . . zoning," I explained, waving my hand dismissively.

He cocked an eyebrow. "Well, whatever you're reading must be pretty juicy for that much"—he held up his hands and air-quoted—"zoning."

On my way to the elevator, I silently congratulated myself for diffusing the situation. Nonetheless, I would need to remain on guard. Dalton was like a heat-seeking missile for gossip, and I certainly didn't want him meddling in Forest and Annabelle's business.

Well, *our* business now.

To: Forest Watts
From: Annabelle Watts

Hey, babe, I heard back from Don on the life insurance. He agreed we should go with Sun Life. He'll send the papers later this week for signature. xoxo

To: Forest Watts
From: Annabelle Watts

I managed to get a reservation for four at Atera on Saturday at eight. I invited Celina and Phil Davis to join us—haven't seen them since Tahoe so I thought it would be a good chance to catch up. See you tonight—I'm making paella. xoxo

To: Annabelle Watts
From: Forest Watts

Miss you—hope your sore throat is feeling better. I'll pick up some NyQuil on my way home. Get some rest until I'm there. xoxo

Chapter Seven

PEOPLE ARE LIKE puzzles. My psychology professor taught me that. He'd stood at the front of the lecture hall, holding up a single jigsaw piece to illustrate his point, his loud voice booming, *If you are missing even one piece, you will never put them together properly.* My classmates had rolled their eyes at his clichéd bravado, but I'd scribbled down every word, underlining it twice. It was good news for me. I've always excelled at puzzles. The same cannot be said for people.

I checked the time on my phone now as I hustled to the top of the cracked subway stairs with the herd of commuters: eight A.M. Thirty minutes early for work. Perfect timing. I wrapped my hands around the warm latte I'd picked up near my apartment in order to avoid a repeat of the Starbucks run-in with Ricky and quickened my pace. The wind was picking up, which was going to make standing at the base of the building decidedly less comfortable, but I didn't plan on waiting out in the cold air too long. All that I was after this morning was another piece of the puzzle.

Pictures don't always tell the whole story about a person, do they? Anyone who's ever been on a dating site can confirm this fact. In order to truly know what someone looks like, it is imperative to see him in the flesh, free of filters, cropping, or color correcting. I'd been able to examine dozens of gorgeous photos of Forest Watts online, but relying on those alone to get a full sense of him would be like putting the edge pieces of a puzzle together and not even bothering to take the time to fill in the middle. That would be silly.

"*AMNew York, AMNew York,* free paper, free paper, free paper," the hefty woman sporting the company-issued red vest called out robotically as she passed a folded newspaper to the occasional out-stretched hand. Ignoring her, I cut across the avenue and made my way west. All around me, people were progressing through the banal steps of their morning routines. Whether it was the kitten-heeled woman tapping on her phone to scan her schedule for the day, or the man in the fluorescent construction vest stopping for a bagel and black coffee at the cart on the corner of Fifty-ninth and Lexington, they were all going through the motions they'd per-formed hundreds of times before. For some of them, I imagined, it was like clockwork. Down to the minute. I wondered how closely Forest kept to his morning routine.

Meticulously, I hoped.

I had a pretty good idea what time he arrived at the office, judg-ing from the time stamps on the flurry of email responses I'd come across—eight-twenty A.M. Throw in a few minutes for the eleva-tor ride up and a quick hello to his secretary and that meant he probably pushed through the revolving doors into the lobby at approximately eight-fifteen A.M. Give or take. The cavernous building that housed Levy & Strong was nearly a block wide, meaning there were multiple entrances on both the Fifty-eighth Street and Fifty-ninth Street sides. If Forest walked from Grand Central as part of his routine, he would enter on the Fifty-eighth Street side. If he transferred to a subway instead, he would pop up at Fifty-ninth, entering through the opposite side of the building. It was hard to know which one would be more like him. On the one hand, I could see him as the type of person who would prefer to be on foot rather than in the claustrophobic confines of a sub-way car during rush hour. On the other, he would appreciate the efficiency of a commute that dropped him off mere steps from his building.

It was a coin toss, really.

Pulling up the collar of my wool coat around my ears, I positioned myself in the middle of the wide block, allowing myself the best view of both street corners leading to the entrances. Through the sunglasses I'd slipped on despite the lack of sun, I began scrutinizing the faces attached to the black and camel over-coats that were striding down the sidewalk with the unbridled confidence that comes from gainful employment. There was a woman with a honey-colored pixie cut framing milky white skin; a man with the kind of wrinkles that plant themselves after years of scowling. As I studied each one, the familiarity of the moment sent an unexpected chill down my spine, instantly transporting me back to my first week in New York City.

It was over six years ago, but I could still see the tiny red patches blooming on Dad's cheeks as he mumbled, *Just be yourself, Cassie,* giving me an awkward pat on the shoulder as we exchanged good-byes near the ticket counter of the train station, like he was reluc-tantly reciting a line from a parenting manual titled *Advice to Give Your Daughter Before She Starts Her First Real Job. You too,* I'd replied before stumbling, *I mean . . . I will, Dad.* But, even then, I recog-nized Dad's advice for what it was: obtusely ill advised. Why would I want to be someone that nobody had ever liked? The whole point of moving to New York was to become someone else entirely. And overcoming my inadequate natural instincts was going to take a calculated, deliberate effort. I spent two full days before I started my new job at Nolan & Wright walking the side-walks of midtown, studying the pencil-skirted women who were to become my colleagues, looking for clues on how I could fit into their exclusive club. I paid careful attention to their fashion choices, eavesdropped on their conversations, hoping to nail down the vocabulary and syntax. It felt like I was eight years old again, back on the playground, hovering alone in the fringes, watching the other kids play. But I was certain that if I examined these women closely enough, if I played the game the way they did, I too could wrap myself in camouflage and become someone else. Someone better. Someone who was worthy of being loved. My past could be exfoliated.

The alarm chimed on my phone now, bringing me back to the

present. Eight-ten A.M. My heartbeat kicked up a notch as my gaze flicked back and forth between the street corners. The overcoats were coming fast and furious now, and it was becoming more difficult to scan effectively while still remaining inconspicuous. I let out a frustrated sigh. This plan was not well thought out. If I was going to have any chance at success this morning, I would need to pick a side. I chewed at a scabbed hangnail, considering. If I was a gambling woman, I'd say Forest would arrive on the corner of Fifty-eighth Street sometime in the next two minutes. Shoving my cold hands in my pockets, I made my way toward that entrance.

But I am not a gambler. I have always been a meticulous planner. I hate leaving anything to chance. You would too if you had my luck.

Chapter Eight

I DID NOT win my imaginary bet. Three days of loitering at the base of the building and not a single Forest sighting.

I wasn't stalking him. Really. I wasn't. Reading his emails was what I was being paid to do. I was simply doing my job. It would be fair, though, to say I was spending significantly more time on Google in the evenings.

You might be surprised by how much you can learn about a person with just a few clicks of the mouse. I know I was. Through my strategic Internet sleuthing I'd tracked down his and Annabelle's birthdays, names of their relatives, religion, political party, and a whole host of detailed photographs. From Annabelle's social media photos, I could see that she and Forest liked to ski. Jackson Hole, Whistler, Beaver Creek, #FreshPowder. They celebrated Oktoberfest in Munich every year, #AnnualTradition. They didn't have any children, which wasn't surprising given their busy travel schedule. This meant there was no cherub-faced infant cannibalizing her Instagram. Thankfully. I'd also examined Annabelle's abdomen in every photo and found no evidence of a baby bump so there wasn't an impending arrival. But Annabelle did sit on the board of two children's charities—Off the Streets and New Yorkers for Children—so she didn't lack a nurturing parental instinct. Unlike my mother.

Unfortunately for me, Annabelle seemed to have taken a hiatus from posting pictures online lately. She must be preoccupied. I would have to find out with what.

When I thought about it, I'd probably learned more about Forest in three days than I ever knew about my own father. Although, truth be told, that wasn't a very high bar. Still, he was family.

Of course, anyone with a mild curiosity and a Wi-Fi password could track those details down about Forest and Annabelle. My relationship with them was far more intimate. Exclusive. From Forest's inbox I was getting to know his true self, not just the one he chose to present to the world. His proclivity for online shopping meant I was privy to what kind of books he read, food he ate, even what kind of underwear he wore (boxers, not briefs—Saxx brand). I knew the name of his family doctor, his younger sister, and where his parents lived. All of the connections, intersections, and rhythms of his daily life. And my mountain of information about their lives was increasing with every glorious click of my mouse.

Forest, I'm using a new cleaning service so I changed the alarm code—9 then my birth year. xoxo Annabelle

It didn't take Sherlock Holmes to figure that one out. She should really be more careful.

There were some details about them that couldn't be unearthed no matter how many emails I reviewed or Internet rabbit holes I went down, though. But I was confident enough in my knowledge now to fill in any gaps. Take, for instance, frequency of sex—there's something you won't find online. Forest and Annabelle were probably all over each other at the same rate as horny teenagers, despite the fact that they'd been married seven years. Lucky number seven. That was what Forest had called it when he'd emailed the jeweler to have a necklace made for Annabelle. *I want something special for Annabelle this anniversary—it's lucky number seven.*

I wondered what they did for their seventh anniversary. Did they drink "our" wine? I could picture them with their hands clasped across the table, Forest pulling a velvet box tied up with a bright red ribbon from his suit pocket. *I couldn't wait until the end of dinner to give this to you, Annabelle . . .*

It would be something expensive, but not ostentatious. He knew his wife well.

"Cassie." Dalton's voice broke into my fantasy and brought me back to my unwelcome reality. "Earth to Cassie."

"Sorry." I gave my head a shake. Dalton and I had ventured four blocks from the building to try the latest buzz-y chopped salad spot, but after taking one look at the line we decided it wasn't worth cutting into our minuscule thirty-minute lunch break and were now holed up in a Chipotle choking down lukewarm burritos. "I didn't get much sleep last night," I added, dabbing hot sauce off the corner of my mouth. Which was the truth. No point in adding I'd spent my evening scouring Annabelle's sparse Instagram account, searching for any clues as to what the inside of her and Forest's house looked like. It was important to have a frame of reference. When Forest told Annabelle what time he would be home, what kind of couch was she sitting on when her honey-brown eyes read his email?

Lucky for me, the research skills I'd honed in law school could finally be put to good use. I was able to take a peek at their upholstered dining room chairs thanks to a picture Annabelle posted two Thanksgivings ago (#TableIsReady #SoThankful) and a few clicks later located the chairs at Mitchell Gold for $1999 a pop. Annabelle had expensive taste. I'd bet the inside of their home made *Architectural Digest* look like a Target flyer.

"Hot date keeping you up late?" Dalton lifted a teasing eyebrow as he peeled down the foil on his burrito.

"Not exactly." I rolled my eyes, playing along with his light-hearted tone. Despite the short time we'd been working side by side, Dalton was growing on me. We ate meals together and poked fun at our coworkers, but I was always careful to walk the line between friendly and flirty, not wanting to tip the relationship too far over to one side, which would inevitably put an end to it. If there was one thing I knew about men, it was this: If they think there is *no* chance they can have you, then they won't waste a single minute talking to you. But, on the other hand, if they are one hundred percent *sure* that they can have you, they won't waste a minute talking to you either. As I said, it's a thin line. And it was important for me to walk it. Dalton was the closest thing I had to a work friend. Or any friend for that matter.

"Speaking of hot dates, or lack thereof, I read the most hilarious email from a partner at the firm this morning."

My ears perked up. Dalton had yet to mention Forest again after our initial conversation, and I assumed that the one email he read from Forest's inbox was just a fluke. In fact, I was counting on it. It made me feel privileged, somehow exceptional, to be the one person invited into the Wattses' private world. I didn't want Dalton snooping around in there too.

I've never liked to share.

On the other hand, the date range of Dalton's review folder was current, so if Dalton *did* have access to any more of Forest's emails—if he *did*—well, then I most certainly needed to know.

"Oh yeah, what did it say?" I asked, doing my best to sound casual. As if my stomach wasn't constricting with anticipation.

He leaned across the table, a gleam in his eye. "So, there's a litigation partner named Shelly Murphy," Dalton started. "She's one of the main contacts for Falcon Healthcare so I've read a lot of her boring-ass emails." He rolled his eyes. "Anyway, I came across one today where she was telling a friend about a blind date her sister set her up on." Giddy, Dalton launched into what I could only assume was a story about a blind date gone wrong while I plastered on what I hoped was an interested expression. I should've been relieved—happy even—that this story wasn't about Forest, but my shoulders were still tense.

The more I let myself think about it, the more I realized Dalton *must* have come across more of Forest's emails. There was no way his cache would have only *one* while mine had hundreds. There had to be other emails he wasn't talking about. Was he toying with me?

I chewed my lip as my eyes drifted out the window. The sidewalk was bustling with the usual ravenous midtown lunch crowd. Women with belted sheath dresses, expensive purses, and sensible heels whizzed by in packs. It wasn't too long ago that I had been one of them. How swiftly they'd culled me from the herd. Clearly, they'd sensed there was something faulty with me and, like a cat who eats the weakest of her young, sacrificed me for the good of the group.

I glared at the satisfied, smug expressions on their faces and felt my hands curl into fists. They were flaunting their success in my face with their flagrant, aggressive happiness.

That should be you, Cassie, the voice in my head hissed. *You should be out there with them instead of in here. But you fucked it all up.*

The burrito had gone cold in my hand. Dalton was still talking. I forced myself to focus right when he was delivering the punch line. "So, she goes to meet him at the bar and it turns out they actually know each other but never made the connection." He paused for effect. "He's a VP at Falcon and she fucking hates the guy because apparently he's a 'misogynist asswipe.'" He air-quoted, his grin widening ear to ear.

I raised my eyebrows and fixed my best shocked and amused expression on my face.

"Can you imagine telling a story like that over email?" He shook his head in disbelief. "I mean, some of the shit these people reveal is astounding. This morning I opened an email that had a guy's Social Security number in it. The whole freaking nine digits, out there for the world to see." Dalton flicked his hand in emphasis.

My pulse quickened. Could that be Forest? He was always a little careless about what he put in his email. Trusting. Maybe too trusting for his own good.

His information was safe with me, of course, but was it safe with Dalton?

"Crazy," I replied, picking at the label of my water bottle. "Which lawyer did that?" I struggled to keep my tone nonchalant.

He ran the pad of his thumb across his top lip. "Some first-year associate, I think. Setting up benefits with HR."

I let out a slow, relieved exhale.

Now, to seize the opportunity. "I never get anything juicy in my review. You always get all the good stuff. Remember how you had that email about the guy in the cafeteria about to get fired? By that corporate partner?" I didn't dare say Forest's name for fear of my reddening face outing me. "Have you—"

"Yeah, I've had some humdingers," Dalton interrupted, failing to take my bait. "I like to think it's the universe's way of throwing me a bone. Ninety percent of what I read is so dull I want to scratch my eyes out, so every so often I get rewarded with something good." He crumpled up the empty burrito wrapper and tossed it on his tray. "Anyway, what are you up to this weekend?"

I shifted in my chair, annoyed with his swift topic change. The mere mention of the weekend threw my mood out of whack. In the old days, I would've looked forward to Saturday and Sunday. I would've had plans, errands, an entire to-do list. But that was then. Now the weekend was just forty-eight long, empty hours that needed to be filled. I supposed there were many things I could do with that time. I could go to the Met and take a guided tour. I could go to the gym. I could take in a matinee at the movie theater three blocks from my apartment. But the problem with all those things was they came with the unfortunate side effect of reminding me I had no one to do them with.

"I'm meeting up with some friends," I lied. I could feel my face flush, so I took a long swallow from my bottled water, hoping it would double as a shield.

Dalton nodded. There was a brief moment when the air felt charged and I wondered if he was going to ask me to do something with him over the weekend. *Would I accept an invitation from Dalton?* I wondered, watching his Adam's apple bob as he slugged back his La Croix. At least I would be around another person, connected to the world somehow, like a human being. I didn't need to consider the possibility, though, because Dalton changed the topic again and launched into an idea he had for a TV show about a group of temp attorneys.

"It would be a cross between *The Office* and *Orange Is the New Black*," I heard him say before I tuned out and let my mind drift back to my happy place. Forest and Annabelle.

I wondered what their plans were for the weekend. They were an active couple, obviously, so Saturday would include tennis or a bike ride or maybe even a hot yoga class. Sundays would be reserved for relaxing. According to the invoice sent to Forest's inbox, they had the Sunday *Times* delivered to their doorstep. I could picture them waking in a bundle of goose down and Egyptian cotton, and Forest padding to the front door to retrieve the newspaper from the mat while Annabelle made coffee and warmed two buttery croissants. Then she would sit in their solarium and Forest would come up behind her and lay his hands on her shoulders for a ten-second massage before taking the seat next to her so she could rest her feet in his lap.

I lifted a hand to my shoulder and gave it a gentle squeeze, imagining the weight of Forest's hands. I tried to remember the last time I had meaningful physical contact with another person, the last time someone's skin had touched mine. I once read an article about babies in the neonatal units of hospitals thriving from skin-to-skin contact. "Kangaroo care" the article called it. The babies who didn't receive kangaroo care were far less likely to survive. *Does this apply to adults?* I wondered, running a fingertip down my arm. Was the way I was living right now—void of human touch—literally killing me? God knows it felt that way.

An empty feeling attacked my stomach and spread throughout my insides. It felt like my wanting was swallowing me whole. I tried to tune back in to the conversation with Dalton, but couldn't keep from staring at his hands as they moved, punctuating his sentences. I wanted to snatch them midair and hold them against my shoulder, feel their weight against my body. My skin began to prickle, aching for something—a drink, a pill, anything to neutralize the horrid thoughts in my mind. I silently reprimanded myself for not replacing the little bottle of Bacardi I had stashed in my purse for just this type of situation.

Dalton was still talking, oblivious to the hurricane whirling inside me.

I dug my fingernails deep into my legs, hard enough to leave marks. Then I pushed them harder. The pain spread comfortingly down my thighs.

There, the feeling is gone now, Cassie. You're back to normal. You're back to normal.

Dalton cocked his head. "You okay, Cass?"

No.

"I'm good," I said, rearranging my features into a thin smile as I stood up and grabbed the metal tray with the remains of my burrito. "I just remembered I need to pick something up on the way back to the office."

To: Mary Woodson
From: Cassandra Woodson

Hi Grandma,

Sorry I've been MIA, I've been really busy. I made a career transition—another firm recruited me pretty hard so I made a move. They're still setting me up on their phone system, but I'll give you my number when it all shakes out.
Talk soon,
Cassie

Chapter Nine

"Next stop Fordham. Fordham next stop," the scratchy voice on the speaker announced.

I shifted in the blue pleather seat, my legs jittery with nervous energy. Across the aisle two twenty-something guys each hitched a backpack around one shoulder and shuffled toward the exit. A gray-haired man put a hand on his instrument case to keep it from sliding across the floor when the train screeched to a halt. Outside the window, urban scenery gave way to a landscape of houses, bringing me one step closer. My skin was tingling with anticipation. This was really happening. I was taking the bull by the horns. Thinking outside the box. Picking up the ball and running with it. For once, living up to all the positive clichés that used to appear in my employee evaluation at Nolan & Wright every year.

Cassie Woodson is a dependable team player who doesn't hesitate to step up to the plate.

I should have that stitched on a pillow. Proof I used to be a respected human being. How the mighty have fallen, as Dad would say. But, I supposed you couldn't be a team player without a team, could you? I was totally alone.

No. You have Forest and Annabelle now, I reminded myself. *Team Watts.* And it was time to finally get a look at my winning team in person. Standing at the base of the building every morning had been fruitless and was quickly growing tiresome.

I surveyed the train car, wondering if Forest had ever sat where

I was sitting. Maybe he'd spent time mindlessly picking at the same corner of peeling plastic that my fingernail was picking at right now. I smiled, picturing him walking down the aisle of the train, searching for an available seat before flopping down on this one, wiggling a thumb under his tie, and settling in for the thirty-five-minute journey. This was his route, the one he took back and forth to work every day and here I was, walking in the same footsteps, like some kind of religious pilgrimage. I smiled to myself thinking about Forest as a messiah. Now there was a religion I could get behind.

Of course, Forest wouldn't be on the train today. It was Sunday morning so he would be home with Annabelle enjoying the unseasonably warm fall weather. Hopefully outside on their deck. The front one. Where I could see them.

Fingers crossed.

I rested my head against the dirty train window and closed my eyes for a moment. My stomach was starting to feel sour, the mini Zaro's black and white cookies I'd ingested at Grand Central an hour ago sitting like a brick. They'd looked tasty in the display case, but turns out, they were way too sweet and doughy for my taste.

The clanging and bumping of the train was not exactly helping with my nausea. Nor was it doing anything good for the exhaustion permeating my bones. I lifted my fingers to my temples, rotating tiny circles in an attempt to counteract the headache pressing against my skull. The woman with the flowered scarf in the opposite seat looked up from her novel and frowned. Clearly the pain in my head was somehow bothersome to her. I dropped my hands to my lap and sat up straighter, avoiding her gaze. Out of the corner of my eye, I noticed a tiny, disapproving shake of her head before she returned her attention to her book.

Screw you and your ugly fucking scarf, I wanted to scream.

God, my head was hurting. I really needed to get more sleep. Insomnia was wreaking havoc on my central nervous system. Last night, I tried to focus on the TV to put me to sleep, but it didn't work. At two forty-five A.M. I'd staggered through my kitchen on a scavenger hunt for something stronger than the pinot grigio I had optimistically thought would do the trick. Flinging open cupboards, I cursed myself for my failure to plan ahead. How stupid of me to think a few bottles of wine would be enough to get through an entire weekend. I was on the verge of giving up the search when I came across a dusty, half-empty bottle of Jack Daniel's in the back corner underneath the sink. Gratefully, I'd brought the bottle to my lips, tilted my head back, and let the familiar spicy warmth slide down my throat.

It is remarkable, really, how that oaky taste was still linked to certain memories, forever imprinted on my cerebral cortex like an unwanted tattoo. All it took was one gulp of the dark amber liquid and I was right back there, at the post-work dinners I used to share with Landon. We'd be sitting across a reclaimed-wood table at the latest trendy downtown restaurant, his eyes studying the menu, mine studying the perfect angles of his face. At the end of the meal, without fail, Landon would order two glasses of scotch on the rocks. Never a blend, of course. Always a single malt. Unlike the cheap version I'd chugged last night like my life depended on it. I never even *liked* the taste of scotch, but I would still sip the single malt that Landon ordered for me with a shit-eating grin on my face, marveling like an idiot that this Golden Boy had chosen me—basic, boring Cassie Woodson. Of course, if I'd kept my Greek mythology classes in mind, I would've realized I was more like Icarus than Aphrodite.

Fucking prick. God, Landon was a fucking prick.

Time is not the healer it's cracked up to be.

The screech of the train's brakes startled my eyes open with the speed of being roused from a bad dream. I blinked a few times, getting my bearings. There was a niggle at the back of my mind. A tiny voice I couldn't quite make out. A cold clamminess on the back of my neck. *Think, Cassie, think.*

Last night.

After the scotch.

An unpleasant sensation rose up within me. I had done something. My head spun for a second and I gripped the edge of the seat and tried to breathe deeply to keep from tipping over. What had I done? Frantically, I tried to recall every move I'd made last night. I remembered sitting on my sofa and watching television. The volume was low. I couldn't remember what I was watching, but at some point the phone was in my hands. I was desperate to tell someone something. Who? Had I placed a call? Or maybe pecked out an email?

The oxygen thinned out in the train.

Oh god, oh god, oh god.

I pulled the phone from my pocket with shaking hands and navigated to my sent folder, mentally begging it to be clear.

My shoulders slumped with relief. The last email that was sent from my account was the one I'd written to Grandma yesterday afternoon.

Still, there was an uneasy feeling lodged in my throat.

My trembling finger slid to the green-and-white phone icon. Had I talked to anyone last night? I bit my lip and tapped on the list of recent calls.

No. No. No.

I shook my head vehemently, as if trying to shake the very truth of what I was seeing out of my brain. The call log showed I'd made three calls last night: at 3:05 A.M., 3:08 A.M., 3:17 A.M. All to Landon's phone. My stomach twisted. Judging from the length of the calls, the first two were hang ups. The third one, I'd left a thirty-six second voicemail.

My nails dug into my palms. This was certainly going to violate that stupid restraining order.

"*Shit!*" I hissed under my breath.

The lady with the flowered scarf let out a disgusted huff before gathering her book and purse and moving to a seat two rows back.

Good riddance, lady. Go hang yourself with that ugly scarf.

I groaned and stuffed the phone into the side pocket of my purse, trying to jam down any thoughts of Landon along with it. But I couldn't quite get to the safe place in my head. It was too late. My heart was already racing; my throat was tight. I knew what came next. I could feel it building, that painfully familiar feeling. Whenever I got it, the memories of my last day at Nolan & Wright started coming in relentless waves, like an army on attack, blitzing through my brain.

The sounds come first. John Dwight's horrified scream vibrating in my ears.

Cassie! No! What did you do?

Then come the images. The blood-soaked, perfectly pressed white dress shirt. The blade in my hands.

I was slipping.

I pressed my palms into my eye sockets hard enough to fill my vision with multicolored dots.

The train wailed and shuddered to a standstill at what I could see from the white sign on the platform was the Woodlawn station.

Only two more stops.

I reached into my pocket and pulled out the blister pack of Robitussin Maximum Strength. I pushed five pills through the foil into my sweaty palm. It usually only took three or four to quiet my racing mind, but fuck it. Five it was. I stared down at the capsules, my nausea intensifying. What was it Dad used to say when he swallowed a pill? *Open the latch, it's coming down the hatch!* I wished I had something as strong as the pills he used to pop. But I would need to go see a doctor to get anything close to that potency. And that was out of the question. I was not some faulty transmission that needed fixing. I was valedictorian, for god's sake! Unfortunately, the only other way to get meds like that was to steal them. And what kind of person would steal pills from her own father's medicine cabinet?

You.

"Once," I said out loud.

I threw the pills in my mouth and swallowed them dry. I closed my eyes for a moment, waiting for the sweet numbness to spread over me like a heavy blanket. It seemed to take longer these days. After a moment, the chatter in my mind got quieter and I forced myself to unfurl my fists, rubbing my aching palms on my pants. Time to focus on more important things.

I slid my hand into my bag, closing my fingers around the rim of the smooth three-ring black binder, and inhaled deeply.

Forest.

Everything there was to know about Forest was now literally at my fingertips. I'd spent Friday night typing up every morsel of information I'd gathered about Forest into one pretty Word document (discreetly labeled "miscellaneous.doc" in the unlikely event anyone else ever used my laptop) complete with headings and bullet points. It was a labor of love that took me over eight hours. Thirty-two thousand six hundred and fifty words. Thirty-one pictures. Ninety-two bold-faced, underlined headings. **Names of Friends, Family Details, Annabelle's Likes** . . .

I'd printed the meticulous document, three-hole punched, and carefully slotted it into the rings of a binder I'd purchased from the CVS across the street at four in the morning. It was a thing of beauty, really. In my hunt for useful information, it was like a taxidermy deer head I could hang on my wall.

I flipped it open and Forest's face stared back at me from the smudges of my printed images. I let the sight of his warm brown eyes fill all the nooks and crannies of my mind where Landon once dwelled, let it burn inside me like a pilot light.

There was Forest in his firm photo, dressed in a navy dress shirt and striped tie, a gleaming smile on his lips as if he knew I was admiring his gorgeous face. There he was with Annabelle, resplendent in red silk, his hand positioned protectively on the small of her back as they posed together in front of a vinyl wall at a charity function at the Met. I closed my eyes and imagined for a moment the way Forest looked at Annabelle in that dress from across the room.

Here. Now, here's my favorite one of them—a candid of Forest and Annabelle at the 2016 Friends of the High Line Benefit, both of them smiling as they look at something off-camera, heads tilted at the exact same angle, as if everything about them is always perfectly in sync. I chewed on a hangnail, wondering what or who was bringing such a joyful crinkle to their eyes. I wished with every fiber of my body that it was me.

Cassie, you made it! We've been waiting for you! Come get in the picture! I could picture Annabelle's wide smile as she beckoned me over.

No longer cast out. I was wanted. Cherished. Part of what made them whole.

"Bronxville next stop. Next stop Bronxville," the train conductor's voice blared. I leapt out of my seat, tucked the binder safely away, swung my bag over my shoulder, and staggered to the exit.

Finally, I had arrived.

Chapter Ten

"WHERE TO, HONEY?" the gray-haired taxi driver asked.

"Nineteen Woodland Drive," I replied breathlessly, wiping a bead of sweat off my forehead with the back of my hand and pulling the car door shut. I'd run up the stairs, two at a time, anxious to get to the taxi pick-up spot before any of my fellow passengers. I'd briefly considered taking a stroll around the area first and popping into The Grind, a coffee shop Annabelle had mentioned in an email to Forest *(I'm at The Grind having a cinnamon latte with Lizzy, will call you back when we're done!),* but now that I was here, mere minutes away from Forest and Annabelle's home, the magnetic pull was too strong to resist.

I could probably find my way through the inside of their house if I wanted to. I'd studied the floor plans and cross-referenced them with Annabelle's Instagram photos. My favorite room, hands down, had to be the elegant dining room with the gilt chandelier and two-sided fireplace. It was the perfect mix of modern and traditional, just like them. And a far cry from the particleboard Ikea coffee table I ate off of in my apartment.

Of course, I wasn't going to go inside their home. Not today. I only wanted to observe them in their natural habitat. They had to leave their house at some point, and I was prepared to wait it out. I had comfortable shoes and snacks. I would stop by The Grind on the way back. A latte would hit the spot.

The driver threw the car in reverse. I noticed him peering at me in the rearview mirror over his glasses so I sat up straighter, trying to project an air of confidence, pulling out my phone as if I was one of those people who received important messages all the time instead of just emails from Seamless offering me ten percent off my next order.

Please don't talk to me, my mind pleaded. *Please don't be one of those taxi drivers who needs to have a conversation.* All I wanted to do was gaze out the window, take in every detail of my surroundings, and fix them in my memory. The post office was coming into view now. I remembered seeing an image of it when I was searching the area around the train station on Google Earth. Annabelle probably mailed her Christmas cards there. Tasteful, custom letterpress I was sure. I lifted a hand to the passenger window and pressed my fingers against the glass, resisting the urge to tell the driver to stop so I could hop out and rest my hand on the door handle. I so badly needed to see what they see, touch what they had touched.

I slid my thumb down the screen of my phone, wondering if there was a way I could somehow angle it to take a stealth video of the ride. I wanted to capture every image of their world, save them for later. That way, I wouldn't miss a single thing.

The car stopped at a red light and out of the corner of my eye, I could see the driver studying me in the rearview mirror. The edges of my mind curled with uncertainty. Could he tell I didn't belong here? I smoothed down the flyaway hair on top of my head, realizing I was probably red-faced and sweaty after running up the stairs and had the appearance of someone who had fled a burning building. No wonder he was gawking.

"I haven't had you in my car before." His voice sliced through the silence, startling me. I looked up, catching his eye, and something moved uneasily in my stomach. I ignored it and returned my gaze to the window. Maybe if I didn't say anything he would take a hint.

"It's usually the same crowd coming off the trains," he continued in a thick New York accent as the light turned green. "All the regulars. But I haven't seen you before." There was a question in his tone, but I had no intention of answering it.

"Yeah, I don't think I've been in your car before," I replied distractedly as my eyes stayed fixed on the window. Outside, the cafés and small shops that had dotted the streets around the train station had given way to tree-lined sidewalks and brick colonial houses with meticulously maintained yards. It was certainly a lot different than the neighborhood I grew up in, where the lots were so small you could reach out your window and touch the house next to you. Everything seemed easier out here, lighter. Even the air felt like it contained more oxygen. I wanted to roll down my window and fill my lungs with it.

It was exactly how I pictured Forest and Annabelle's neighborhood would be.

I closed my eyes and crushed a surge of longing.

The driver cleared his throat, drawing my attention back to him. He gave me an unnerving smile. "So . . ." He paused and something in the way the air in the taxi shifted made the tiny hairs on my arms stand at attention. "How do you know Forest?"

The words landed like a grenade. Everything outside the window swirled and dropped on its side. The car was still moving, the radio still playing, but the only sound I could hear was my own breath quickening.

Of course, my mind screamed. Of course he would know Forest. Forest must use the same fleet of cabs every day rushing home from the train station to Annabelle. And he would be the friendly type of person who would engage the taxi driver in small talk. *How are the kids? How's your mom's back? I remember she was in the hospital. . . .*

That would be so Forest.

I stared at the driver's reflection in the mirror as he raised his eyebrows expectantly, tapping his thick thumbs against the steering wheel to the beat of the music. *Say something, Cassie,* my mind implored. *Anything.* But the words lodged in my throat. After what felt like an hour but was probably only a few seconds, I sucked in my cheeks to wet my mouth enough to speak. "I'm sorry?" I stammered, pretending I hadn't heard him.

"You're going to Forest Watts's house, right?" He flicked on his blinker and turned down what I could see from the sign was Woodland Drive, Forest and Annabelle's street. "I have Forest in my taxi a lot. Really nice guy. And his wife . . ." He snapped a finger, presumably trying to come up with her name.

Annabelle, my frantic mind silently filled in.

"Annabelle!" His smile widened.

Had I said her name out loud? My heart was pounding so hard I could feel it in the back of my skull now.

"Are you her sister? I can see some resemblance."

Sister.

For a moment the sheer exhilaration that this stranger had put me in the same gene pool as Annabelle Watts knocked any other thought from my head, but swiftly the reality of my situation kicked in. This guy knew Forest. What the hell was I going to say to him when we reached Forest's house? The homes on this street weren't really houses, they were estates. It would look odd if I told the driver I didn't want him to pull into the long, winding driveway and instead asked to be dropped off at the curb. So odd, in fact, that he'd probably mention something about it to Forest the next time he saw him. *I picked up a woman from the train station who said she was going to your house but then wanted to be dropped off across the street.* Oh god, maybe Forest and Annabelle would get spooked and report the incident to the police.

Bile crept up in the back of my throat.

Getting in this taxi had to be the stupidest thing I'd ever done.

Not even close, the unforgiving voice in my head whispered in response.

Pinpricks of stress were gathering in the middle of my forehead making it hard to think. The numbers fixed to mailboxes of the homes we were driving past were getting smaller and smaller. We'd be at 19 Woodland Drive in no time. I felt as though I was being driven off a cliff.

Oh god, think, Cassie. Think!

"I forgot something at the train station!" I blurted, patting the backseat frantically for effect. It was not hard to fake being in full-blown panic mode.

He jammed on the brakes, his eyes swiveling from the road to the rearview mirror again. "Something important?"

"Yes, yes, my, um . . . roller bag." My voice sounded unnaturally high-pitched. I tried to lower it. "How scatterbrained of me. Can you turn around here?" I tapped on the window with a trembling finger, pointing to the large driveway out the right-hand side. "I should get back there right away."

"You don't want me to take you to your sister's house first? Let them know what happened?"

My stomach flipped like a pancake. *Sister*. He had no idea how long I would be replaying that scenario in my mind fantasizing about it. Or how much I would kill to make it a reality. "No, no." I shook my head. "I want to get back to the station as soon as possible so no one walks away with it."

He nodded. "Probably a good idea." He pulled the steering wheel and made a quick three-point turn.

I swiveled my head to look out the rear window. Like a heat-seeking missile, my eyes landed on a large red mailbox with silver numbers affixed to the side. My stomach lurched. Number nineteen.

Come outside. Walk to your mailbox. Let me see you.

"I'll get you back to the station, sweetheart. You can't have a suitcase sitting on the platform. Ever since 9/11 the cops will swoop right in thinking there's a bomb in there." He made a blowing up motion with his hands. "That's how they'll get us next time, you know? The terrorists. They won't need planes, they'll just put bombs in suitcases and they'll put them everywhere."

I nodded, feeling my cheek quavering. I didn't dare respond, for fear of how my voice would sound, but I was grateful he was talking about something other than Forest now. Who would've thought a conversational pivot to terrorists would land me in safer territory? I clenched my sweaty hands together hard enough my knuckles turned white. *Please don't let him mention this to Forest. Please don't let him mention this to Forest.* I silently begged a god I didn't believe in.

My hands were still trembling minutes later when I pulled the handle to the back door and leapt out of the taxi at the train station.

"Tell your sister Annabelle that Glen says 'hi'!" the driver called out after me as I speed-walked away from the car, trying not to break into a run. When I was finally out of sight, I bent over a garbage can and threw up.

To: Forest Watts
From: Cassandra Woodson

This email was written but not sent and has been saved as a draft until further action

Forest,

We haven't met before, but I'm a good friend of your sister, Courtney, from back in our days at BU. I'm going to be in New York tomorrow for a quick visit and she mentioned I should come out and meet up with you and your wife. Courtney always speaks fondly of you so it would be great to put a face to a name! Would you mind if I pop by around noon? It would be lovely to meet you and Annabelle in person.

Warmly,
Cassie

To: Cassandra Woodson
From: Landon McKinley

First of all, were you outside my apartment building last week? My doorman thinks he saw you standing out there for over an hour.

Second, I received a drunken voicemail last night and I'm pretty sure it was from you. Between the slurring and swearing it was hard to tell. You need to stop this, Cassie. Seriously. I don't want to have to call the police. Again.

Chapter Eleven

THE CLOMP CLOMP of my scuffed pumps echoed as I swiped my employee ID and pushed through the turnstile. *Pull it together,* I repeated in my mind as I ran a hand over my flyaway hair and surreptitiously wiped the sweat beads from my chest. I couldn't remember falling asleep last night, but I must have. One minute I was looking at the TV with bleary, stinging eyes, the next minute a horn was blaring from the street below, dragging me into consciousness like a splash of cold water to the face. I deserved a medal for how fast I'd made it here, despite the headache throbbing behind my eyes. I cupped my palm around my mouth as I scurried to the elevator bank and did a quick breath check. My nose crinkled. The smell of gin was still lingering. I had stopped at the liquor store on my way home from my disastrous trip to Bronxville yesterday and bought a fresh bottle. A big one. What else was going to calm the trauma of what happened?

Trauma? said the nasty voice in my head. *Puh-lease, you drama queen.*

But it *was* traumatic. I thought I'd put my relationship with Forest and Annabelle in jeopardy. What if the taxi driver had pulled into the driveway and deposited me right there on the doorstep, leaving me no time to prepare and get a good story in place? That would've been catastrophic. Next time I went out there I would be smarter. I would walk from the train station, rather than take a taxi. It wouldn't take more than twenty minutes. Thirty tops. I just needed to wait a week or two for that nosy taxi driver to forget my face in case he was lurking around the train station.

I'm very forgettable. Just ask my mother.

I rooted through my purse for my tin of cinnamon Altoids and popped four in my mouth, cringing as they dissolved on my tongue. The intense taste always made my eyes water. I pushed the button for the elevator and shot a quick look at the clock—eight forty-five. Hopefully Ricky would be too wrapped up in his work to notice I was fifteen minutes late.

"Oh good, I'm not the only one running late this morning," Dalton panted, hopping into the elevator behind me as the doors were closing. His hands were full with two venti-sized Starbucks cups, and I could feel my nerve endings pulsing under my skin, aching for a sip.

Dalton gave me a quick once-over. "Here, you look like you need one of these," he said, extending his hand.

"Really?" I eyed the cup like some kind of crack junkie about to get a fix.

"Yes, really, but I'm rescinding the offer if you don't take it." He jiggled the cup impatiently.

"Thanks," I said, accepting the cup. Unexpected tears prickled the back of my eyes as I wrapped my fingers around the warmth. I couldn't remember the last time another person had given me anything. "I didn't have time to stop to pick anything up on the way, so this is perfect." I smiled, blinking rapidly as I raised the cup in a toast.

"Anytime." Dalton took a gulp from his cup and I followed suit.

"Wait a sec." I cleared my throat and pointed to the sticker affixed to the cup that read MOBILE ORDER: BROCK.

Dalton gave a mock scoff. "Hey, if an entitled fuck named Brock can't be bothered to line up and order his coffee like the rest of us then I can't be bothered to refrain from taking his drink while waiting for my own."

I laughed as Dalton lifted his hand and made a "hey, what can you do" expression. I wasn't sure if it was the rare genuine laughter escaping from my mouth or the taste of the sweet, sugary drink, but I could feel some of the tension that had built up over the weekend slowly seeping from my body. By the time we entered our poorly ventilated work space (which Dalton had termed Alcatraz) I was feeling something close to calm. Which was why I was caught completely off guard when I saw Ricky's lanky body striding like a bandleader toward us.

"You guys are fifteen minutes late," he boomed, pointing to the imaginary watch on his wrist. "That's going to be one less bathroom break for each of you today."

"No worries, Ricky, I'll just piss into this if I need to." Dalton raised his coffee cup.

Ricky narrowed his eyes and pointed a menacing finger at Dalton. "Watch it, funny boy. Don't think I won't call the temp agency and have you replaced tomorrow." Ricky glared as if he was a bar brawler waiting for Dalton to throw the first punch, before turning his attention to me.

"Cassie, I need a word." He tilted his overly gelled head toward the side door, which led to a small break room.

"Sure," I answered, trying to keep my expression neutral. This couldn't be about being fifteen minutes late or Dalton would be included in the reprimand. I glanced over at Dalton, who raised his eyebrows in a way that asked, *What's going on?* I shrugged my shoulders and followed Ricky, taking a deep, practiced breath and exhaling slowly, controlled.

The urge to flee was causing beads of sweat on the back of my neck.

I briefly considered telling Ricky I needed to go to the bathroom. ASAP. "Women problems," I'd say by way of explanation so he would be too embarrassed to question me. Then I'd walk right to the elevator, down through the revolving doors, and disappear into the anonymity of New York City.

Gone.

But that would sever my tie to Forest and Annabelle. Sure, I would still have Google, but any idiot could track that information down. Our connection was different. It was private. Personal. The thought of putting that in jeopardy was so frightening it suddenly felt like a real physical threat, like an armed hitman looming behind a door.

I fixed an innocent expression on my face.

Act natural. Nothing to see here.

"Cassie," Ricky started after closing the door. The tiny room had a rickety table with two folding chairs and a fluorescent light flickering overhead, making it look more like an interrogation room than a break room. Ricky even had the look of a small-town detective with his cheap suit and slicked hair. I would've found the whole scene hysterical if I hadn't been so utterly terrified.

"Do you know why I've called you in here?"

"Um . . . because I was late?" I willed my voice to stay even. Any shake would make it seem like I had something to hide.

"No, but that can't happen again." He glared at me long enough to hit the point home before continuing. "The reason I called you in here is I was reviewing everyone's stats from last week . . ." He trailed off into a moment of heavy, accusing silence.

A bead of sweat dribbled down my back. Shit. So, there *was* some kind of employee surveillance in place. Even the extra strength Tylenol I'd popped this morning couldn't quell the rising panic.

Ricky crossed his arms over his chest. "You were at the bottom, Cassie. You only reviewed two hundred files a day."

Shit.

I clenched my hands together to hide the tiny shake and cleared my throat. "Well . . . um . . . last week I came across a lot of documents that were multiple pages long—some of them as many as fifty or sixty pages and they were extremely dense too." I scrunched my eyebrows together, an exaggerated expression to demonstrate the complexity of the task. "So I needed to take a little extra time before marking them nonresponsive. I know you said when in doubt I should come to you, but you're so busy and I didn't want to waste your time, so I reviewed those ones diligently. Maybe more diligently than necessary because it definitely took me longer than it should've." My voice held steady. I sounded in control. *Nothing to see here.* "You were so right, Ricky, there are a lot of complicated aspects to this project."

Ricky's hawkish face softened, clearly pleased with my deferential attitude and the fact I'd referenced one of his instructions. "Look, I get that you're new here and still learning the ropes, but the higher-ups have set a pace for us and they're always watching." He lowered his voice and pointed to the ceiling, as if from thirty floors above they could see and hear us, like an omnipresent, all-knowing god. "They are *always* watching," he repeated.

I resisted the urge to remind him that by the nature of our project it was actually *us* who were monitoring *them.*

"If we're going to meet their expectations, Cassie, we need to be getting through over five hundred documents a day."

"Five hundred," I echoed, standing up straighter in an attempt to physically convey I was up for the challenge. "I'll increase the pace today. I think I'm past the learning stage at this point."

"Learning stage," Ricky repeated suspiciously and eyed me as if he was an interrogator trying to get his subject to break down and confess. The fluorescent lights flickered, illuminating the thick silence. I felt my underarms grow damp but fought to maintain the neutral expression on my face.

Reluctantly, Ricky broke the silence. "Well, you'd *better* pick up the pace today. We're only as strong as our weakest link."

I gave an obedient nod as my insides sagged with relief.

"I'm going to be keeping my eye on you, Cassie." Ricky opened the door to the interrogation room, indicating our conversation was over.

I let out a long exhale, only now realizing how shallow my breath had been. I noticed Dalton trying to catch my eye on my way back to my workstation, but I kept my head down.

Ricky's skeptical gaze was burning into my back.

To: Cassandra Woodson
From: Pamela West

Dear Ms. Woodson,

Thank you for your interest in the NYU Law Alumni Association. In order to register you for our LAA annual luncheon at Cipriani, I first need to get some information from you. I can't seem to find your name in our alumni database—would it be possible you are in there under your maiden name? As well, I'll need to have your graduation year. If you could pass that information along, I can get you registered!

Regards,
Pamela West

Chapter Twelve

"Please tell me the part where he called you the weakest link again," Dalton said with a chuckle, wiping the ketchup from the side of his mouth with a napkin. We were in our usual spot in the cafeteria, our nightly dinners having become a ritual I was surprised to find myself looking forward to.

"Shhh . . ." I cautioned. "He'll hear you!" I shot a glance in Ricky's direction, but he was absorbed in something on his phone, earbuds firmly in place, as he chowed down on his gravy-coated chicken. It had been a week since he'd pulled me into the interrogation room, but that didn't stop Dalton from wanting to hear the story again.

It *was* pretty comical when I thought about it now, my body no longer pumped full of the disorienting fight-or-flight adrenaline that had flooded through me in the moment. Ricky thought monitoring how many documents I reviewed would make my work more efficient. But there was a problem with Ricky's stats: They didn't tell him whether I was actually *reading* what was on the screen before clicking "nonresponsive." Now that I knew he was scrutinizing our total number of documents reviewed, it was easy for me to game the system. A few mindless taps on my mouse and I could make ten, twenty, one hundred documents a day disappear from my "to be reviewed" folder, padding my numbers just enough to avoid suspicion.

"And what will Ricky do if he hears me? Fire me?" Dalton gave an exaggerated eye roll. "He's never gonna do that, Cassie. Trust me. He's like one of those Southern housewives who yells at her cleaning lady because she didn't fold her laundry the way she likes. Those women never actually *fire* the cleaning lady because they know if they do, they'll be hand-scrubbing their underwear themselves." He dipped a crinkle-cut French fry in his pool of ketchup and popped it in his mouth, as if he'd unarguably proved his point.

I wrinkled my nose. "Are we the underwear scrubbers in this analogy?"

Dalton hooted and slapped his knee. Out of the corner of my eye I noticed a table of polished associates stop their conversations and shoot us a look.

I shifted uncomfortably in my chair.

"Yeah, I guess I consider us the underwear scrubbers." Dalton scratched his cheek pensively, oblivious to the glares. "I never thought about it quite like that, but that sounds about right. Listen—" He licked his index finger before wiping it on a napkin. "Ricky won't fire me and even if he did I'm fully prepared for my eventual unemployment."

I lowered my voice hoping he would follow suit. "Why? Is this project ending? Do you know something I don't?"

"No, but you are aware at some point clients are going to realize the mindless monkey work we do can be done by a computer, right? We're not exactly splitting the atom around here." Dalton pointed his fork at me. "You have to be prepared, Cass, like a temp law Boy Scout, for when our jobs are inevitably eliminated. And I don't mean only this gig. I mean all temp gigs." He gave an ominous look. "I, for one, am prepared. I have my expenses down to only fifty percent of my paycheck and I bank the other fifty."

I considered this. "How do you manage to bank half your salary and still live in the city? Do you have one of those rent-controlled apartments?"

"I live with my mom. Rent free." He shrugged like it was no big deal, but I noticed the faintest blush. "That's what mothers are for, right?"

A sharp bolt of pain passed through my chest. One toss-off comment like that was all it took to remind me Dalton didn't know me very well. He assumed all mothers were like his, perfectly content to have her adult child under her roof so she could do his laundry and surround him in a blanket of maternal love.

Maternal love. Ha. I wanted to laugh out loud at the ridiculous concept.

Dalton's forehead wrinkled. "Are you okay?"

"Yep." I ran a fingertip under my eyes. "The stir-fry's extra spicy tonight." I took a long gulp of my drink, using the cup as a shield. When I lifted my gaze Dalton was examining me, his head tilted to one side.

"What?" I asked, picking up my napkin. "Is there something on my face?"

"You look kind of different today. Glowy or something," he mumbled, his voice uncharacteristically quiet.

"It must be the makeup." I shrugged, pushing my straw in and out of its plastic lid, suppressing a tiny grin.

It wasn't the makeup. It was Forest. After all of my efforts, I had finally, blessedly seen him in the flesh. And it was all thanks to an innocuous email I unearthed from Forest to his friend Shane. *I'm telling you, buddy, I get a Fireball from Juice Press every morning and I haven't been sick in years.*

Boom.

The email was practically an engraved invitation. I couldn't just ignore it, at least not when all I had to do was google the Juice Press locations in the city, copy down the addresses of all twelve spots, and pick a new one to wait outside every morning.

It only took me three days. At 8:02 A.M. this morning outside of the Fifty-ninth Street location, my patience was finally rewarded. Forest Watts, his hands tucked in his pockets as he strode down the pavement, passed mere inches from my body on his way for his daily pressed juice. It took all my willpower not to run over to him and rub my hands over his face to ensure he was real. Instead, I stood on the corner, content to observe him from afar. His tall frame. The spread of his back and shoulders under his cashmere coat. How he lifted his right hand to run through his hair. I watched as he peered at his phone, waiting for the light to change, wishing I could claw inside his head. See what he was seeing. Was he reading an email from her? Were they talking about having "our" wine with dinner? His expression gave nothing away. Every nerve in my body stood at attention as my eyes followed him across Fifty-ninth Street, right up to the entrance to Juice Press. I waited for him to come out, a plastic bottle of brightly colored juice in his hand, and followed at a close distance. Forest had a determined stride. I liked that about him. It showed he knew what he wanted. We had that in common. One block, two blocks. I got bolder, sped up until I was three paces behind. On a whim, I raised my phone and snapped a picture of him from behind. *Smile!* I wished I could call out. *Click.* A keepsake to add to my growing collection. We walked on, into the lobby of the building, only to part ways at the elevator bank. *Higher-ups, this way. Temps, that way.* "I'll see you soon!" I wanted to call out, giddy by our first ever face-to-face interaction. It would definitely not be the last.

My unrelenting thirst to be in his orbit again galvanized me for what I was about to do now.

I picked up my fork and pushed the pile of rice around my plate. Steam bloomed from it for a second or two as I worked up the nerve to speak. "Hey . . . um . . . I came across a few emails from that guy you told me about, the run-Forest-run guy?" It was the first time I'd said his name out loud, to another person at least, and it tasted delicious in my mouth. Sweet and smooth.

Dalton stared at me, his expression inscrutable.

"The one who terminates people?" I clarified, raising the end of the sentence like I was asking a question, hoping Dalton would take the prompt and start talking.

"Oh yeah?" He popped another French fry in his mouth.

I wiped my sweaty palms on my lap, feeling piqued. "Yeah, nothing too interesting, but it's just weird, you know? I don't know why his emails are part of our review." I forced myself to keep my eyes on Dalton's face so I could assess his reaction. "Have you . . . have you seen any more of his emails in your folder?" He said nothing and for an agonizing moment I wondered if I'd been too bold with my questioning, but then he swallowed and I realized he was simply having trouble clearing his mouth.

"I've seen a few," he said, running his tongue around his teeth and swallowing again. "Quite a few."

A small part of my chest collapsed. *No. No. No. Forest was mine. Only mine.* My face muscles contracted as I struggled to remain expressionless. I wanted to take back my question, to stay tight inside the bubble that Forest and I had created together and not let Dalton seep in through the gaps.

But now he had gone and popped the whole fucking thing.

I felt an unsettling flare in my cheeks. *Breathe, Cassie. Breathe. He doesn't know Forest and Annabelle the way you do.*

Although, maybe he had some information about Forest that I didn't have.

My pulse kicked up another notch. It was important to choose my next words carefully. Saying the wrong thing here could be entirely misconstrued.

"Um. Have you seen anything juicy in his emails?" I cleared my throat to mask the tremor in my voice. "Like is he terminating anyone else?" Dalton cocked his head and eyed me quizzically for a millisecond too long. Sweat snaked down my spine.

"Probably," he said. "But I get the feeling that's not all he's doing to a coworker if you know what I'm saying." He raised his eyebrows suggestively.

I choked on my Diet Coke.

"You okay?" Dalton asked, peering.

I nodded, before giving my chest a light pound and dabbing my watering eyes. "Wrong pipe," I croaked. A hot bullet of anger lodged itself in my throat. Was Dalton implying what I thought he was implying? Because if he was. If he was then that was fucking ridiculous.

Dalton was peering at me curiously.

My mask was slipping but I pushed it back on firmly.

"What makes you say that?" I asked, forking a bite of oily chicken into my mouth, trying to sound like this was all just breezy office gossip, as if I didn't want to hurl my tray across the cafeteria. "Did you read something?"

He smiled and licked the grease off his fingers. There was an unpleasant gleam in his eye. "Well . . ." He drew out the word for effect. "Have you seen any emails to his secretary?"

"No," I lied.

"He got a new one. About a month ago."

Forest had a new secretary? This was new information. This I did not know. My knee started to bounce.

"Her name is . . . wait for it . . ." He paused, grinning. "Wednesday Walters."

"Wednesday?" I repeated in a maniacal tone, louder than I intended.

Dalton gestured for me to lower my voice before leaning in and lowering his. "You don't hire a secretary literally named after hump day unless you're hoping to hook up with her. It's like hiring someone named Bunny." He arched a triumphant eyebrow, as if this comparison alone proved his point.

I clutched my napkin with a rigor-mortis-like grip. This man was obviously delusional. How had I not realized this before?

"I wonder if she's called Wednesday because that was the day her parents conceived her?" Dalton chuckled and looked off into the distance as if contemplating the idea.

"So, did you see something in an email to Wednesday Walters to back up your ridiculous theory?" I struggled to keep the anger out of my voice.

"Well, no." He shrugged, a wounded look flickering across his face.

"Then you don't know what you're talking about, do you?" I snapped, surprising myself with the force of my voice.

"Whoa." Dalton held up his palms. "I didn't know I was hitting on a sore spot here, Cass. I mean, what's it to you?"

Heat rose to my face, but I rearranged my features to ensure my expression was neutral and shrugged casually. "I just don't think it's good to spread rumors about people you know nothing about." I forked in another mouthful of chicken, barely tasting it.

Dalton eyeballed me for a moment. "Oh, I know nothing, huh?" He planted an elbow on the table, and began counting off on his fingers. "I know the guy has a lunch meeting every Monday, I know he eats tacos every freaking Tuesday . . ."

I opened my mouth to speak, to tell him that just because he could recite a scheduling item and a food preference didn't mean he could soil a person's reputation, but Dalton continued.

"Oh, and he goes to the same midtown bar every Friday night for drinks. So, I would say I know this guy pretty well, actually." He took a triumphant bite of his hamburger and a blob of ketchup affixed itself to the corner of his mouth.

I was twisting the napkin so hard now it was starting to resemble a rope. I couldn't focus through the blinding veil of my rage. But then slowly, syllable by syllable, my mind caught up with the words that Dalton had vomited from his mouth.

The hairs on the back of my neck stood up.

Forest goes to the same bar every Friday night? Now we were getting somewhere.

I lifted the straw to my lips, structuring a question in my mind. "Which bar?" I asked, taking a sip even though there was nothing left but melting ice.

Dalton's mouth was full so he gestured he needed to finish chewing. My stomach twisted tighter with each chew. Bringing Forest up with Dalton had been a huge risk, but now at least there would be a payoff. A valuable one. After a moment, Dalton swallowed hard, dabbed the side of his mouth, and said, "I don't remember what it was called. Just follow the hordes of boring dudes with too much money."

It was everything I could do not to reach across the table, wrap my hands around his throat, and squeeze the life out of him.

"I'm going to get a refill." I stood abruptly on wobbly legs and picked up my cup. My heart was beating so fast and loud now that I needed a second to regroup. The edges of my mind were starting to feel blurry, my last shred of self-control slipping from my grasp. Out of the corner of my eye, I saw a group of temps pick up their trays in unison. For once, I was relieved our dinner break was over. I couldn't sit here another minute and listen to Dalton's delusions.

He didn't know Forest from a fucking hole in the wall. If he did, he would know there was no way Forest would ever cheat on Annabelle. Of that I was absolutely sure.

Wasn't I?

Chapter Thirteen

FIREBALL.

That is the name of the cold-pressed juice that Forest picks up every morning. It was also what was sitting in my stomach as I casually stood in the Juice Press on Fifty-ninth Street the next morning, staring into the refrigerator for what was going on eighteen minutes. It wasn't simply the anticipation of seeing Forest's face when he inevitably walked through the door for his morning juice. Today, I was taking it up a notch. Today, I wanted to hear his voice. And I wanted him to hear mine. I just needed to come up with a way to make that happen.

Maybe I could casually peek over his shoulder as he picked up his juice and comment on the benefits of the Fireball. *All those antioxidants!* "I have one every morning!" he'd respond, his long-lashed eyes burrowing into mine. A smile tugged at my lips thinking about having Forest's attention on me. *God that would be incredible.* I snuck another anxious look at my watch. If Forest didn't come in soon, I was going to be late for work. Or possibly arrested for loitering in this small juice bar now that the morning swell of people had died down and my presence was more conspicuous.

"You need any help?" The cashier sporting the messy man bun called out from behind the counter. "The Doctor Green Juice works wonders for detoxing after a rough night out." He flashed a knowing smile.

"Thanks," I answered, annoyed by the passive-aggressive implication that I looked like I had tied one on last night, when in fact I'd spent it on my couch with my friend Google. Although, in Man Bun's defense, there was gin involved and I probably hadn't pieced together more than four hours of sleep. My eyes were red enough that I probably *did* look like my body was attempting to metabolize toxic levels of alcohol, but I'd only had three drinks—four max— and I'd stuck to clear liquid, which doesn't leave me feeling hungover. No, these bloodshot eyes had nothing to do with the gin and everything to do with the fact that they'd been glued to my computer screen all night scouring every last corner of the Internet.

The accusation thrown around by Dalton had been infuriating, yes, but it also produced another unfortunate side effect. It allowed a troublesome thought to wiggle its way into my consciousness: Why weren't there any *recent* photos online of Forest and Annabelle together? The last picture of them I could track down was from six months ago, around the same time frame of the emails I was reviewing. When I'd flipped open my laptop last night, I had been desperate to lay my hands on anything current, as if Forest and Annabelle's happy marriage was the subject of a ransom demand and I was insisting on proof of life from the kidnapper.

I'd spent hours and clicked on every possible hit for Annabelle and Forest Watts, but despite disappearing down an Internet rabbit hole the size of the Grand Canyon, I never found a single piece of photographic evidence proving Annabelle and Forest had even been in the same room any time in the past six months. A tornado of dread swirled inside as I went down every possible path, including considering the possibility that Annabelle could've died in some tragic *Love Story*–type scenario sometime in the past six months, making Forest a grieving widower. But that theory was quickly debunked when I came across a list of participants in last week's Spin-o-Thon Fundraiser for Heart Disease, proving Annabelle was very much alive and well and still committed to charitable work. Reluctantly, I considered some scenarios that could erode a previously impenetrable relationship—infidelity, fighting, boredom—but dismissed them all. Forest and Annabelle's love was too strong for that.

I did scour Wednesday Walters's Instagram account. If she was

Forest's new secretary, then I most certainly needed to know her. She was older than I'd imagined, probably late thirties, I estimated as I examined a photo of her with a cocktail in her hand sitting on a hammock with two other doppelgängers. *#ThisIsWhatFridayIs-For,* the caption read. I scrolled through the ninety-seven likes, most of which appeared to come from men. Her Twitter profile mentioned she had a highly sensitive peanut allergy, which I jotted down in my notebook. It was nice to know there was a weapon to draw should I need it. She wore a scrunchie in her hair in two of the pictures—a scrunchie! She certainly was not a woman who could ever, ever be a threat to Annabelle.

When I'd opened my eyes this morning, I could feel the shame sloshing over me like cheap wine from a glass. It had been disloyal to give Dalton's harebrained theory any weight at all. I needed to atone for my mistake and recommit myself to Forest and Annabelle, like a lapsed Catholic returning to confession. And standing here in Juice Press seemed like a good first step.

"Or if you're looking for a good immune booster, the Volcano is our newest product." Man Bun gestured to the far-left side of the refrigerator. "All the anti-inflammatories of the Fireball, without the addition of orange juice, so fewer calories."

"Great," I answered, smothering my annoyance that Man Bun was now implying I needed to watch my calories while boosting my immune system. I opened up the fridge and grabbed a Fireball hoping to get him to shut up already. Peering at the label, biding time, I considered the fact that Forest might be skipping his juice this morning. Maybe he had an early meeting or was home sick. With my adrenaline waning, I decided I would have to come back and try again tomorrow. But first, in order not to look completely crazy and be able to show my face in here again, I was going to have to waste eight dollars on a six-ounce bottle of juice that surely tasted like dragon piss.

"Just the Fireball then?" Man Bun asked as I put the juice on the counter.

I nodded, barely containing my irritation.

"Good choice. There's a guy who comes in here every morning and has one of these. Says he never gets sick."

As if on cue, the jingle of the bell as the door swung open filled the store. And like how an animal can sense a change in the earth's magnetic field, I knew it was him.

"Speak of the devil!" Man Bun called out. "I was just telling this customer about your Fireball habit."

Goosebumps dotted my arms. I turned around, my heart thunking in my chest, and there he was. I had spent so many hours staring at his photograph, memorizing the way his hair fell around his forehead and the pattern of the lines around his eyes and now those eyes were directed at me. The heat radiating from them made my insides melt like plastic.

"As habits go, it's not the worst one to have, right?" He lifted an eyebrow.

His voice was deeper than I'd imagined, like the sound of a soothing bass. I'd pictured it more baritone. I liked it.

"Definitely not the worst habit to have," I replied, my hands tightening around my overpriced juice. Looking directly at his face was as intense as staring at the sun, and I had to avert my eyes for a second to keep them from watering.

"It has to be better for you than smoking." He smiled. It was that same charmingly boyish smile I'd seen in his photos, but there was a structure to his face that the pictures didn't capture. The way his cheekbones framed his chiseled mouth, how his eyebrow pulled up slightly when he spoke. I wanted to memorize all of it. I needed to keep this conversation going, somehow capitalize on the opening he'd given me.

"Or hoarding," I replied cautiously. "Although . . . umm . . . I guess you could be hoarding juice bottles," I trailed off.

There was a brief pause before he threw his head back and laughed. A hearty, throaty, full guffaw. I hadn't imagined that laugh from him. His photos made him seem more like the soft-chuckling type. But this sound was like a thunderclap that exploded from his mouth. I could hardly believe this glorious sound had been released in response to something I'd said. Something that wasn't even particularly funny.

Forest cocked his head to the side, studying me, and I could swear I saw a twinge of recognition on his face. For a second I thought he was going to ask if he knew me from somewhere, to which I would have been both overjoyed and horrified.

"Have you tried one before?" he asked, pointing to the bottle in my hands.

I shook my head tentatively, not daring to take my eyes off him. It felt as if a rare butterfly had landed on my arm and if I so much as breathed too hard, it would float away.

"Ahhhh, well, then I bet you'll be a convert. The first few sips are tough because of the burn from the Tabasco, but after that you'll be hooked."

I smiled. There was a glint in his eye when he spoke that reminded me of a sunbeam ricocheting off ice. I wanted to reach out, to touch him, to run my fingers through his hair. Anything to feel the physicality of him. To prove to myself that he was really there.

"It burns so good, right, Atticus?"

"It sure does!" Man Bun (who I now realized had a real name) called out.

I wasn't ready for this encounter to be over. I tried to say something, anything, but the words refused to launch from my mouth.

Forest grabbed a bottle from the refrigerator and tossed a ten dollar bill on the counter. "Keep the change," he instructed, tapping the bill lightly with his hand. He turned and locked eyes with mine and flashed that megawatt smile again. It felt like my stomach was being lowered into a warm bubble bath.

"Enjoy the burn!" he said. Then he winked at me. *Winked*. Like the two of us now had a secret.

I somehow managed to squeak out a "thanks."

He raised his hand in a wave, which I returned, despite the numbness in my limbs. With all of the stars twirling around in my head I almost missed it, but just as Forest was lowering his hand back into his pocket my eyes fixed on the fourth finger of his left hand.

The tectonic plates in my life shifted underneath me.

Forest Watts wasn't wearing a wedding ring.

Chapter Fourteen

No.

No. No. No.

It's not true. It can't be true.

Forest and Annabelle were a match. They were a set. They were a perfect partnership. I was as certain of that as I was the earth was round.

And yet.

I'd spent the last hour sitting here at my workstation, ignoring my computer screen and instead scrutinizing every photo on my phone to locate one with Forest's left hand visible. It was possible Forest never wore a ring. Maybe he had something against jewelry. An allergy perhaps. But every picture confirmed what I already knew. Forest Watts did indeed wear a scuffed platinum band on his left hand. That is, he wore one six months ago, when the pictures were taken. Forest's naked ring finger today coupled with the fact that he hadn't been photographed with Annabelle since then could only mean one thing: Some time between then and now Forest and Annabelle had separated. This excruciating revelation made it hard to breathe. It felt like someone had clamped a wrench around my lungs and wouldn't stop twisting.

I swiped to my favorite picture of Annabelle and Forest together. It was the same one I used as the screensaver on my laptop because I loved how their bodies fit perfectly together, like slotting in the last piece of a puzzle. *You complete me.*

Pressure built up behind my eyes. This felt worse than a death. And I would know.

I blinked rapidly, trying not to surrender the tears that were threatening to spill forth with humiliating force. I could feel it building, that familiar gut-wrenching ache. I would know this feeling anywhere. Betrayal.

Forest and Annabelle had betrayed me.

How could this happen? How could this *fucking* happen?

I enlarged the picture on my phone with my thumb and index finger, examining Annabelle's face, as if her eyes could somehow transmit hidden clues. I tugged my earlobe and considered, for the first time, whether she looked a little generic with her updo and black satin gown. Her smile did appear to be a little forced and, now that I took a closer look, it didn't even reach her eyes. Had it always been like that? I wondered what else I might have missed about Annabelle. I swiped to the next picture. I felt a kind of quickening, a momentum building in my chest as I studied the photo. Forest was gazing at Annabelle with rapture, but her attention was focused on the lens of the camera. Why wasn't she even *looking* at him? This detail I'd neglected to notice was now so glaringly obvious. An undercurrent of panic hummed beneath my skin as I flicked through the remaining photos, trying to locate one where Annabelle's eyes were focused on Forest.

Look at your fucking husband, Annabelle! my mind screamed. *He fucking adores you. I fucking adore you.*

I dropped my phone in my lap and pressed my fingertips to my eyelids.

A picture is worth a thousand words.

It was as if someone had typed the truth on a slip of paper and shoved it in my palm. All at once I knew. Annabelle did this. It was *her* fault. She must be one of those women who was incapable of being satisfied, a closet narcissist who woke up one day and decided she wanted someone richer, taller, or more prominent in the community. I imagined her testing the waters with other men, ensuring she would have a safe landing place if and when she decided to pull the chute on her marriage. Then, only once she was certain she had another man willing to cater to her every whim, she opened up that cherry-red door of theirs and walked out of Forest's life forever.

What had I been *thinking* to not realize this before?

You weren't thinking, I told myself. *You were under Annabelle's spell, just like Forest was. It's not your fault. And it certainly isn't Forest's fault either.*

And then something changed inside me. Like a switch, flipped. I didn't admire Annabelle anymore. I hated her.

An unfocused, primal rage swept over me. *How could you? How could you?* My mind screamed as I stared into what I could now understand were her vacant, loveless eyes. *You ungrateful bitch. You are an ungrateful bitch who never deserved Forest!* Loathing bubbled like molten rock in my stomach, a volcano barely contained. If I saw her right now, if I saw her, I didn't even want to think about what I would do to her. Because the truth was, she hadn't only ripped apart her own life, she'd ripped apart mine too. And that was self-ish. Selfish people did not deserve to be walking around this earth unscathed. And yet, they were everywhere, trampling thought-lessly on every heart in their path. It was a fucking injustice.

Annabelle thought she could mistreat people with impunity. She needed to be taught a lesson.

My phone vibrated against my leg and I jumped like a startled rabbit.

Dalton's eyes swung from his computer screen to the phone in my lap. A smile played at his lips as he pulled out an earbud. "You wouldn't be using a contraband item at your workstation, would you?" he teased.

Officially, according to the sign Ricky had written in black Sharpie and posted on the wall, phones were now "prohibited from being in your viewing area during work hours." Unoffi-cially, all temps clung to their phones like an appendage.

I wrestled my breathing under control. "Ha, ha," I replied, forcing my mouth into a shaky smile and unclenching the fists I didn't realize I was making. One of my nails had broken through the skin, leaving a tiny trickle of blood on my palm. I lifted it to my mouth and discreetly licked away the metallic taste. Dalton didn't seem to notice, though, because his attention was on my phone which, I realized a second too late, was still zoomed in on a photo of Annabelle's face.

I fumbled with the phone, jabbing at a text bubble on the screen, thankfully making the photo disappear.

To Cassie,

I've just finished reviewing the numbers for last week and noticed you reviewed the most files in the group (behind me, of course, but top for temps). Keep up the good work!

Sincerely,
Ricky

I glanced over to Ricky's workstation and his grinning face was staring back at me. Unease pricked at my skin. Was he sending this message as some kind of test to see if I would follow the rules? Or did he know I wasn't reading the files I said I'd reviewed? But as I was considering this possibility Ricky flashed an enthusiastic thumbs-up in my direction. Despite Ricky's strict adherence to rules, he wasn't going to reprimand me for looking at my phone during work hours. There were some benefits to being on Ricky's good side, I supposed.

I smiled tightly in return and lifted a hand in an awkward wave of acknowledgment, as if Ricky was a guy across the bar who had bought me a drink.

Dalton cleared his throat, a glint of mischievousness twinkling in his eye. "Hey, Ricky," he called loud enough to be heard across the room. "I hope you're not texting someone right now when the sign on the wall clearly states that phones are prohibited. You wouldn't want me to come over there and have to perform a citizen's arrest." He wagged an accusing finger.

A few scattered snickers peppered the room. Ricky glared at Dalton, answering only with an annoyed huff, but I noticed his cheeks turn crimson.

"You're terrible," I whispered, my cheek still quivering from adrenaline. "Now stop being so nosy. Eyes on your own paper." I swatted him away from my phone, feeling increasingly unnerved by Dalton's snooping. The last thing I needed right now was his curious eyes seeing something they shouldn't.

I set my phone facedown on the table. With a shaky finger, I clicked open the next document in the review folder, forcing myself to go through the motions. I tried to focus, but everything around me seemed to be vibrating with unease. I could feel Ricky's eyes swing from his computer back to me. Was he watching me or was I being paranoid? Slowly, with purpose, I read each line of the uninteresting email on my screen for his benefit.

Charlie, take a first crack at this and circle back with me ASAP, the email read. It was exactly like the emails I used to receive when I was at Nolan & Wright, back when I was one of the higher-ups. I swiped the arrow over the "nonresponsive" button, sneaking a look at Ricky to ensure he saw that, yes, I was indeed working. But he'd already returned his attention back to his computer. I clicked and watched the email disappear. I couldn't help but wonder about my own Nolan & Wright inbox, somewhere out there in cyberspace. I imagined a temp scrolling through my personal emails. Was there anything in there I wouldn't want someone to read?

My knuckles tightened around the mouse.

Of course there is, stupid, the nasty voice in my head hissed.

The words of Landon's final email to me began to assault my consciousness.

Cassie . . . I didn't mean for this to happen.

I squeezed my eyes shut, hard enough that tiny rainbow dots spotted the darkness. When I opened them, it took me a second to register what I was seeing on my computer screen.

To: Forest Watts
From: Jesse Maynard

I need a beer. See you at Elwood's tonight?

I held back a gasp.

Is this? Is that?

I scrambled to pick up my phone and tapped open my calendar. My finger was shaking as I slid it across the screen, scrolling until I reached the day, nine months ago, when this email was written.

February 8, 2019. It was a Friday. Elwood's was the bar that Forest visited on Fridays.

A smile twitched at my lips. I could feel a renewed sense of purpose sweeping through my body, as if a floodgate had been lifted.

There was only one explanation for this email being in my review folder today: It was a sign. I was looking at things all wrong. Being angry at Annabelle wasn't going to give me back what she took from me. What she took from *us*. It was a Band-Aid on a bullet hole. I needed to consider the total picture. Annabelle's departure left a gaping hole in the perfect world Forest had created. If I ignored that reality simply because I was angry it would be lunacy. It would be blind masochism.

At some point the vacancy in Forest's life was going to be filled. Should it be filled by some opportunistic secretary who wore scrunchies in her hair?

No.

It should be filled by me.

Chapter Fifteen

I PULLED OPEN the heavy mahogany door and felt the familiar swell of warmth, light, and chatter rush over me. Hip and generically modern, Elwood's was your typical trendy midtown bar frequented by cocky bankers, lawyers sporting button-downs and hearty laughs, and girls with hopeful eyes in slippy dresses—the type of bar I used to follow the herd of associates to after work when I was still one of the group. Even back then these kinds of places weren't my desired scene, but I would sip my overpriced cocktail and pretend otherwise. I have a lifetime of practice when it comes to masking what I feel behind a plastered-on smile. There would always be one member of our group who would deem the crowd a "sausage fest," and we'd chuckle at the worn-out joke as we continued downing drinks and reverting to our tried-and-true topic of conversation: gossip about our colleagues. I'm sure those assholes had a heyday when news spread about me. The whole situation probably provided them happy-hour fodder for weeks. *Holy shit, did you hear about Cassie? I could've predicted that one . . . she always seemed a little crazy to me . . . a little off, ya know?* I'm sure Landon nodded his head in agreement, making some joke about how he was a magnet for the crazy ones. It would be just like him to find a way to point out that women were drawn to him while simultaneously trashing them.

I raked my hand through my freshly blown-out hair now, as if I could physically force the past out of my mind. That was the old me. I was shedding her like a dead skin.

I had prepared for this evening as if it were a military campaign. I was strategic about my wardrobe, precise about my goals. I applied makeup like war paint. I wasn't going to settle for anything other than total victory. The war documentaries Dad used to watch had taught me that.

Glancing around the bar, I caught sight of my reflection in the mirror tiles on the wall. My once mousy-brown hair was transformed by three-hundred-dollar highlights, my thick eyebrows expertly plucked. I'd even managed to chisel some cheekbones on my heart-shaped face thanks to strategic contouring.

I smiled and tugged at the hem of my dress. I wasn't used to wearing a dress this short, but I knew what Forest liked.

Wear the shorter one, you married a leg man:) His words were immortalized on a special page in my binder titled "Forest's Preferences." He'd written it in response to an email from Annabelle and I remembered the giddy feeling in my stomach as I scrolled down and noticed there was an attachment—a photo of two stylish dresses laid out on her bed with a message that simply said, *Red or black?* I had, of course, recorded every morsel of information I could collect from the photo, right down to the color and pattern of their duvet cover (a lush, wavy ocean blue which definitely looked more Frette than Macy's). Thanks to the clarity of the photograph (taken, no doubt, with the newest iPhone camera—Annabelle always had all the latest tech, I imagined) I was able to zoom in on the labels and read they were both made by Reiss. All it took was a few clicks of my mouse to discover that both dresses were available at Bloomingdale's, a mere four blocks from Levy & Strong. I was only going to take a little look, maybe slide my hands down the fabric, but once I was in the store it became clear to me that it would be crazy *not* to try them on.

The lipsticked saleswoman complimented my taste when she hung the two dresses on the hook in the dressing room. Still, a tiny part of me wondered if she was eyeing me suspiciously as she swung the door shut. But that would be silly. Trying on dresses wasn't a crime, was it?

When I'd peeled off my boxy blouse, stepped into the red, off-the-shoulder dress, and felt the soft material against my flesh, I could feel my old, uninteresting self fleeing my body like some kind of exorcised demon. And when I looked in the mirror and saw the way the expensive fabric clung against all the best parts of my body and the color transformed my complexion, I knew I had to make the dress mine. I tried not to think about how many hours of temping it would take to pay off the bill as the sales associate swiped my credit card and handed me the receipt for my $610 purchase.

It was only money after all.

The makeup was a little trickier to get just right. Annabelle tended to mix up her color palette depending on the occasion. I had to bring four different photos to Sephora in order to ensure they understood the precise look I was going for. "Do you *know* the woman in the pictures?" the nosy sales associate asked as she led me through the aisles to the higher-priced cosmetics. "Because it would be easier if you asked her what brand of makeup she's wearing. Then we'd at least have a starting point."

"That would spoil the surprise," I answered, thinking on my feet. The sales associate looked puzzled. "The woman in the pictures is a good friend of mine and I'm getting her a birthday present," I explained. She shrugged her shoulders and directed me to the shade of lipstick she thought Annabelle was wearing in two of the photos (Dior in Red Iconic) while I smiled to myself, pleased I'd diffused the situation. With the commission that woman was making on my purchases she should probably learn to keep her stupid questions to herself.

I'd maxed out my credit cards, skipped out of work two hours early to prepare, but look at me now. Just look at me. I *am* Annabelle. Someone people aspire to be.

I checked the time on my phone—half past eight. Not long now.

A man shuffled past me, balancing four highball glasses in his hands, making his way to a table full of happy people in the corner who looked like they could star in a beer commercial. I was starting to feel self-conscious about standing here alone in the crowded bar, without a single person to talk to. I needed a social prop. I could feel the anxiety collecting under my rib cage. Suddenly, the only sound in the room was the dull ringing in my ears. My eyes darted to the door.

Drink.

I needed a drink.

That would settle things down.

I rubbed my perfectly matte red lips together, smoothed my hands over my dress, and threw my shoulders back. Annabelle wasn't the type of person who would retreat. And now, neither was I.

I HAD JUST ordered my second drink when he walked in. I was perched against a barstool (my dress only allowing for perching rather than sitting), listening to a guy with one too many buttons undone on his shirt drone on about his job in finance. I had no interest in talking to Boring Finance Guy, but he provided a good shield so I feigned interest while impatiently sipping my drink and scanning the room like a police helicopter searchlight.

When I spotted Forest's silhouette by the door, it was like the headliner had finally appeared onstage at the sold-out show. A spark of joy flared in my chest, spreading throughout my body. I wanted to jump up and whoop, but I managed to suppress my excitement and watch him out of the corner of my eye for a few beats. A visible aura surrounded him, like an infrared image, and he managed to look even more breathtaking than the last time I saw him. He hesitated at the entrance, scanning the crowd and giving a few halfhearted waves. I bit my lip, wondering who the lucky recipients of his attention were. With the proximity to Levy & Strong there must have been a lot of his colleagues here. Smirking, I remembered the intimate details of their lives I was privy to on a daily basis. Little did they know there was a lowly temp in their midst who could easily out their embarrassing secrets at any moment. *Aren't you the one who went on that really bad date, but still thought she should give you a blowjob anyway?*

"I work in venture capital, so I have to be able to spot potential, which is something they can't teach at Harvard Business School. It's something that has to come naturally," I heard Boring Finance Guy blather. I nodded distractedly and watched as Forest took a step toward the bar. His movements were like music. Like a symphony.

My vision tunneled until he was all I could see.

"Excuse me," I sputtered to Boring Finance Guy, before throwing back my drink and making a beeline to the end of the bar. Adrenaline was zipping through my veins, but I felt a calmness descend upon me. I had a script. I had a strategy. I could not be more ready. It was like I'd spent months training for a race and now was standing at the starting line, finally getting the chance to run it.

Forest squeezed through the crowd, exuding the type of quiet confidence that made the women nearby raise their eyes from their drinks and take notice. I quickened my pace and leaned over the bar next to Forest just as he raised his hand to wave the bartender over.

"Can I get a 50/50 martini please?" I called out to the bartender, a little louder than I'd intended, pretending I was oblivious to the fact that Forest was about to order. I tried not to look in his direction—not yet at least—but, like a flower to the sun, I turned my head a fraction, just enough to see Forest staring at me, a curious expression on his face.

"Make that two of those," he said, holding up two fingers before turning back to me, grinning. My fingertips tingled under the full beam of his attention. "We have the same taste in drinks."

"Great minds," I replied, returning the smile. All that time spent reviewing my notes in the past few days had paid off. I knew Forest better than he knew himself.

I watched the bartender pour a clear stream of gin into two glasses, top it with vermouth, and slide an olive through a toothpick. Out of the corner of my eye I could see Forest watching me, his gaze traveling down the length of my body. I stood completely still to let him take all of me in.

I had constructed myself brick by brick to suit his tastes. He should be pleased with what he saw.

"I'm Forest," he said, sticking out his hand, flashing that eye-wateringly gorgeous grin of his.

"Cassie." I put my hand in his and let it linger. A throng of butterflies rose up en masse from the pit of my stomach and took flight inside my body.

"Nice to meet you, Cassie." The bottles behind the bar, lit from below, cast a warm shadow across his face and all I wanted to do was dive naked into the delectable dimple that appeared when he smiled. Judging from the hair twirls and lusty looks over rims of Technicolor martinis from the other women in the bar, I wasn't the only one who noticed Forest was the lone diamond in a room full of cubic zirconia. The two doe-eyed blondes next to me dressed in black pants so tight you would think they were suctioned on were smiling openly at him now, trying to catch his attention. *Move along girls,* I wanted to snarl. *He's mine.* I hopped up on the barstool and crossed my legs to their best advantage, shifting my body to block the doe eyes out. I noticed Forest sneak an appreciative look at my legs when he thought I wasn't watching, and I silently congratulated myself for my quick thinking.

The bartender slid our drinks across the smooth wood, and Forest raised his in a toast. "To us, the only people here who know how to order a good drink."

"To us." I clinked his glass. I found myself counting the inches between us. Ten, twelve tops. He was so close I could taste my future.

"Bottoms up." He gave me a playful wink, a move I would normally cringe over, but Forest somehow managed to make it look cool. I took a gulp of my 50/50 martini and winced. *Good god, this drink is terrible.* I forced my face to look pleased and took another sip; this one went down easier. I could smell the spicy scent of Forest's aftershave mixed with laundry dryer sheets and it tickled the back of my throat. I inhaled a long, deep breath, trying to fill my lungs with his scent, and briefly wondered if I could ask him what brand of aftershave he was wearing. I wanted to sprinkle it on my sheets. Of course, if all went as planned, our toiletries would soon be lined up side by side on our his and hers vanity.

A sliver of excitement wove its way through my chest.

"So, do you work in the neighborhood, Cassie?" he asked, wriggling a finger beneath his tie. The sound of my name on his lips felt like butter—no, better than butter, it felt like silk—and I had to take a second to collect myself. It was important to stick to my well-planned script.

"Is that a variation on 'Do you come here often?'" I replied in a coy tone, reciting my rehearsed line with the same confidence and charm as the fifty times I'd said it in front of my bathroom mirror. Practice makes perfect. Thank goodness I recalled the advice from the *Cosmo* article "Flirting Tips No Man Can Resist." *Answer his first question with a flirty question.* This was playing out exactly as I'd imagined. I was filled with the same feeling I used to get when I would look down at a final exam, certain I'd studied enough and knew all the answers.

Forest must have noticed and found my confidence charming because he threw his head back and laughed. That rumbling, genuine laugh of his that sounded like music.

"Now that you mention it, that's exactly what it sounds like." His eyes were creased with humor and gazing directly into mine, and if I couldn't still feel the lacquered barstool against my leg I would swear I was levitating. He tilted his head and was looking at me the same way I'd seen him look at Annabelle in a photo online. I never, ever wanted it to stop.

I watched his thumb unconsciously rub across the stem of his glass and sent a little plea out to the universe. If I could just have this man for my own I could be happy.

"So, do you?" Forest leaned in close enough for me to feel the brush of his breath against my skin. "Come here often?" He raised a playful eyebrow, oozing confidence like warm honey.

I love you was all I wanted to say, so I took a sip of my drink. "First time." I returned his flirtatious tone. "You?"

He shook his head. "I work nearby, and there always seems to be someone from my firm leading the charge to come here."

I forced my facial expression to convey that this was news to me, that I didn't know the exact address of his building and the floor he worked on. That I didn't work in a bunker full of temps in the same building.

"We're going to need another round," an enthusiastic patron

called out to the bartender, jostling Forest and causing his arm to brush up against mine. Even though it was only for a second, his touch set off an explosion of sensation inside me. It was the first time I'd been touched by another human in months, unless you counted Ricky's sweaty handshake on my first day. It felt good. So pathetically good.

Thankfully, Forest was oblivious to the fireworks bursting inside my body because he continued talking.

"I'm a lawyer, probably like half the people in this bar." He gestured with his finger to the crowd in a way that managed to be both self-assured and self-deprecating. I followed his gaze around the room and noticed the doe-eyed blondes had slipped away, presumably recognizing defeat, and in their place were two bros who were giving new meaning to the term "manspreading." One of the bros looked familiar to me, but in my distracted bliss it took me a second to place him.

Was that? Is he?

My stomach jumped into my throat.

Fuck. Fuck. FUCK.

Standing inches away from me was Dean Reilly, an associate at Nolan & Wright. I'd never worked directly with Dean, but he was notorious for getting remarkably drunk at firm events and groping the secretaries. He was the type of guy who would like nothing better than to have a good, loud laugh at the woman who he'd read about on all the legal blogs, and would be about as discreet as a neon sign. *Hey, you're the crazy girl that used to work in my office? Holy shit, I've heard about you!*

The heat rose in my neck. This guy could ruin this whole damn thing in an instant. I darted my eyes away, praying he didn't recognize me, but his mere presence was like being confronted by the Ghost of Christmas Past. My thin veneer of confidence began to evaporate.

"A lawyer, huh. That's interesting!" I replied in a high-pitched maniacal tone, shifting on my stool so I had my back to Dean. I felt exposed, like one of those dreams where you stand up to give a presentation and realize you don't have any clothes on.

"It must be a great time to be doing M&A," I yammered nervously, trying to disguise the panic that was swiftly rising inside me. "I mean, with all the deal flow, especially in the technology industry." Forest cocked his head to the side and gave me a quizzical look. Something about the way he was looking at me now set off the panic button in my chest.

"How did you know I do M&A and specialize in the tech industry?" he asked.

Oh shit.

Dean had knocked me completely off my game. My face was beet red now and the alcohol was kicking in and I might as well have revealed to Forest that not only do I know what type of law he does, but I also know exactly how much money he makes doing it.

Fuck!

I took a sip of my drink, buying time to compose myself. "Oh . . . um . . . just a guess. It seems every lawyer does M&A these days," I said, inwardly holding my breath. "Especially in the tech industry."

Forest nodded slowly, his brow furrowed.

I could feel my heart beating in my throat.

Just as I was contemplating putting my drink down and making a run for it, Forest's serious expression broke out into a grin. "I didn't realize I was getting so predictable. How can I expect to impress someone as gorgeous as yourself if I can't throw you a curveball?"

I could've collapsed with relief. Not only did he not notice my slipup, he said he was trying to *impress* me. ME! I beamed, repeating his sentence in my mind, committing the words to memory.

Someone as gorgeous as yourself.

"Hey!" a drunken voice called over my shoulder, interrupting my internal revelry. "Hey!" he repeated, tapping me. My entire body tensed. I tried to ignore him, but if there was one thing I knew about men like Dean Reilly it was that they refuse to be ignored. Ever. Reluctantly, I turned around. He was peering at me, not kindly.

"Do I know you from someplace?" he slurred. My cheeks simmered. He looked sloppy and aggressive. An unsettling hatred for him bubbled up from somewhere deep inside me, threatening to spill over with frightening force. I imagined gripping his ridiculously trendy craft beer bottle by the neck, smashing one side of it against the bar, using the jagged edge to slice through his jugular.

At a minimum, it would make him shut the fuck up.

No. I had Forest to consider. And bloodshed wasn't a good look for me. That much, I knew.

Inhale. One, two, three . . . I swallowed hard, forcing down my anger like an overstuffed suitcase. It was crucial I play this right. I rearranged my expression and let out a deep sigh as if I dealt with drunk assholes hitting on me at bars all the time and it was all just so tiresome. "I don't think so," I answered, hoping against hope he was too drunk to place me without my usual tailored suit, punishing ponytail, and makeup-free face.

"Yeahhhh." He wagged an aggressive finger at me. His face was close enough to mine I could smell his stale beer breath, and all I wanted was to be smelling Forest's spicy smell again.

Why was it that no matter how much I wanted to erase it, my past was always there, staring me directly in the face, literally breathing its putrid breath all over me?

Drunk Dean scrunched up his face, as if he was squeezing out the answer from an old sponge before slapping his hand down on the bar. "I got it!" He pulled back, his squinty eyes zeroing in on me.

I froze like a tiny rabbit when it senses danger nearby. Right before it's swallowed up by a predator.

Drunk Dean looked smug, like he was about to let us in on the secret to world peace. "I went to law school with you," he slurred, his lip lifting in a sneer.

Wrong.

"I don't think so," I said, struggling to steady my voice, viscerally aware of Forest watching our conversation. Did he notice how hard I was breathing?

"Yeah, I'm sure of it." Drunk Dean glared at me. "Where did you go to law school?"

I could feel the rage coagulating in my throat. "I didn't go to law school," I snapped, immediately regretting it. My plan had been to keep my answers about my career as vague as possible. There was safety in the gray area. But now, in my knee-jerk reaction to halt Dean's trip down memory lane, to silence this asshole for good, I'd done the opposite. How was I going to walk this back once Forest and I were in a relationship? He would eventually find out I'm a lawyer. My panicked mind was already whirling with possibilities. Maybe I could play it off like one of the lies women tell to drunks at a bar when they don't want to deal with them anymore—like a fake phone number. Maybe Forest and I would look back at this moment and laugh.

"Wait a minute . . ." Drunk Dean's voice sliced through my thoughts. He was smirking now, sharp and sarcastic, as I sat paralyzed with fear, my heart banging inside me like the clapper of a bell.

"You . . . you're the one . . . you used to work at—"

"Listen, buddy." Forest held up a firm hand, interrupting Dean. "She's answered your question, she doesn't know you and you don't know her. So, we're going to get back to *our* conversation." He gestured from me to him. "And you get back to yours."

Dean eyeballed him, nostrils flaring, for a tense moment before muttering "whatever, asshole" and pushing back through the crowd, stumbling away.

I waited to exhale until he was out of sight. Relief—warm, glorious relief—swept over me. It was as if I'd somehow managed to make it across a wobbly suspension bridge one second before it collapsed.

Forest followed Dean with his eyes before turning his attention back to me. "Well, he sure was a charmer." He was grinning, gleaming with self-satisfaction, like a dog who had retrieved a stick, and it was not lost on me that he had just, quite literally, chased the demons from my past away. I stared into his face, his strong, perfect face, and was overcome with a kind of primitive joy I didn't even know existed. It was like suddenly having access to a missing limb.

"Thank you," I said shakily, but Forest waved me off. There was an awkward beat of silence before he spoke.

"So, this is now going to sound really creepy thanks to that jerk, but I've been thinking I know you from somewhere and I think I figured it out." He drained the last of his drink and set the glass on the bar.

I willed my smile to not change. To not even flicker. This had not been part of my plan. We were veering off script.

"Juice Press," Forest said, raising his eyebrows as if to ask, *Am I right?*

"Juice Press," I echoed more loudly than I'd intended, cocking my head slightly to give the impression of wracking my brain. "Well, I do go there every morning on my way to work so maybe I've seen you there?" My voice trailed up, as if that would've been a fun coincidence, not the culmination of hours of plotting.

His smile widened.

Words kept spilling from my mouth.

"My office is actually in the same building as Juice Press, so it's a great place to work if you have a pressed juice addiction. Which I do. My coworkers are always teasing me about it. I'm a legal recruiter, which is the reason I know a lot about the M&A market." So many details, tumbling out unedited. "I . . . um . . . I place a lot of M&A lawyers. That's the bulk of what I do. I love it. Most days." I lifted my glass to my lips to prevent any more words from escaping.

Forest was looking at me, his expression inscrutable.

"Well, I should get your card then," he replied after a moment. "Never know when I'll need a legal recruiter to help with a job switch."

"Oh . . . umm . . ." I stammered, tapping the stem of the glass with my fingernail. I'd somehow managed to give myself the one career where Forest would ask for a business card, and what on earth is more mood killing than talking about the current state of the M&A market? Avoiding his gaze, I stared into my martini glass as if it held the secret to how to turn this conversation around. "I . . . um . . . don't have any cards with me now. I was just at a conference where I handed a bunch out."

"Ah." Forest nodded, a tiny smile playing at his lips. "Well, that is a very effective way to avoid giving your number out to random strangers in bars." His eyes were glinting now.

For a single reckless beat, I considered telling him the truth. *You're not a stranger to me. I've known you for a while now, and I know more about you than any man I've ever dated and I think I might love you more already. I'm certain I do.* My heart was aching to end this charade and tell him everything.

No. Strategic. Careful. Don't be stupid, Cassie.

I fiddled with the cocktail napkin on the bar and cleared my throat. "I can . . . I can give you my number . . . I mean, if you want it." I lifted my eyes to meet his, and right then, to my utter and delighted surprise, Forest dipped his head, paused for a moment as if asking permission, and kissed me. Every nerve in my body ignited. His tongue grazed my lips and I parted them, letting out an involuntary groan. I didn't care that I nearly knocked over my drink in my enthusiasm to return the kiss or that we were surrounded by people and neither, apparently, did he. He rested his hand on my back and pulled me closer. Desire spread through me like hot liquid, and I had to resist the urge to bite him, to swallow him whole, to consume his cinnamon-flavored flesh. I wanted every part of his skin touching mine. I wanted . . .

Forest broke off the kiss and leaned his forehead against mine, his chest visibly rising and falling. Everything inside my body seemed to speed up, while everything outside my body—the bartender rattling the martini shaker above his head, the lithe brunette tilting her frothy pastel drink to her sticky lips—slowed. I couldn't hear anything but the sound of us. Breathing in. Breathing out.

I tried not to move a muscle, fearing if I did I might wake up from this dream to discover that none of it was real.

"Do you wanna get out of here?" he whispered, winding his fingers through mine. I could feel his hot breath in the tiny hairs on my earlobe.

I looked directly into his eyes, feeling emboldened in a way I'd never felt before in my life. I nodded. Yes. That was exactly what I wanted.

Dalton Sever: *Hey, Cass. So, did you really have a doctor's appointment this afternoon or was that just something you made up for little Ricky so that you could leave work early?*

Dalton Sever: *What are you up to tonight? There's something I really need to talk to you about. Can you call me?*

Dalton Sever: *Hello?*

Chapter Sixteen

I SMOTHERED A yawn as I padded into the bathroom, the linoleum cold under my bare feet. My eyes were dry and gritty, reminding me that I'd spent most of the evening face-to-face with the glow of my laptop. I popped a few drops of extra strength Visine and placed my phone on the edge of the sink, peering again at the maddeningly blank screen. Its silence was beginning to feel like it was mocking me. *No change from when you checked five seconds ago, Cassie!* Letting out a deep sigh, I peeled off my pajamas, turned the knob as far left as possible, and stepped beneath the spray.

There could be any number of reasonable explanations for why Forest hadn't contacted me yet, I reminded myself as the water soaked my hair. I imagined him typing a message, but forgetting to hit "send." Or maybe it was as simple as phone problems. He could've dropped it on a subway track or mistakenly left it at the counter of a deli and when he came back it was gone. People lose their phones all the time.

I picked up a bar of soap and ran it along my already reddening arms. My showers had become punishingly hot lately, as if I could somehow burn the filth of failure away, layer by layer. I dropped my head to let the water course over the knots in my shoulders and down my back.

The evening hadn't gone quite as planned. Obviously. If it had, I wouldn't be standing here in this shower by myself. Forest would be in here with me, whispering into my ear, *Ready for round two?* But I was alone. Again.

It had started out well—better than I could have imagined—with Forest's hand on the small of my back as he led me out of the bar into the night air. Our chemistry—oh god our chemistry—was electric and we barely made it outside before we were kissing again, Forest's arms around my waist, hands traveling down my backside. Any concern I had about the admiring glances of prettier women or the interrogating eyes of Drunk Dean dissolved like an aspirin on my tongue as Forest's lips traced a trail across my collarbone.

It was easy. A key slipped right into a lock. I should've known nothing is ever that easy for me.

I'd tried to stay present in the moment, to enjoy the bolts of pleasure that were coursing through my body, but my anxious mind kept running through every word we'd exchanged in the bar, in an effort to keep straight what I was supposed to know about him versus what I'd gathered from his email and Google. I could not afford another screwup.

We introduced ourselves. Did he tell me his last name? I don't think so. Lawyer, he told me, but did he ever mention the name of the firm?

"You're shivering," Forest had growled in my ear, rubbing my arms. "Let me grab an Uber." He pulled out his phone, unlocking it—eight, nine, nine, five. Or was it eight, nine, nine, two? His hands on my body made it difficult to focus.

"Where should we go?" he asked.

"We can go back to my place," I heard my voice say, before mentally kicking myself for being so forward. That surely was not a very Annabelle-esque thing to do. Annabelle was subtle. Elusive. She wasn't going to make things easy for you. "For a drink," I added lamely.

If I had been thinking clearly, I would've realized that suggesting my apartment, with its overflowing recycling bin of colored glass bottles and unwashed bedding balled up on the couch, was not going to be a turn-on for a man used to his professionally cleaned home and Frette sheets. But my pheromones were firing faster than a machine gun, making clear, rational thought nearly impossible.

"Perfect." Forest began pecking at his screen. I seized the opportunity to examine his profile, trying to commit every part of him to memory. I'd never noticed how long his eyelashes were—their blond tips not visible in photographs online. And there was a tiny, thread-like white scar that slashed through his left eyebrow, which served only to highlight the remaining perfection of his face. I wondered how I missed that detail before, but then the bar was dark and I'd been completely hypnotized by the sound of his voice. I made a mental note to ask him how he got the scar, feeling an odd sense of disappointment that there was a fact about Forest I didn't already know. I took a deep breath and reminded myself that I would soon know every part of him.

The Uber arrived comically fast, as if it had been waiting around the corner eager and prepared to respond to Forest's beck and call. One more thing that had fallen seamlessly into place. I imagined this was what a life with Forest must be like: smooth and effortless, like reclining in the first-class cabin after I'd spent years vying for an armrest in coach. Forest opened the door of the black SUV and gallantly gestured for me to slide in. I stumbled a bit up the step, shaky on my highest pair of heels (the ones I'd chosen to reach Annabelle's statuesque height) but Forest reached out a hand, steadying me. "I got you," he whispered and his warm breath sent a shiver down to my toes. The glow of happiness surrounding me at that moment could have lit up all of New York City.

We had only driven two blocks when his phone rang. The first time, he checked the screen, silenced the ringer, and turned his eyes back to mine. But when his pocket vibrated seconds later, he pulled it out and peered, frowning. The light from the screen illuminated his face and I noticed he had a tiny patch of facial hair near his left ear that was a little longer than the rest. A spot he'd missed while shaving. He wasn't aware of it, but I was.

"I haaaaate to do this," Forest groaned after a moment, looking up from his screen with contrite eyes.

"You have to go?" I said, painfully familiar with the look of someone who is about to let me down.

He exhaled a heavy sigh and traced his thumb on my palm. "I'm really sorry, but I have to go back to work. I have a deal blowing up."

"You lawyers are all the same," I teased, trying to keep my tone light, as if disappointment wasn't spearing me in the gut.

Men don't like when a woman shows emotion. Landon taught me that.

"Ohhh!" Forest clutched his heart. "Slotted into a category with other lawyers—ouch. I promise I'm not married to my work like the rest of them." He held up his hand as if swearing on a Bible, and I could think of nothing else other than Forest being married to me.

"Here," he said, digging in his breast pocket and pulling out a business card. "My cellphone number is on this. Shoot me a text so I have your number, and we'll figure out a time when I can take you out." He flashed that dimple again. "We can grab dinner, and I can learn more about you other than just your pressed juice preferences." His fingers trailed down my arm as he let go.

I offered to have the car drop him off at his office (careful not to mention I knew the exact location of his firm), but he insisted on having the driver pull over so he could get out and walk. "I need the fresh air to clear my head or I'm never going to be able to focus on work tonight." Then he popped out of the car and the driver pulled away and I was left with his business card and a head full of anxiety about what I was supposed to say in the text I send him. I'd stayed awake until the sun came up as I suffered through every incarnation of what to write in my silly little greeting.

Hey, it's me!

Hey, it's Cassie here, nice meeting you.

I wished I could call a tribunal or workshop it, but I finally settled on *Hope you didn't have to work too late! xo Cassie* and hit "send."

Two days. Forty-eight hours. An entire fucking weekend of compulsive phone checking and there was still no response to my carefully composed message. I was like Charlie Brown with the football; just when I thought Forest was going to be mine, he was snatched away from me at the last minute. I wondered now if maybe I'd played the whole thing wrong. Maybe I should've made another plan to meet while we were still in the car. Maybe I should've been flirtier in my text. Maybe I was too forward, too boring, too ugly, too . . . me.

I shut my eyes and let the water run down my face. I reminded myself Forest was attracted to a woman like Annabelle. A woman comfortable enough with herself she doesn't need the reassurance of an immediate response. If I wanted to make Forest love me, I needed to adapt, chameleonlike, into Annabelle. In every possible way.

People are drawn to familiarity. You can't graduate magna cum laude with a bachelor's degree in psychology and not know that.

I would plan better for next time. Preparation was key.

I'd already spent all weekend visiting gallery after gallery, studying Annabelle's favorite artists (according to her Instagram posts). My knowledge of art didn't extend past the generic prints of the New York skyline currently adorning my walls, but Forest was used to someone who could distinguish a Warhol from a Lichtenstein. And I was nothing if not diligent. Particulars like this would be important. I was sure of it. I could already picture Forest grabbing my hand and guiding me up the stone steps of the home he and Annabelle used to share, through the cherry-red front door, and into the foyer. I would casually comment how I love the texture on the David Allan Peters painting he has hanging above the console table. *The way he carves the canvas seems to bring order to the abstract,* I would say earnestly, tilting my head just so. Forest would watch me, lift an intrigued eyebrow, and marvel how we have the same taste in art. Then, he'd pull me toward that glorious bedroom of theirs, realizing how effortless it is to fit me into his perfect life.

I would be totally ready to integrate into his world.

It's all in the details.

The wailing from an ambulance five stories below jarred me back to the unwelcome present. My throat was tight with tears. There was a physical gnawing inside me, as if the very life was being squeezed from me with each second that passed without hearing from him. I was five years old again, waiting by the phone on my birthday, hoping my mother would call. I squeezed a slug of shampoo into my hand and rubbed it into my scalp hard, physically purging the memories from my mind. I imagined my brain rejecting them, like a foreign antigen.

I stepped out of the shower and wrapped a towel around my pink skin, pulling it tight. Rubbing clear a circle in the fogged mirror, I examined my reflection, tilting my chin left then right. The moisturizer I'd been using thanks to Annabelle's Amazon purchasing history was doing wonders for my complexion and eating regularly had put some color back into my cheeks. It was amazing, really. With Forest in my life, I was looking better than I ever had before. I was like Humpty Dumpty finally being put back together again.

I tucked my hair behind my ears and tried out the Mona Lisa smile Annabelle had perfected in her photos. A slight turn up of the left corner of my mouth. Then my eyes, purposely evasive, as if I'm hiding a juicy secret. A small raise of my brow. I placed my hand on my hip like she does, and posed as if someone in the mirror was taking my picture.

Not bad. I deserved to be loved, didn't I?

Landon would say no.

My mother would say no.

I yanked open the medicine cabinet and extracted a jumbo-sized bottle of extra strength Tylenol. I shook four into my palm, dipped my head under the faucet, and swallowed them down. Then I reconsidered and popped one more. After a moment, the sharp, jagged edges in my mind started to become smoother, as if being rubbed with sandpaper.

There. That was better.

Robotically, I blow-dried my hair and dressed with my eyes fixed on my phone.

Still no text.

I flopped on my bed, flipped open my binder, and scanned everything I'd added over the weekend. It was amazing, really, how many new nuggets of information I'd been able to gather from having Forest's mobile phone number. I found a long-dormant Facebook profile with the name FoWa using his number on the account. All along I had assumed Forest shunned social media because I'd scoured Facebook, Twitter, and Instagram and come back frustratingly empty. It turned out he'd used a pseudonym for his social media accounts. I liked that he wanted to keep his personal life separate from his clients and coworkers.

I clicked open my pen now and scrawled, *Who is on his friend list?* on the page I'd created for information about his Facebook profile. Even with the pseudonym, Forest still managed to have over seven hundred friends. I didn't even *know* seven hundred people. Unfortunately for me, his Facebook settings were private so doing any investigation on his friends was going to be tricky. He'd been tagged in two photos that were public—both posted by someone called Richard Storm. The photos were of a group of people sitting down at a large, distressed-wood table in what looked like a ski lodge, everyone pink-faced and dressed in fleece zip-ups. Annabelle was in both pictures, but the date on the pictures was from 2015. I'd done a reverse image search (something I never even knew was possible until I had googled "what information can I gain from a photo") and found the photos had also been posted on Instagram by the same friend with the hashtags #VailPowder #StillCanShred. Someone with the handle @stacisutherland had commented, *Wish I could've been there!* You and me both, Staci Sutherland.

I pried my attention away for a moment to survey surfaces of my bedroom in search of my keys. If I didn't get moving, I was going to be late to work. I checked the bathroom in case I'd taken them in there while on autopilot but they weren't there either. I rubbed my temples, trying to think clearly, to physically push away the haziness from my head. *I had my keys with me when I came home from the gallery yesterday. I must have left them on the kitchen counter when I grabbed a drink from the fridge.*

I shimmied into my shoes and flipped on the overhead light on my way to the kitchen. Then I froze.

The living room was instantly flooded with the unforgiving glare of the halogen bulb, illuminating every detail of the horror show in front of me. Slowly, my eyes swept around the tiny room as if seeing it for the first time. Empty beer bottles littered the area rug, yellow stickies with words like "GPS?" and "social media accounts?" were affixed to the walls, torn pages with haphazard notes scratched across them covered my coffee table, a Chinese-food-encrusted paper plate was poking out from underneath my couch.

My apartment didn't look like this when I went to sleep last night. Did it?

The details of the later hours of the evening were murky. I wasn't even sure I recalled using my laptop last night, although clearly, I had. I bent down and moved an empty takeout container I had no recollection of ordering off the keyboard.

I shook my head. It hurt, and I regretted the movement instantly.

"Fuck," I shouted into my empty living room. The sound hit the walls like a fist. I was so sick of this life. I wanted the one Forest had promised me when he'd kissed me. One where my weekends are spent drinking "our" wine instead of whatever shit I'd consumed last night. After everything I'd been through, I was entitled to some kind of cosmic reward. I hadn't endured the nightmare roller-coaster ride of the past year for nothing.

No.

I was going to be the one living in that elegant, red-doored house with Forest, safe in the knowledge I was a permanent fixture in someone else's life. Finally. Then all of this—the terrible temp position, losing my job, everything with Dad—it would all be nothing more than a dusty exhibit in the museum of my memory. One I didn't plan on visiting.

I extracted my keys from underneath a couch cushion and did one last check of my messages before dropping my phone in my purse. I got up, determined, and pushed my sleeves into my coat. This wasn't a decision for Forest Watts to make. It was destiny.

If Forest Watts didn't realize we belong together, then I would take matters into my own hands.

To: Cassandra Woodson
From: Mary Woodson

I don't understand your last email, Cassandra. What do you mean you're moving to Bronxville?

To: Cassandra Woodson
From: Matt_999666

Is this the same Cassandra Woodson that was in that viral video a few months back? In the lobby of an office building? I'll pay you good $$$ to come over to my place and star in our own little video. I like my girls fucking crazy like you.

Chapter Seventeen

"Happy Monday!" A middle-aged woman in a tight skirt chirped as she shuffled past me on the carpeted corridor.

I flashed a fake smile in return, cradling the accordion file against my hip, and tried to wrestle my breathing under control. It was imperative to blend in, and her asinine greeting had the potential to bring unwanted attention to my presence. I threw a look over my shoulder to determine if any suspicions had been roused, but no heads were lifted in my direction, no eyes were trailing me. Printers still whirred, phones still rang. Nobody seemed to notice the unknown temp embedded among the higher-ups. Thankfully.

Sometimes the best ideas are right under your nose. Or in my case thirty floors above my workstation. If I wanted to track down Forest's whereabouts, what better place for me to start than where he spent the majority of his time?

The plan was surprisingly simple. Minutes before Ricky's iPhone alarm was set to chime, filling the bunker with the sound of the Star Wars "Imperial March" and indicating the beginning of our lunch break, I excused myself and signed out on the "shit breaks" clipboard. Once safely ensconced in the stairwell leading down to the lobby, I dialed Forest's office number. "Mr. Watts will be away from his office until one-thirty," his secretary had advised while I patted myself on the back for having the foresight to maintain a list of Forest's top clients. It made it easy to impersonate an assistant whose boss was entitled to know the precise time that

Forest was expected to return. But her response only confirmed what I'd already expected—Forest Watts's office would be gloriously empty for a full hour.

Dalton might have been wrong about a lot of things, but he was right about this: Forest did, in fact, have a weekly lunch meeting every Monday. The only surprising part was that it took me until this morning to realize how this detail could be used to my advantage.

I wondered how long Dalton had waited for me to come back from the bathroom before cutting his losses and heading out to eat his shredded pork burrito solo. Hopefully not long enough to tip Ricky off that one of his loyal foot soldiers had gone MIA.

My heels thudded on the geometric-patterned carpet now, past a gaggle of secretaries huddled around a box of Dunkin' Donuts and two gray suits engaged in a firm handshake inside a small conference room. I threw my shoulders back and swallowed down my rising panic. Outside the floor-to-ceiling windows, the treetops in Central Park were coming into view, which meant I'd reached the north side of the thirty-fifth floor. Forest's office would be in my sight line. I paused outside a vacant corner office, the perfect spot to perform some reconnaissance. I brushed nonexistent lint off my pants as my eyes scanned the faces in the line of cubicles until they landed on hers.

I took a moment to study her from the far end of the hallway. She had more wrinkles than in her Instagram photos, thanks no doubt to the various filters she employed, but her overly plucked eyebrows were unmistakable.

Wednesday Walters.

I watched as she shuffled papers from one pile to another, picked one up, peered at it, sighed, and tossed it in the trashcan. I was biding my time, waiting for an opportunity to slip by her while her attention was absorbed elsewhere, but I couldn't believe my luck when she rose from her chair and hitched her purse over her shoulder.

"Can you watch the phone?" I heard her call out to the woman in the opposite cubicle before her velvet-scrunchied ponytail swished out of view.

A bubble of excitement formed in my stomach. This must be how it would feel to stumble upon the Hope Diamond while the guards were asleep.

I took a deep breath, readying myself to scurry down the corridor, past the office doors as covertly as possible. I was well practiced at being invisible. A quick stop in the copy room had provided me with the accordion file and enough stapled documents to slide inside it to make it appear important. Anyone who's worked in an office knows that if you're carrying a file and walking with purpose you could probably murder someone and still slip away unnoticed.

My heart was pounding at double speed by the time I made it to the brass nameplate that read FOREST J. WATTS, but I couldn't resist lifting my free hand to the cold metal and grazing each letter with the tips of my fingers before lowering it to the handle, pushing the door open, and stepping inside.

Forest's office had the same spicy scent as his skin, and I fought the temptation to put my nose right up to the upholstered furniture to fill my lungs with him. Instead, I conducted a swift mental inventory, wishing there was time to record it all: two paintings on the walls (one abstract, the other a bold-colored cityscape), shelves—Lucite deal tombstones, an elaborate beer stein, a plaque with the large words FORTY UNDER FORTY. The only framed photograph in the office sat behind Forest's desk—a shot of him crossing the finish line at the New York City Marathon.

No pictures of Annabelle, not that I expected any, but it was reassuring to see she wasn't lingering in his life like a bad smell.

There was a Bloomingdale's shopping bag in the corner, and I quickly pushed aside the tissue paper to get a look at what he'd purchased—two sweaters (John Varvatos, size large) and a brown leather belt.

I was a carnivore for details, but the clock was ticking.

I moved to his desk, pulled a yellow Post-it with penciled numbers off his monitor, which, judging by the fact that there were ten digits, was his attorney billing number. I folded it in half and slipped it into my pocket.

You never know what will come in handy.

"Good afternoon, Levy & Strong, Bill Grossman's office," I heard a secretary murmur into her headset from down the hallway. I stopped, statue still, and held my breath. I felt like a soldier who'd parachuted into enemy territory and could be discovered at any second. My head was shouting at me to retreat, but there was no way I was exiting his office empty-handed. I needed something. A clue. Why wasn't Forest contacting me? More important, where and when could I see him next?

I hated uncertainty.

Yanking open a drawer, I shuffled aside pens and energy bars, and extracted a bright yellow tube. I narrowed my eyes to inspect the label. *EpiPen 0.3 mg Epinephrine Auto-Injector.* Forest had an allergy that required an EpiPen? This I did not know. I wondered if Wednesday tried to bond with him over their mutual ailments. I slipped it in my pocket and moved on to the next drawer. A bowl of loose change, two bottles of water, a near-empty container of prescription pills that I slid into my pocket before hip-checking the drawer back in place.

I checked the time. Only ten minutes left in my lunch break. I couldn't be late getting back to the bunker or Ricky would surely send a search party out looking for me. Swiftly, I shimmied around to the front of the oversized desk and began sifting through the mail in the black metal letter tray marked IN in a last-ditch effort to find something useful.

"Can I help you?" An icy voice smacked me from behind.

My heart crashed to a stop.

I took a moment to rearrange my features, to wipe the palpable terror from my face, before turning around. There she was, flashing those same chemically whitened teeth I'd seen on Instagram. They were even brighter without the filter.

"Oh." I cleared the wobble in my voice. "No, I'm good. Thanks. I'm just dropping this off in Forest Watts's inbox." The weight of the items I'd swiped felt like a brick in my pocket. I shifted my weight to disguise the bulge.

Wednesday's eyes traveled from my face to the accordion file I was clutching like a life preserver, then back to my face. Her brows furrowed accusingly. "Are you new here?"

My brain felt full of static, like a television that had lost its signal. It took a few seconds to find the words and force them out of my trembling mouth. "Yes, well, um . . . I'm the temp filling in for Brad Baker's assistant while she's on maternity leave."

Wednesday crossed her arms over her surgically enhanced chest. "And what did you say your name is?" Her tone was accusatory. She knew as well as I did that I hadn't.

I forced myself to maintain eye contact, wishing I could control my heartbeat. Sociopaths can do that.

"Caroline." My smile stayed stapled in place. I purposely didn't offer up a last name. The less information Wednesday had about the temp she discovered in Forest's office, the better. Although, I was willing to bet my monthly salary she couldn't pick Brad Baker or his secretary out of a lineup if she had a gun to her head. I knew from experience the corporate department didn't fraternize with the litigation department in large firms. Sure, they had the same employer, but they might as well be working in different cities with how infrequently their paths crossed.

Wednesday tilted her head, assessing me.

One second.

Two seconds.

If Forest came back from his meeting now, what in the hell would he think of this scene playing out in his office? The thought lodged in my throat, making it hard to pull a breath into my lungs. I was beginning to feel light-headed.

After what felt like an eternity, she spoke. "Well, Caroline, in this firm we give all deliveries for partners to their assistants. Never do we put them directly on their desks." She emphasized "never" as if she was dispensing lifesaving advice. "I don't know how things are done at the other firms you've temped at, but that's how they're done here. *All* of Mr. Watts's correspondence goes through me."

My body swelled with rage and I almost had a moment of weakness as the urge to wrap my hands around her throat threatened to overwhelm me. She thought she was Forest's gatekeeper, but I was Forest's future girlfriend for fuck's sake! Forest didn't need protection from me. But now was not the time to set her straight. I had to get out of this office and back to the bunker. I compressed my lips together, biting back my anger.

Blind naïveté was the only workable option here. I arranged my expression accordingly.

I lowered my head in what I hoped came across as deference. "Sorry, when I walked by your cubicle nobody was there, so I just figured you might be sick." I gave an apologetic shrug.

She eyeballed me for a beat before sticking out her palm. "Well, lesson learned, I guess. I'll take that now."

I hesitated. Sweat began to bead on my forehead despite the chill in the room. There hadn't been any time to read the printouts when I'd gathered them from the recycling bin earlier. I had no idea what Wednesday would see if she looked inside the file now. This was not part of the plan.

Wednesday huffed and flicked her fingers with impatience. Reluctantly, I relinquished the accordion file. I clasped my hands together so she wouldn't notice how hard they were trembling on my way out of Forest's office.

As I scurried past Wednesday's cubicle, I wondered how many of the prescription pills sitting in my pocket I would need to dissolve in her coffee to make her forget this whole encounter ever happened. Although, when I thought about it, a peanut or two would certainly do the trick.

Sometimes, the ideas that flew through my head scared me.

Chapter Eighteen

"So, I still don't get it." Dalton dropped his tray on the table. "You ate lunch by yourself in the cafeteria yesterday and now you wanna eat here again today?" He slid into the chair across from me, gesturing to the floor-to-ceiling windows. "I feel like we're prisoners forgoing our fifteen minutes of outside time in the courtyard."

I shrugged, twisting a noodle around my fork. "I'm just getting tired of wasting what little time we have searching for the right place to eat. We've got any type of food you want right here." I shoveled a forkful of noodles into my mouth to punctuate the point. The truth was the cafeteria was the last place I wanted to be, but it was necessary to throw Dalton off the scent of my mysterious absence during our lunch break yesterday.

Two broad-shouldered men in striped dress shirts strode past our table, trays of piled-high pasta in hand. "Carb loading," the taller one called out to a James Franco look-alike sitting at a booth in the corner before plopping down beside him. I noticed the shorter one had the same jet-black hair as Forest, and for a split second an instinctive flicker of panic ignited in the bottom of my stomach. An encounter with Forest in his firm cafeteria now would be relationship suicide. How would I ever explain what I was doing here? But logically, I knew that wouldn't happen. Partners had their own dining room and no self-respecting partner would ever be caught dead in here. Seeing Forest's hair color in the cafeteria now could only be one thing: a promising omen.

I needed something positive after my frustrating voyage to his office.

Dalton eyed me dubiously. "Have you heard of a little thing called Stockholm syndrome, Cassie Woodson?"

My shoulders bristled. Dalton had only ever referred to me by my first name. I purposely never uttered my last name in front of him. Or anyone for that matter. And Ricky had introduced me to the group as "the new girl from the temp agency" on my first day of work. Hearing "Woodson" fly off his tongue made me wonder if he'd tracked it down in order to google me.

"It's not like we have to eat lunch together every day," I snapped, feeling a sudden burst of irritation. I saw him pull back into himself a tiny bit, and felt satisfied. Ignoring his wounded expression, I tapped a finger on my phone, waking the screen for the third time since we sat down. I was like a gambler in Vegas with her eyes glued to a slot machine waiting for the winning pull.

Come on, Forest. My mind pleaded. *Come on.*

"Fine by me," Dalton muttered, glaring at me. He unclenched his jaw to take an angry bite of his hamburger. Ignoring him, I tapped on my missed calls in the event that my phone wasn't working properly and had not alerted me to the fact that I'd received a call at some point between when I'd paid for my food five minutes ago and now.

No new calls.

No new texts.

I wanted to smash my stupid phone into a million pieces. And sitting here eating my oily cafeteria lunch was only making my mood drop farther. I didn't want food. I wanted Forest. Everything else was a waste of energy. Breath.

I drummed my nails, briefly debating whether I should bite the bullet and send Forest a quick, innocuous text. *Hey, I had a great time on Friday!* I could say.

No. I needed to play the long game. I could not be desperate. I must be cool. Like Annabelle. Annabelle wouldn't send a follow-up text begging for attention. All she had to do for attention was exist.

Forest was clearly testing my endurance.

"For someone who can't take her eyes off her phone right now you're not exactly quick to respond to your texts, are you?" Dalton said in a tone that reminded me of a petulant child.

I looked up from the screen and peered at him through my eyebrows, confused. For a moment, I wondered if he meant I'd somehow missed a text from Forest. But that wasn't possible. Seeing the frown on Dalton's face now, I was hit with the vague memory of tapping open a message from him at some point over the weekend. Maybe there was even more than one. I couldn't for the life of me remember what they said, though, or whether I'd replied. Based on his agitated expression now, I hadn't.

"Sorry." I sighed, shaking my head. "I completely forgot to text you back. My weekend was really busy." There was a long pause, and I could almost hear the cogs turning in his brain.

He crossed his arms, tilting his head to one side. "Oh right, you were hanging out with 'friends,' right?" He air-quoted "friends," as if the scenario was ludicrous.

His words hung in the air for a long beat. My face flushed with anger and humiliation. Who the hell did he think he was, implying that I was incapable of having any friends? But after a moment, I clued in to what he was suggesting. It wasn't that he thought I was inventing a group of friends. No. He thought I was *seeing* someone. I opened my mouth to correct him, but stopped myself.

I am. I am seeing someone.

A smile spread across my face.

"Busted!" Dalton called out.

I responded with a mischievous shrug. There was no point in trying to conceal it when I could still feel Forest's lips on my neck.

Dalton blew out a puff of air, the corners of his lips curling up. "I knew you were covering something. You're not a very good liar." A flash of something that looked like irritation crossed his face, but only for a moment, then it was gone. He picked up his drink and took a long slug. "So, who is he?"

I crossed my arms, holding the backs of my elbows rather than tucking my fists under my biceps, just as I'd seen Annabelle do in a photo. Her mannerisms were becoming second nature to me. "Um . . . no one you would know. He's someone I've known for a while now." My voice thinned out. This conversation was veering into a dangerous minefield. One that I wasn't prepared to navigate. "Anyway, what were you texting me about?"

Two tiny red patches bloomed on his cheeks. "Oh . . . I had something I wanted to ask you about. Just . . . wanted to get your advice on something." He looked away and something guarded came over his expression, like a curtain falling across a window. "But don't worry about it, I figured out what I'm going to do." He took a large bite of his hamburger, slid his phone out of his pocket, and jabbed at it with an index finger.

My shoulders loosened, for once relieved we weren't talking about Forest. Nothing good could come from Dalton sniffing around my personal life. I picked up my phone and reviewed the Google search I'd done on amoxicillin, the prescription drug I'd found in Forest's drawer. It had such a wide use it was hard to pin down what Forest had taken it for, but the prescription had been filled at the CVS around the corner, so that could be useful to know.

"Are you fucking kidding me?" Dalton's angry voice sliced through my thoughts.

My heart stopped. But when I raised my anxious eyes from the screen, I noticed Dalton's attention was somewhere else. I looked over my shoulder to locate the subject of his sudden wrath, relieved it wasn't me.

"Would you look at that asshole over there giving Rocco a hard time." He threw a hand toward the grill station and I could see a smug-looking guy in an expensively tailored dress shirt narrowing his eyes at Rocco, a friendly cafeteria worker, seemingly giving him a few choice words. "I see this all the time with those entitled pricks," Dalton huffed. "There's a million choices on the menu and they lose their shit because they don't get something they want." A red-hot flush was sweeping over Dalton's face. He looked like a steam whistle ready to blow.

I could see Rocco shrugging his shoulders, not entirely bothered by the encounter, but Dalton continued, his voice trembling with fury. "These guys think they're fucking gods, and everyone around them is supposed to serve them." He jabbed a finger on the table. "They just take for the sake of taking, and they don't give a shit about anybody but themselves."

I eyed him cautiously. Dalton was one of those people who thrived on being low-key annoyed, but this was taking it to a whole new level. The vein in his temple was bulging now. I wanted to warn him to be careful.

Losing your temper can be a costly mistake.

"What's up with you today?" I asked, lowering my voice in the hopes that he would follow suit.

"What's up with *me*?" He pressed an indignant palm to his chest. "Oh, because clearly being annoyed that some asshole is pulling rank on Rocco is something that's *my* problem? Geez, Cassie, you seem to want to defend these guys an awful lot. What are you *obsessed* with them or something?"

I glared at him, trying to conceal the terror ricocheting inside my head. I could feel the heat rising to my face like mercury in a thermometer. I didn't dare look around to see who'd overheard Dalton's tirade. I took a moment to rearrange my expression. Indignation. Indignation is important when you're accused of something for which you are innocent.

"What are you talking about?" I snapped, crossing my hands over my chest to hide the tiny tremble. "You sound like a crazy person right now. You think I'm obsessed with some random lawyer who is yelling at Rocco right now? Who, PS, does not seem nearly as bothered by whatever is happening over there as you are. Maybe *you're* the one who's obsessed."

"You know what?" Dalton leapt up so quickly he sent a pile of napkins tumbling to the floor. "I don't feel like sitting here anymore. We still have . . ." He shot an aggravated look at his watch. "Ten minutes left before we need to be back in the bunker, and I think I need some fresh air." He grabbed his tray off the table and huffed over to the garbage without another word.

I watched him elbow through a crowd of people at the elevator.

Dalton was about as inconspicuous as a wild boar. It was important to remember that. I blew out a long breath, pushed my tray of unfinished food away, and tapped my phone again, watching the screen until it went dark, then black.

Late afternoon, I was back at my workstation pecking out a list of places Forest and I could potentially have our next meetup. Juice Press was too transparent. Equinox had potential, but I had to find out which one he frequented first. There was a good chance Wednesday would have that information, but I needed to give it at least a week before I attempted to use her as a source. She would surely have her guard up now.

Every second Forest and I were apart felt like a waste of time. But it was crucial my next move be well thought out. An impulsive decision can change the course of your life.

"Hey, where's your buddy boy over here?" Ricky's voice interrupted my thoughts. I looked up from my screen to see him hovering over me with his thumb pointed in the direction of Dalton's seat.

"Hmmm?" I lifted my earbuds away from my ears, which I'd gotten into the habit of wearing during the day, not that I had any music on. They gave me the feeling of being in a more secluded space, rather than an overcrowded storage room that doubled as a work space, but Ricky clearly didn't get the memo about my silent body armor.

"Dalton," Ricky repeated huffily. "Your dinner buddy. Where'd he go?"

I took a quick peek at Dalton's screen, which had gone black with the firm logo spinning across it. I shrugged. "Bathroom, I guess." I glanced at the time in the left-hand corner of my screen, unintentionally raising my eyebrows in surprise: 4:27 P.M. Normally, Dalton's bathroom routine was as precise as a train schedule—sign out at 3:30 P.M., back by 3:45 P.M. on the nose—although, it didn't coincide with any need to actually use the facilities. "If I don't break up the hours of tedium between lunch and dinner exactly down the middle, I'll stick a freaking pen right in my eye just to avoid reviewing one more document," Dalton had explained. But today Dalton had been gone for nearly an hour, which was the reason Ricky was staring at me now like a disapproving school principal.

Looking back, this should have been the first sign that something was amiss.

"I think he, um . . . must have left for the bathroom later than usual today," I said, blushing slightly now that I was acknowledging the fact that I knew the exact time my coworker typically signed out on the "shit breaks" clipboard. There went my last shred of dignity.

Ricky gave an exaggerated eye roll. "Don't even try to cover for him, Cassie, you're only dragging your own professional reputation through the mud. Your little buddy will never get another temp job with the reputation he's made for himself at this one. *Don't* let the same happen to you." He jammed a finger on the top of my computer in emphasis.

I resisted the urge to tell Ricky that I'd already hit rock bottom in the career reputation department.

"New bathroom-break rule, everyone," Ricky called out, shooting a forbidding glance around the room. He looked slightly unhinged with his angry red face and gelled hair sticking up on the left side. "If you're any longer than five minutes, you're going to see your pay docked. This isn't freaking *Romper Room,* people."

I watched as he huffed his way back to his workstation muttering, "You'd think I was a freaking babysitter, for heaven's sake."

I waited until he was back at his desk before I picked up my phone to send a quick text to Dalton to warn him Ricky was on the warpath. Dalton may be convinced Ricky would never fire him, but I wasn't so confident. I swiped my screen and winced as it went black.

"Shit," I muttered. A morning spent robotically tapping and waking my phone had left my battery completely depleted. I tossed my phone back in my purse. Dinner was only a few short hours away and I could charge it in the cafeteria then.

Maybe it's for the best, I told myself. A watched pot never boils.

But all thoughts of Dalton's bathroom break, depleted batteries, or anything else went completely out the window when I clicked open a new document and the email popped up on the screen.

> To: IT
> From: Forest Watts
>
> I'll be out of the office from 12–2 so you can perform the work on my computer then.
> User ID: FWatts
> Password: AMFW072912

My breath caught in my throat. Holy. Shit.

I shot a frantic look around the room, as if my computer had sounded a loud warning bell—*ALERT confidential password has been revealed ALERT*—but their eyes were fixed on their screens. I returned my attention to the monitor, pressing hard on my thighs to keep my hands steady.

All I had to do was record the user ID and password in my notebook and I would have the tools to gain full access to Forest's account. Then I most certainly would find an email that would indicate where he would be and when.

My skin began to tingle with pure exhilaration as I reached down for my Longchamp tote.

"Shit," I breathed, realizing that this morning I'd made the unfortunate decision to switch out my usual utility purse for a cute, small cross-body one in an effort to look casual and light, the way I imagined Annabelle to be.

That meant no notebook and no pen.

My eyes darted around my work space for something to write with, but clearly the higher-ups had decided not to issue any office supplies to a group of temps whose sole purpose was mouse-clicking because the only writing utensil in the entire bunker was dangling from a string off the "shit breaks" clipboard.

My mind went into overdrive trying to figure out my next move. With a dead battery on my phone, I didn't have the option to take a picture of my screen. AMFW072912—I could possibly memorize it, but what if I screwed it up? There would be no way to retrieve the email once it was gone. I grabbed my stupid, tiny purse off the floor and anxiously rooted through it in an effort to find something—a pen, a marker, or even an old eyeliner—anything that could be used to write. There was a tampon, an old ChapStick, a half-eaten granola bar in a wrapper, but not one freaking writing utensil. I pressed the heels of my palms to my eyes in frustration. The guy with the long comb-over in the row behind me eyeballed me curiously before returning his attention to his screen.

The blood was thumping in my ears now. I felt like the seconds were ticking away in a championship game and I was the one holding the ball, poised to score the winning touchdown or fumble and lose it all.

My eyes darted to the bathroom-break clipboard. I couldn't exactly rip the pen off the string without being noticed, but maybe I could sign out and dash to the Duane Reade across the street. But signing out now after Ricky's tirade and with Dalton still gone would likely trigger Ricky's attention. The last thing I needed right now was Ricky's attention.

Would Ricky believe me if I told him I'm going out for a cigarette? He'd probably demand proof in the form of me producing a package of cigarettes he knew I didn't possess. Why oh why hadn't I listened to my former secretary and taken up smoking? "People underestimate the benefits of smoking," she'd explained while tapping a pack of Marlboro Reds against her palm. "Sure, it takes a few years off your life, but when you're a smoker you get to take a break and go outside with no questions asked." I would've gladly exchanged pink lungs and twenty years of my life for a freaking pen right now.

I pushed my chair back and leapt up. Water. He couldn't deny me the basic human need of water. I gave a few halfhearted coughs and put my palm to my chest before shimmying down the row of mouse-clickers and heading to the interrogation room.

"Just grabbing my bottle of water from the fridge," I whispered by way of explanation as I walked past Ricky's computer in response to his inquisitive look. He glared at me as if stemming dehydration was a piss-poor excuse for getting up from my workstation.

I quickened my pace.

The buzzing of the overhead lights in the interrogation room sounded like a ticking time bomb as I frantically scoured the room, under the table, behind the water cooler, and in every cupboard.

Not. One. Fucking. Pen.

I pressed my palms into my eyes. *Think, Cassie, think!*

And that's when the call came in.

Chapter Nineteen

THE RING SLICED through the break room. It had been months since I'd heard the blare from a landline telephone—with its shrill, high-pitched tone—and the sound was so foreign to me that it took me a second to figure out what it was.

Brrrrriiiing! The third ring ripped me out of my thoughts and, like a Pavlovian dog, my entire body tensed. I had once received the worst news of my life over the phone.

A shiver of dread whipped down my spine. There was no way this could be good.

Ricky thundered into the interrogation room, breathing so heavily you would think the twenty-foot sprint he'd done from his desk was the length of a marathon.

"Is . . . is there a *phone* ringing?" he puffed, wide-eyed.

I nodded, staring at the black telephone circa 1995 I only now noticed was affixed to the wall of the break room. Judging by Ricky's expression, this was the first he'd learned of the phone's existence as well. The higher-ups never called us. Ever. Ricky received his instructions via email and as far as I could tell that was the only communication any of us in the bunker had with anyone above us. Once, Ricky had unintentionally revealed to me that he'd never even met the partner we were working for face-to-face. "I don't think he wants to waste my time with status meetings. He knows how crazy busy we are around here," Ricky had explained in the same way my high school friend used to justify all the reasons the guy she hooked up with wasn't texting her.

The caller ID screen glowed green now and flashed *Conference Room 37F*. Ricky and I stared at each other in what can only be described as confused horror. *The call is coming from inside the house! I repeat, the call is coming from inside the house!*

Ricky cleared his throat and picked up the receiver. "You have Ricky Sandos here, head staff attorney at Levy & Strong, also known as staff attorney extraordinaire, at your service." He winced and pinched his nose, as if he'd inadvertently revealed he still wet his bed to whoever was on the other end of the line. I chewed on my cuticle, eyes fixed on Ricky, as he nodded his head and uttered a few "uh-huhs." His face was stiff and I noticed his neck growing splotchy. The air was charged, and I instinctively knew, the same way a cat can sense an impending hurricane, that whatever was happening on the other end of the phone was not going to be good news for me.

"Yes, I understand. You have my absolute assurance. Yes, the minute I get off the phone. Okay, right away," Ricky said to whoever was on the end of the line. He swallowed hard and hung up the receiver, staring at it for a few seconds, as if it was an alien life-form performing mind control.

"Who . . . who was it?" I prodded, breaking the trance.

"It was . . . uhhh . . . it was one of the partners upstairs. We need to halt our review." He raised the end of the sentence like he was asking a question.

I focused on keeping my face still. My heart pounded so hard in my chest I was sure it was visible through my shirt.

"We need to halt our review," he repeated with more authority, as if he'd answered his own question definitively.

"Has . . . has the case settled?" I asked, trying not to let panic seep into my tone.

He shook his head. "There's been some kind of glitch, apparently with the keyword search. A word they used to catch any communications involving one of the subsidiaries ended up flagging one of the partners' entire inbox."

I focused on keeping my expression neutral, but every muscle in my face was twitching. "Did they say which one?" I asked.

He shook his head. "Just that we need to immediately stop our review and send everyone home for the night. They're going to run a new search and create a new database fixing the glitch for the morning."

"Wow, that's a pretty big glitch." I forced an unnatural calm to my voice.

Ricky nodded. "Talk about a huge false positive. I never came across anything like that in my review so I don't know what they're talking about. Did you?"

I shook my head, hoping my eyes didn't betray me. As I suspected, Ricky's review folder evidently lacked any of Forest's emails.

I followed Ricky on shaking legs as he strode out the door, back to the group.

"Listen up, everyone," Ricky announced, his drill sergeant voice trembling with adrenaline. "We're shutting it down for the night. Sign out of your computers immediately. Don't even finish the document you're reviewing. It's a direct order from the higher-ups."

My hands were still trembling when I slung my purse over my shoulder and pushed in my chair. I barely had time to sneak a peek at my screen before Ricky was pacing the rows, ensuring everyone had completely signed off the system.

"Don't dillydally, people. I need to lock up for the night," he bellowed. It felt like we were going to be made to clasp our hands behind our necks like captured enemy soldiers.

"Hey, what's going on?"

I looked up to see Dalton's perplexed expression as he gestured around the room. His face was sheet white and sweaty, as if he'd been hit with a bad bout of food poisoning.

"Where have you been?" I whispered, pressing myself against the table in an attempt to get out of the way of the guy Dalton referred to as "the Mute." Tell a group of temps to go home for the night and they'll stampede toward the doors faster than shoppers rushing a Walmart on Black Friday. "Are you okay?" I asked, peering at his clammy face. "You look like you're sick."

"Yeah, yeah. All good." He dabbed a bead of sweat off his forehead. "But what's the deal with all this? Did you finally lead a mutiny or something?"

"We're being sent home for the night."

"Seriously? Why?"

"I'll fill you in on the way out," I answered distractedly, my stomach twisting with dread as I wondered what my review folder would contain tomorrow. Or would *not* contain.

"Can you grab my bag?" Dalton gestured with his chin to his workstation. "And throw this in there too?" He slid his phone across the table and I tucked it in the side pocket of his backpack.

"Holy crap, what do you keep in here?" I joked, lifting the dead weight off the floor and hefting it over my shoulder.

"Well, it might help if you held it upright, Cassie." His lips twitched with humor as I shuffled down the row and passed over the heavy sack.

We filed into the elevator with the other temps and rode down in silence. The air was thick with a nervous energy as fingers flew across phone screens like tiny gnats. Everyone around me had somewhere else to be. My hands were itching—practically aching—to send a message to Forest, as if he was a dose of heroin I suddenly needed to inject into my veins.

The doors opened in the lobby and someone muttered, "We'd better still get paid for these hours," as we pushed through the turnstiles. The security guard looked up from his paper and raised a curious brow.

"What's with the mass exodus?"

"I've staged a walkout," Dalton responded. "Tell those assholes to improve working conditions or we're not coming back." He raised a triumphant fist as the security guard hooted and clapped.

"You're definitely going to get yourself fired," I teased, a tiny quaver in my voice, as the revolving door deposited us into cool early evening air.

"Underwear scrubbers, Cass. Never forget the underwear-scrubbers theory," Dalton reminded me, an impish grin on his face. "And besides, I don't think I'm going to need this job anymore."

"Really? You got another gig?" My stomach sank with disappointment. If I was shut out of Forest's emails tomorrow, Dalton was the only source left for any inside information.

"Which way are you walking?" he asked, ignoring my question.

"Subway," I responded, pointing east, silently hoping Dalton would suggest grabbing dinner. It wasn't only that I hoped to press him for information about Forest, but I was also filled with a sudden, desperate need for company. It had been a while since I had to eat alone during the week and the mere thought of it was filling me with dread.

"I'll walk a few blocks with you." He fidgeted with his employee ID as he pulled it over his head and tucked it in his pocket. He seemed far more jittery than usual, and I briefly wondered if us being alone together outside of office hours was making him nervous.

I filled him in on the phone call Ricky took in the interrogation room while we walked, and Dalton listened, rapt.

"So, he never told you which lawyer's inbox was caught up in the cache of emails?"

"No." I cleared the shake in my throat. "But it must be that guy Forest's, right? I never saw anything in his email that would explain why they were caught up in our review. Did . . ." I faltered. "Did you?"

He shook his head. "No, but I didn't read them too closely."

I nodded, biting the inside of my mouth.

Dalton's eyes darted behind him. "Listen, Cass, I don't want you to think I'm abandoning you or anything, but I don't think I'm going to be at this gig much longer."

"Not this again." I rolled my eyes with as much playfulness as I could muster. "Our jobs are going to be redundant, yada, yada, yada."

He pushed a hand through his disheveled hair and for a moment I thought he was going to say something, but he pressed his lips together and looked away.

We passed a man perched up against the wall with a sleeping dog's chin resting on his lap and a sign that said SEEKING HUMAN KINDNESS beside him. Dalton reached into his back pocket, pulled out a twenty-dollar bill, and dropped it into his cup without missing a step.

I raised an eyebrow. "You're feeling magnanimous today."

"I'm a lucky guy." He shrugged. "Not in the ways I thought I would be, but sometimes you gotta make your own luck." He shoved his hands back in his pockets.

I nodded, thrown by the pensive edge in Dalton's voice. His emotions were all over the place today. We stopped in front of the subway entrance and for a moment there was a beat of uncomfortable silence.

"Hey, um . . ." I readjusted my purse over my shoulder. "Do you want to go grab dinner somewhere?" I forced an unnatural cheer in my voice.

"Oh, uh . . . I . . ." Dalton rocked back on his heels, avoiding my eyes. "I actually have something I need to do. I mean, I'm meeting someone soon."

"Oh." I tried to hide my surprise. Did Dalton have a girlfriend this whole time and I never heard about her? Surely he would've mentioned that. But he seemed so cagey and uncomfortable right now that there was no way the person he was meeting was just a friend.

"No problem!" I replied, a tad too manically. "I mean, I have stuff I should be doing too." I gestured to the subway stairs with my thumb as if I had a whole to-do list waiting for me down there.

"Another time though, okay?"

"Sure." I nodded enthusiastically in an attempt to cover my embarrassment. You would think I'd be used to rejection by now. "See you tomorrow then!" I turned and headed down the subway stairs, already feeling the crushing weight of the emptiness of my apartment.

Later, of course, I wondered what would have happened if I'd been paying better attention to the things Dalton was saying to me that night. If I'd just inquired more.

If only.

Chapter Twenty

"CAN I HELP you?" Ricky removed his earbuds and eyed me suspiciously. I couldn't blame him. This was probably the first conversation anyone in this room had ever initiated with Ricky. On purpose, at least. But these were desperate times that called for desperate measures.

"I, um . . . I have a question that I'm hoping you can help me with," I said, jittery from the extra coffee I downed this morning in an effort to offset a night of relentless insomnia. Or maybe my body was already experiencing the symptoms of intense withdrawal from Forest's emails, being that it was eleven in the morning and I had yet to come across a single one.

"A question?" Ricky popped up from his seat like an actor who'd just heard his name called at the Academy Awards. "I'm always telling people to come to me with questions, but they seem to think they know it all. But there's really no room for error on this project, you know? I mean, look what happened yesterday with the whole . . ." He raised his eyebrows and gestured with his thumb to the interrogation room before lowering his voice to a whisper. "We can't afford to have another mistake after that one." His eyes darted around the room, as if there was a possibility of one of our temps being a plant from the higher-ups, before adding in a low voice, "Not that *we* were the ones responsible for it."

I nodded, pleased Ricky had brought the subject up himself.

This was going to be easier than I thought. "Did they tell you anything more? I mean, about what happened?"

He shook his head. "Nothing other than an email early this morning giving the green light to instruct everyone to start reviewing documents again." His forehead wrinkled. "But I'm sure they'll fill me in on the details soon." He nodded earnestly as if agreeing with himself.

"Did they tell you the name of the lawyer who had his personal emails caught up in the data set?" I lowered my voice, despite the earbuds jammed in my fellow temps' ears. "In case I come across any today I want to be able to . . . um . . . report it."

Ricky eyed me for a beat longer than necessary. "No, but if you come across anything that doesn't look like it should be part of our review you should always report it to me immediately."

"Of course." I nodded, matching his earnest tone.

"I've asked a few temps if they came across any emails that obviously shouldn't have been in our data set, but nobody will admit to anything." He glared over his shoulder before crossing his arms and puffing out his scrawny chest. "Keep your ear to the ground, and let me know if you hear of anything."

"I will." I cleared my throat to mask the tiny shake. "But chances are whoever reviewed them wouldn't have even noticed they didn't belong. I mean, we review a lot of personal stuff, right?"

Ricky let out a short, mirthless laugh. "There's a difference between personal stuff and reviewing someone's entire inbox. It doesn't take a genius to know the difference and somebody in here should've brought it to my attention so I could've alerted the higher-ups before it went on as long as it did. It was an invasion of privacy if you ask me." I could tell from Ricky's expression he was much more disappointed he'd lost out on his opportunity to look like Superman to the higher-ups than he was about any invasion of privacy.

Ricky tossed another glare around the room before returning his attention to me, raising an ominous eyebrow. "I just hope the higher-ups investigate."

My spine tensed, one vertebra at a time. I never even considered the higher-ups would do anything more than rerun the keyword search. But now that Ricky mentioned it, surely there was a possibility someone would want to smoke the snooping temps out of their holes. Maybe even bring them to some kind of humiliating justice.

The last thing I needed right now was another altercation with the police.

Jesus Christ, not another one.

Beads of sweat sprang underneath my arms. As if sensing a change in the air, a messy-haired temp in the row behind Ricky raised his eyes from his computer and peered at me for a moment too long before returning his attention to his screen.

"Do you think they'll do that?" I asked, struggling to keep the worry out of my tone.

Ricky shrugged. "I would. I mean, can you imagine having your whole inbox out there for some stranger to read?" He gazed into the distance as if imagining the possibility before snapping his attention back to me. "Not that I have anything I need to hide," he said curtly, the tips of his ears turning pink.

"No, of course not." I tried not to imagine how many bodies were buried in Ricky's personal email. "But it would still feel like an invasion," I added, trying to fill the air, which was suddenly charged with awkwardness. "I would imagine . . ."

He nodded before straightening his posture, as if physically composing himself. "So, what can I do you for?" I must have looked puzzled because he added, "The question you said you wanted to ask me?"

"Oh, right." I surreptitiously wiped my palms on my pants. This conversation had not gone the way I'd planned when I walked over here. I needed to get the information I came for and get back to my workstation. "Um, I was reviewing an email and it had the name of an entity that I think is a subsidiary of Falcon Healthcare, but I wanted to check before I mark it responsive. Can I . . . can I borrow the list?"

"Sure." He picked up a stapled document beside his keyboard.

Falcon Healthcare had over two hundred subsidiaries around the world, all neatly typed into one list for the temps to consult, if needed. The list was normally kept at the front of the room, next to the "shit breaks" clipboard, but it had been at Ricky's workstation all morning, which made me think Ricky must've been scouring the document looking for the name of the mystery partner who'd had the grave misfortune of sharing a name with a Falcon subsidiary.

"What's the name of the entity?" Ricky asked as he passed me the stapled pages.

"Oh, it's, um . . ." My eyes glanced to the side and I noticed the messy-haired temp was once again watching me, his expression blank, and even though it was only one person I had the sudden feeling that all eyes in the room were laser focused on me, waiting for my answer. My anxious mind spun.

"GenTech Inc.," I answered, giving the first company name that popped into my head.

"GenTech Inc.," Ricky parroted slowly. I couldn't tell if he was eyeing me doubtfully or if a hint of dubiousness was just a part of Ricky's default expression. My insides clenched. GenTech Inc. wasn't a Falcon Healthcare subsidiary. It was the name of a company that a client of Nolan & Wright had purchased two years ago. I was the senior associate on the deal and it had consumed my life for months. I dug my nails into my palm, trying not to think about how the partner on the deal had given me a hearty pat on the back, telling me how proud he was of me, as if he *knew* those words were my emotional kryptonite.

Ricky clasped his chin with his thumb and forefinger and furrowed his brow. "Sounds kinda familiar. But we might as well have a look." He gestured with his head to the list in my hands.

I could feel myself grimace, but swiftly rearranged my expression to mask my disappointment. My plan had been to bring the list of subsidiaries back to my workstation where I could study it in peace, but Ricky was looking at me expectantly now, like this was a mystery we were going to solve together. So, under Ricky's watchful eye, I flipped open the stapled list.

"Hm." I furrowed my brow as I ran my finger down the page and scanned the alphabetized company names.

Don't be here. Don't be here, my mind pleaded.

Hope. I was still holding out hope for a lucky coincidence, that another partner was the reason they'd rerun the keyword search and Forest's emails would somehow, inexplicably remain under the radar, giving me an opportunity to keep reviewing them. How else was I going to learn the details about why Forest and Annabelle's marriage had ended? I couldn't come straight out and ask Forest. Not right away, at least. And with every minute that passed without word from Forest, it was getting harder to ignore the shreds of doubt that were beginning to ravage my thoughts. *What if I'm wrong? What if Forest and Annabelle's marriage isn't over after all?*

I struggled to keep a neutral expression when my finger slid down to the *F*'s. My eyes stopped about three quarters down the page.

Forest Biotech Inc.

An invisible hand reached into the pit of my stomach and squeezed. There it was—the reason Forest's emails had been flagged for our review and the answer to the question I'd been wondering about since day one was now literally at my fingertips. Falcon Healthcare had a subsidiary called Forest Biotech Inc. Whoever ran the search must have made an error and left off the word "Biotech," inadvertently picking up the entire inbox of Forest Watts. And now that the error was discovered, a new, corrected search was run.

I was locked out of Forest's email. Forever.

"Is it there?" Ricky asked, peering over the top of the page.

"Nope." I flipped the list closed and quickly handed it back to him like it was evidence of a crime and I didn't want to be the one left holding it. "It's not there. But I'm glad I took the time to check. You can never be too careful, right?" I let out a little, awkward laugh.

Ricky was evaluating me now, the gears in his head turning, so I forced myself to maintain eye contact. Objectively, there was nothing to worry about—looking up an entity on the subsidiary list was just a normal, run-of-the-mill thing temps did all the time. Still, my pulse raced as Ricky continued to hold my gaze, peering through his eyebrows as if attempting some sort of Jedi mind trick.

"It is *always* better to be safe than sorry, Cassie," he said with an intensity that bolted me to the ground. I had the distinct feeling we weren't talking about reviewing documents anymore. For a second I wondered if Ricky was toying with me. Maybe the higher-ups had asked him to look into which one of the temps had Forest's emails in their review folder and he was in the process of doing that on the down low.

Don't be stupid, I told myself. Ricky wasn't the kind of person who could do anything covertly. If the higher-ups ever asked him to do that, he'd probably carry around a comically oversized magnifying glass in order to show everyone he was heading up an investigation.

"Okay, well, I better get back to my desk then," I said trying to lighten whatever was happening here between us. "Thanks, for the help, Ricky."

"No problemo," he responded in a tone that bordered on chipper, making me wonder if my guilty mind had simply imagined the strangeness. I turned on my heel, suddenly eager to get back to my chair.

"Oh hey, Cassie? I have a question for you too." There was a hint of smugness in his tone.

I froze. Instinctively my eyes darted toward the exit. *I can make a dash for it if it comes to that,* I told myself. *I can be out of here in three seconds flat.*

As casually as possible, I turned back around. Ricky's expression was hard to read, but it reminded me of a TV lawyer about to begin a cross-examination.

"Shoot," I replied, flashing a tight smile, struggling to keep my face impassive.

He crossed his arms over his chest. "What is it, exactly, that you see in that guy?"

My rib cage tightened around my lungs.

I could feel a tiny tremble in my cheek so I took a moment to slide my mask back in place. "I'm sorry?" I said, tilting my head to one side.

"Dalton. I mean, it's nearly lunch." He pointed an angry finger to the clock on the wall. "And the guy still hasn't even bothered to come to work. How can you even associate yourself with someone like that?"

I shrugged one shoulder, my fight-or-flight adrenaline slowly being expelled from my body like helium from a balloon. "He's probably just sick and couldn't make it in today."

Ricky scoffed. "Yeah, sick of *working*." He plopped back down in his chair, stuck his earbuds in, and returned to mouse-clicking.

Back at my workstation, I dug through my purse for my phone and fired off a quick text to Dalton. *You're really testing this underwear-scrubbers theory today . . .*

I kept my eyes on the screen, waiting for a response, but it remained maddeningly blank.

Cassandra Woodson: *Where were you today? Ricky was on the warpath. Call me.*

Cassandra Woodson: *Earth to Dalton. Are you awake? Why aren't you answering my messages? Call me.*

Chapter Twenty-One

I RAN MY finger down the nylon, skull-printed leggings, keeping my head down to make myself as inconspicuous as possible, as three ponytailed blondes strode past me.

"Welcome, warriors," the tank-topped woman behind the desk sang. "Are you ready to get high on sweat?"

I struggled to keep my eyes from rolling. God, I hated fitness cults. But I reminded myself I was supposed to be blending in with this bunch, not standing out. That was already going to be tricky since I was outfitted in dowdy work attire and lacked an expensive gym bag thrown over my shoulder. There hadn't been enough time to return to my apartment and prepare.

"Are you here for our Midnight Ride?" Tank Top called out in my direction after the gaggle of blondes made their way into the locker room.

I took a moment to rearrange my face before turning around.

"Yes, I'm really excited for this." I forced a cheerful note into my voice. I refrained from asking the obvious question—why the "Midnight Ride" was at nine P.M. and not, say . . . midnight? Semantics clearly didn't have a place in this cult. And I knew my best course of action here would be sweetness. The old "catch more flies with honey" saying. "It's really great that you guys are one of the sponsors. It's for such a good cause."

"Such a good cause," Tank Top parroted, nodding. I would bet a million dollars she couldn't even name the charity she was raising funds for tonight. But I could. It was called Art Start—bringing fine arts education into public schools in low income neighborhoods in New York City. Or as Annabelle referred to it on Instagram, *supporting the next generation of artists!!*

Every relationship has its obstacles. It was important for me to determine if Annabelle would be ours.

With no word from Forest yet, there was only one way to extinguish the spark of doubt that had ignited in the back of my thoughts, threatening to blaze into an inferno: I needed to track down Annabelle. If I was able to manufacture an opportunity to interact with her, it would give me the chance to casually ask a few strategic questions. Narcissists like Annabelle can't help but talk about themselves. I could say something like, *Watts? That's an interesting last name. Is it German?* And she would say, *Oh, it's my ex-husband's name.* It would be a litmus test. Using the word "ex" is an acknowledgment to the world that the relationship is indeed in the past. I should know. I've spent a lot of time in that category.

I didn't allow myself to consider my next steps if Annabelle was unwilling to concede that she was firmly in Forest's rearview mirror. As Grandma used to say, *Cross that bridge when you come to it.*

I'd spent my lunch and dinner breaks today on Instagram visiting the profiles Annabelle followed, searching for comments she might have left on their posts. Social media really can be a road map to someone's whereabouts if the right amount of detective work is involved.

Now that I wouldn't have access to Forest's emails anymore, I needed to get creative.

Annabelle had been an Instagram "like" whore lately, tapping the tiny heart ninety-six times in the past three days, I'd discovered in my research. Vacation photos, sunsets, inspirational sayings—she wasn't discerning. However, there was a higher threshold for which photos she deemed worthy of a comment. Annabelle doled out her Instagram comments the way Grandma doled out compliments—infrequently and without sincerity. I'd studied each one until I had her writing style memorized—she always dropped the pronouns at the beginning of her sentences *(Love this!! Wish I could be there!!),* never used a single exclamation point when she could use two, and shunned emojis. But, of course, her diction wasn't the reason for my social media scavenger hunt. I was trying to decipher whether any of her comments would provide a hint as to where I could finally see Annabelle in person.

A comment she posted at 6:37 tonight did just that.

Can't wait for the midnight ride tonight! Such a great cause!! she'd written in response to a photo posted by @ArtStart. A few clicks of the mouse later and I'd discovered that the charity ride would be held at the Spirit Cycle near Grand Central at nine P.M. Cost: $250. Participants could enter to win one of ten door prizes, the top being a painting donated from the collection of Annabelle Watts (estimated value $8,500).

They don't call it the Information Age for nothing.

"Your name?" Tank Top asked, bopping her head to the loud beat of the music thrumming through the speakers.

I briefly debated giving a fake name before nixing the idea. I would have to use a credit card to pay for the ticket which would reveal my name. "Cassie Woodson," I answered, hitching my purse up on my shoulder.

She put down her canned energy drink and peered at her computer, wrinkling her nose as if smelling something bad. "I don't see you here on the list, Cassie."

I squeezed the strap of my purse. Just once—one fucking time—I wanted to be "on the list." Any list.

"Um . . . I tried to register this afternoon, but online registration was closed." Tank Top's eyes wandered over my shoulder as I spoke. She was already bored with me. "My friend Annabelle Watts is going to be here, so I was hoping to join her?" I added, sweetening the pot.

Surely dropping Annabelle's name would give me some level of clout.

Tank Top waved to the two Lycra-clad women with sharp-edged pixie cuts who were bypassing the desk and heading right for the locker room. "Welcome, warrior leaders!" she called out before turning her attention back to me. "Unfortunately, our midnight charity ride is sold out." She jutted her lower lip. "Has been for weeks. The incomparable Valentine Lee is leading the ride, so it was a really popular ticket." She tilted her head, considering. "But if someone doesn't show up and there's a free bike I could see what I can do."

She said this like she was offering possible entry into a private party at the White House, so I forced my mouth into a smile and responded, "That would be great if you could."

"Just wait right over there." She gestured to a rack of slouchy black T-shirts with MY RIDE OR DIE CREW IS BETTER THAN YOURS scrawled across the front in fluorescent pink. "And you can fill this out while you wait." She tapped an iPad and passed it across the counter to me.

I took a few steps to the side and began entering my information—*Name. Preferred Warrior Name. Email Address. Password. Create Account.* When I was finished, I rested it on the counter and examined the price tags on the T-shirts, trying to keep my eyes from widening when I read $68. If all went as planned and I was bestowed a bike for this charity ride I was going to have to drop a ridiculous amount of money for something to wear.

More money flushed down the toilet.

But it would be worth it, I told myself. Meeting Annabelle in person was an important part of safeguarding my relationship with Forest. Know thy enemy, as they say. And when else was I going to have a chance like this practically fall into my lap?

I swiped my phone, checking Annabelle's Instagram to see if there was any indication that she'd arrived before me and was already inside. No new photos. No new comments. Not even a new "like."

"Welcome, warriors!" I heard Tank Top call out. I turned my gaze to the door and my heart came to a stop. Her head was turned, looking at something on the opposite wall, but I would recognize that long neck and ballerina posture anywhere.

Annabelle.

She was flanked by a pair of rail-thin brunettes donning matching pink Sweaty Betty headbands. I watched as her friends gave their names and she waited demurely for her turn, her hands in the pockets of her glossy black coat. She wore pale-blue patterned leggings and her hair was pulled back with delicate wisps falling around her face. Her makeup was subtle and her lashes were curled with expertly applied mascara.

Jealousy burrowed its way under my skin like a tick. There wasn't a single flaw on her entire body. Not one fucking blemish. It was enough to make you want to drive a sharp object through her temple.

"Annabelle Watts," I heard her say and it wasn't until I saw Tank Top turn her eyes toward me that I realized my error.

Shit.

"Oh, Annabelle, your friend's been waiting for you over there." Tank Top pointed a fire-engine-red fingertip in my direction. Annabelle's head swiveled.

The Earth stopped spinning on its axis.

Everyone's eyes were now firmly fastened on me. Annabelle's friends tilted their heads curiously. Venomously. Annabelle's expression was one of confusion, and I didn't miss the way her eyes darted to the left, consulting her mental Rolodex. But it only took a second before she repositioned her face into a seemingly warm smile. Her finishing school, thank-you-note-writing, always say "nice to *see* you" rather than "nice to *meet* you" manners would prevent her from admitting she had absolutely no clue who I was.

"Oh, hi there," she said smoothly. Her voice was breathier than I'd imagined. I thought it would have a sexy rasp to it, but it didn't. I made a mental note. She took a step closer to me, and I inhaled the sweet smell of her floral perfume.

"Cassie," I filled in, as if she had simply forgotten my name. I forced my mouth to return her smile, but couldn't keep my cheek from trembling. *Could she tell?* I wondered. Did she have some sixth sense that I was her ex-husband's new girlfriend? I watched her eyes, but they gave nothing away.

"I'm so glad you could come tonight, Cassie." The sound of my name coming out of Annabelle's mouth made my vision blur, as if I was suddenly seeing everything through frosted glass, and I had to rest my hand on the clothing rack to steady myself. "We're going to make a lot of children happy with the money we raise," she added, lifting a delicate hand to her collarbone, toying with the silver cross pendant hanging from her neck.

I struggled to focus my gaze.

Is that?

Is that a fucking RING on her finger?

Why the fuck is there a ring on Annabelle's finger?

I looked away, blinking rapidly and dabbing at the corners of my lids. My anger felt like a rabid dog on a short leash and I had to press a fist into my stomach to stop it from churning.

No. It couldn't be. It couldn't be.

My breaths were coming rapidly as I shot another look at her hand, zeroing in on the spot where her solitaire, princess-cut diamond (three carats? It was difficult to tell from the photos online . . .) usually sat.

My knees buckled with relief. The glint from the pendant against Annabelle's knuckle had made it look like a ring, but now that my eyes were fully focused I could see the fourth finger on Annabelle's left hand was conspicuously, gloriously bare. The corners of my lips pulled up as I imagined her engagement ring being stripped from her finger the way a disgraced Olympian is stripped of her medals.

I wondered if she returned it to Forest. I made a mental note to find out.

"You guys are all set," Tank Top said, returning a credit card to one of the skinny brunettes, jostling me out of my head.

"Are you coming inside, Cassie?" Annabelle gestured with her head toward the locker room and a wisp of hair fell artfully over her eye. "It's going to be a fun ride."

My pulse was pounding in my neck now. "Oh, I'm—"

"Unfortunately, she's not registered," Tank Top interrupted, jutting out that infuriating lip of hers again. "And you ladies are the last to arrive so all of the bikes have been filled."

"Bummer," Annabelle breathed, her eyes traveling over my face, clearly still trying to place me. "Next time for sure, though.

Nice to see you again, Cassie." She flashed her perfectly straight teeth.

I stood motionless, watching her follow her cohorts into the locker room as my stomach clenched with desperation. It felt like the last helicopter was leaving Saigon without me on it. Any chance I had to talk to her was slipping away. "Annabelle!" I heard her name boom out of my mouth like a cannonball.

The entire group halted. Even Tank Top stopped bopping to the music and turned her attention to me. Annabelle's headbanded friends raised their eyebrows in question, but she motioned for them to go ahead.

"Yes?" She crinkled her pert little nose. Her expression was perplexed. Or was it annoyed? It was difficult to decipher with how skilled she was at concealing her emotions.

Manipulative bitch.

"We met at the New Yorkers for Children fall gala last year," I blurted, my voice trembling. "Back when you were still with your ex-husband."

Her glossy mouth dropped open, and I derived a small amount of cold, hard satisfaction from throwing a stone into her perfectly balanced façade. Tiny, almost imperceptible red patches bloomed on her cheeks. If you weren't familiar with her skin tone, you might not even know they were there. But I did.

"Of course," she breathed, giving a terse goodbye nod before spinning on her heel and disappearing into the locker room. It was only when the door slammed shut behind her that I realized my hands were shaking so hard I'd unintentionally pulled two shirts off their hangers. I left the heap of clothes on the tiled floor and avoided Tank Top's gawking eyes on my way out. It wasn't how I'd planned this evening to go, but I'd managed to accomplish something.

I'd eliminated Annabelle from the equation.

To: Cassandra Woodson
From: Edward Rossi

Hi, Cassandra,

I'm an old friend of your dad's from back in our army days. I heard about what's happened with your dad. He was always a bit of a loner, but one of the strongest in our unit. We are thinking of you.

Ed

Chapter Twenty-Two

MY STOMACH FELT full of acid as I placed my phone beside my dinner tray, facedown. The image on the home screen—a shot of the lighthouse in Montauk which usually made me feel calm seemed to taunt me now. The original photo included Landon and me on the beach, arm in arm, grinning like fools on Montauk Point, but I'd long since cropped us out of the picture, leaving only the charming lighthouse and beautiful waves behind. The nautical image had always been meditative to me, but now, sitting here at a table alone in the cafeteria, it seemed to eyeball me judgmentally, whispering, *One more person. One more person has cropped you out of his life.*

I hadn't seen Dalton in two days, not since we'd walked to the subway together. Two days with no one to talk to, nobody to eat dinner with, and nothing but my thoughts to keep me company. And I would be the first to admit, my thoughts made very, very bad company.

"This happens all the time," Ricky had explained this morning. "Temps take new gigs at other firms without ever bothering to inform me they're leaving. They think they can make more money or have better hours somewhere else so they jump ship and don't come in one day." He let out a disgusted scoff before his eyes went wide. "Wait, didn't he even tell *you* he was peace-ing out? Even after you risked your own reputation by covering for him?" I shook my head, embarrassed about going to Ricky to track down the whereabouts of my supposed friend. Truth be told, though, I don't know why I was surprised. I had a long history of short friendships. People in my life seemed to view a relationship with me like a quart of milk or a pound of ground beef—good for a defined period of time before it needed to be discarded into the trash. Judging by the fact that Dalton hadn't answered any of my six texts and two phone calls, our friendship had clearly reached the end of its limited shelf life.

A burst of laughter from a table of four alpha males in the corner stirred me back to the present. I glared at them, suddenly hating them for their overt display of self-absorbed entitlement. They certainly hadn't spent the previous evening chasing vodka with cough syrup in an effort to quiet the voices in their heads. If Dalton was here he would deliver a perfectly cutting quip about frat boys or trust fund babies.

I missed him, I realized. At the very least, I missed having another human being to talk to. Looking at the people paired up at other tables made me feel like a child with her nose pressed up against a store window.

I pecked out two words to Dalton now. "Fuck. You." Then I hit "send" and stared at the screen, waiting for the three dots to appear in response. Not surprisingly, they don't. I picked up my fork and chased a wilted onion around my plate before surrendering and pushing the tray away. The knot in my stomach was not going to be dislodged by ingesting another bite of cafeteria food.

I hated myself for continuing to contact Dalton, as if maybe my texts had somehow, inexplicably gone astray. Couldn't I take the hint after the first one went unanswered? Or the second? He hadn't even bothered to answer my message about the book he'd left at his workstation. *You may have moved on to bigger and better things, but what are you going to read when you get there?* I'd written and attached a photo of his copy of *A Confederacy of Dunces* in my hand. Nothing but radio silence in return. He was done with me.

I drummed my fingers on the table as a strange little tingle of worry traveled down my back, but just as quickly I shrugged it away.

I tapped my screen awake again. No message from Dalton. No message from Forest.

I'd loitered outside of Juice Press this morning. And yesterday morning. And the one before. No Forest. I'd even gone inside, purchased a Fireball, asked Man Bun if he'd seen Forest. He hadn't. To say I was desperate to read Forest's emails again would be an understatement. I would've gladly given my full paycheck just to lay eyes on him again.

Being kept from Forest for this long was like being forced into a straitjacket and wrapped in shackles. I drained my Diet Coke and slammed it on the tray. The old adage is clearly bullshit. Good things do *not* come to those who wait. It was time for Plan B.

I rooted through my purse and pulled out my black three-ring binder and a pencil, surreptitiously scanning the cafeteria in the unlikely event someone was watching me, but I probably could've jumped up on the table and danced to "All the Single Ladies" Beyoncé-style before anyone would've bothered to turn their eyes in my direction.

There were small benefits to being invisible.

I rested the binder on my lap and began flipping through the pages. There was a list of every restaurant he'd ever made a reservation for on OpenTable, but there weren't any patterns that could point me to which day he'd be returning. He'd recently purchased golf gloves on Amazon, but there were seventy-eight golf courses within a one-hour drive from New York City (I'd googled), so that information wasn't helpful either. I cracked one thumb knuckle, then the other one. I was a detective dealing with a particularly frustrating cold case. I needed a new tip, some other piece of information about Forest and his whereabouts.

My knee began to bounce as I flipped to the last page of the binder titled "Forest's Password."

After I'd arrived home on the night I'd parted ways with Dalton at the subway, I had immediately signed on to my computer, brought up the document title "miscellaneous.doc," and typed what I'd been repeating in the back of my mind since it flashed on my screen. AMFW07. It wasn't the whole password, I knew I was missing four numbers, but it was all my foggy, anxious mind could recollect at the time.

I chewed the side of my fingernail, my eyes fixed on the first four letters so intently they began swimming around the page. *A-M-F-W.* It reminded me of the doodles I used to do in grade school when I would be sitting by myself at recess, dreaming of being the girlfriend of the most popular boy in our class, Johnny Doyle, certain the partnership would be the cure for all that was wrong in my life. *CW + JD*, my thirteen-year-old self would write, surrounded by a giant heart.

The pencil dropped from my hands. I flipped the pages frantically, stopping on the page with the details of Forest and Annabelle's wedding announcement. *Forest Watts married Annabelle Murphy.* With shaking hands, I picked up the pencil and scrawled across the bottom of the page *Forest Watts Annabelle Murphy. AMFW.* I underlined it twice, nearly ripping the paper with the force. Uncurling my fingers and giving my wrist a shake, I reminded myself this was long before our relationship started. And the important thing was that I'd cracked part of the code.

I was one step closer.

I turned my attention to the numbers in the password. There were six digits in total. It could be a license plate. Or maybe a phone number.

No, stupid, a phone number is seven digits.

I traced the zero with my pencil, wondering if I would be able to see Forest's license plate number from the street or if I would need to gain access to his garage to take a look.

It would be a project for this weekend.

"You coming, Cassie?" A voice sliced through my thoughts like a serrated knife. I looked up to see Ricky looming over me.

I snapped to attention like a schoolgirl caught talking in line and slammed my binder shut, stuffing it in my bag. "Is it time?" I said, unable to control the maniacal tone of my voice. "I always forget when dinner ends."

Ricky gave me a sideways look before waggling his phone and pointing an obnoxious finger on the screen. "Seven o'clock. Same time as every other night you've been here."

"Right." I nodded, struggling to keep my expression impassive as my eyes ran over the picture on his home screen—a shot of Ricky winking and giving the camera the double finger guns pose. I briefly debated whether I should toss off a comment about the photo in order to distract him when my gaze narrowed like the lens of a camera, zeroing in on the numbers on the screen, directly below the clock.

Bingo.

I leapt from the banquette and grabbed my tray with shaking hands.

"If you set an alarm on your phone like I do you won't need me reminding you," Ricky grumbled, but I barely heard him above the noise in my head.

As I filed into the elevator with the other temps, my whole body was buzzing with such excitement I could've wrapped my arms around all of them for a group hug.

Like a successful illusionist, I'd found a way out of my strait-jacket.

Chapter Twenty-Three

I KEPT MY head down when we entered the bunker after our dinner break, in an effort to make myself as inconspicuous as possible. I felt like Offred from *The Handmaid's Tale* in a room full of Eyes, and I wished I could wear one of those white bonnets with wings to hide the anxiety I knew was etched all over my face.

"Let's finish the day strong, people," Ricky called out to the room as we dispersed to our workstations in silence. He dropped his stockpile of granola bars beside his computer, and I watched out of the side of my eye, waiting for him to complete his post-dinner routine—pop open his nightly Mountain Dew, crack his neck once on each side, and dive back into his mouse-clicking. I shuffled down the row slowly, hoping Ricky would be fully engaged in document review before I reached my workstation, but in an unexpected break from the script, Ricky clapped his hands together and announced, "I need to make a call, everyone—a *management* related one," he emphasized, peering around the room like a teacher looking for a star student to put in charge in his absence. Presumably seeing no one who fit the bill, he nixed the idea and strode toward the interrogation room, phone in hand. "No one should take a bathroom break in my absence," he called over his shoulder.

I felt a tiny flutter of happiness, barely believing my luck.

I shimmied down the aisle to my workstation and then, as nonchalantly as possible, bypassed my own chair and took a seat at

Dalton's workstation instead. Surreptitiously, I surveyed the room to determine if anyone noticed my musical chairs act, but earbuds were planted firmly in place and eyes were already glued to the glowing screens.

Plan B was now set in motion.

The groundwork had been laid, but it was Ricky who had slotted the final piece in place. When he had so obnoxiously pointed to his phone screen, my eyes had landed on the six digits beneath the time—11/7/19—and the penny dropped.

Dates. Dates are six digits.

Forest's password had six numbers and started with 0-7, which meant it had to be an important date in July. I knew Forest well enough to narrow it down to two: his wedding anniversary or his birthday.

Dalton's wobbly chair squeaked as I shifted my weight, and I felt my heart thump against my rib cage. *There's a reason they give us defective, loud chairs,* I remembered Dalton saying. *It's one more way they can keep track of our movements, like we're dogs with one of those jangly ID tags.*

It was a good thing Dalton wasn't here now. Signing on from his computer instead of my own meant nothing could be traced back to me, Temp 021. And with my coworkers' general aversion to interacting with human beings, I was confident they wouldn't notice my choice of computers.

I wiped my sweaty palms on my lap, staring at the firm logo swirling around Dalton's computer screen. I felt like I was standing with my toes on the edge of the high diving board deciding whether I should jump. My breath quickened. Breaking into Forest's email was technically hacking which was technically a federal crime. I could picture the woman from the temp agency *Cassie, I knew you couldn't get a reference from your former employer, but I never imagined you were a criminal!*

But if I let this chance slip through my fingers it might not come again. The case we were working on could settle tomorrow, for all we knew. If that happened, the temps would be unceremoniously dismissed and, just like that, my connection to Forest would be severed.

I shot a glance at the interrogation room. Ricky's call would be ending soon. It was now or never. My pulse began picking up speed until it was thudding like a tribal drum imploring me, *Do it. Do it. Do it.*

I swiped the mouse before I could change my mind and tapped the cursor on the rectangular box beside "User ID." If the risk of getting arrested was the currency I had to pay to read Forest's emails again, I was willing to pay it. My fingers flew over the keys as I typed in "FWatts" and hit "tab." I paused before typing in the password, considering which one I wanted to try first, before deciding on Forest's birthday and hitting enter.

Big bold words flashed on the screen: ***The username or password is incorrect.***

My stomach dropped. Too many failed sign-in attempts would likely lock Forest out of the system which would certainly cause IT to investigate. If the next one didn't work, I would have to throw in the towel.

The cursor pulsed like a racing heartbeat.

I watched my fingers as they pressed the keys—072912. Then I held my breath and hit Enter.

Please, please, please.

Dalton's computer hummed, the blood rushed in my ears, and then, much to my surprise and utter delight, tiny icons popped up on the screen like beautiful, twinkling stars.

My lungs expanded with fresh oxygen. I was in.

WITH MY PULSE racing faster than a car in the Indy 500, I clicked open Forest's Outlook and frantically scanned his inbox. It suddenly occurred to me I had no plan of attack. Of course, I wanted to go back through all of the emails in the past six months and read every sliver of correspondence between Forest and Annabelle, but I couldn't risk being in Dalton's seat when Ricky came back into the room. I had to be strategic. My next "chance" encounter with Forest had to be my top priority. I needed to find an email that would point me in the direction of where Forest would be and when.

I shot a look at the clock on the wall. The second hand seemed to be moving at warp speed. I felt like I was Jason Bourne trying to diffuse a deadly bomb before it blows.

Tick, tick, tick.

I scrolled down the inbox and began speed-reading the subject lines. *Project Blackbird SPA, CLE Webinar, RFI—Employment Lawyer in Texas . . .*

My vision blurred. This wasn't getting me anywhere. I had to open something. I clicked on an email with the subject line *Meeting request.*

All hands meeting—Project Spearhead, it read. *Conference Room 26A. Please confirm your availability.*

Click.

Forest, Can we set up a call for Tuesday morning?

Click.

Forest, Please find the revised SPA attached.

Click.

I shot another glance at the interrogation room. I had to move quicker.

I navigated to his "sent" folder and scanned the screen for Wednesday Walters's name. Emails to his secretary would most certainly have scheduling information. Rolling the mouse, I clicked on the first email to Wednesday I saw. *Please print attached and file.*

Shit, I mouthed silently. I grabbed the back of my neck and squeezed. It was stiff with tension. This was nothing like reviewing Forest's emails from the safety of my own computer. The stress was nauseating.

Keep clicking and reading Cassie, my mind screamed. *Stop being a coward, for once.*

Frantic now, I scanned the inbox for any email which wasn't work related and clicked—an email from his ticket broker confirming Rangers tickets for a game in January. It didn't include any information on where the seats would be located, but it was something. I grabbed my pen and scratched down the details.

Click.

An email from his tailor saying his suit was ready for pickup.

Click.

Amazon wanted to know how many stars he would give *The Longest Winter.*

Click.

His sister wanted to remind him about his mother's birthday.

Click.

My wrist ached from scribbling every word down.

Tick, tick, tick.

God, I wished I had the time to settle in and read every last one. Reading his words again was like taking a mouthful of air after being held under water too long.

Keep moving, Cassie!

My eyes zipped around the screen as I scrolled through what appeared to be useless work-related emails. My knee was bouncing with nervous energy. There had to be something here that would be helpful. There *had* to be. I scanned the left-hand side of the screen, reading the names of the files Forest had created for organizing his inbox, hoping to find one titled "Personal" or "Scheduling."

Apollo Correspondence, Project Diesel, CLE . . .

My eyes landed on the word in the lower left-hand side of the screen. Then I froze.

Holy shit.

The corners of my mouth twitched. Of course. How could I have been so dumb? I was so fixated on Forest's emails, so utterly consumed with the information that would be available to me with access to his inbox, it hadn't even occurred to me what else I would have access to.

His calendar.

Everything there was to know about Forest's schedule could be found right here in his Outlook calendar, which was now a click away. I wasn't going to find out where Forest would be *one* single time. I was going to find out where Forest would be every second of every glorious day.

Feeling invincible now, I picked up my phone, readying myself to transfer any pertinent information from Forest's calendar into my own.

I don't know if it was because I was completely engrossed in the task at hand or if he really was stealthy like a ninja, but when Ricky walked up behind me, he didn't make a sound.

Chapter Twenty-Four

THERE WAS NO way to know how long Ricky had been standing there behind me before he opened his mouth.

"Cassie."

The sound of my name coming from over my shoulder was like a hammer on a patient's knee, automatically kicking my reflexes into high gear. I X'ed out of my window faster than a game of Whac-A-Mole and spun around.

Looming over me, staring with an intensity that sent a chill through me, was Ricky.

I gripped my armrests in an attempt to stabilize my sudden vertigo and forced myself to look him in the eyes, trying to conceal my suspiciously shallow breathing. My thoughts were spinning, trying to land on any excuse I could present to explain away the fact that I was sitting in a seat which wasn't mine, signed in to a corporate partner's account, but the only words my rattled mind could hold on to were "ACT CASUAL."

Act fucking casual, Cassie!

"Cassie," Ricky repeated, and I noticed now his chin was quivering. Was he crying? Was this going to turn into one of those "this is hurting me more than it's hurting you" situations? If it was, maybe there was a way I could somehow play on his sympathies. Ricky was going to see to it that I was fired for this, no doubt about that, but maybe I could convince him not to report me to the agency. Or, god forbid, the police.

What have you done, Cassie? What the hell have you done this time?

"I, uh . . . I don't know what to say here." Ricky slid off his glasses and rubbed the bridge of his nose.

I struggled against the sudden, overwhelming urge to get up and run.

"Ricky, I was just, um . . ." It felt like there was a noose tightening around my throat, making my voice come out low and raspy. I was just . . . what? *I was just signed in to a partner's account by fucking accident?*

But then again, it was possible my reflexes were fast enough and Ricky hadn't seen anything. I snuck a peek at my screen. My heart rose into my throat. Clicking the X had closed Forest's Outlook, yes, but that still left me on Forest's home screen, which, I realized now, looked completely different from a temp's home screen based on the sheer number of icons. Nothing says "Very Important Employee" more than a rich garden of icons greeting you when you sign on to your computer. It could not have looked more different than the barren screen that greeted me every morning when I signed on as Temp 021. I crossed my arms over my chest and arched my back in an attempt to occupy as much space as possible, shifting my body in front of the monitor. "Working. I was just working." I gave him my best attempt at a smile, but could feel my cheek quiver. "Trying to get my numbers up. Like you always say, it's all about the numbers," I babbled.

Beads of sweat pricked on the back of my neck, dampening my hair.

Ricky seemed oblivious to my jumpiness as he let out a long sigh and rubbed his chin, a gesture I remember the doctor doing when he gave us the news about Dad. The way Ricky was looking at me now sent a fresh jolt of fear through me.

Whatever was coming had the feel of an oncoming train.

"I don't know how to say this, Cassie, but I just called the temp agency that placed Dalton here. I wanted them to know . . ." He took a shuddering breath. "I guess I wanted them to know that he'd stopped coming into work without any notice and maybe they would put something on his permanent record." His voice cracked. "I didn't think he was a very good worker. He was always coming in late and being disobedient. I thought it was important for me to take initiative and give feedback to the agency because that's what good managers do."

I searched Ricky's face for any clue of where this conversation was going. There was something about the look in his eyes now that made every hair on my body snap to attention.

"What did they say, Ricky?"

"I didn't expect . . ." he trailed off.

"What did they say, Ricky?" I repeated, my tone firmer than intended. I could taste the sweat on my upper lip.

Ricky raised his eyes to the ceiling, blinking rapidly. "Well, they said he's, um . . . they said that he's . . . gone."

My eyes narrowed. "What does that mean—gone?"

"Dead," Ricky whispered.

My ears took in the word, but my brain didn't process it right away. I was suddenly self-conscious about my reaction, worried I was showing my relief that we weren't talking about what was on my computer screen. Ricky's lips were still moving, but it was impossible to hear him over the roaring in my head.

"Wait." I held up a hand, interrupting him. I tugged at the neck of my sweater, trying to catch my breath, to get some air. This was ridiculous. Dalton was simply ignoring my texts, that's why he wasn't responding. People ignored me all the time. It didn't mean they were deceased, for god's sake. When my voice finally emerged, it was tight. "You told me he'd switched jobs—that's why he didn't come back to work."

"Well, that's what I thought he did, but . . ." Ricky shook his head and rested a sweaty palm on my shoulder. "I'm really sorry, Cassie."

My nails dug deep into the flesh of my palms. There it was—the platitude I was so painfully familiar with. *I'm really sorry, Cassie.* The words cracked open the past. I could feel it oozing inside me. This was real. This was happening. Again.

"But how?" I sputtered.

Ricky crossed his arms, hugging himself, and dropped his head. "They said he killed himself," he whispered.

His words knocked the wind out of me. I gulped a few shallow breaths, but I couldn't seem to push oxygen all the way down to my lungs. It took me three tries to get the words out. "But Dalton wouldn't do that. He wouldn't kill himself. He had . . . he had plans."

Ricky closed his eyes and gave a somber nod. "I would never have thought it either. He certainly didn't give out any signs, right?"

"No," I shot back, not wanting to chew on the question.

He stared at the wall for a moment before dabbing his eyes with an index finger and turning his attention back to me. "Listen, I need to make an announcement to the group, but I wanted to come and tell you first. I know you guys were friends."

I nodded. *Were.* Another relationship moved into the past tense. Tears stabbed the backs of my eyes.

"Hey." Ricky's brow creased. "Wait. Why are you sitting here?" He tapped on the back of my chair. It took me a beat to remember I was sitting in Dalton's seat, still signed in under Forest's username.

"Oh . . . um." I swallowed the beach-ball-sized lump in my throat. "My computer kept freezing and I didn't want to bother you with it, so I figured I would just use this one." Out of the corner of my eye, I could see the firm logo now dancing across Dalton's darkened computer screen.

Ricky peered at the offending computer screen beside me before leaning over and shaking the mouse.

I held my breath as the screen glowed.

"But you're still signed in on your computer." His eyebrows knitted together. "You were able to sign in on both computers?"

I nodded, not daring to speak.

He drew back and folded his arms over his chest. His eyes slid back and forth between the two computers. It felt like an eternity before he spoke. "That's weird. I'll have someone from IT look at it."

I nodded. In my haze, it took my mind a second to catch up to the danger of having IT anywhere near this room. "Oh, um . . ." I cleared the tremor in my voice. "Don't worry about it. It looks like it might have resolved itself. You must have the magic touch."

He paused for a moment, an inscrutable expression on his face. Then he pointed an index finger in my direction. "Is that yours?"

My entire body went rigid.

"It must have fallen out of your pocket or something." He bent over and picked up a black iPhone, camouflaged in the shadows from the table, and tapped at the screen. "Looks like the battery is dead." He held it out to me.

I sat immobilized, eyeballing the phone, as if Ricky was trying to hand me a live snake. "That's . . . it's . . . not mine," I sputtered. "I think it's Dalton's."

Ricky's eyes widened to saucers. He uncurled his fingers and looked down at the offending device. "Holy moly. Holy flipping moly." He blushed, raising his gaze to me and added sheepishly, "Excuse my French." The gears were shifting in his mind as he turned the phone over in his palm. "It's weird that he left this here. Almost like he wanted us to find it."

"Yeah." There was a niggle in the back of my consciousness, an itch waiting to be scratched. I thought back to Tuesday night, after the review had been put on hold. I remembered now how Dalton was standing on the other side of the table when everyone was stampeding to the door. He'd held his phone out to me and asked me to put it in his ridiculously heavy backpack. I'd slid it into the side mesh pocket, but it must've fallen out when I threw the bag over my shoulder.

Guilt exploded like a bomb inside my chest. Dalton hadn't purposely left his phone behind like some breadcrumb on a trail for us to find. It was here on the floor because of my carelessness. Maybe if Dalton had had his phone with him he would've used it to reach out to someone for help.

"You should go home, Cassie. You really don't look good." Ricky cut through my thoughts, giving my shoulder a quick, awkward squeeze. "There's only an hour left here anyway. Come back tomorrow when you're feeling better."

I nodded. My insides felt like a dishrag being wrung out.

"I . . . I won't dock your pay for the time off," Ricky added in a tone I'm sure he thought was benevolent.

With my hands still shaking, I waited for Ricky to walk away before I signed out of Forest's account and shut down Dalton's computer.

THE GIN AND tonic fizzed on my lip as I brought it to my mouth and slugged back another gulp. I'd slept-walked home from the subway, reeling from the severe turn of events, but managed to have the foresight to stop at the bodega across the street, picking up a bottle of tonic water, cheese, and Triscuits as if I was some kind of lonely retiree. Then I'd thrown a new, jumbo-sized bottle of Tylenol PM into the basket. There was no way the gin alone would do the trick tonight.

I let out a long sigh, sank farther into the couch, and turned up the volume on the TV, filling my terminally silent apartment with the sound of Simon Cowell's voice crushing another person's dreams on *America's Got Talent*. God, I hated this show. But I didn't have the energy to find something better. I twisted open the child-proof cap of the Tylenol PM and popped five pills in my mouth before reconsidering and popping a sixth. My stomach was gnawing with hunger, reminding me I'd skipped dinner. That was an error in judgment. One of many.

Leaning forward, I pushed the box of crackers aside, slid the knife off the coffee table, and inspected the tip of the blade, giving it a gentle tap with my index finger. I wondered if having this in my hand now would violate that ridiculous order of protection, the one that had been slapped against my chest by a hefty process server who looked like he was straight out of central casting. *Are you Cassandra Jane Woodson?* he'd opened with in his thick New Jersey accent. My chest constricted at the memory now. It was all so NCIS-like that it was almost comical. Almost.

Your failure to obey this order may subject you to mandatory arrest and criminal prosecution.

No, when I thought about it now, the order only specified firearms as "prohibited weapons." Not knives. Which meant I could have a stockpile of machetes in my apartment, so long as I wasn't in possession of a single device that could discharge a bullet. Chalk that up as reason number thirty-two why the whole thing was so patently absurd. As if I couldn't inflict just as much damage with this blade in my hand. If I wanted to, I could lift the cold stainless steel to Landon's neck, soundlessly slip it into his jugular, and watch him bleed out without ever handling a single firearm.

No fucking piece of paper could save him from that, now could it?

"It's a 'no' from me," Simon Cowell declared from my television.

I blinked rapidly, as if waking from a bad dream, and looked down to see my hand had formed a tight fist around the knife's wooden handle. I loosened my grip and downed the rest of my drink, tipping the bottle for a refill, omitting the tonic this time. Turning the knife over, I rested it on the block of aged cheddar cheese. I couldn't remember what possessed me to buy this at the bodega. I don't even like cheddar cheese. It was Dad who believed we could subsist on it.

As the blade sliced down, thoughts of Dalton began flitting through my mind despite my attempt to avoid them. He had been so agitated in the cafeteria on his last day of work, but seemed to have recovered by the time the lunch break was over. I could picture him in the lobby after we were sent home for the night, joking with the security guard about a walkout. I replayed our conversation on the way to the subway, frame by frame, like a sportscaster analyzing the final play of the game. My mind zeroed in on his earnest expression as we walked down the sidewalk together. *Listen, Cass,* I could hear him saying. *I don't want you to think I'm abandoning you or anything, but I don't think I'm going to be at this gig much longer.*

I felt a sharp pain and looked down to see I'd cut myself. I watched the blood spring to the surface before stuffing my finger in my mouth, wincing at the metallic taste. The edges of the TV started to look fuzzy as my mind continued spinning through the same frantic loop. *I don't want you to think I'm abandoning you or anything, but I don't think I'm going to be at this gig much longer.*

A terrible awareness boiled up from deep in my gut. Dalton had warned me. He had fucking warned me. It was as if a co-anchor suddenly paused the screen, our final play, shouting *there* and penning a circle around Dalton's troubled face. *There was the moment he told* you he was going to take his own life.

I pressed the heels of my palms into my eyes as shame burrowed its way underneath my skin like a parasite. This was my fault. Dalton had been living a happy little life eating pancakes with his mom and saving half of his salary to prepare for his future until he came into contact with me. I couldn't ignore the truth anymore—there was something dreadfully, dangerously wrong with me. It was as if I were some kind of negative magnetic charge for people, constantly repelling them away.

My mother, Landon, Dalton, Forest.

I picked up my glass and hurled it across the living room, watching it shatter. "FUUUUUCK," I shouted until my throat was hoarse. Self-loathing was spreading like a brushfire inside me. I would've given anything to rewind time, to be back at Nolan & Wright, sitting in my windowed office, secure in the knowledge that I was a rising star at the firm. That I was *someone.* Someone Dad would be proud of. I tried to picture the look on Dad's face if he could see my life now, if he knew what I had done. He'd probably think my mother had the right idea when she'd left me behind.

The squeal of brakes from a taxi five stories below shook me back to the present. I dragged my fingers through my hair, tugging hard at the roots. The knife glinted invitingly from the coffee table. Sitting here alone, confined to my own thoughts, suddenly felt as hazardous as an oncoming train.

I had to get out of here.

I had to find Forest.

I had to make him want me.

Nobody wants you, the nasty voice in my head hissed.

I could feel my precarious grip on mental stability slipping, the hard-won recovery I'd managed in the past month dissolving like a castle made of sand. Bleary eyed, I grabbed my phone and swiped my finger along the screen, searching my contacts for someone, anyone I could call. But unless I wanted to make an appointment with my hairdresser, there was nobody who was going to be happy to see my number on their caller ID. With a trembling finger, I tapped open my message to Forest.

Every cell in my body froze. Was that? Oh god, was it?

A little gray bubble with three ellipses had magically appeared below my text.

I blinked rapidly, hardly able to trust my own eyes. I was struck by the same range of emotions I imagined someone would get if she'd been wandering in the desert for days and stumbled upon a glass of water—an unmitigated thrill followed by the uncertainty of whether what you are looking at is indeed a mirage. I rubbed my eyes and looked again. It was still there. It was real. Forest Watts was typing a message to me this very second. My hand clamped around the phone like a vise.

Praise be. The wait was finally over.

Chapter Twenty-Five

"First text received—9:38 p.m.," I scrawled on a fresh piece of paper, marveling how it had taken me all day to realize that I hadn't yet recorded the timeline of our correspondence in my binder. It wasn't like me to make such a glaring oversight. But I guess happiness was not an emotional state my mind was accustomed to.

All those hours I'd spent reading Forest's words, imagining they'd been written for me, and finally it had happened. Forest's fingers had pecked out a message meant solely, miraculously for me.

Sorry I had to cut our night short. Work has been crazy—maybe I need a good legal recruiter in my life. ;)

I chewed the tip of my pen, ignoring the sound of the mouse clicks around me. I was experiencing the same flutter in my chest as when his message first popped up on my screen last night, like a butterfly wing softly stroking my insides.

This is how it feels, I realized. *This is how it feels to need someone and actually have them show up for you.*

It was as if I'd received a vaccination that would keep me safe from every dark thought, every horrendous memory that had once infected my brain.

I couldn't resist running my thumb down the screen of my phone now, like I was running a finger down Forest's bare chest. I could picture myself in bed beside him, my head resting on the nook just under his shoulder, tracing my fingers over the soft skin between his pecs, as we marveled over the forces of fate that had brought us together. We'd laugh about this text exchange, maybe I would even tell him how I'd agonized over my response and he'd say, *Me too! That's why it took me so long to get back to you!*

"Dinnertime, folks," Ricky announced, jostling me out of my fantasy. He clapped his hands like he was gathering a class of pre-schoolers to the alphabet rug for circle time. "Let's get moving—it's 'pierogi night,' and last time they ran out because you guys were too slow." He cast an accusing look around the room as if each one of us shouldered some responsibility for depriving him of his favorite Polish dumpling. His face softened when his gaze landed on me. I averted my eyes, busying myself with rearranging the items in my purse. I'd successfully avoided Ricky's pitying glances all day and refused to be the recipient of one now. I'd had my fill of pity.

I waited for him to turn his back to me before I hitched my bag over my shoulder and shuffled to the door with the herd. Even though I'd already committed our entire exchange to memory, I couldn't resist rereading the carefully constructed response I'd sent back to Forest last night. *If you've been working this hard then you need more than just career advice to destress.* It was important to match his playful tone without appearing desperate, to keep the conversation going without being the one to force it. It was a difficult needle to thread, but I patted myself on the back for threading it seamlessly. It was something Annabelle would write. Only it probably wouldn't have taken Annabelle ten minutes and an entire bottle of gin to compose the message. But, whatever. After I'd pressed "send" on the message, my phone had buzzed almost instantly with his response: *Agreed—know any good ways to relieve stress?*

I might . . . I'd fired back, working off instinct rather than thought. I did a happy little shimmy on my couch when his reply popped onto my screen moments later: *I'm intrigued :) Free for a drink Monday after work? This deal should ease up a bit by then.* The stale air in my apartment had felt like champagne in my lungs when I inhaled a deep breath and wrote back *I think I could make that work.*

"The button isn't pressed. Someone press *L,*" a nameless temp muttered as we crammed into the elevator. I peeled my attention away from my phone and peered around at the blank faces, which resembled a busload of inmates being processed on their way to Rikers. I felt distanced from them now, as if I was above all of the banality, floating, looking down on a different, luckier version of myself. Only it wasn't dumb luck that had brought me Forest. Like everything else in my life I'd worked my ass off for this. But unlike everything else, I was not, under any circumstances, going to fuck it up.

The doors pinged open and I thrust my hands in the pockets of my dress pants, head down, and moved briskly through the lobby. This walk between our elevator and the elevator that served the upper floors was like a game of Russian roulette now that Forest could recognize my face. I'd managed to avoid a run-in thus far, but I was petrified that one of these days was going to be the unlucky pull.

If I had enough money in my bank account, or rather any money in my bank account, I would've quit this job and eliminated the risk of being outed. There was certainly nothing left for me here now that both Dalton and Forest's inbox were gone. But the consistent paycheck was crucial to maintaining the person Forest was falling in love with. He was used to Annabelle, which meant he'd grown accustomed to perfectly manicured hands, fresh balayage highlights, and the type of poreless skin that can only be achieved with regular facials. I couldn't expect him to settle for Nice'n Easy and Maybelline. We boarded the second elevator, and I pulled my phone out, rereading each message one more time. After I'd hit "send" on my flirty *I think I could make that work,* Forest had responded, *Great—let's go someplace quiet—without all those irritating lawyers.*

What did you have in mind? I'd typed, hoping I didn't sound too 1990s soap opera.

I know a great South African wine bar in the UES—Kaia. Meet you there at nine p.m.? he'd responded.

I knew Kaia Wine Bar well; it was across the street from my apartment, and I walked past it every day on my way back from the subway. There was always a happy couple cozying up on the barstools by the window, wineglasses in hand, but I'd never gone inside for obvious reasons. The whole atmosphere didn't exactly scream, *Lonely, single women welcome here*. Forest must've known Kaia was close to my apartment—he'd been the one to give my address to the Uber driver. He clearly had the same plans as I did for the end of the night.

Perfect, I'd typed back. And it was. *He* was. We were perfect together.

I would spend my weekend preparing for our date. I'd already done my research for when our conversation inevitably turned to careers and had my talking points primed: I worked at BLG Legal Recruiting, placing midlevel and senior associates in large law firms. Mostly corporate finance.

Another plate on a pole, spinning.

Of course, there would be the whole three years of law school and the bar exam to gloss over. Not to mention the five years working as an associate at Nolan & Wright.

My lies were multiplying like rabbits. But I would gladly do whatever needed to be done to keep him. No matter what it was.

I bypassed the pierogi station in the cafeteria and treated myself to an assortment of sushi instead. *I could eat my body weight in sushi and still not be full,* I remembered Dalton proclaiming over dinner one evening, and the memory of the grin on his face as he told a story about a deliveryman's horrified expression upon discovering the two large bags were for one person made the backs of my eyes prickle. I dabbed at them with my sleeve, refusing to surrender to the tears that were threatening to spill forth, and willed my body to ignore the stabbing feeling in my chest as I put the bento box on my tray.

Mind over matter. Grief does not exist if you do not allow it. Grandma taught me that.

I must have been deep in my head because my whole body startled when I felt a light tap on my shoulder as I was reaching for a bottle of Poland Spring in the refrigerator.

"Whoa, sorry, Cassie. I didn't mean to scare you." Ricky held up his palms before peering over both shoulders and lowering his voice to a whisper. "I just wanted to let you know I have some new intel on the, um . . . situation."

"Intel?" I repeated, my tone piqued as I rearranged my tray and continued toward the line for the cashier.

He looked momentarily annoyed that I wasn't playing along, but fell into pace beside me. "Yes, I figured you would want to be briefed on the latest. So, yesterday I went down to the police station to deliver the phone." He air-quoted "police station," as if it had been a cheap imitation of what he'd imagined it should be. "And when I gave it to them, the guy was really thankful, so I asked if he could provide me a little insight into what we were dealing with here."

A tiny snort escaped, despite my attempt to conceal it. Dalton would've loved to hear about Ricky's effort to cozy up to the police. I could picture him folding over in laughter, not even able to get words out until he gasped back a few deep breaths.

I balled my fists, flexed them a few times.

God, I hated the feeling of missing people. Every time you thought about them it was like ripping off a fresh, painful scab. Which was why it was better practice not to think about them at all.

Oblivious, Ricky continued. "Apparently, Dalton's mother doesn't believe he would've killed himself and wants them to open up an investigation." He emphasized the word "investigation," raising his eyebrows significantly. "So, of course I offered to be interviewed to assist with collecting background data, but they told me that wasn't really necessary at this time. The guy said it was a pretty open-and-shut case." He shrugged his shoulders as if to say he didn't agree with that decision.

A small piece of my heart broke thinking about Dalton's grieving mother. How unfair the world is, really, when the doting mother loses her only child but the mother who couldn't give a rat's ass about hers is allowed to have a daughter who is still very much alive.

Karma is clearly a myth.

"Anyway, I did my civic duty and gave him the phone we found, so mission accomplished." Ricky puffed out his chest.

I retrieved my card from the cashier and headed toward the condiments station, relieved this conversation would be over soon. I could feel a headache gathering in my temples despite the Tylenol I'd popped an hour ago. Ricky followed a step behind me, his lips still moving.

"It's really a sad situation," I heard him say, before he put his tray down near the packets of soy sauce and rested a sweaty palm on my shoulder. "If you need anything, I'm here."

"Thanks, Ricky." I gave what I hoped was a somber nod.

"If you ever need someone to walk home with, I live just two blocks from where you do, so I would be happy to accompany you." The question must have been written on my face because he quickly added, "The addresses of all of the temps are written on the sign-in sheet."

Interesting. There was something I'd never noticed. Evidently temps weren't entitled to the common courtesy of privacy.

"That's okay. I don't usually go home straight after work," I lied.

There was an awkward pause before he spoke again. "I can . . . I can have dinner with you tonight if you're in need of some company. Totally on a professional level of course." He held up both palms as tiny red patches bloomed on his cheeks.

"Oh, um . . ." I tried to keep my face from betraying what was really going on in my head. Dinner with Ricky was right up there with clipping someone else's toenails in terms of my "last things I want to do" list. What I really wanted was to use that time to study every last morsel in my binder. I needed to be pin sharp for Forest. But something told me it was critical to stay on Ricky's good side.

"Sure." I nodded. "That would be great." I marveled at how smoothly the lie rolled off my tongue.

As Ricky slurped a pierogi into his mouth and launched into a story about cafeteria health codes, my mind shifted back to Forest. I wondered if he was still in the building now or if he was working on preparations for our date. Maybe getting a haircut or buying a new shirt. Not that he needed to. I would take him how he is. Always. After all, he'd saved me from myself last night.

My life belonged to him now. And his belonged to me.

Chapter Twenty-Six

I WOKE UP to the soft creak of my queen-sized bed as he rolled over, adjusting the pillow underneath his head. I yawned and rubbed my eyes as the world came into focus. My nightstand with the vase of fresh sunflowers I'd purchased as part of my cleaning spree in preparation for Forest (because I knew he used to buy sunflowers for Annabelle). The crisp sheets on my bed were new too, my way of exorcising any demons that were stubbornly clinging to the old ones. I'd even burned a candle that smelled like morning dew, like a wonderful new beginning. Anything that could reveal a morsel about my past—the banker's box full of items from my office at Nolan & Wright I had yet to weed through, the old law books I'd used to study for the bar exam—was now somewhere at the bottom of my garbage chute. The victims of my weekend pre-Forest purge. It was cathartic, really, sweeping away my past and ushering in my new chapter.

His body was illuminated by the morning sun leaking in around the blinds now, and I let out a soft, satisfied moan as I settled into the area between his arm and chest. Even though I'd only slept a few hours, every part of my body felt infused with fresh vitality. Euphoria was hissing in my veins, and I wished there was a way to mainline it every morning. I closed my eyes and listened to him breathing, tracing the lines of his chest like it was a love letter written in Braille just for me.

"I need to go," he whispered in a gravelly morning voice as he ran the pad of his thumb down my arm. It was an intimate gesture, the kind of thing he probably did in the early days with Annabelle, and it sent a trail of fresh goosebumps down my body.

"What time is it?" I whispered, tilting my head to meet his eyes. They looked different in the morning light and reminded me of warm maple syrup.

"It's five in the morning. I have to get home or I'll never make it to my morning meeting on time." He planted a lingering kiss on my mouth, groaning, before gently extracting his arm, careful not to pull my hair, and shifting a pillow beneath my head. I could see the beginnings of an erection as he reluctantly rolled over and sat up.

I did that, I thought triumphantly.

I watched as he picked up his wrinkled shirt off the floor and slid his arms into the sleeves. I remembered how quickly we had taken it off last night, both of us fumbling with the buttons as we'd crashed around my apartment. It was the perfect end—the cherry on top—to an incredible night spent sipping wine in a dimly lit corner of Kaia, our bodies leaning in to each other on the leather banquette, like one of those couples I had so longed to be every time I walked past the window after work.

"I wish I could stay, but if I'm late to this meeting my client will flip," Forest said, fastening the last button on his shirt. "Then I really will need the services of a legal recruiter." He grinned and took my hand, lifting it to his lips. I could feel myself melting like butter on toast.

"I don't mix business with pleasure," I said, a sleepy smile spreading across my face. I loved the little groan that came from the back of Forest's throat whenever he kissed. It was soft, barely perceptible. I don't think he was even aware of it. But I was.

I snuggled against the pillow and admired his toned, muscular body that I now knew so intimately. Those weekly sessions with the trainer at Equinox were working some kind of magic to be giving him definition like that. I wondered if it would look suspicious if I started seeing the same trainer. Although, we would probably be working out together soon enough.

A tiny, irritating voice in the back of my mind warned me not to put the cart before the horse. It certainly wouldn't be the first time I'd mistaken a one-night stand for a full-blown relationship. But this time was different. Forest Watts was mine now.

For better, for worse. For richer, for poorer. In sickness, in health. Until death do us part.

Unlike Annabelle, I would take those vows seriously.

"Ah well, I wouldn't want to do anything to interfere with the pleasure then," Forest replied, smiling and running a hand down my bare stomach, sending a delicious chill down to my toes.

I propped myself up on an elbow. "You sure you don't want to come back in here? It's nice and cozy." I pulled back the duvet, hoping it was coming across as sexy rather than desperate.

"I wish I could." Forest dropped another kiss on my head, and it took all my willpower not to wrap my arms around his shoulders and pull him back into bed with me. "Mmm . . . You smell so good," Forest growled in my ear as he nuzzled my neck. I beamed in response, thankful I'd sprung for the pricey L'Occitane shea butter soap—the same soap Annabelle used. I'd done a late-night shopping spree after I received my most recent paycheck, purchasing every grooming item I'd come across in the *Amazon Order Confirmation* emails in Forest's inbox. For someone who lived so close to a shopping area, Annabelle certainly did her fair share of online shopping. Not only had I been able to purchase the same soap, but also conditioner, lotion, and even the same toothpaste. Her grooming items of choice were higher end than what my bank account would've liked (ninety dollars for a tiny container of eye cream?), but if that was what Forest was accustomed to, then that was what I needed to give him. It would make the transition to a new relationship seamless. I would smell like home to him.

"You get some more sleep," Forest said, flashing that dimple as he tucked his shirt in and smoothed his palms over his pants. "I'll call you later, and we can make a plan to grab some dinner this weekend. Hey, have you ever been to Maison Thai?"

I shook my head, hoping my expression didn't betray my delight. That was the same restaurant he'd told Annabelle he would take her to.

"You'll love it. It's a tiny hole in the wall, but you've never had better Thai food. I'll see if I can get a reservation."

"Perfect." I tried to stifle my excitement. "Happy" doesn't even begin to describe how I felt. "Buoyant" maybe. Like I was floating.

"Great." He held eye contact for a beat longer than usual, a move so loaded with intimacy that it made me feel light-headed. He slipped his phone into his back pocket and gave a little wave on his way out of my bedroom.

I waited until I heard my front door close before I moved. Then I leapt out of bed and padded over to my closet. Standing on my tippy toes, I pulled my leather satchel off the top shelf. I'd stashed it there before heading out to meet Forest last night.

Out of sight, but never out of mind.

I sat back on my bed, pulled my legs up into a lotus position, and slid my binder out. The one positive about Forest leaving my apartment earlier than I'd hoped was it meant I could finally record every new tidbit I'd gleaned about him, which I'd been itching to do all night.

Most of what Forest told me wasn't news to me (he was a runner, he enjoyed historical fiction . . .), but I did my best to act as if it was. (*Oh, do you run short distances or long? Wow, the New York City Marathon! That must have been amazing!*) But then there were the parts of our conversation that were completely unexpected. The ones that sent the hairs on my arms straight up. He had knee surgery last year. He's deathly allergic to shellfish. Which explained the EpiPen.

These I did not know. These could be useful.

I had excused myself to go to the bathroom halfway through the evening and disappeared into a stall to record every new piece of information into my phone. It would've been careless to rely on memory alone. Sitting on a cold toilet seat, my fingers flew across my screen, typing my stream of consciousness into an email draft. *He loves Wes Anderson movies and coincidentally attended the same high school as him (in Texas? double-check IMDb). His mother was recently diagnosed with dementia and he wishes he could live closer.*

As Dalton said, knowledge is power.

Unfortunately, I barely had enough time to get my thoughts down before there was a hard knock on the bathroom door, reminding me that I was occupying the only women's bathroom in the small wine bar. Flustered, I ran my hands under the sink in case whoever was waiting for the bathroom needed a sign that I was finishing up, opened the door to an impatient-looking older woman, and returned to the table.

I slid the pen out from the inside pocket of the binder now, flipped to a blank page, and began writing as if my memories would vaporize if I paused, even for a moment.

Mole on right shoulder.

Picture of a ski mountain on home screen of phone.

I wrote with the focus of an Olympic athlete and didn't stop writing until I had filled two full pages with new material. Later, I would type it all into the saved document and print out a fresh copy with the new information included. It was important to keep the binder up to date.

"There," I whispered, tucking a strand of hair behind my ear and surveying my work. One incident from the evening rolled around in the back of my mind, gnawing at me. It was the one part of the night I had yet to write down. The one part of the evening I wished I could forget.

Forest had just topped off my glass (a rich Malbec that tasted like warm sunshine) when it happened. Given that my level of preparation for our date rivaled my preparation for the bar exam, it was shocking to be caught off guard by anything, much less something so simple. I had extensively googled legal recruiters, could've talked about my fake career all night long without a single misstep, and swore to myself I would keep everything else as close as possible to the truth. I had also binge-watched *Homeland* because Forest used to watch it religiously with Annabelle, researched the charities where she sat on the board, and could've regurgitated the plot of every novel they'd purchased in the past year.

Brick by brick, I had molded myself into someone Forest would love. But I'd missed a step in my preparation. A critical one.

"I have a confession, but you have to promise not to think I'm crazy," Forest had said, a smile twitching at his lips as he returned the bottle of wine to the table. "But . . . I feel like I know you. And I don't mean from the other night at Elwood's."

My wineglass froze midsip.

"Please don't get creeped out." Forest chuckled, misinterpreting my suddenly tense shoulders. "I just mean . . ." He paused, his brow furrowing. "I feel so comfortable with you. Like I feel like we've already known each other for a while. Does that make sense?"

I did my best not to let my facial expression betray exactly how much sense it made.

My diligence had paid off.

"No, I know what you mean," I breathed, placing my hand on top of his. "I think we just . . . click." I have never been happier than I was right then. Which was probably why I didn't foresee what was coming.

"We do." His head cocked to one side. "Where did you come from, Cassie—" he paused.

And that was the moment. That was the moment I should've prepared for.

"Wait." An impish smile teased the corners of his mouth. "I just realized I don't know your last name. That kinda blows a hole in my theory about knowing you well, doesn't it?" His face broke out into a wide grin.

My eyes were focused on his lower lip—his perfect lower lip—completely oblivious to the land mine I was about to step on.

"Okay, let's do this officially." He put down his wineglass and held out a smooth hand. "Forest Watts."

I placed my hand in his. "Cassie Wood—"

Boom.

The word hadn't yet cleared my lips when an explosive detonated in my mind. Even with all my research and all my preparation, there was still something I hadn't considered. My name. I couldn't tell Forest my real name. I'd googled myself before. I knew the sites that would come up if someone typed "Cassie

Woodson" into a search engine. I was painfully aware of the things written about me.

No matter how much effort I put into reinventing myself, there was no way to escape my past.

"It's Cassie Wood," I repeated, choking back the second syllable.

Forest's deep brown eyes glittered as he said, "Well, nice to meet you, Cassie Wood."

And then the next thing I knew we were kissing and it didn't matter how complicated it would be now that I'd given Forest a fake name in addition to a fake career. I saw it as another hurdle cleared, not a potential future problem. But with the judgmental morning light shining in my eyes now, I was beginning to realize just how deep of a hole I'd dug for myself. A career could be fudged, but a last name? That was going to be tricky. Although, it wasn't like Forest was going to demand ID. He had no reason not to trust me.

I took a deep breath now and scribbled *Cassie Wood,* underlining it twice before slamming my binder shut.

Worry slivered under my skin, but I tensed my muscles to squeeze it out. There would be plenty of time to figure it all out later.

Forest's smell was still lingering in my bedroom. I closed my eyes, straightened my back, and inhaled through my nose, holding it for a second before exhaling out my mouth. Forest was the air that I breathed now, and the realization filled me with a greater sense of harmony than any yoga class ever could. Namaste. I opened my eyes and looked at my clock. Six-thirty. If I didn't start moving I was going to be late for work.

I jumped in the shower and was barely in there long enough to feel the water before I was toweling off and buzzing around my apartment, trying to locate where I'd stuffed all my clothes in my hasty cleanup. Anything that could be described as "business attire" was out of view, as if Forest would've somehow been able to sniff out the scent of failure on them. I located a pair of black Theory pants still in the dry-cleaning bag at the back of my closet, threw them on, pulled a sweater off a padded hanger, shimmied into it, and ran a brush through my hair. Catching sight of myself in my dresser mirror, I paused.

My once bloodshot eyes were bright white, the sallow skin replaced with a flushed glow. It was like I'd been a caterpillar before and now I was finally emerging out of my cocoon as a butterfly.

I leaned in closer, my forehead almost touching the glass. "You did it," I whispered, my lips curling into a smile. "You really did it." I had been drifting along, lost, like a boat without a compass until Forest appeared. He was like the lighthouse in Montauk, shining brightly and guiding me in the right direction.

My phone vibrated on the table, startling me.

Forest.

I darted over, thrilled he wasn't going to wait one second longer to text me. I wondered if it would be something cute like, *Last night was fun ;)* or maybe asking me out again tonight. Or, better yet, he was standing outside my apartment right now, two hot cups of coffee and a bag of bagels in hand. God that would be incredible. Part of me wanted to savor the anticipation of not knowing, stretch it out like a piece of taffy, but I couldn't last more than a few seconds before picking up my phone and taking a peek. My eyes struggled for a moment to register what I was looking at. Then the phone fell from my hands as if I'd been electrocuted. The clang of the hard case hitting the floor echoed off the four walls.

The name on the screen wasn't the one I expected. The name on the screen wasn't *Forest*. It was *Dalton*.

Chapter Twenty-Seven

I COLLAPSED ONTO the couch, my eyes fixed on my phone on the floor, as if there were a danger it could somehow come to life and attack me, like some twisted B-rate horror movie. Why the hell would someone be contacting me from Dalton's phone? Oh god, what if it was the police? I knew from experience I did not play well with law enforcement.

I leaned over, my heart like a hammer against my rib cage, and wrapped my fingers around the phone, steeling myself for whatever it was that I was about to read.

> *Hello. This is Dalton's mother, Elena. I see that you and Dalton exchanged some text messages. Were you a friend of my son?*

I drew in a sharp breath, as if someone had kicked me in the stomach and knocked the wind out of me. Even the police would've been better than this. What could Dalton's mom possibly want with me? Unless, of course, she knew that Dalton had warned me he was about to kill himself and I'd ignored him.

The knots in my shoulder blades tightened.

No. That couldn't be it. How could she possibly know about that?

I reread her message. *Were you a friend of my son?* My eyes drifted up to the ceiling, considering my response. *I think so? Kind of?* It wasn't like we hung out on Friday nights or spent birthdays together like friends on television shows did. But when I thought about it, if I didn't consider Dalton a friend, then would *any* of my previous friendships really qualify?

Yes, I typed as fast as my shaking fingers would allow, wanting to end the overanalysis. I watched with shallow breaths as the gray bubble appeared underneath almost instantly.

Can I call you? I really need to talk to you, but I am not good with this silly thing.

"Call me?" I groaned, panicked. My eyes darted around my living room as if something around me could come to my rescue. I could think of no greater horror than being forced to talk to someone else's mother, and it probably didn't take a psychologist to figure out why. I've never been able to interact with them without worrying they would somehow discover my own mother hadn't wanted me and conclude there must be something defective about me, like a malfunctioning TV that gets returned to the store. I've always been aware of an edge in their voices when they spoke to me, as if conveying, *If you were mine, I would've walked out on you too.* And if there was one mother, other than my own, who would surely find me to be deficient, it would be Dalton's mom.

I stiffened at the sound of Grandma's voice piping in my head. *Your mother was not well and having a baby made her problems worse.*

It was suffocatingly familiar, this feeling, as if I was being confronted with an old, horrendous photo from the past. I knew what it felt like to be told I was the reason someone was gone. I knew that feeling well. And I didn't want to revisit it.

I pushed myself off the couch and slid on my shoes, readying myself to leave for work, but unsettling images began to assault my consciousness: Dalton's grieving mom hunched over her son's iPhone, tears running down her cheeks, waiting for a response that wasn't coming. I closed my eyes and dragged a deep breath, feelings of guilt bumping up against my need for self-preservation.

You owe this woman something, Cassie, the voice in my head hissed. *At the very least you owe Dalton.*

I grabbed my phone and pecked out a response with my thumb before I could change my mind.

Sure.

Moments later my phone buzzed in my hand. Even though I was expecting the call, I still froze for a moment, like a gazelle who senses danger from a rustle in the bushes. Then, holding my breath, I pressed my index finger to the screen, swiped, and lifted it to my ear.

"Hello? Is this Cassie?" the voice on the other end asked. It was hard to hear her over the blood suddenly rushing in my ears.

It took me a couple of tries to find my voice. "Yes. This is she."

She cleared her throat. "My name is Elena, and I'm calling because I saw you and Dalton sent each other some texts." She emphasized the word "texts" like she'd learned a new vocabulary word and was trying it out on her tongue. It reminded me of something Dad would do, and I felt a sharp pang of longing, like a paring knife slicing into my insides.

"I wanted to ask you something . . ." She choked up.

I chewed my fingernail, my pulse accelerating. What text had I sent Dalton that she would have a question about? I pulled the phone away from my ear and tapped the screen in a frantic attempt to reread the messages I'd sent him last week. Nine unanswered blue bubbles stared back at me.

> *You're really testing this underwear-scrubbers theory today. . . .*
>
> *It's almost dinner—are you coming in today?*
>
> *Ricky has informed us we can't have beverages (yes, he used the word "beverages") at our workstations anymore and you're not here to lead the rebellion.*
>
> *Hey—did you get my voicemail?*

You may have moved on to bigger and better things, but what are you going to read when you get there? (ransom picture of the book you left behind attached . . .)

Temp022, if that is your real name, have you disappeared?

Fuck you.

Fuck you.

Fuck you.

My eyes squeezed shut for a few erratic heartbeats. I didn't remember sending the last three texts. I shuddered to think what I might have emailed him.

"You said you were friends with my son," Elena continued. "How did you two know each other?"

I began pacing the small room. "Um . . . we worked together, um . . . well, beside each other, for a little while."

"I see." She dragged a shuddery breath. "Well, you were probably upset when Dalton stopped responding to your messages."

"Oh . . . um . . . about those messages. I didn't mean to—" I faltered, tiny shards of shame collecting in my throat.

"Cassie," she interrupted. "I don't know if his employer told his coworkers this, but Dalton passed away last week."

I froze midstride. Her voice was so swollen, so full of pain that my throat constricted. "They told us," I whispered, raspy. "I'm really sorry." I squeezed my eyes shut. It sounded grossly inadequate. Those are words you utter when you bump into someone on the subway. There should be an entirely different vocabulary you use for someone whose entire life has just shattered around her. Although, in my own experience, it's better to be abandoned by a loved one for death than for no reason at all.

"Oh. You already knew." She paused, the silence short but weighted. I could hear her thinking, *Did* you *have something to do with this?*

Of course you did, the nasty little voice in my head whispered. *You drove your mother away. And now Dalton too. You're toxic to everyone in your orbit.*

Even Dad knew that. It was probably what killed him.

I kicked the leg of the coffee table, relishing the pain radiating in my toe.

"Well, we had a service for him, but the only people who came were family so I just assumed . . ." she trailed off.

I squeezed my forehead, rubbing my temples with as much force as my fingers would allow. Guilt began crawling on my skin like an army of ants. "I wish I would've known about the service. I definitely would've come," I lied.

There was a pause before she spoke. "I see." She didn't. She sighed in a way that seemed to ask *What is wrong with you?* and it was times like this that made me wonder if there really was something wrong with me. The answer tasted bitter so I didn't chew on it very long.

I closed my eyes, the weight of my lids suddenly too heavy. "I can't even imagine how hard this is for you, Elena," I heard myself say. "Dalton was such a great person." Finally, something true.

"He was," she whispered.

"Please know how missed he is by . . . everyone." My voice cracked. The backs of my eyes stung with tears fighting to push out with frightening force. It had been a mistake to pick up the phone, I realized. I'd let my guard down and now the memories were going to pounce and drag me back through the debris of my life. I needed to end this call ASAP. "Thank you for reaching out, Elena." I cleared the shake in my throat. "I unfortunately need to head off to work. I really hate to cut the conversation short, but—"

"They say he did it to *himself*," she interrupted, choking on her words. I sat motionless, not daring to speak. She heaved a deep breath and blew it out slowly. "But that's not true. I know it isn't. Ever since Dalton's dad died, he's been the one looking after me. Not that I need looking after, but in Dalton's mind I do. He wouldn't do this. He wouldn't." She went quiet and I could feel her evaluating me in the silence. Judging me.

You did this.

You're toxic.

You're poison.

I heard the squeal of a bus pulling away from the curb below, and all I wanted was to be on it. Anywhere else but on this phone right now. I was drifting too far from shore. I needed a lifeline.

Hang up! Hang up! my mind screamed.

"You were Dalton's friend, his only friend I could find. I have something I really need to ask you, Cassie." I could practically hear her wringing her hands, the same way Grandma used to when she delivered unwelcome news. "But I don't want to do it over the phone. Would you come over to our apartment?"

I collapsed onto my couch, resting my forehead in my hand. Every impulse in my body told me to say no. I knew the smells of a home cursed with emptiness and sorrow. I'd seen the red-rimmed eyes, the hair hanging listless around a puffy face, the distant gaze, the haunted expression.

"Please," she whispered, small, heartbreakingly soft. "There isn't anyone else I can find that knew him well. Just you."

"Okay," I heard my voice respond.

She let out a shuddering sigh that sounded something like relief. "Can you come tonight?"

"Um . . . well, I don't get out of work until eight-thirty tonight. So that's probably a little too late . . ." I trailed off, picking at the edge of a scab on my knuckle until a prickle of blood sprang through.

"Come after work then. I don't get a lot of sleep anymore anyways." She let out a humorless laugh. "Do you have a pen to write my address down?"

"Just a sec." I glanced around my living room. My pre-Forest cleaning purge meant all my sticky notes and pens had been stuffed in shoeboxes in my closet, so I padded a few steps into my kitchen and pulled open the junk drawer, digging out a pink highlighter and an old receipt.

"The address is 405 East Sixty-third Street, Apartment 8G."

"Okay, 405 East Sixty-third Street, Apartment 8G," I repeated back to her, hesitating before I flipped over the receipt and jotted it down.

"You'll come?" she asked.

No.

"Yes. I'll come."

"Good. See you then." Then the line went dead.

I slid the phone in my pocket and leaned back against my laminate counter. "Fuck," I whispered, pressing the heels of my hands into my eye sockets as if I could physically crush the thoughts from my head. I ran the kitchen tap until it was cold, filled a glass, and drank it down in one gulp, the cool wetness soothing my suddenly parched throat. Reconsidering, I pulled a bottle of vodka from the fridge, tilted it to my lips, and swallowed back what remained. I shuddered, wiped my mouth, and set the bottle down on the counter, stroking it as if it were a magic lamp and a genie was going to pop out. I would've given anything for Dalton's mother to be right. For Dalton not to have taken his own life. For it not to be my fault. But as much as I tried to force that theory together, it was like jamming in the wrong puzzle piece. I couldn't make it fit.

If only Dalton had befriended someone else, someone who didn't come into this world with the power to ignite mental illness in her own mother. Maybe then he would still be alive.

Sadness ballooned inside me until it felt like it might burst through my skin. Without thinking about what I was doing, I made a beeline to my laptop, opened a browser, and navigated to the Bloomingdale's website. A few frantic clicks later and I'd purchased the belted wool trench coat I'd seen Annabelle wear in an Instagram photo, the one where she's standing with her hands in her pockets, looking artfully off to the side, accentuating her long neck and razor-sharp cheekbones. One of the comments to the photo read *Impossible not to LOVE* with three heart-eye emojis. Breathing quickly now, I clicked a few more times and threw in the oversized Chloe sunglasses too.

There.

I crossed my arms over my racing heart, examining my receipt, my shoulders rising and falling with each breath. It was $985 I didn't have, but it was a small price to pay. Now *I* was the woman who was impossible not to love. I wasn't repulsive to everyone around me like some kind of noxious gas. I wasn't responsible for Dalton's mother's pain. And I was adored by Forest Watts.

Closing my eyes for a moment, I focused on the pinpricks of light dancing across my lids and willed images of Forest and my new life to sweep through my mind, like a windshield wiper, swiping away everything else.

It was vital not to lose sight of the goal. I'd come too far.

I pushed off the couch and grabbed my coat off the floor by the front door—its resting place after Forest had pulled it off and tossed it in a mad rush to undress each other last night—and stuck my hand in the pocket. Frowning, I checked the other one. I was sure I'd put my keys back in my coat pocket after using them to open the door last night. I ran my eyes along the surfaces of my living room, but they were spotless thanks to how I'd stashed everything I owned out of sight. I moved aside the couch cushions and slid my hand underneath, feeling around for the purple fur pom-pom keychain Grandma had given me for Christmas last year. "Because I know how much you like purple," she'd said when I'd opened it. I hadn't owned anything purple since my 'N Sync super fan days, but I thanked her and continued to use the keychain nonetheless. My brow furrowed. How was it I had a perfectly clean apartment for the first time, maybe ever, and I couldn't locate the one thing I needed? I padded into the kitchen, found the spare key in the junk drawer, and slid it into a zippered pocket in my purse. I briefly debated bringing my Forest binder with me before nixing the idea. I couldn't risk having it in my purse all day in the event of an impromptu invitation from Forest. Men in happy relationships did things like that.

Love makes people spontaneous.

Pausing at my front door, I retreated into my bedroom, slipped my hand into the back pocket of the pants I wore last night, and retrieved the platinum card. My eyes scanned the black letters on the front.

Forest J. Watts.

I let out a long exhale. Just looking at his name really did make everything else feel better.

Chapter Twenty-Eight

"PLEASE SELECT FROM one of the following options," the robotic voice droned on the other end of the line. "For account balance, press one. For payments, press two. To update your account information—"

Panting up the last few subway stairs, I jabbed at the zero to interrupt the recording. I needed to speak with an actual human.

"We'll transfer you to an account representative. For faster service, please enter your card number."

My heart rate kicked up a notch as I ran my index finger along the edge of the thick platinum card, turning it over in my palm, and carefully tapped in the unfamiliar digits with the other hand. An overplayed Adele song began crooning in my ear. I exited the station and headed up Lexington Avenue.

"Good morning!" A perky Southern accent cut through the hold music, startling me. "American Express card services, am I speaking with Mr. Watts?"

My eyes widened. She was cutting right to the chase. I cleared my throat, lowering it an octave, and threw a look over my shoulder before responding. "Yes, this is Forest Watts calling."

"And how can I help you today, Mr. Watts?"

"I'm just calling because I wanted to confirm my last few transactions with you." I turned the corner, averting my eyes from my reflection in the store window. "I left my credit card behind at a restaurant yesterday and didn't pick it up for a few hours so I wanted to make sure there weren't any unknown charges."

A pause at the other end of the line. Some typing.

Taking Forest's credit card last night hadn't been part of the plan. But after he had signed the check at Kaia and closed the leather bifold holder, rising to his feet, I'd spotted the telltale platinum rounded corner still peeking out the side and realized he'd forgotten to retrieve his credit card. That left me with two options—I could tell him or I could take it.

Carpe diem, as Robin Williams would say. Seize the day.

All I had to do was formulate an excuse to return to the table when we were on our way out of the restaurant ("forgot my umbrella!"), grasp the corner of the credit card between my index finger and thumb, and slip it into my back pocket in one smooth motion. Technically, it wasn't stealing. He'd left the card behind. There was a difference. And who knows what the waitress would've done if she got her hands on it?

Forest was lucky to have my vigilant eye in his corner, keeping his finances safe.

"I can assist you with that, Mr. Watts," she said.

I felt the edges of my mouth tug upward. The feeling of being referred to as a Watts was surprisingly enjoyable, and I had to resist asking her to repeat it, substituting in the word "Mrs." this time. *What can I help you with, Mrs. Watts? Would you like to be added to your husband's account, Mrs. Watts? Secure a payment for a platinum wedding band perhaps?*

"Mr. Watts?" her Southern accent repeated, cutting through my fantasy. "Are you still there? Did you hear my question?"

"Sorry, you cut out for a moment," I mumbled, keeping my voice low.

"Can you give me the last four digits of your Social Security number, sir?" There was an irritated edge to her chirpiness now. "I need to have that to access your recent transactions."

"Nine-two-eight-two," I rattled off from memory.

"And your code word?"

I froze midstride. Shit.

"Um . . . oh geez, I never remember those things." I gave a forced laugh, an "I'm much too important for petty code words" chortle. "My secretary is the one you should be asking, but she's away on vacation. Clearly, I'm lost without her."

I could hear the lipsticked smile spread across her face, charmed by a powerful, rich man in need of the help of a woman. "Well . . ." She drew out the end of the word. She was flirting now and there was a part of me that wanted to reach through this phone and wrap all five fingers around her neck and squeeze. "I can give you the first letter if that would be helpful, Mr. Watts. It's *C* as in Charlie."

I beamed. For once, it was my lucky fucking day. "Is it Campbell? That's my dear mother's maiden name."

"Right!" she squealed like I'd won a prize. "Okay." Her fingernails clicked against the keys. "How far back do you want me to go?"

"How about you just tell me the last . . . let's see . . . ten transactions." My stomach tensed. Anyone who's ever watched a Lifetime movie knows the first sign that a man is cheating is suspicious, unaccounted-for charges on his credit card statements—expensive jewelry, perhaps a dinner at a romantic restaurant. I didn't suspect Forest would have these, but finding out what he was spending his money on recently would certainly go a long way in confirming that there wasn't another woman creeping around in Forest's life.

I remember what happened the last time a man blindsided me.

Trust, but verify. That's my motto now.

"Okay, the last charge I see here is at Kaia Wine Bar for $147.92. And the one before that . . ."

I pressed the phone so hard against my ear that the back of my earring came close to puncturing the soft skin of my neck as she rattled the last ten purchases made with Forest's Amex—a charge from Equinox, two from Uber, a few midtown lunch spots. I forensically took in every iota of information. A monthly payment to Verizon. Nothing suspicious, nothing that would point to another woman in the picture. When she was finished, I shuffled to the side to avoid being run over by agitated commuters and exhaled a sigh of relief.

"Thanks so much. It sounds like I was just being overly cautious." I unfurled the fist I didn't realize I'd been making with my other hand and looked down at my palm, noticing my fingernails had dug four angry-red little crescent moons into my flesh.

"Well, you can never be too careful, can you, Mr. Watts? Is there anything else I can help you with?"

I paused for a moment to consider whether now was a good time to gather all the remaining crumbs of data—his account balance, linked payments—before deciding it would be more productive to do that at home, where I was free to record everything with ease. I'd already taken a photo of the front and back of the card so I could return it to Forest before he realized it was missing and canceled it. It only remained useful to me as long as it was valid. And now that I knew his code word it would be easy to call back whenever I needed to.

"Nope, you've been very helpful. Thanks." I clicked the "end call" button, slid my phone back in my pocket, and pushed off the wall. Gazing down the sidewalk, I realized with slight shock I was standing in front of Levy & Strong, having walked all the way to the office on autopilot.

I dropped the Amex in my purse, pulled out my laminated ID badge, and pushed through the revolving doors into the marbled lobby of Levy & Strong. My mind was whirring as I swiped my employee ID on the sensor on the turnstile, pushed through, and, without thinking about it, slipped the card over my neck and headed for the elevator.

Every other day I waited to put the ID over my head until I was out of the lobby, safe in the confines of the elevator, on my way to the bunker.

Every other day but today.

I retrieved my phone from my pocket, comforted by the weight in my hand, and tapped "Forest Watts" into Google. I was still feeling slightly off balance from the phone call with Dalton's mom this morning and needed the sight of Forest's face to settle my nerves like a Valium. The same images I'd pored over for tens of hours popped up on my screen and, just as they had the first time I laid eyes on them, they made my whole body exhale, like someone had placed a warm, fluffy blanket over my insides. Who needed therapy when I had Forest? There was Forest's firm headshot; there was the picture of him at the Stamp Out Cancer gala last year. I scrutinized the details in the photo—the shine on his cuff links, the exact positioning of Annabelle's hand on his forearm—picturing myself in her place. Not long now. Maybe our first photo together online would be a simple selfie posted on Instagram, our heads pressed together with a setting sun in the background, #instalove #happy #bestday. Or maybe it would be one of us dressed up in our finest attending a benefit for a charity near and dear to our hearts.

Have you met Forest's new girlfriend? people would ask. *I've never seen him so in love before. They're perfect together.*

"Cassie?" someone called out, cutting through my fantasy like a machete. My stomach lurched.

Oh god. I knew that voice.

Then, for an instant, time froze.

Today was the day. Today was the day I pulled the trigger with a bullet in the chamber.

Chapter Twenty-Nine

WITH MY HEART in my throat, I slowly turned around. There he was, looking back at me, mirroring the surprised expression I knew I was wearing.

Alarm sounds blared in my head. *This is not a drill. I repeat: This is not a drill.* This was worst-case scenario, the disaster you prepare for but never think will actually occur in your lifetime. My entire house was burning down to the ground, and despite my meticulous preparation, my mind was inexplicably, horrifyingly blank. I forced myself to take a breath, wishing the floor would stop moving beneath me so I could steady myself.

"Forest," I stuttered.

His eyebrows twisted together. "Cassie? What are you . . . what are you doing here?"

Gray suits were whizzing past me, making me dizzy. "Um. Well . . ." My mind kicked into gear and began spinning like a compass trying to land on the right direction. I was a juggler trying to keep all my lies in the air without dropping any. Any wrong move and they would all come tumbling down on top of me.

Think, Cassie. Think!

I considered telling him the story I'd prepared for a potential lobby run-in. The words would surely pour out of my mouth effortlessly with the number of times I had practiced them in front of my mirror at home. *I'm here for a meeting with HR about placing a candidate at a law firm in the building.* But that would only work in a situation where I was not wearing my employee ID card around my neck, the one that, I noticed now, Forest currently had his eyes fixed on.

His brow furrowed deeper in confusion as all the blood in my body rushed to my head. I knew the words that were written above my photo in bold capital letters: LEVY & STRONG—TEMPORARY EMPLOYEE.

The harsh reality hit me like a baseball bat to the head. There was simply no way to keep all of my stories going. The only decision I had to make was exactly how much truth I was going to reveal. I drew a shaky breath and reverted to the advice every lawyer gives his client during cross-examination: Answer only the question asked.

"I . . . um . . . I work here." My voice quavered. Something flashed in his eyes and he looked so baffled, so utterly blindsided, that my heart broke a little bit.

"But . . . wait." He pushed a hand through his hair. "No, you don't."

Regret balled in my throat. Forest wasn't some attorney cross-examining me and trying to trip me up. He was the love of my life, and if I didn't start explaining fast I was going to lose him. "Forest," I began, my voice already bordering on pleading. My eyes were darting around the crowded lobby as if someone could throw me a life preserver. A woman in a red suit strode past us, briefcase swinging, peering curiously at Forest so I lowered my voice. "I know this looks weird. I've been meaning to tell you. I just haven't had the—"

"Meaning to tell me what?" His eyes narrowed.

Inhale. Exhale.

"I've been meaning to tell you I wasn't entirely honest about my career, but I can explain."

"Cassie?" A voice sliced through the air, stopping me dead. I would've sworn my predicament couldn't possibly get any worse than it already had.

I was sorely mistaken.

"What's the holdup, Cassie?" Ricky pointed to his watch and took a few steps closer to me. I stared at him openmouthed, my heart ticking like a bomb against my ribs. "T minus four minutes until you have to punch the clock!"

Oh god. I wished the floor would open up and swallow me.

"I'll be . . . I'll be right there, Ricky," I answered, struggling to steady my voice. Out of the corner of my eye I could see Forest peering at me, then frowning, then looking up as though consulting his memory. For once I wished I could be safely in the bunker with Ricky rather than standing here in the lobby with Forest.

Ricky's gaze moved from me to Forest, who he seemed to be noticing for the first time. Realizing he was in the presence of a higher-up, Ricky straightened his posture, smoothed down his cowlick, and puffed out his chest like an army cadet ready to salute a senior officer.

"Ricky Sandos, sir." He stuck out a palm. "Head staff attorney and a loyal foot soldier." I lowered my head, inwardly cringing.

Forest shook his hand, his eyes narrowing as if trying to determine how Ricky fit into this candid-camera moment. "Good to meet you, Ricky Sandos. Uh . . . Ricky, could I have a second with Cassie here before she heads up?" He grinned tightly before adding, "Official firm business."

Ricky tilted his head and something flickered across his face. Confusion? Jealousy? Recognition? It was impossible to tell because it was gone before I could put my finger on it. Ricky cleared his throat and gave a brusque nod. "Of course," he said, his eyes ping-ponging from Forest to me. "Cassie, I'll sign you in and will see you when you, uh . . . arrive." He hitched his messenger bag up on his shoulder before quickly adding, "Whenever that may be." I half expected him to bow to Forest before departing, but instead he just furrowed his brow, like he was trying to solve a particularly hard riddle, and gave a wave.

Forest's eyes followed Ricky as he walked away. Then, he took my elbow and led me to a quiet corner by the far elevator bank. He peered over his shoulder to ensure we were out of view before opening his mouth.

"Cassie, what the hell is going on here?" he hissed with quiet ferocity.

"I . . . I haven't been completely honest with you, Forest," I stuttered.

"Yeah, I gathered that already." His tone was hard, impatient, and hearing it felt like someone was running a sharp blade down my chest.

I could feel my veins rushing, the blood thumping in my ears. Dreaded possibilities raced through my mind with gale force. Forest could figure out every lie I'd ever told him and decide he didn't want to see me again. Then, I would never walk hand in hand with him up that cobblestone path and through the cherry-red door, content in the knowledge that I had finally found my happy ending. Forest would be one more person who chose to abandon me. One more in a long list of people who had no trouble leaving me in the dust. I would walk out of this lobby now and the only thing waiting for me at home would be punishing, unrelenting silence.

My stomach twisted with dread.

The mere thought of returning to my apartment alone right now felt as hazardous as stepping in front of an oncoming train. What I said right here was make or break, do or die. For both of us.

I couldn't live without Forest, and I knew he wouldn't want to live without me.

I forced myself to stand up a little straighter, struggling to emit a sense of composure. "Forest, I'm sorry." I let out a resigned breath, shaking my head. "When I met you that first night and you told me you were a lawyer, I . . . well . . . I was recently laid off from the small firm I'd been working for and was a little embarrassed about it. I didn't want to talk about how the partner I'd worked for had mismanaged funds, and had to lay off three associates including me. So, I told you I was a legal recruiter, when the truth was I had just *met* with a legal recruiter that day about a new position. That's why it was on my mind." Words kept escaping my mouth, each phrase seemingly necessitated by the previous one. "I didn't want to admit I was looking for a job because I didn't want you to think . . ." I shook my head. "I don't know what I was thinking. And when I was placed at this job here at Levy & Strong, um, the Monday after I met you, it completely slipped my mind that you worked here. I mean, I'm not even working anywhere near you." I let out an odd little laugh and gestured to my faraway elevator bank. "So it didn't click in my head that you worked here too. Not until last night when you were talking a bit about your job and then I realized my mistake." I reached out for his arm, tracing my thumb around his wrist, doing my best to resurrect images of the two of us together in my bed last night. Maybe if I could get him thinking about our sexual chemistry he would forget everything else.

"I'm sorry I wasn't honest with you. I was going to tell you, really." I paused, staring directly into his eyes, trying to gauge his reaction. Forest was still listening, he hadn't stomped away. This was working. I licked my lips. "The project I'm working on is drawing to a close this week, so I was waiting to tell you until I knew where I was working next. It's just that—"

Forest held his hand up, silencing me. His jaw was rigid as he stared at me for what felt like hours but was probably only a minute. "So, you *weren't* working here the night you met me at Elwood's?"

I shook my head, trying to ignore the dizzy feeling sweeping through it. "No, I would've told you if I was."

Forest's expression was inscrutable and I wished desperately I could slip into his head as easily as I'd been able to slip into his inbox. He swiped a hand down his face. "Well, when exactly did you start working for Mr. Staff Attorney Extraordinaire then?" I opened my mouth to answer but he kept talking. "You know what? It doesn't matter when you started working there. Here. Whatever." He shook his head. "Listen." His tone softened and he glanced over his shoulder before setting a hand on my waist. "I like you. It doesn't matter to me what you do for a living, but I don't want to be lied to. Is there anything else you're not telling me?"

I took a tentative step closer to him, as if I was close to the edge of a precipice. "No." I shook my head. "That's it. No more lies," I said, forcing the tremble out of my voice and miming an X on my heart with my fingertip. "I swear to god."

If there was a god, it certainly would've struck me down with a lightning bolt on the spot. But if there was one thing I knew about the truth it was this: It is highly overrated.

Forest's face was impassive. I wanted to claw inside his mind, uncoil his brain, see what he was thinking. A muscle in his cheek twitched. Oh god, he was angry now. Really angry. But before I could throw myself at his feet and beg for mercy, he inhaled long and deep, blew it out. "No more lies," he echoed.

I could've collapsed with relief.

"No more lies," I repeated. His eyes were fixed on mine. I held his gaze, repressing the distant drumbeat of concern.

He cocked his head, the lines on his face softening. "So, are you working on any of my deals?"

I shook my head. "No, it's a small litigation thing, so our paths never cross." My voice remained steady despite the flush I knew was creeping across my chest.

Forest stuffed his hands in his pockets and rocked back on his heels. He was eyeing me now, evaluating me, like he was trying to determine how much he could trust me. I willed my facial muscles to stay relaxed. To not even flicker. Looking calm is very important when trying to convey innocence.

Finally, he broke the silence. "I wonder if HR would have anything to say about me dating one of our temps."

I let out a nervous laugh, not sure if he was being serious. Restrictions on workplace romances weren't something I'd considered. "Well, I just got a call about another job that I'll probably take."

His expression changed and broke out into a wide grin. "Well, we should celebrate then," he said. "Are you free tonight?"

"Tonight?" My voice was practically manic. The relief that Forest wasn't leaving me was so profound, I was coming undone. For once in my life, I hadn't screwed up as royally as I'd feared and had, somehow, managed to dig myself out of a sinkhole the size of a house. It was all so wonderful—so completely unprecedented—that it took me a second to determine why my mouth wouldn't cooperate.

Elena. She was stationed in the back of my mind, like a cocked pistol, waiting. If I didn't go over to her apartment tonight it would surely destroy her. And the list of people I'd destroyed was already long.

"Tonight works," I said, chewing the inside of my cheek. "I just . . . I might have to do something really quickly after work, but I could meet right after that."

"Something . . ." Forest trailed off, the ends of his lips twitching up.

I waved my hand dismissively. "I just need to do something for a friend, but it won't take long."

"Well, let's do it tomorrow instead then. I wouldn't want you to feel rushed. And that way I can work late tonight and get some stuff off my plate."

Shit. I'd been stupid to let my conscience interfere here. Now it would look weird if I reversed course and insisted on tonight. Although, when I thought about it, wasn't being unavailable for last-minute dates a very Annabelle-esque thing? Perhaps it would end up working in my favor.

"Sure." I nodded. "Tomorrow probably does work better. You never know how long these things will take."

Forest eyed me dubiously for a beat. "You're a mysterious woman, Cassie Wood."

You have no idea.

"I think you like a little mystery," I said, working my face into a smile to conceal the chaos that was pinballing around in my mind.

The corners of his lips twitched. "How do you know me so well?"

I held his gaze, hoping my eyes didn't betray the answer. *I know you better than you know yourself.*

A lightbulb suddenly flicked on in my head. "Oh, I almost forgot." I cleared the tremble from my throat and reached into my purse, seizing the opportunity. "This must have fallen out of your pocket because I found it on the floor of my bedroom this morning."

Forest's eyes widened. "I didn't even realize it was gone." He shook his head as he slid the platinum card back into his wallet, in between—I narrowed my eyes to get a better look—his New York State driver's license and a red Bank of America card.

"What would I do without you, Cassie Wood?"

Die. You would die without me.

"Just wait until you get the bill for all the online shopping I did this morning." I gave what I hoped was a playful wink.

There was that laugh bursting out of his mouth again. God, I loved that sound.

"I'll text you later, and we can make a plan for tomorrow," he said before turning toward the elevator bank and giving a little wave.

"Perfect," I replied, my smile broadening. But as I stood there on shaky legs watching him walk away, I couldn't help feeling like I was hanging on by a thread—one that was frayed enough it could give at any second.

Chapter Thirty

I PULLED THE bottle of vodka out of the brown paper bag, grabbed a tumbler from my sparse cupboard, and poured the liquid up to the top, not bothering with the tonic. I raised the glass in a mock toast before taking a long swig, relishing the heat hitting the back of my throat and trailing down into my empty stomach. I should be filled with happiness tonight—my day had started by waking up next to Forest. There wasn't anything better than that. But, unfortunately, that was where it had peaked. To say today didn't go as planned would be a gross understatement.

"Everything okay?" Ricky had called out from his chair the second I entered the bunker after my run-in with Forest in the lobby. Three quick strides later and he was right in front of me, peering at my face as if he'd been stranded in the bunker for months and I'd just arrived with news from the outside world. To his credit, I probably did look like I'd survived a perilous journey to get there—red-faced, sweaty, distracted—but Ricky was kind enough not to mention anything about my appearance. "Yeah, everything's fine," I'd answered a tad too manically, squirming like Pablo Escobar when the drug-sniffing dog is making his way down the customs line. "I think that guy in the lobby got me confused with another temp. He asked me about some due diligence for a deal of his, but I told him I was working on an e-discovery for the litigation department." I shrugged, avoiding Ricky's eyes. "They must think we all look the same up there," I added. There was an

odd look on Ricky's face but it passed too quickly for me to identify it. I was steeling myself for a barrage of questions from him,
maybe even a full-on interrogation underneath the hot lights of
the break room. *Cassie Woodson, how did you come to make the acquain-
tance of a full-blown higher-up? And can you get me a meeting with him?*

Surprisingly, Ricky didn't direct another question my way. Instead, he let out a relieved sigh and murmured something about
being thankful we weren't in trouble. His normally tense face had
a softness to it, and I briefly wondered if he was going to give me
a hug or cry or something equally out of character, but he merely
turned and went back to his workstation, reinserting his earbuds.

I took another swallow of my drink, wincing, and leaned against
the counter, rolling my neck to ease the pressure that had been sitting on my spine since the morning. God, that was a close call with
Forest. Too close. There was absolutely no way to stay in this temp
job now. Not when the lobby had become a perilous minefield for
my relationship. I would have to call the temp agency tomorrow
and request a new assignment. Sure, it might mean forgoing a paycheck for a few weeks, but there was no other choice.

All of my eggs were in one basket now—his.

I yanked open my fridge, searching for anything that could
quiet my growling stomach. I felt a tinge of regret about leaving
work early, two hours before the dinner break. Maybe I should've
at least stayed for one last free meal, but nearly being outed by
Forest had triggered some strange fight-or-flight primal instinct,
and my body had chosen flight. Ricky hadn't even questioned me
when I told him I wasn't feeling well and needed to leave, which
was completely out of character for Inspector Ricky. "If you need
me to, I can come by after work and bring you anything you
need," he'd offered, but I'd demurred. "I'll consider myself on
standby then," he'd called out as I slunk out of the bunker. Maybe
he thought I held some kind of power with the higher-ups, and I
guess when I thought about, I did. After all, I was Forest Watts's
girlfriend, wasn't I?

I retrieved a vanilla yogurt container from the back of the top
shelf and lifted the lid to take a whiff, before tossing it in the gar-

bage. If I couldn't remember when I'd purchased it, it wasn't a good sign. I tucked a half-empty box of Wheat Thins under my arm, plucked the bottle off the counter, and moved into the tiny living area, glass in hand. The silence in my apartment was pressing down on me.

I should be with Forest tonight, I thought as I carefully set the bottle on the coffee table and collapsed on the couch. *Not here alone with nothing but a box of Wheat Thins to keep me company.* And I *would've* been with Forest if my mouth had just formed the word "yes" immediately instead of hesitating. Instead, I now had twenty-four excruciating hours ahead of me until I saw his face again. And there would be no room for error next time. Forest had made it clear he wouldn't be handing out second chances.

Sliding my hand into my pocket, I pulled out the canary-yellow labeled cylinder I'd been carrying around with me ever since I'd procured it from Forest's office. A bubble of excitement formed in my stomach as my eyes ran over the illustration of the needle entering the line-drawn leg. I felt a strange kinship with this little inanimate object. After all, it had the power to save Forest's life and Forest was the person who had saved mine. A smile tugged at my lips as I rolled it back and forth between my palms. My limbs were beginning to feel loose and careless, and I almost knocked over my glass as my hand formed a fist around the tube. Sucking a breath between my clenched teeth, I yanked off the blue activation cap. My vision was bleary, but I could see the glint from the silver tip as I lifted it above my shoulder and jammed it into my upper thigh.

A loud click filled the room.

I began counting to ten, just as the instructions had advised. Closing my eyes, I imagined Forest being in anaphylactic shock after eating an inconspicuous piece of shellfish and his life being saved with the liquid that was now pumping into my body.

I wanted to experience everything Forest experienced. Feel what he felt.

That's what love is all about isn't it?

Eight. Nine. Ten.

I jerked it out and tossed the capsule on the living room floor, breathing heavily. The pounding in my chest felt quicker, and I pictured myself suddenly being superhuman. Now that I had this inside me, a piece of Forest was inside me too. It would get me through whatever the evening was going to throw at me.

Staring down at my glass of Absolut, I noticed there were ripples forming on the surface from my trembling hands. I took another slug and rolled the citrusy liquid around on my tongue, narrowing my eyes to read the address scrawled in pink highlighter on the crumpled receipt beside my laptop, where I'd discarded it this morning—*405 East 63rd St 8G.* The apartment Dalton had shared with his mom wasn't too far from the building that housed Levy & Strong, I realized now, and walking to the subway with me hadn't really been on Dalton's way home. One more thing I never knew about Dalton.

It made me wonder what else I might have missed.

The screen of my MacBook glowed invitingly from the coffee table. I dropped my fingers on the keyboard, navigated to Google, and typed "Dalton Sever" into the search field and hit "return." The blue line slid along the top of the screen as I held my breath. When it reached the end, I leaned forward, squinting. There weren't nearly as many hits as there had been for Forest, and it made me wonder if there was a direct correlation between a person's visibility in the virtual world and a person's value in the real world. Although, when I thought about it, I would've gladly severed a limb to have a digital footprint as sparse as Dalton's right now.

I rearranged myself on the couch, tucking my feet underneath me, and clicked through the websites systematically. New York Law School listed Dalton in their graduating class of 2011. His name came up in the directory of lawyers admitted to the New York bar. Neither of those tidbits was news to me. Dalton had told me he was born and raised in New York, and we'd gone through the mandatory "where did you go to law school?" conversation. With some digging, I found a Twitter profile with no tweets and a scant Facebook page with a profile picture of a fluffy golden retriever and two hundred and ten "friends." The irony didn't escape me that not one of these supposed "friends" had exchanged a text message with Dalton recently. After clicking around a few more dead ends, I sunk back into the couch, resigned to the reality that Dalton didn't leave many shards of his history behind online.

I tapped a fingernail against my glass, deciding what to do next. If there was one thing my time as a temp had taught me it was this: Everything you need to know about a man can be found in his inbox. Everything.

I set down my glass, pulled back the sleeves of my sweater, and began to type with grim determination. I retrieved Dalton's email address from his Facebook profile—dsever123@gmail.com—and from there I navigated to the log-on page of Gmail. The cursor flashed like a taunt as I wracked my brain for any personal detail Dalton had dropped in conversation that might be useful in deciphering his password. I leaned forward and typed—*Yankees1, BarackObama1, MartinScorsese1*—but every attempt was met with bold red letters on the screen telling me my haphazard guesses were incorrect. I chewed at a loose piece of skin on my lip. This would be so much easier if it didn't require a password. I swiped my cursor to the "Forgot My Password" link. My finger hovered over the trackpad as I wrestled with a tiny internal gut check. Surely, I was going to hell for this.

But that fate had already been sealed, hadn't it?

I double-clicked.

My leg bounced as I scanned Dalton's first security question. *What is your mother's maiden name?* I felt like a student sitting in the front row of the classroom, holding her hand high in the air. *Oh, pick me! I know this one!* Dalton told me a story once about how his mother's last name had been Dick ("A common Scottish last name," he'd explained in a mock earnest tone) and how she told him the only reason she ended up marrying his father was so Dalton didn't have to go through life with the name Dalton Dick. "I come from a long line of Dicks," he'd joked. I typed in "Dick" and hit "return." One down, two to go.

Where were you born? The cursor blinked, waiting for an answer.

I shook my head in disbelief. For someone who was so concerned about Amazon and Apple whittling their way into his brain and deciphering every word he was reading, Dalton's inbox wasn't exactly Fort Knox. I typed in "New York" and hit "return."

What was the name of your first pet? I tugged my lower lip, thinking. Dalton never mentioned a pet, not even the cute golden retriever who was featured in the photo in his Facebook profile picture. I shrugged and typed "Sandy." He looked like a Sandy, but apparently was not. I gave it a few more guesses—Daisy, Max, Buddy—before slamming my laptop shut in frustration.

Fuck it, I whispered underneath my breath. This was futile. I wasn't even sure what I was hoping to find.

I squeezed my eyes shut. There was only one way to prevent the emotional shrapnel from Dalton's suicide from being permanently lodged in my consciousness. I needed to go see Dalton's mom tonight and listen to her grief-fueled, crackpot theories on what happened to her son—however misguided they were—and that would be my penance. Maybe if I properly punished myself this way, the reservoir of guilt still curdling in my stomach would dissolve. It wasn't like I had anything else to do tonight.

Still, a vague sense of unease gnawed at me.

I leapt up from the couch and slammed my glass down hard enough to make the table shake. I grabbed my purse off the floor, where I'd tossed it when I walked in, and checked the inside pocket to ensure my spare key was there. It was only six, but I was eager to get this meeting over with. And something told me Elena wouldn't mind if I arrived early.

Chapter Thirty-One

IT IS A testament to how distracted I was that I didn't immediately notice him standing there, a mere ten feet away from me, gripping the pole and sucking up all the oxygen in the subway car. I would've thought my body was programmed to sense his presence, the way an antelope can smell a cheetah on the horizon.

But, then again, he'd always had the uncanny ability to blindside me.

I was devising a game plan as I barreled down the fractured concrete stairs, readying myself to meet with Elena. If I hadn't been in such a rush to get it over with, the whole incident could've been avoided. A mere fifteen seconds later and I would've missed the train and waited for the next one. Instead, I swiped my Metro-Card, pushed through the turnstile, and sprinted through the closing metal doors a second before they slammed shut.

We made it two stops—all the way to Sixty-eighth Street—before I saw him. I was pinned against a pole, my nose buried in the armpit of a large man with pastel pants and an obnoxiously patterned belt, doing my best not to inhale. "This is Sixty-eighth Street, next stop Fifty-ninth Street," the recorded voice announced over the loudspeaker as the doors slid open and a stream of impatient commuters bumped through the crowd to exit the train. The loud noise of someone dropping a stainless-steel travel mug stirred me out of my racing thoughts and I lifted my eyes from my phone. That was when I noticed the man standing on the other side of the subway train, his shoulders back, legs spread, claiming all the available airspace as if he was the only one in the whole goddamn subway car entitled to it.

No. No. No.

I squeezed my eyes shut hoping it would make him disappear. It didn't.

Three million people in this city. Three million fucking people in this city and I had to be on the same train with Landon McKinley. Landon. Fucking. McKinley.

I could feel anger wrap its way around me like a boa constrictor, tightening its grip.

The last time I saw Landon's face, it was dripping with blood, the result of what the alarmist in human resources called a "sharp projectile." *This is a sharp projectile,* the alarmist had explained with the self-important look every head of human resources gets whenever there is an HR issue that has been elevated to senior management. *A sharp projectile is a weapon. You were brandishing a weapon at work, Cassandra.*

But if I'd had a weapon with me at work that day—a real one—Landon wouldn't be standing here now, would he?

I glared at him, my face prickling with heat. He didn't even live on the Upper East Side, so what the hell was he doing on the 6 train? Landon was strictly a West Side New Yorker, the result of spending his childhood days at an elite boys' school on West Seventy-fifth Street and somehow still being too stunted to stray too far from the mothership as an adult. It helped that his parents had gifted him a two-bedroom co-op with views of Central Park for his twenty-first birthday (which Landon confided in me he thought "should've been bigger"), which pretty much tells you all you need to know about Landon and his family.

My eyes narrowed as Landon dipped his head and whispered in the ear of the woman standing beside him, who I only now noticed. She was wearing a purple headband and fitted dress and looked like she belonged on the set of *Gossip Girl* instead of bustling through the midtown rush. She was exactly the type of boarding school, blue-blooded tight-ass I always feared Landon preferred. Purple Headband flashed Landon a smile, and it occurred to me she must be the reason he was here, on *my* subway, invading my space like an enemy soldier. My anger thickened to a spiky knot in the center of my chest. I glared at Purple Headband, curious whether she had any idea what she was signing up for. A part of me wanted to call across to her, over the heads of the other passengers, *You're hooking up with an asshole, sweetie.*

She turned her head a fraction, stifling a tiny little yawn, and I caught sight of her sharp cheekbones and softly lined doe eyes.

The hairs on the back of my neck rose one at a time.

I knew her. I fucking knew her. She was the summer associate who had assisted on a large transaction I'd spearheaded for John Dwight, my former mentor at Nolan & Wright. I'd never given her a second thought back then, but of course, my attention was consumed by other things.

Anger rose from deep in my stomach into my throat.

Look at her. Just look at her standing there in her childish fucking headband. I wanted to go over there and rip it off her head, beat her over the head with it, and tell her how fucking stupid she was. And I wasn't the only one who thought so either. I remember John Dwight had referred to her work as "inept." *Make sure you keep a close eye on the work of that summer associate, Cassie. I've seen her research and she's inept.*

Yet, here she stood with everything that used to be mine. My job. My man. My fucking subway.

So, who's really the inept one, Cassie? the nasty little voice in my head snarled.

I bit down on the inside of my cheek hard enough to draw blood. Suppressed memories that had been growing inside me like a cancerous tumor began erupting into my consciousness.

If I closed my eyes, I was right back there, sitting at my sleek desk, listening to the buzz outside my office on the thirty-seventh floor. That was my happy place, really. It wasn't the actual work that gave it that designation, but it was the *feeling* I had every morning when I walked through the doors. In my office, I was enveloped in the world of concrete, solvable problems. When back home in Lancaster, Dad's health issues had become insurmountable.

"I'm afraid the cancer is terminal," the doctor had informed us with a well-practiced sympathetic face while Dad and I stared at him in stunned shock. I'd brought Dad to the hospital that morning, the morning of Christmas Eve last year, because his frequent back pain had become so debilitating he was having trouble getting out of bed. "Come on, Dad. You can't live like this," I told him as I helped his reluctant body into the car. For once, Dad didn't object. I thought it would be a pinched nerve or a slipped disk, something that could be treated with prescription painkillers and rest. What it turned out to be was stage-four pancreatic cancer, a tumor that had grown large enough that it was pressing on a spinal nerve.

I'm so sorry to have to deliver this news.

Landon and I had been seeing each other for eight months by then, and he was the only one I told when I returned to the office a week later. I was nervous how people would react if they knew. I've always loathed the look of pity in a person's eyes. I didn't want people asking me if Dad had smoked, in a veiled attempt to comfort themselves that the same thing couldn't happen to them (he hadn't). I didn't want to hear about the latest nutritional supplement or homeopathic therapy. I wanted my happy place to stay that way, so I leaned in further with the desperate hope that maybe if I didn't talk about the illness and instead kept moving, kept working, and never stopped to catch my breath, I could keep the world spinning fast enough that Dad wouldn't fall off it.

The squealing of the train's brakes roused me from my thoughts, and I gripped the pole tighter to steady myself. *Don't think about it, Cassie. Do not think about it.* I couldn't afford to be clawed back into the past. I stared down at my knuckles as they turned red, then white. For a long moment, my mind went blank, the sound of murmured conversations and the rolling of the train lulling me into some kind of meditative state.

Like a moth to a flame, my eyes slid back to his familiar face, the same face I had imagined gazing into on my wedding day.

The train lurched. Memories began to crash into my consciousness like a tsunami. I squeezed my eyes shut so hard my head hurt, but they came swift and unrelenting, until I was unwillingly dragged into the undertow. Then I was right back there, back to my last day at Nolan & Wright.

Dad had been sick twelve weeks by then. He'd decided against chemotherapy, at the advice of his doctor, and opted for symptom management instead. "Palliative care," the oncologist called it. Grandma called it "giving up." *Forget this medical mumbo jumbo, Cassandra, what your dad is doing is giving up.* But Dad was unwavering about his decision. He knew there was no point in treatment that would never cure him and would probably make him feel worse. And so, after Christmas, our new reality—symptom management—began.

Grandma moved in and I tapped into my savings to pay for a home nurse to help. It stretched my finances, but I knew that my earning potential at Nolan & Wright would offset it, in time. I rearranged my schedule to be able to take the Amtrak down every Friday night after work, spend the weekend with him, and take an early morning train on Monday to be back in the city and at my desk by eight A.M. If there was an evening where I could get out of work by six, I'd pop down for an evening midweek. "Go back to New York and focus on your job, Cass," Dad pleaded. "Don't get yourself fired just to sit in a room and stare at me."

For a short time, the cancer diagnosis had actually seemed like a gift. Thanks to the medicine, Dad was in less pain and was more eager to get off the couch and go outside. "I feel so good I just may change my mind and live!" he'd joked with uncharacteristic levity. We went for walks, saw movies, and talked more than we ever did when I was young. I had the attentive, present parent I'd always wanted. But the tumor stubbornly took over his body and his medicinal arsenal eliminated his appetite. He dropped thirty pounds, his cheeks caved, and eventually his twiggy legs couldn't support his weight for more than a few minutes at a time.

"I don't have to go back to the office," I offered as Dad got weaker. "I can take leave from my job and be here full-time."

"Nonsense." Grandma waved me away. "Your father made me promise him you wouldn't do anything to risk losing your job. And besides, if he sees you here during the week he'll think it's time . . ." She trailed off, as if we had some control over when the end would come.

The thing about grief, though, is it can sneak up on you. It's like a mosquito trapped in your room while you're trying to sleep. You can swat it away, but eventually it comes back, buzzing in your ear, refusing to be ignored.

On the morning of my last day at Nolan & Wright, I couldn't bury my head under the pillow anymore. I was sitting on the 5:02 A.M. train from Lancaster Station, ready to return to the office after a weekend with Dad. I'd taken my usual seat in the third car, next to the window, and pulled out my laptop to review a contract I'd spent the greater part of the weekend drafting. Despite trying to force myself to focus, my mind kept returning to the sight of Dad's paper-thin skin when I'd kissed him goodbye and the disoriented look on his face when his eyes fluttered open. It was suddenly so gut-wrenchingly clear that the end was near, and even though I knew it was inevitable, it still crushed me. As the train pulled away from the station and started its trek to New York City, an email pinged into my inbox. *I don't want there to be any mention of your mother in his obituary, Cassie,* Grandma wrote. *She did this to him. She was toxic.* Reading her words, anguish slammed me like a rough wave on the beach, knocking me off balance.

My mother *was* toxic. But *I* was the one who had made her that way. I was the reason my dying father was alone. It was me who was the toxic one.

By the time the train finally rattled into Penn Station three hours later, I'd pushed every last salty tear out. The other suited commuters typed away on their personal devices in an attempt not to stare, but I could see their horrified expressions as I hid my face in my palms to shield my snotty, splotchy shame. I stood up and grabbed my roller bag before the train stopped, wanting to be the first one out the door, like I was escaping the scene of a crime. My stomach was aching, reminding me that I hadn't eaten in more than twenty-four hours, as if it was me who was slowly dying inside instead of Dad.

I told myself to pull it together, stop being weak.

Stop being like your mother.

Striding down the platform, I remember feeling something close to relief to be on my way back to the office, far away from the constant rhythm of bad news, where nobody talked about pain management or tumors, where I could just be around Landon and push the rest of the world away. And that's the part that kills me the most when I think about that day, how I was so damn *eager* to see Landon, so wholeheartedly sure he was going to be like a warm, comforting blanket I wanted wrapped around me.

I skipped my usual coffee stop and did the half-run, half-walk all the way to work, desperate to make it to the polished marble lobby of Nolan & Wright, like it was an oasis in a desert of misery. My whole body exhaled when I finally stepped into the elevator and pressed the button for the thirty-seventh floor. I'd made it. I pulled out my phone seeking protection behind its glow and punched out a quick text to Landon. *I'm here early. R U around? I really want to see you.*

Then I saw the email in my inbox.

To: Cassandra Woodson
From: Landon McKinley

The past few weeks have been so hard for me trying to find a good time to tell you this—you're never around and I can't keep putting it off. I just have to say it. I've been seeing someone else. I didn't mean for this to happen, but I really hope it doesn't interfere with our working relationship. And I hope we can still be friends!

I still remember how he finished the email with a fucking exclamation point, like his friendship was some sort of prize I'd been lucky enough to win.

Too numb to realize what a terrible idea it was, I made my way down the carpeted corridor to Landon's office, gripping my phone so hard my knuckles were aching. I found him sitting at his desk, munching on a bagel slathered with cream cheese and scrolling through Twitter like he didn't have a care in the world. Like he dumped girlfriends via email every day. Like he hadn't just gutted me like a fish.

He looked up from his screen and greeted me with a startled smile. "Hey, Cass, you're back early. I . . . uhhh . . . I thought you were coming back Tuesday."

I stared at him, my chest rising and falling with each humiliated breath. Words were swarming around in my head, but I couldn't grab on to any of them. After a few beats of silence Landon's plastered expression fell, presumably reading my face and realizing I wasn't going to follow his lead and pretend like the rug hadn't been ripped out from underneath me.

"Cassie." Landon cleared his throat, shifting nervously in his chair.

The fury bubbled up from underneath like lava. "Are you fucking kidding me?" The words erupted from somewhere deep in my gut, surprising me with their force.

"Cass." Landon rose slowly and held out his hands in the "don't shoot" position. His eyes were wide, as if I really was holding a weapon in my hands.

"Are you fucking kidding me," I repeated louder this time, strengthening the grip on my phone like it was a more aggressive version of a stress ball. "The past few weeks have been so hard for YOU?"

"I'm sorry. Really. I didn't know how to tell you in person." His tone was slow and deliberate, like he was a negotiator trying to talk me in from the ledge. "I thought this way would be better. For both of us. You've . . . you've been getting a little too intense for me lately." He shot a frantic look outside his door. "Come on, Cass. People will hear you. I know you don't want people to hear you."

I know you don't want people to hear you. It was as if his words set off an explosion in my head, blowing away all the bullshit.

Boom.

My father's illness was a nuisance for Landon. *He'd* been the one who had encouraged me to keep it repressed. *I know you don't want to talk about it,* he'd say when I'd call him late at night, emotionally exhausted. *I'm sure you don't want the people at work to know, right?* he'd counseled, rubbing my arm with false sympathy. He never asked me any questions about my dad and would change the subject if he ever came up. *I wish I could come with you,* he'd say, jutting out his lower lip when he waved goodbye to me on Friday nights, even though there was no good reason why he couldn't.

The truth hit me with the weight of a grand piano. Landon had never wanted our relationship to be anything more than casual. And yet, he'd still wasted my time pretending he had. Time I could've spent with my father. Time I would never, ever get back. It was all so clear standing there looking at his ridiculously phony face. Crystal. Fucking. Clear. And so, I did something I'd never done in my twenty-nine years on this earth.

I snapped.

It's scary how many details I remember now. That's the thing I hate most about the way my brain works, the way it stores and catalogs the worst moments in my life on a giant hard drive so I'm forced to obsess over them whenever I close my eyes at night.

I remember how sweaty my palms were when the phone left my hand. I remember Landon was wearing his cuff links that double as a compass and the needle was spinning as he raised his arms in an attempt to shield his face. I remember I could hear a conversation from a cubicle outside of Landon's office and right at the moment the phone slammed into the left side of Landon's face the secretary had said "Bingo!" to whoever was on the other end of the line, like she was somehow narrating the whole incident. I remember how it felt like the floor dropped from underneath me when Landon put a shaking hand to his mouth and his fingers came back bloody. I remember picking up the scissors from his pencil holder, my body shaking with rage and rejection, lifting them high into the air, and swinging the blade down with every ounce of strength I had left. I can still hear the sound of the crack as it made contact with the polished desk, hard enough to leave an inch-long gash. My memories get a little hazy when I try to pinpoint what part of Landon's body I was trying to connect with, but I'm pretty sure it was his heart.

"What the hell is going on here?" John Dwight's voice had boomed from the doorway. I remember John's wide eyes as they took in the sight of the blood dripping onto Landon's perfectly pressed white shirt. I had no idea so much blood could come from one person's lip. There was something in Landon's palm, something small and white. It was only when I took a good look at his face that I realized one of his teeth was missing.

An hour later, I was sitting at a polished conference room table across from human resources and John Dwight. "There is a zero-tolerance policy in instances of workplace violence, and we have to adhere to it," the woman from human resources informed me, like she was reading verbatim from her training manual of *How to Fire a Mentally Unstable Employee*. "When you throw something, it falls under the definition of a dangerous projectile—a weapon," she said, waving my confiscated phone in emphasis. John stared at me with sad eyes, like his favorite puppy had just taken a bite out of the neighbor's hand and was going to have to be put to sleep.

I sat silently, my face red hot, the shame sharp and painful.

Workplace violence. Brandished a weapon. Security will usher you out.

A breakdown. That was what I heard people whispering. *She's having a breakdown.* Like I was some kind of rickety old car turning to rust.

It was as if my life was an Etch A Sketch and someone had given it a swift, hard shake and everything—the career I loved and worked so hard for, the colleagues I considered friends, the paycheck I desperately needed—had all at once disappeared.

The sound of the static-filled loudspeaker startled me back into the present. "This is Fifty-first Street. Next stop Forty-second Street, Grand Central."

"Shit," I hissed. I missed my stop.

A woman with a punishingly tight ponytail looked up from her phone and gave a tiny, judgmental shake of her head. Ignoring her, I white-knuckled the strap of my purse as I watched Landon reach down for Purple Headband's hand and file out the open doors. He looked so happy. He looked so goddamn happy, and he didn't deserve to be. I wondered what he would think now if I called across the train, *He's dead now, motherfucker. My dad died and I wasn't there because I came back to see* you, *you piece of shit.*

My breath was coming fast and hard, and I could feel myself dropping into something familiar and dark. I wasn't in control of my own body as I followed them out the doors onto the platform. The voices in my head were so loud I wondered if everyone around me could hear them, but Landon was oblivious to anything else around him, which was par for the course. I wanted to drag him by his hair and pull him down the stairs that he and Purple Headband were now ascending, hand in hand. I imagined my closed fist hitting his cheek repeatedly, until I heard his bones crack, slicing through his skin from the inside. And then I would keep hitting him.

Landon needs to pay. The words repeated in my mind like a battle cry as I reached down and wrapped my fingers around the neck of a brown beer bottle that had been discarded in the corner of the steps. I'd closed the gap between us now, and was about five stairs behind them when the phone in my pocket buzzed, stopping me midstride. Frozen, I watched as Landon practically skipped his way to the top of the stairs. I didn't realize the bottle had fallen from my hands until I heard the loud clang of it rolling down the stairs.

"Move it," a messy-haired man huffed as he shouldered past me, and I stumbled, steadying myself with my palm on the cold concrete wall. Dragging in a deep breath, I seized my phone from my pocket and pressed it to life with trembling hands. My vision was too blurry and raw to make out any words. I dabbed away the moisture in the corners of my eyes with my sleeve and peered down at the screen again.

Last night was fun. Completely snowed under here at the office tonight, but can't wait to see you tomorrow. Eight p.m. at Maison Thai? I made a reservation.

I folded forward on myself, nearly crumpling to the ground. *What the hell did you almost do, Cassie?* The relief that I hadn't gone through with anything stupid was so intense it was as if I'd narrowly escaped a burning building. I closed my eyes for a moment and waited for them to stop tearing.

Landon didn't deserve happiness. But I did. And I had finally found it. I wasn't going to let anything—or anyone—get in the way of it.

HuffPost, March 24, 2019 (Archives)
Footage of Lawyer's Swift Exit Goes Viral

Cassandra Woodson, a New York based lawyer, became Internet famous on Tuesday for the worst reason: A video of her being escorted out of her office by police went viral.

Woodson was captured on a smartphone yelling profanities at the police officer who had been called to the scene to escort Woodson out of the building after she allegedly assaulted a coworker.

"You'll f***ing regret this," Woodson is heard repeatedly saying to an unnamed person off-camera.

The video spread across social media, and within hours, Twitter users had identified the woman in the video as Cassandra Woodson.

Woodson had been employed as an associate of the prestigious midtown firm Nolan & Wright, according to their website. A spokesman for Nolan & Wright confirmed Woodson is no longer employed at the firm.

Chapter Thirty-Two

THE ELEVATOR DOORS opened slowly on the eighth floor, as if giving me one last chance to change my mind. *You can do this,* I repeated to myself as I made my way down the carpeted hallway, peering at the letters on the doorways and rotating my wrists as if preparing myself to deadlift two hundred pounds. I was being ridiculous, I realized. It wasn't like Elena's anguish was some kind of highly contagious disease. Nevertheless, I was filled with a peculiar feeling about this meeting, one I couldn't shake off.

A heavyset woman opened the door marked 8G before I finished knocking, my sweaty hand still raised when she appeared. She had Dalton's pleasantly round face and warm almond-shaped eyes, but hers had an emptiness behind them and reminded me of Grandma's on the day of Dad's funeral. The skin on her face sagged, as if it knew it would never be called upon to form a genuine smile again.

"Cassie?" she said, brushing a strand of gray, matted hair from her face.

I nodded, blinking rapidly, struggling to push away the visceral reaction. I remembered how it felt—not even being able to gather the energy required to take a shower. I remembered it with almost perfect clarity. She was a living, breathing reminder of my own grief after Dad died, the grief that was still stuck inside me like a splinter. One I had no intention of ever picking at.

Yet, here I was.

"Nice to meet you, Mrs. Sever," I answered, hoping she didn't notice the tiny tremor in my voice.

"Elena," she replied, waving her hand as if shooing a fly. "Thank you for coming, Cassie." She stepped aside and gestured for me to enter the apartment. I followed her in, my footing unsteady.

The apartment was what a realtor would describe as "cozy," with its well-worn flowered couch and built-in bookshelf, cluttered with knickknacks and framed photos. But the unpleasant, musty scent that permeated the air suggested the person who lived there felt anything but cozy. It smelled like grief and helplessness. My body remembered that stale air on a cellular level. I could picture sitting on the side of Dad's bed, dipping my finger in a jar of Vaseline, and sliding it across his sandpaper-dry, bloodied lips.

A pressure began building behind my eyes now, and I realized it was tears welling up.

"Why don't you sit down in here and I'll grab us some tea," Elena offered as she shuffled across the parquet floor.

"Oh, that's okay. I . . . um . . ." I stuttered. "You don't have to . . . um . . . I was just . . ." Elena's sad brown eyes fastened to me, and suddenly I had the desperate feeling an animal must get when a door swings shut on a cage.

Breathe in. Breathe out.

"Sure, yes, tea would be good. Thank you." I smiled tightly. She assessed me for a moment before turning and heading into the galley kitchen.

I pulled a deep breath as I stepped onto the living room's frayed rug and perched tentatively on the edge of the couch, gazing around the cluttered room. There were collections of vases and porcelain angels, dusty books, and candles that had never seen a match. My eyes fell on a silver framed photo of Dalton, dressed in a cap and gown, smiling in front of the New York Law School sign. He looked so fresh faced and optimistic. It was like one of those pictures you see flashed up on the news after another senseless tragedy, the kind that make you stop and look closer, thinking, *He had his whole life ahead of him.* I averted my eyes and blinked hard.

Elena came back into the room and placed a steaming, rose-patterned cup and saucer in front of me before lowering herself into an armchair.

"Thank you." I lifted the cup to my mouth and took a sip. It burned my top lip. I took another sip, relishing the pain.

Elena assessed me over the rim of her teacup.

"Good tea," I said awkwardly. There wasn't a sound in the room and the silence stretched out, filling the space between us and ringing in my ears. Elena's eyes had an accusing quality to them, like she knew I was some kind of poisonous apple—toxic to the core. Sweat started to bead on the back of my neck, and it smelled like vodka and regret. I should never have come here. Why on earth did I agree to this? I looked down at my cup, as if the answers might be found in the tea leaves, and noticed it had begun to clatter against the saucer.

"So, you worked with Dalton?" Elena said at last.

I nodded, setting the saucer on the table as delicately as I chose my words. "I didn't work with him very long. I was pretty new to . . . um . . . the position, but I got to know him because we ate dinner together most nights."

She gripped her hands tightly together in her lap. "He never mentioned you to me. But he probably thought I would ask too many questions, which I guess I've been known to do." Her voice cracked and trailed away. She looked dazed, like she'd just been pulled from the wreckage of a car accident, and I was hit with a penetrating sadness for her. I wanted to reach over and squeeze her hand, say something that would ease an ounce of her pain, but I knew better than to believe words would help.

The clock in the hall ticked. I twisted the silver stacked ring on my finger. Questions skittered through my mind, each more inappropriate to ask than the last. I pressed my lips together. The less I said, the better.

"Can I ask you something, Cassie?"

"Of course," I answered, clutching the armrest to keep from fidgeting. The air in the room seemed to tighten.

"Did you and my son do drugs together?"

"What? No!" I shook my head, shocked. "Never. Dalton and I would just talk. Sometimes we texted. We looked out for each other at work, but that was it," I stuttered. She was staring at me with unflinching scrutiny, her wrinkled lips compressed. I reached up to smooth down a flyaway hair, suddenly self-conscious about how I looked.

"Well." She blew out a breath of air and gazed out the window. "The police told me my Dalton must have been a drug addict."

My brow knitted as I tried to process this news. I couldn't think of a single thing Dalton had ever said or done that would point in that direction. But people can surprise you, can't they? And, from my experience, it's never a good surprise. "Why would the police think that?" I asked to fill the unpleasantly thick silence that had descended between us.

Elena snapped her gaze back to me. I could see the muscle flex in her jaw as she clenched her teeth. "Because his body was found on a street in Bushwick with a baggie in his pocket. They say he jumped."

A sharp, involuntary gasp escaped from my mouth. *Oh, Dalton.* I swallowed down the nausea that burned in my throat. "I . . . I had no idea. I'm so sorry."

She shut her eyes as if the effort to keep them open had become too much. "They think Dalton jumped from one of the buildings, and apparently it's a neighborhood where people go to buy . . . those things." She flitted her hand through the air agitatedly. "But when I went to the police station I told them they were wrong and they needed to investigate. Well, they took out their silly pens and wrote down what I was saying on their clipboards, but did nothing. All they gave me was the belongings Dalton had on him and a number for a therapist, as if I'm the crazy one." Tears welled up in her red-rimmed eyes. "They don't understand a mother's intuition. I tried to tell them the kind of person my Dalton was. There wasn't a single day that passed where he didn't make me proud. Always so proud . . ." She trailed off, letting the statement hang heavy in the air.

I swallowed the emotion lodged like a razor blade in my throat.

Part of me wanted to tell her that the kind of person Dalton was really had nothing to do with what happened to him in the end. And at the same time, I felt an overwhelming sadness no one had ever said something similar about me. Not even when Dad was dying did I hear those words—*I'm proud of you, Cassie.*

Dark clouds of memories began expanding in my skull. I could feel myself becoming unraveled. I bit the pink flesh inside my cheek until I could taste the metallic tang of blood. I needed to turn off the spout on my emotions to prevent myself from unspooling any further.

"Did you ever see Dalton do anything illegal, Cassie?"

I dabbed my eyes with the sleeve of my sweater. "No, never."

She kneaded her temple with her fingertips and nodded. "That's what I thought." She blew out an annoyed puff of air. "Do you know what that's like—to not only be told that your loved one is dead but to be told he must have been suffering long before he died?"

Yes.

I pressed my lips together, having the good sense to realize that the question was rhetorical.

"And drugs . . ." She shook her head. "Dalton didn't even like to take Tylenol. If he was doing drugs it's like I didn't even know the person who was living right here under my roof . . . like I didn't even know my own son. That thought is"—she paused, turning her eyes to the window before whispering in a small voice—"that thought is just more than I can bear."

After what felt like hours, but was probably only a minute, Elena swung her gaze back toward me, as if suddenly remembering I was still sitting there. "I need you to do something for me, Cassie."

As if sensing a shift in the air, an aging golden retriever lumbered into the room and rested its chin on Elena's knee. I recognized it as the same dog in Dalton's Facebook profile photo, albeit a little older and grayer now.

"Good boy. You're a good boy," Elena whispered, patting him gently on the head.

"What do you need me to do?" I asked, my voice hoarse.

She gave a little cough to clear her throat. "I know that Dalton didn't kill himself. I know it here." She tapped a wrinkled fist to her chest. "But I want to hear what you think happened to him. Do you think Dalton killed himself?" There was a desperate, beseeching edge to her voice that was ripping my insides apart.

I pressed my tongue into the burn on the roof of my mouth, weighing the cost of telling her about my conversation with Dalton on the way to the subway with the benefit that this information might provide some level of comfort. Then I considered the possibility that she found it more comforting to maintain a shred of doubt. The truth can hurt. Of that, I was certain.

I looked away, avoiding her anxious eyes. God, I hated making decisions. They paralyzed me. Probably because I didn't have a successful track record for making good ones. "I don't . . . I don't know," I stuttered, copping out.

The room was silent again, the only sound being the soft jingle of the metal tags around the dog's neck. Suddenly, an idea sliced through the fog in my mind with such force I drew in a sharp breath: I knew where I could get more information about Dalton. Maybe even enough to give her clarity without revealing my final conversation with Dalton. Elena peered at me curiously.

I brought a fist to my mouth and gave a few coughs. "What's his name?" I asked, gesturing to the dog as casually as I could.

The edges of Elena's mouth turned up slightly. "Buckwheat. Dalton gave him that name."

"Is he, um—" I paused, battling the tremor in my voice. "Is he Dalton's first pet?" I watched her eyes and noticed a tiny flinch. I'd said something wrong. She knew why I was digging for this information. I suddenly felt wretched.

Her forehead creased, and she appraised me for a moment before she spoke. "Do you realize you're the second person who has asked me that?"

The tiny hairs on my arms stood up. "I am?"

She nodded. "The day after Dalton's body was found, one of his friends from your office came here to pay his respects." She went silent for a moment, staring into her teacup. Then she added quietly, "He said he thought Dalton had probably been depressed for a while."

My eyes widened. "Someone from Levy & Strong came here?"

She answered with a somber nod. "He was here for about an hour. I showed him some of my photo albums." Elena gestured to the stack of leather-bound albums piled beside the coffee table. "He asked about Dalton's friends, but I didn't know about you then. I . . . I didn't have Dalton's phone until a police officer dropped it off." She closed her eyes and gripped her armrest. "That's when I saw his texts to you. Dalton didn't talk about his job with me very much so I never got to know any of his coworkers."

I listened, rapt, and utterly confused. It had to have been Ricky, but why wouldn't he have told me?

A strange sensation traveled through me, all the way down to my toes.

"I guess there were *some* things about Dalton that I didn't know," she said, then sighed, moisture welling up in her eyes. It beaded and spilled over before she could dab it away with her balled tissue. "I'm sorry." She swiped at the tears running down her cheeks. "I didn't call you over here to blubber in your face."

"No, no, it's no problem at all," I said, looking away, trying to process what she'd said. Ricky thought Dalton had been depressed? How would he possibly know? And why the hell would Ricky be asking about Dalton's pets? I shifted my weight on the couch. My back was aching, and I realized I'd been sitting rigid with tension since I arrived.

"Ricky didn't tell me he was coming over, so I'm just a bit surprised," I said to fill the silence.

Her forehead creased into a frown. "No." She shook her head. "No, the man's name wasn't Ricky. It was—" She paused, her face scrunched. "Graham." She nodded resolutely. "It was Graham."

"Graham?" I repeated, realizing with slight shock I didn't even know the names of my fellow temps. My mind flipped through images trying to place a face to the name. "Are you sure he worked with Dalton in his current position and not at . . . um . . . a different firm?"

"I may look old to you, but my memory is fully intact." Her tone was slightly piqued.

I sucked in a slow breath, feeling the blood drain from my face. "Sorry . . . it's just . . . I don't think I know Graham."

She cocked her head, considering me. "But you said you were in the same department as Dalton."

I shifted nervously. "It's a big office, so I guess I'm still getting to know people." There was no use letting her know there were seventeen of us packed into a room small enough I could probably identify each one by smell.

"Well . . ." She let out a shuddery breath. "He was tall and had kind eyes and told me how much he enjoyed working alongside Dalton. He said they ate lunch together sometimes in the cafeteria so you must have crossed paths."

Stunned silence was all I could manage in response. My thoughts flew in different directions like a bag of marbles dumped on the floor. Was the Unabomber temp named Graham? Did he have some affection for Dalton I never knew about? Or maybe the guy Dalton had nicknamed Inspector Gadget on account of his long raincoats? I think I saw them talking at some point.

Still, I couldn't shake the crawling sensation that there was something I was missing.

Buckwheat trotted over to me and put his nose in my crotch before resting his head on my leg. I patted him on the head distractedly, suppressing a bubble of unease.

Elena pointed to Buckwheat and started to tell a story about Dalton with him as a puppy, but I couldn't focus on the words coming out of her mouth with all the questions tangled in my mind like spaghetti. None of this made sense. Why would one of the temps come over here and want to know all these details about Dalton, including the answer to his security question for his email? Elena must have misunderstood. This Graham guy had probably asked a question about Buckwheat and she interpreted it to be the same question I'd asked.

"He's not always so friendly with strangers, you know," I tuned back in to hear Elena say. She gestured to Buckwheat, who had now plopped his body against my legs. "He must know you were a friend of Dalton's."

I ran my hand along Buckwheat's back, shook my fingers, and watched the tiny hairs settle on the floor before I spoke again. "Was he the same way with Graham too? So friendly?"

She nodded and I breathed a small sigh of relief. Whoever was here had probably been an animal lover, simply curious about Dalton's pets. I could picture the conversation—Graham saying something about having a dog like Buckwheat when he was growing up. Elena telling a story about Dalton choosing Buckwheat out of the litter as a child. It had to be something like that.

I cleared the shake in my throat. "I can see why Graham had so many questions about Buckwheat. He's a sweetheart."

"Well, we didn't really talk about Buckwheat. Buckwheat sniffed him and went back to sleep." She gestured to an overstuffed dog bed on the kitchen floor. "No, Graham wanted to know the name of Dalton's *first* pet—just like you."

I focused on keeping my face still, despite the hurricane swirling inside me. There was no doubt about it, whoever Graham was, he wanted to access Dalton's email. The only question was why? My head was spinning as I tried to rearrange my thoughts, to put them in some kind of order to make sense of this conversation.

"Dalton must've talked a lot about his animals at work," Elena said, her unsteady gaze resting on Buckwheat.

I forced a nod. There was a new sensation creeping over me, burrowing its way deep under my skin. It wasn't anxiety or shame or grief. It was foreboding.

A police car wailed from eight stories down, and my head whipped toward the window. It took a minute for me to reorient myself. "I'm so sorry, but I should really get going," I stammered, placing my cup of now-cool tea down on the saucer. "Thank you for getting in touch with me. It was nice to meet you in person." My words came out unsteady. I don't even know how they managed to emerge from my bone-dry mouth. "I can see why Dalton always spoke so fondly about you." I was getting to my feet when Elena spoke.

"I just realized I didn't give him the right answer to his question." She was looking over my shoulder and I followed her gaze to a framed photo of a gap-toothed boy holding a large ginger cat. I stood there wavering like a flame as she continued. "I thought his first pet was Perry Mason. That's what he called our cat. But when I think about it now, that wasn't right." She paused, putting her hand gently over her mouth. "His first pet was actually a gecko. Dalton called him Gilligan. Gilligan the gecko." She smiled sadly. "Dalton watched way too much TV as a little boy, but he loved those old programs. He's always been an old soul." Her eyes squeezed shut and the corner of her mouth quavered a little. "I can't believe I forgot about Gilligan. He loved that little lizard. But then Dalton loves all animals." She brushed a tear from her cheek with the back of her hand before inhaling a deep breath. Her face softened as she reached for my hand, cupping it between her palms. "Thank you for coming over tonight and trying to help me find out what really happened to my Dalton. You're the type of girl who must make your parents very proud, Cassie."

Somehow, I managed to squeak out, "Thank you, Elena," before I showed myself out.

Chapter Thirty-Three

I SLID ONTO the barstool, set my venti latte down, and arranged my purse in front of me to double as a shield from passersby. The last thing I wanted—or frankly needed—at this point was a caffeinated drink, but I figured if I was going to be sitting here for the next few hours it was better to order something so I wouldn't stand out.

I peeled the lid off my cup and watched the steam bloom, struggling to still my trembling hand. Whether it was the epinephrine I'd injected into my thigh earlier or the natural adrenaline produced by my body after that strange conversation with Elena, it was hard to tell. Either way, sleep was not going to come easily tonight. That much I knew.

I would have to fill my evening hours in other ways.

I lifted the cup to my lips and sipped, gazing out the floor-to-ceiling window. Outside, there was an end-of-the-workday buzz in the air, as the midtown crowd skittered to Grand Central, the Q train, their classic six apartments on the Upper East Side, or to a nearby bar to meet friends. Everyone had somewhere to go. I took another sip, wondering where Forest was at this very moment. Sitting in his high-backed leather chair in his office, working late, if he was being truthful.

And I intended to find out if he was.

The upside of there being a Starbucks on every block in New York City was that it meant there happened to be one with an unobstructed view of the entrance to Elwood's. It certainly made my monitoring more comfortable. Of course, I didn't expect to see Forest enter his favorite bar tonight. But if I'd learned anything from Landon it was this: Never let your guard down. My relationship with Forest was still new, after all, and needed to be nurtured the same way I would a small animal. I wouldn't let a newborn kitten loose in the middle of New York City without any supervision, would I? No.

As Ricky said, better safe than sorry.

"Tall caramel macchiato for Allison," the barista called out.

I checked the time on my phone—7:05 P.M. It was still early. That conversation with Elena felt like it had taken days when in reality it had been less than an hour. I plucked a few napkins from the dispenser, wiping a bead of sweat from the side of my eyebrow, before returning my attention to the entrance to Elwood's where three Wall Street bros dressed in matching black coats were approaching the door. They were shorter than Forest. Inferior.

I drummed my fingers on the lacquered bar. Out of the corner of my eye, I could see two forty-something women peering at me, the one with the short hair leaning in to whisper something to her friend in the off-the-shoulder blouse before their eyes darted back to me again. I turned my face away from them, running a palm over any flyaway hair, and began digging through my purse, searching for my earbuds. Music would pass the time. Pushing aside my wallet, my knuckle grazed the spine of a brightly colored paperback, and it took me a second to remember what it was. Dalton's book. I'd taken it from his workstation on the first night he was absent from work.

I stared at it for a few seconds as if it was an oracle, before slowly easing it out of my purse, a sharp corner gently scraping my palm.

"I don't know why people ever read e-books," I remembered Dalton pontificating one night in the cafeteria as he gestured to another temp who was bent over a Kindle at a nearby table. "You're basically handing Amazon or Apple a blueprint of your brain. I saw this 20/20 on how one day they'll be able to determine every word your eyes have ever read. Count me out of that Big Brother shit!" He'd held up his paperback book in triumph.

Peeling back the cover now, I leafed through the pages, my thumb stopping on a dog-eared page in the middle of the book. I felt a shiver travel across my skin as I lifted the triangle. How tragically optimistic it was of Dalton to hold his place. He'd clearly expected to finish reading it. Running my finger along the crease, smoothing it out, I noticed there was something written on the inside of the small triangular fold. I tapped the screen of my phone to turn on the light, angling it to avoid a shadow, and squinted to read the lightly penciled notation: *1227 Himrod St.*

I stared at the address, frowning. There was something wiggling beneath my consciousness, a nagging sense of déjà vu I couldn't quite place.

A quick Google search on my phone revealed the address belonged to an apartment building located in Bushwick, not a neighborhood I've ever set foot in.

So, why did I feel like I'd been there before?

An unpleasant sensation gripped my insides as questions ricocheted around in my head. Was this the building that Dalton jumped from? Why did he have this address written in his book? A few taps on my phone revealed that there were three apartments currently for rent at 1227 Himrod Street, a landlord's phone number attached. I enlarged the screen with my index finger and thumb to get a better look at the landlord's name. Graham Ricci.

My body went corpse cold.

I lifted my cup and took a shaky sip of my latte, stiffening at the sound of Elena's voice when it piped through my head. *Thank you for coming over tonight and trying to help me find out what really happened to my Dalton. You're the type of girl who must make your parents very proud, Cassie.*

I squeezed my eyes shut. *She couldn't know,* I told myself. *She couldn't know those words were my emotional kryptonite.*

"Sir," the barista called out, startling me. "Sir, your credit card didn't go through." I looked up to see a white-haired man shuffling back to the register, looking sheepish. I watched as he jammed his credit card into the reader, muttering under his breath, and an awareness suddenly flooded through me like a tidal wave. I was already in possession of a road map of Forest's whereabouts tonight—his credit card number. I didn't have to sit here alone, babysitting this door to determine whether Forest was telling the truth about working late. I could just as easily find out what he did tonight by calling his credit card company. That method would also eliminate the risk of being spotted.

I tossed what was left of my latte in the garbage and threw a glare over my shoulder at the middle-aged women on my way out. Wrapping my scarf around my neck, I stared down the street toward the subway station, debating my next step.

I had an entire evening ahead of me to kill.

Chapter Thirty-Four

I CHECKED THE numbers on the front of the six-story tenement building against the address scrawled on the page one last time before slipping Dalton's book back into my bag and taking a deep breath.

I wasn't sure what I was doing here. But given the strangeness of the conversation I had with Elena and the utterly bizarre fact that the landlord of this building had the same name as the person who claimed to work with Dalton, something had compelled me to come.

According to the text I'd sent Graham Ricci, I was here because I was interested in viewing one of his rental apartments. I'd expected he would want to arrange an appointment for later in the week, giving me time to figure out my plan. Or possibly talk myself out of it. What I didn't expect was his response: *You can come by any time in the next hour.* Clearly, Graham wanted to strike while the iron was hot. From the looks of the building, I could understand why.

"Spare any change?" the homeless woman leaning against the redbrick building called out, shaking a dirty cup in my direction. She was rail thin with wispy hair and looked old—too old to be sitting here on a hard sidewalk—and I was hit with the same feeling I always get whenever I see someone who would be my mother's age.

Is this where she wound up? Is this the reason she never came back?

I dug my nails into my palms hard, then pushed them a little deeper, relishing the pain.

"Focus," I whispered underneath my breath. The homeless woman was staring at me now with dull gray eyes, and as much as I wanted to ignore her my conscience wouldn't let me, so I reached into my pocket and stuffed a few crumpled bills into her outstretched hand. She mumbled thanks and I noticed what few teeth she had were blackened. My heart pinched so I averted my eyes to the littered coffee cups and plastic bags on the sidewalk.

Up until now I'd had my doubts that drugs played any role in Dalton's decision making. But there wasn't anything I could see in the neighborhood that would conflict with the conclusion the police made. This block looked like it could be used as a set for a *Law & Order* spin-off. It was amazing to me there were still pockets like this in Brooklyn, where most neighborhoods now came equipped with a Whole Foods and an Urban Outfitters.

I watched as a stocky man with a large tattoo on his neck walked down the sidewalk, checking his watch before ascending the small staircase and unlocking the dirty glass door. He disappeared inside, and I waited for him to be out of view before I approached the list of lightly penciled names next to the numbered buttons on the side of the door. I located the one labeled LANDLORD and paused for a second before resting my index finger on it and pressing.

Static blared from the speaker.

"It's Cassie, here to see the apartment," I bellowed, my voice trailing up, unsure if it was a working intercom. There was a loud buzz, and the lock on the door unclicked.

The smell in the lobby—a mix of cigarette smoke and Chinese food—hit me like mustard gas as the heavy door slammed behind me. I could hear the faint sound of someone yelling through the air vent, but for the life of me, couldn't figure out what they were saying. It suddenly occurred to me that there was not a single person in the world who knew where I was right now.

A tiny prickle of fear ran down my spine.

If Neck Tattoo came back down the stairs, shanked me in the throat, and dumped my body in a dumpster, would anyone even come looking for me? It's not like anyone from my temp agency would be surprised if I didn't show up for work again considering how I'd walked off the job today. They probably wouldn't even attempt to reach me. Forest would think I'd ghosted him, and even if he did suspect foul play, he didn't know my real name. I pictured my body being pulled out of a dumpster, the police trying to identify me against any missing person report and, finding none, eventually burying me as Jane Doe. The thought seemed melodramatic and silly, but then again maybe not.

I pulled out my phone, deciding I should at least send someone an email with my whereabouts. With the cursor pulsing in the "To:" box like a heartbeat, I was hit with the same anxious feeling I get whenever I have to put down an emergency contact person on an insurance form. My mind was agonizingly blank. I briefly debated sending Forest a text, but realized how crazy a *hey, in case you can't get ahold of me, come look for me in a tenement in Bushwick—here's the address* would sound, so I made the split-second decision to send the email to myself.

I am going to 1227 Himrod Street. If I don't come back, please come looking for me there.

I hit "send," feeling ridiculous yet still slightly reassured to have my whereabouts out there somewhere in cyberspace. Even if it was just my own inbox.

I coiled a strand of hair around my finger, wondering how long Graham was going to leave me waiting. Not that I had anywhere else to be. Tonight was all about tying up loose ends. Tomorrow, I would shower the smell of this lobby off my body, blow-dry my hair, and turn back into the person Forest was falling for. The new me. The person who would always, always have an emergency contact.

My phone buzzed in my hand, startling me. I looked down at the screen, surprised to see a text from Ricky.

To Cassie,

I wanted to check in with you to see how you are feeling. Please confirm your status.

Sincerely,
Ricky

I reread the message twice, exhaling a tiny snort. Leave it to Ricky to compose a text message with the formality of a letter sent home from a soldier in World War II. Still, I felt an unexpected surge of affection for the staff attorney extraordinaire. This text checking in on me was more concern than my own parents had ever shown. Tucking the phone in my pocket, I made a mental note to fire off a friendly response as soon as I was out of this creepy building. The less time spent in here the better.

The door to the stairwell banged open and a large figure appeared.

"You're here to see the apartment?" he asked, it sounding more like an accusation than a question.

I nodded, too afraid to speak. The tattoo on his neck was even more imposing close-up.

Neck Tattoo scrutinized me for a moment. "I'm Graham, the landlord here. You can follow me." He gestured with his hand down the hallway.

My feet stayed firmly planted on the tiled floor. Neck Tattoo was Graham? But Elena's description of Graham had been that he was tall with kind eyes. How could she possibly fail to mention the large, colored tattoo on the side of Graham's neck, which I was now close enough to see was a bloody skull on top of a woman's body?

"Oh, um, wait," I stammered, my brain needing to catch up with my escalating heart rate. There was no way I was following this guy behind a closed door. "I, um . . . I just realized you don't have an elevator and my husband and I have a newborn so we have a stroller." I emphasized the word "husband" so he knew there would in fact be someone in this world who would come looking for me if I went missing. "I think a walk-up might be too difficult for us."

He rubbed the back of his neck, annoyed. "So, do you want to see it or not?"

My eyes darted to the exit, and I briefly considered making a break for it. But I'd made the effort to come here and didn't want to return to my apartment empty-handed, without silencing the questions screaming in my head.

I needed to change course.

"Can I ask a few questions about the building first?" He stared at me wordlessly, so I forged ahead. "I think my friend used to come here a lot. Do you remember seeing someone named Dalton?" I kept my eyes on his face, studying it for a tell—any fraction of movement, any indication that the name was somehow familiar to him. But there was nothing. Not even a quiver. "I think he might have known you . . ." I trailed off.

His steely expression was difficult to read. After a moment, he answered. "Lady, there's a lot of people who come around this building. I don't check ID. Do you want to see the apartment or not?"

I looked down at my hand, clutched tightly around my phone. There was an ache in my head, running from temple to temple. What was I doing here? I'd convinced myself that tracking down Graham would somehow help. Help Elena. Help lift the heavy weight of remorse hanging like a noose around my neck. Help *something*. But that was silly. This guy wasn't the same Graham who'd gone over to Elena's house. Certainly not with that neck tattoo.

"Sorry, but I don't think it will work for us," I stammered, backing away toward the exit. "I'd better get home to my husband."

As I pushed through the door, I heard him mutter, "You're crazy, lady."

A small part of me was terrified that he wasn't wrong.

Chapter Thirty-Five

THE DOORMAN LOOKED at me strangely, lifting a caterpillar-like gray eyebrow, when I asked him for a Post-it note.

"I have a delivery for someone in the building," I said by way of explanation, swiping my hair behind my ears and running a fingertip underneath my eyes. "And I just want to make sure she gets it."

He slid a scuffed yellow block across the desk, rooted through his drawer, and placed a pen on top. "Make sure you write the apartment number and your name."

I did as he instructed, adding, *Elena, Dalton left this book at work so I wanted to return it to you. I hope you are able to find some peace and comfort.* I peeled the note off and stuck it in the top left-hand corner of the cover, sliding my finger over the edges to make sure it was secure. Then, I feathered through the pages with my thumb, ensuring no stray bits of paper from my purse were stuck inside, and placed it in the doorman's waiting hands.

Moral compass satisfied.

That's what I should've done to begin with, I told myself as I stepped back through the sliding doors, into the crisp evening air, and started my journey uptown on foot. I'd allowed myself to get caught up in Elena's grief-fueled theory which had been stupid of me. Dalton was dead. As tragic as it was, there wasn't anything that was going to change that.

I pulled a hair tie from my wrist and twisted my hair in a hasty ponytail to get it off my damp neck, and rummaged through my purse, extracting a pastel yellow tube of hand cream. I squeezed a bean-sized amount into my hands, rubbing it across my parched skin. I kept walking, periodically lifting my moisturized palms to my nose and inhaling the scent that Molton Brown called "Orange & Bergamot" and what Annabelle's Instagram had termed *#heaven*.

A breeze cut through the air, raising goosebumps on my arms. I picked up the pace, suddenly desperate to get back to my apartment.

"Focus, Cassie. Focus," I muttered to myself, jamming my hands in my pockets and cutting across Lexington Avenue as the crosswalk signal counted down. But despite my best efforts, my thoughts kept creeping back to Elena, like a loose thread my subconscious insisted on pulling. Why was she so convinced that Dalton hadn't committed suicide? Was Dalton really a drug addict? And who the hell was the person who had gone to see Elena?

I moved the pieces in my mind, sliding them around to see where they fit. Graham told Elena he worked with Dalton. Maybe it was someone Dalton had been friendly with before I'd arrived. Maybe they'd had some kind of a falling-out. Those sorts of things happen all the time among work colleagues. It wouldn't preclude Graham from visiting Elena after Dalton's death. Maybe he went over there because he felt guilty. I certainly knew what guilt could do to a person.

Still, it didn't explain why Graham would want to access Dalton's email.

My purse pounded against my side as my mind filled with wild scenarios, none of which were good. I was so lost in thought that I didn't even realize I'd stepped into traffic until a taxi driver jammed on his brakes, blaring his horn. I leapt back to the sidewalk, my pulse racing.

"Watch it!" a pudgy man in an ill-fitting coat huffed as he dodged out of my path. He muttered something under his breath and shook his head at me in frustration.

"Sorry," I mumbled, putting a palm to my chest in an attempt to slow down my out-of-control heartbeat. I was starting to feel dizzy, like I'd just stepped off a merry-go-round. My mind was spinning like a tornado, the blaring question in my head getting louder and louder, refusing to be ignored. No matter how many times I turned it over, I couldn't make any sense of it.

Who the hell was Graham and why did he want to break in to Dalton's email?

People were blurring past me now, and the sounds of the city—horns honking, people yelling—were drilling into my temples, giving me vertigo. I blinked hard, trying to chase away the stifling panic that was prickling on my skin, but it fought to stay close.

I know that Dalton didn't kill himself. I know it here. Elena's voice reverberated in my skull.

Suddenly, everything went quiet. It was as if someone had taken a remote control and hit "mute" on the city noises that buzzed around me, leaving me in deafening silence. I couldn't swallow. Or breathe. Or think. My eyes darted over my shoulder, seized by the fear that someone was watching me, stalking me like prey. Was Neck Tattoo following me? My breath quickened to the point I feared I might hyperventilate and pass out right there on the corner.

Breathe in. Breathe out. I focused on each rise and fall of my chest as panic threatened to consume me. A string of mini explosions began going off in my head, one on top of the other, clearing away the clouds in my mind and leaving behind the glaring truth: Something was wrong.

My eyes squeezed shut. Memories of Dalton were floating around in my mind like tiny dust particles. Scenes that had previously been blurry were now appearing in sharp focus. I could see every tooth in his broad smile, the way his Adam's apple bobbed when he laughed. There he was sitting across the table from me in the cafeteria, lifting a single eyebrow with mock shock in that funny way he used to do. There we were walking to the subway together on the last day I saw him, his hand running along the stubble on his chin when we stopped at the top of the stairs. I zoomed in on his face as if the memory was an iPhone video that I could somehow double-tap in order to get a closer look. For the first time, my mind focused in on the tiny tremble in his cheek and the bead of sweat at his hairline. I turned up the volume on the last words he said to me and could suddenly hear with perfect clarity the way his voice shook when he told me he had to meet someone. That was right before he looked over his shoulder anxiously. Or maybe, when I thought about it now, I'd misinterpreted the situation. It wasn't anxiety etched on his face when he looked over his shoulder.

It was fear.

Every nerve in my body tightened. Suddenly a realization wrapped itself around my throat with surprising ferocity, choking me.

I don't think Dalton jumped. I think somebody pushed him.

Chapter Thirty-Six

I DON'T REMEMBER whether I jumped in a taxi, rode the subway, or simply ran the twenty blocks back to my apartment without stopping. The next memory I have is my shaking hands as I struggled to maneuver the key in the lock of my front door and then tumbling all three deadbolts behind me once I finally managed to get inside. My breath was coming so fast and hard it felt like I was going to throw up a lung.

I triple-checked the security of my door and slid down the wall until I was in the fetal position, resting my head against my knees. The tears that had been threatening to escape finally slid down my face. I closed my eyes for a second and tried to untangle the knot in my head. Events from the past few hours popped up like a slideshow—the sadness etched on Elena's face, the bewilderment when I heard another coworker had gone over there, the sight of the address written in Dalton's handwriting. It had all been so disorienting in the moment, but now, after a few minutes in the quiet safety of my apartment, the static in my head was beginning to clear, leaving me to wonder if there wasn't a reasonable explanation I'd somehow overlooked. With my panic receding, my budding theory about Dalton's disappearance was starting to feel less like a realization and more like a wild, paranoid idea.

I swiped angrily at a tear with the back of my hand. "Stop being crazy, Cassie. Stop being crazy," I repeated in time with my rapid breaths.

After I had made the promise to Grandma as a teenager that I would not end up like my mother, I remember checking a book out of the library called *25 Signs of Mental Illness*. "It's for a research paper at school," I'd explained to the librarian who raised a questioning eyebrow as she scanned the barcode and slid the tome across the counter into my young hands. In her defense, it was pretty heavy reading for a thirteen-year-old. I remember locking my bedroom door, pulling the book out of my backpack, and crawling onto my bed, hoping to commit every page to memory, certain that if I knew the warning signals I could nip any troubling behavior in the bud. Most of what I read confused and scared the crap out of me and had long since been intentionally swept from my memory, but I could still see the large, boldfaced words on the first page: #1—*AN IR-RATIONAL FEAR OR SUSPICIOUSNESS OF OTHERS OR A STRONG NERVOUS FEELING*. I remember wondering how the hell anyone could know for sure if a fear was rational or not. But sitting here on the floor of my apartment now, it occurred to me that thinking your depressed coworker did not commit suicide—as he hinted he would—but instead was murdered would probably meet the threshold of an irrational fear.

My running nose made a wet streak on my pants as I raised my head and stared blankly at my small apartment. I rubbed my eyes, but it didn't fix the blurriness. The lights were off, but the room was lit by a dim glow coming from a tiny light left on in the kitchen. My gaze fell on the coffee table and the glint from the half-empty bottle of Absolut caught my eye.

Surely, I didn't drink all of that. No, I would remember.

I rose from the floor and in four quick strides I was at my lap-top. It was time to put my ridiculous theories about Dalton to rest. If Graham really had been wanting to break in to Dalton's email, then there would have to be something in his inbox this Graham guy would either want to know or would *not* want others to know. There was only one way to find out what that was.

My fingers flew across the keys as I answered the first two secu-rity questions with ease. Staring at the third question on the screen, I hesitated. My hands hovered over the keyboard, then dropped to my lap. I rocked back into the couch and pressed the heels of my palms hard into my eyes until tiny colored dots filled my vision.

I let out a long sigh and rubbed the back of my neck, returning my gaze to the screen. The cursor blinked aggressively in the rectangular box below, challenging me. *What is the name of your first pet?*

"Screw it," I whispered. I whipped the arrow to the X in the corner of the screen, and let it hover there for a moment, readying myself to click the mouse and put all of this behind me. My whole body tingled, like I was standing too close to the edge of the cliff.

Forget about it, Cassie. Click the stupid mouse, close the screen, and walk away.

I raised my index finger, but before I had time to think about what I was doing, some greater force took control and my fingers landed on the keyboard with the quickness of a snake striking its prey. My hands were surprisingly steady as I pecked out the letters g-i-l-l-i-g-a-n and hit "enter."

My stomach rose like an elevator into my throat.

Reset your password, the screen instructed. My mind was laser focused now as I created a new password for Dalton's account and retyped it beside the prompt.

Just like that, I was in.

A trove of new, unopened messages filled Dalton's inbox. It struck me as eerie that even though he was dead, his inbox lived on. Emails still poured in. I held my breath as my eyes sifted through the names of the senders—Seamless, Travelocity, Xbox Live—nothing that didn't look like junk mail. Nothing that was going to answer any questions.

But these emails had all come in *after* Dalton had died. I jabbed my finger on the trackpad, sliding farther down Dalton's inbox, past a long string of unread messages, my pulse quickening as the gray box scrolled down the side of the screen. It felt like it took hours, but in reality, it was probably only seconds before I reached the last email that Dalton had opened and read. The subject line was blank, but the sender's name was in bold. I blinked rapidly, not daring to believe my eyes.

Then, for a moment, time stopped.

What. The. Fuck.

With a trembling finger, I tapped open the message.

> To: Dalton Sever
> From: Forest Watts
>
> Relax. Let's talk. Call me at (646) 995-7787

I stared at the screen, trying to make sense of what I was look-ing at. *That was MY Forest. MY Forest had emailed Dalton?* The air around me was suddenly thin. I couldn't get enough oxygen into my lungs.

Why the hell would Forest be sending an email to Dalton? They didn't even know each other. Did they? My vision tunneled on the light gray numbers in the top corner of the screen. A date stamp—*November 5, 2019 4:13 p.m.* I knew that date. It was etched in my memory like a scar. It was the day our review was put on hold and we were sent home for the night.

Gears were turning in my head, shifting, trying to sort this through. Forest had emailed Dalton on the same day we got the call to stop reviewing documents. Was Dalton the one who had alerted Forest about the glitch? Why would he do that? Out of nowhere a memory from that afternoon punched me full in the face. Ricky, coming over to my workstation, demanding to know why Dalton had been out of the bunker so long. *Hey, where's your buddy boy over here?* I remember I looked at the bottom corner of my screen, wondering why Dalton had been gone for more than fifteen minutes, bucking his usual bathroom break routine. I could see the time in my mind's eye with perfect clarity—4:27 P.M.

This email I was looking at now was sent during the time Dal-ton was out of the bunker.

My hand seemed to be moving on its own volition as I scrolled down to see what Forest had been replying to when he wrote *let's talk,* but there was nothing. This email from Forest to Dalton stood alone.

Uneasiness clawed at the back of my neck. Why would someone send an email telling a person to relax with no context? More important, why would Forest email Dalton at all? None of this made sense.

With panic running through me like electricity now, I used the cursor to highlight Forest's email address and pasted it into the search field of Dalton's account. The only way to know why Forest was contacting Dalton was to see if there had been any other correspondence between them. I clicked "return" and almost instantaneously the search revealed four emails—two in Dalton's sent box and two in Dalton's inbox. A quick scan showed the emails were all from the same day, mere minutes apart. I leaned in closer until my face was inches from the screen, as if proximity could somehow provide more clarity. My pulse was pounding at triple time as I clicked open the first one.

> To: Forest Watts
> From: Dalton Sever
>
> You don't know me, but I know you. And I know your secret on Himrod Street. I can't promise I'll keep it. What's it worth to you?

Click.

> To: Dalton Sever
> From: Forest Watts
>
> I don't know what you think you know about me, but you've got the wrong guy, chief.

Click.

> To: Forest Watts
> From: Dalton Sever
>
> No, I'm certain I've got the right guy, chief. I saw the address 1227 Himrod Street in your emails and couldn't help doing a lit-

tle research. The building was purchased in 2018 by Woodland Co for $2.2 million. In 2019, Woodland sold it to an LLC for $5.2 million. Quite the appreciation after less than a year! I was curious who owned Woodland Co, and then I found the answer in your email. Congratulations on the sale. Odd that you made such a large amount of money on a sale to a shell company where neither the owner nor the source of funds can be traced. Hm.

Do I need to go on, chief?

Click.

To: Dalton Sever
From: Forest Watts

Relax. Let's talk. Call me at (646) 995-7787

My heart was beating so fast I thought it might break through my ribs. Questions swirled in my mind as I struggled to take a breath, to calm myself so I could think this through clearly, but there was too much resistance in my chest, like I was wearing a lead vest. Beads of sweat began dampening my shirt. I raised my fingers to my temples as if they could somehow sort out the muddy mess in my head.

What the fuck, what the fuck, what the fuck, what the fuck? I whispered, like a broken record that couldn't stop skipping, as I scanned each email again. And again.

Suddenly, a realization reached up and seized me by the throat and all at once I knew why the address in Dalton's book had felt familiar to me. I'd seen it in Forest's emails.

The living room floor dropped out from underneath me and I was in free fall. Everything was spinning so fast now that I didn't even feel his hand wrap around my shoulder until he squeezed.

Chapter Thirty-Seven

My body bucked in shock before my head whipped around.

He was standing behind me, smiling the same relaxed smile I'd seen him flash when greeting someone on the sidewalk, as if him being in my apartment right now was the most natural thing in the world. He was wearing a white button-down shirt and his head was haloed by the glow from my laptop, giving him the appearance of an angel here to deliver some kind of message, making me wonder whether I was hallucinating.

Little black dots filled my vision. *Not real. Not real.*

"You look surprised to see me," he said in a low gravelly voice. It sounded like his morning voice, the same one I'd spent hours fantasizing would be greeting me every day when I woke up. My stomach flip-flopped.

"Forest," I breathed, leaping to my feet. "What are you doing here?"

He tilted his head. "Waiting for you, Cassie."

I blinked at him, lost in my mental haze. I was ten steps behind. It was as if someone had hit control-alt-delete and rebooted my brain. My short-term memory had been wiped completely clean and all I could focus on was the fact that Forest Watts was here, in my apartment. His smile was like a gravitational pull and I inched closer, closing the gap between us, and laid a tentative hand on his waist, as if touching him too hard might make him disappear.

"I . . . I didn't know you were here waiting or I would've been home sooner."

"Yeah, it was a shame we couldn't meet up tonight to celebrate that new job of yours, but"—the corner of his smile slipped and he gestured with his head toward my laptop—"looks like you were doing a little research here instead, Cass."

I turned my head and in an instant, my spell of adoration was broken and replaced with a shot of paralyzing panic. My coffee table was littered with notes about Dalton from my online investigation mere hours ago. My eyes darted across the surface in a frantic search. Was there anything here about Forest? I couldn't remember. It was too late to hide them now. My Forest binder—oh god, where was my Forest binder? I was off balance, hurtling back down to earth as questions ricocheted in my mind. *How long has Forest been standing there? What has he seen? What can I tell him to cover this up?* Finally, my thoughts landed hard on the pavement with a single question: *How did Forest get into my apartment?* I didn't let him in, and he wouldn't have been able to get past the three deadbolts which I could see out of the corner of my eye were all still firmly in place.

A prickle of unease crept down my spine.

I looked at my hand resting on Forest's waist and that was when I saw it. The tuft of purple fur peeking out of the pocket of his pants. My keychain. The one I couldn't locate this morning.

Forest followed my gaze. "Oh this." He laughed dryly, sticking his hand in his pocket and pulling out my keys. He tossed them on the couch. "I took those while you were sleeping last night." There was a steely edge to his voice. One I didn't recognize. "You didn't even notice me leave the bedroom, did you?"

I shook my head dumbly. My voice seemed inaccessible.

"Well, I figured it was only fair that I have a chance to look around your apartment on my own. I mean, you know so much about me, Cassie, shouldn't I find some things out about you too?" He popped his index finger on my nose, the same way you would do to a child, but it somehow seemed aggressive.

Instinctively, I moved a step back.

It took a couple of seconds before his words registered over the pounding of my heart. *Shouldn't I find some things out about you too?* Fuck. What had Forest found out about me? I was like a fish dropped on the dock, floundering, trying to find my way back into the ocean. I opened my mouth to speak, but before I found my voice my frantic eyes landed on the object in Forest's other hand. It took me a moment to process what it was. Then, all of the oxygen was sucked from my lungs.

The binder.

I could barely choke out the next words. "Forest, I . . ." I started, my tone already pleading, but he held up his hand, cutting me off. His expression darkened, like a cloud passing over the sun.

"Now, this." He held up the binder the way an evangelist would hold up the Bible. "This is the best piece of investigative reporting I've ever come across, Cassie. If you give up your career as a temp you have a promising future as a journalist."

Blood flooded my cheeks. I was frozen, unable to move, or even to breathe.

He licked his thumb and began leafing through the pages. "Let's see here. What nuggets of information does this include? We have 'Forest's Likes,' 'Information about Forest's House,' 'Forest's Facebook Friends.'" He lifted an amused eyebrow before continuing. "'Emails to Annabelle,' 'Annabelle's Clothing' . . ." he trailed off. I felt my chin tremble as tears stabbed my eyes.

"What kind of person has the *time* to put something like this together?" he scoffed.

A hot rush of shame burst over my chest. It was as if someone had slid a blade into my stomach and with one twist had hollowed out my insides.

He kept flipping before stopping on the final page. He laid a palm across and tapped gently. "It isn't until we get to this page here that we realize just how thorough your research has been." He held up the page titled "Forest's Password."

The tears that had been threatening to escape finally slid down my face. With a wrenching effort, I stammered, "I can explain."

"Oh really?" Forest choked out a laugh. "How can you possibly explain all this?" He leaned in closer, until we were nose to nose. "Cassandra Wood-*son*." He spat out the second syllable of my last name like it was a swear word.

My heart twisted so tight I could barely breathe.

He slammed the binder shut and tossed it on the couch. "You're not the only one who knows how to use Google. I know all about you too. And it looks like I'm not the only one who has some secrets, huh?" He raised his eyebrows. "Some pretty fucked-up ones too."

I shuffled back, stumbling over the leg of the coffee table. I had to get out of here. I needed time to formulate a plan to fix this. Fix us.

I felt as if a noose was slowly tightening around my neck.

Forest wrapped a hand around my forearm, and I let him pull me toward him. "You need to tell me, Cassie, since you know everything about me. How does this fit in?" He nodded toward the email still open on my laptop.

My vision blurred. Whether it was tears clouding my eyes or Forest's words making me dizzy I wasn't sure. My brain was so overwhelmed with juggling my own lies, I couldn't figure out where mine ended and Forest's began.

Relax. Let's talk.

"Come on, Cassie. I want to know." He tightened his grip on my arm. "What are you going to write in your little binder about that?"

I wanted to tell him that whatever was in those emails didn't matter to me. I would take him as he is. *For better, for worse. Until death do us part. Always.* I lifted my gaze and saw his face contorted into something ugly I didn't even recognize. With his clenched jaw and bulging cords in his neck, he looked nothing like the man I'd woken up next to. I swallowed hard against the acid rising in my throat. Somehow my voice found its way outside my head, and it sounded only slightly strangled. "I don't . . . I have no idea about any of that. And it's not something I *want* to know anything about."

Forest snorted and folded his arms over his chest. "Oh, of course, you have *no* idea." His words agreed but his tone did not.

He tilted his head and regarded me thoughtfully. "What am I going to do with you, Cassie? I've been sitting here in your apartment just asking myself that question. What am I supposed to do with you?"

"Forest." I held my shaky palms up. "I had no idea you guys even knew each other. Dalton and I were never really that close. Really. You're the only one I care about." My voice broke. I could feel my heart breaking along with it.

He closed his eyes and let out a long sigh. "Then why, my dear, if you are as blissfully ignorant as you claim you are, did you go to the building in Bushwick?"

I heard my breath catch. How did he know I went to the address in Dalton's book? Had he been following me?

"I . . . I didn't know . . ."

"Don't lie to me." He raised his voice, cutting me off. He was staring at me with an intensity that sent a chill down my spine. "I know you went over there, Cassie. You want to know how I know?" He leaned closer, his hot breath brushing my ear. "Because I have *your* password too."

My throat closed up.

"Dear Diary," he mimicked. "I'm going to 1227 Himrod Street. If I don't come back, please come looking for me there." He let out a humorless laugh and leaned back, eyeing me from top to bottom. "Hasn't anyone ever told you that you shouldn't have the same password for all of your accounts? Otherwise, when you create a customer account to take a spin class anyone can get your information."

My heart crashed to a stop.

Annabelle. Annabelle must have come out of the locker room and lifted my email and password from the iPad I left on the counter. My mind reeled, desperately trying to fill in the details. Annabelle couldn't have known I would be at Spirit Cycle that day. I hadn't purchased a ticket in advance and didn't even know about it until she posted about it on Instagram.

Holy shit.

Annabelle had set me up.

I felt a wail rise up through me but fought it, my knuckles pressed against my lips. I should've known Annabelle had something to do with this. Women like her were always screwing things up for people like me. Just because they could.

"You just couldn't keep your nose out of other people's business could you, Cassie?" Forest shook his head with mock sorrow. "Unfortunately, neither could your friend. He sees one address in an email of mine—which he wasn't supposed to be reviewing in the first place—and feels the need to go all fucking Hardy Boys."

I stopped breathing. I was absolutely frozen.

"Unfortunately for all of us, his stupidity didn't end there. That idiot calls me, tells me he's found out all this shit about me." His breathing was fast, but his voice was steady, like he was narrating a movie in his head. "And then he tries to shake me down for money like I'm some kind of fucking sucker who will pay him for his silence." He lowered his voice to a whisper. "I wasn't the sucker here, Cassie. Your friend was. All he managed to do was alert me to the fact that my emails were being reviewed by a bunch of hopeless temps. Which I put a stop to, of course. I even got the moron who made that little fuckup happen fired. And your friend, well, I guess things got a little messier than I'd planned."

My head ached as I tried to process what Forest was telling me. I struggled to rearrange his words until they fell into digestible sentences. Dalton had tried to blackmail Forest.

Things got a little messier than I'd planned.

The full impact of what he'd said spread over me one inch at a time, until I had the whole picture. I fought back a whimper. "You . . ." I croaked, my throat like sandpaper. "Did you do something to Dalton?"

Forest's eyes blazed and terror wound its way through my veins.

"Did you . . . did you kill him?" I heard a tiny voice ask. I was so deep in the pit of my fear that it took me a second to realize the voice was mine.

Forest grimaced and rubbed the side of his jaw with his hand, but didn't answer, which was answer enough.

Everything went dark.

"Your friend should've stayed in his own fucking lane. He did this to himself."

The sounds of the city diminished and the room fell silent, save for the sound of Forest's breathing, ragged and shallow. I was certain he could hear my heart pounding against my rib cage. He glared at me for a moment before his face contorted into something bordering on manic. It was dark and ugly and sent a fresh wave of terror zipping through my insides.

"You!" he exclaimed, wagging an aggressive finger at me, his pupils huge. "Now, you surprised me, Cassie. After I put a stop to my emails being public domain for lonely temps, I still had a problem, didn't I?" He arched a condescending eyebrow. "I had no idea who else had read my emails, which meant I needed to track down a list of names of the people hired to work on that project." There was a sly look on his face now, like a magician about to let you in on the secret to how he made the rabbit disappear. "Now, imagine my surprise when one of the names on the list is Cassie, which just happened to be the same name as the girl who'd showed up at the same bar as me and ordered the exact same drink."

An icy fist wrapped around my heart and squeezed.

He scoffed. "I knew there was something wrong with you the first time I saw you in Juice Press and you couldn't take your creepy eyes off my hand. You were like a fucking predator trying to sniff out unmarried men." He raised his left arm, and I reflexively winced, thinking I was about to be slapped. But when I opened my eyes Forest was smirking, wiggling his fourth finger, flashing the platinum wedding band wrapped firmly around it. "I never wear it on the days I'm going for a workout, but I guess your research didn't tell you that, did it?" He tsked.

My fingernails dug deep into the flesh on my palms. I needed to wake myself from this nightmare.

"Then, when you showed up at Elwood's I was actually worried you were an undercover cop. Why else would you be following me? I even shot Annabelle a warning text so she could start shredding." He exhaled a snort. "But when I saw your name on the list of temps I realized you aren't an undercover cop, you're just a crazy stalker. So, it was my turn to investigate you, find out how much you know. Turns out, quite a lot. And a lot about my wife too. But here's something you don't know." He raised an index finger. "Annabelle outsmarted you. She was the one who came up with the idea to use Instagram to lay the bait and see if you would show up. All it took was one little comment about a fundraiser and—boom—there you were. All starry eyed and stupid enough to leave your email and password lying around for all the world to see." He swept out his arm in a mocking gesture.

I drew in a sharp inhalation of air. I wanted to slam my hand against his mouth and force the words back in. Curl up in a ball and wait for the floor to collapse beneath me from the weight of my pain. The narrative I'd created was being ripped out from my chest, and I felt it as acutely as I would one of my limbs being severed. My head began to throb with a deep, familiar beat. Betrayal. Someone I loved was betraying me. Again.

Forest's gaze roved across my living room, landing on the tiny side table. He smirked, pointing to the empty bottle of Caymus perched in the middle, dried red wax dripping from the taper candle jammed in the bottle's mouth. "Caymus wine? Jesus Christ, how much research on us did you do? I would ask you how you knew about that, but you know what? I don't even want to fucking know." He shook his head. "Jesus, you tried so hard to be her. You think I didn't notice how you smelled the same, dressed the same? It was ridiculous. But someone like you can never, ever hold a candle to my wife. No matter how many hours you spend on that fucking laptop of yours trying to change that."

I physically recoiled, my hands clutching tighter around my stomach, each word out of Forest's mouth striking me like a rapid-fire blow to the gut. He was still speaking, but the words were bending and overlapping in my mind until the hissing sound in my ears got loud enough to drown him out completely. After a moment, I recognized the sound for what it was—Dalton's voice.

These guys think they're fucking gods, and everyone around them is supposed to serve them. They just take for the sake of taking, and they don't give a shit about anybody but themselves.

My eyes burrowed into Forest's flat brown eyes now, searching for the man I knew, but the expression behind them belonged to a stranger. There was physical pain in my temples as a realization settled deep into my bones: The things Dalton had said in the cafeteria were true. This man didn't give a shit about me. He didn't love me. He was no better than Landon, or my mother, or any of the number of people who had fucked me over. *They just take for the sake of taking, and they don't give a shit about anyone but themselves.*

Forest took a step toward me. My mind reeled, trying to figure out what I needed to do next. If I didn't get out of here, Elena would never know the truth about what happened to her son. Forest and Annabelle would get away with everything and live their fucked-up happily ever after. My hands balled into fists as I quickly weighed my options. With three deadbolts on my door, it would be impossible to make a break for it now. Forest would be able to stop me before I even got the first one unlocked. I could scream at the top of my lungs, but if someone did hear me yelling, I doubted they would even come. My interactions with my neighbors had been limited to sharing a silent elevator ride in the morning, and something told me they weren't the type to get involved in what would probably be assumed to be a domestic dispute.

I shuffled backward, inching toward the front door.

It suddenly occurred to me I was still wearing my coat. I could feel my phone heavy in the left pocket.

"But here's where I need you to fill in one of the gaps, Cassie," Forest said, narrowing his eyes. "There's nothing in that binder of yours about the apartment in Bushwick. How did you find out about it?"

"I . . . I really don't know anything about it," I stammered, hearing the unsteadiness in my voice and hoping Forest didn't pick up on it. "The address was written down in a book Dalton left at his workstation. I picked it up for him when he didn't return to work. Just to return it to him."

Forest's head tilted. He was listening.

I rushed ahead. "But he never came back, and I would've dropped it entirely, but I had a weird encounter with Dalton's mom where she told me someone named Graham came to visit her, and I . . . I think . . . I thought maybe . . ." I faltered. Suddenly, a single memory of Elena snapped into my head like a slide loading in a projector: the way her pinky had reached up and gently, unconsciously traced a line through her left eyebrow as she said, *He had kind eyes.* She'd traced the exact spot of the scar that sliced through Forest's left eyebrow.

The truth came to me like the bang of a gun, and I had to force myself not to flinch. Forest was Graham. Forest was the one who went over to Elena's to track down the answer to Dalton's security questions so he could break in to Dalton's inbox, presumably to make sure no one came across the emails I'd just opened. The same emails that were on the screen of my laptop right now.

I softened my tone, struggling against the fear in my voice. "It doesn't have to be like this, Forest. You have to know how much I care about you. You know that I would never tell anyone. I couldn't do that to you." I tilted my face up to his in hopes of conveying my sincerity. "I want us to . . ."

Forest cut me off with a raised hand and I flinched. He scoffed and shook his head. "Don't be so dramatic, Cassie. If you'd kept your nose out of other people's business you wouldn't be in this fucking situation."

I lowered my head as if readying myself for a guillotine and hoped Forest wouldn't notice my hand slipping into my coat pocket. My fingers flexed around the phone. If I could tap in my password I would be able to make an emergency call from the home screen. I'd tapped those numbers out so many times I was sure my body could do it from muscle memory. I slid a fingertip down the slick screen, bringing it to life, and prayed the glow from my pocket wouldn't be noticeable through the fabric of my coat. My finger was shaking as I pressed the first digit of my passcode.

A loud honk from five stories down sliced through the apartment, and Forest threw an angry look out the window. With his body pivoted I could see something poking out of his back pocket. A bolt of silver, glinting in the reflection of the window. I held back a gasp as terror ripped through my gut. It was a knife.

Forest swung his eyes back to me and I froze. He paused, considering me. "You really are crazy, you know that, Cassie?" He took another step toward me, and I could see the rise and fall of his chest quickening. "So crazy in fact, that you stalked me at work, invited me over to your apartment tonight, and then tried to kill me because if you can't have me, then no one can." He rolled his eyes theatrically. "Who would have thought you'd turn out to be such a cliché?" A cryptic smile crept over his mouth. "Although I guess you do have a history of instability, don't you? Lucky for me, you left all the proof of your obsession right there in your handy little binder. It will be really fucking easy for me to prove I had no choice but to kill Miss Boil-Your-Bunny in self-defense."

My blood went cold. I forced myself to maintain eye contact as my trembling finger slid around the screen tapping out the remaining digits, silently pleading for this to work.

Without warning, Forest's hand lunged for my throat. His palms were wrapped around my neck before I even had a chance to scream. I stumbled backward as his fingers pressed into my skin, crushing my windpipe. My legs buckled and a white-hot pain flashed over my eyes, throwing me off balance. Instinctively, my hands flew out to my sides, flailing wildly in an effort to steady myself, to keep my body from falling to the floor where I would have no chance to fight back.

My phone—my last connection with anyone outside this locked apartment—went tumbling out of my pocket.

I choked back a scream as the lit screen plunged from my grasp. It was as if a vital organ was being dislodged from my body. Tiny black dots filled my vision as dizziness engulfed me.

Forest loosened his fingers, a smirk spreading across his face as the phone clanked on the floor. He kicked it out of reach. I could see the white scar above his eye turn an angry red as he leaned in closer, his expression contorting into a scowl.

"You weren't going to make this harder on yourself, Cassie, were you?" His eyes blazed into mine and I could feel his hot, moist breath against my face when he whispered, "Who do you think the police would believe—crazy Cassie Woodson or me?"

He tightened his grip again, harder this time, crushing the scream right out of me.

My throat spasmed with pain. My fingers scrabbled at my neck, clawing his fingers and raking my nails across his wrists as my panicked, wild eyes flicked down in search of something, anything that I could grab on to. I didn't even think about what I was doing when I closed a hand around the one thing within my reach—the binder.

With every ounce of strength I could muster, I swung it toward Forest's head with full force. It made contact on his left temple and sliced through the skin, knocking him off balance. I lunged forward, pressing all my weight against him, and he pitched backward. I watched as he spilled to the floor, clutching his bleeding forehead. If he wailed, I couldn't hear it over the sound of my pulse pounding in my ears.

I pushed myself upright as he made a sweep at my ankles with his hand. Before he could get back up on all fours, I lifted my right foot as high as it would go, directly over his face. Then, for a moment, time stopped. My mind struggled to reconcile this Forest on the floor with the Forest I knew so well. The Forest I loved with every ounce of my being.

This is Forest, a voice in my head whispered. *This is your future. Your lifeline. You'll never survive without him.*

I could taste the blood in my mouth from where my teeth had sliced through my tongue. I wavered. It didn't matter if Forest killed me. Because if he didn't, this abhorrent voice in the back of my mind would eventually finish the job. It was going to continue to grow louder and louder until it cannibalized my entire brain. Just like the cancer that had ravaged my father's insides, cell by healthy cell, stealing him from me. I could see Dad's face in my mind now, hear his voice repeating the words he'd said to me the last time we were together. "Do one thing for me, Cassie," he'd croaked, as I'd shifted his pillows to make him more comfortable. "Don't let the cancer take *your* life too."

I squeezed my eyes shut.

You're the type of girl who must make your parents very proud, Cassie.

A primal sound exploded from my mouth as I, with wild fury, dropped the heel of my shoe square against the bridge of Forest's nose. A loud crack filled the room. Forest let out an animalistic wail as the blood shot out of his nostrils like a firehose, soaking my pant leg. I hesitated for a beat before I somehow forced my feet to move across the living room.

One lock.

Two locks.

Three locks.

My entire body trembled with the massive amount of adrenaline coursing through it, but I managed to untumble them all. I still had the binder under my arm when I finally pushed through the door and opened my mouth to scream. I wasn't sure any sound had come out until I saw the stunned expression on the face of the man at the far end of the hallway as he emerged from the elevator.

"Cassie," he called out, holding up his phone. "I didn't want to barge over here, but you never answered my text."

I could've collapsed with relief. There, walking toward me, as if I'd summoned him with my mind, was Ricky. Staff attorney extraordinaire.

He stopped midstride. His eyes grew as wide as saucers as he took in my blood-soaked clothes. "What the . . ."

"Call the police," I cried, my voice hoarse and desperate, as I staggered toward the stairwell.

One flight down, I yanked open the trash chute. I made sure I heard the binder land in the dumpster before I let the door swing close.

New York Post, **November 15, 2019**
Cheating Manhattan Lawyer Arrested After Assault on Gal Pal

A thirty-nine-year-old corporate lawyer from the prestigious firm Levy & Strong faces multiple charges including aggravated assault and false imprisonment stemming from a late-night dispute at an Upper East Side apartment.

Police responded to a 911 call placed by Ricky Sandos at 9:47 P.M. "I'd come over to check on a colleague of mine because she'd gone home sick and wasn't answering her phone. The next thing I know I see her run out of her apartment with this crazy look on her face and blood all over her legs. It was a dangerous situation, but I was able to stay calm under pressure thanks to my intense legal training," the witness told police. Forest Watts was found inside the apartment and taken into custody shortly thereafter. Sources say the married attorney and the victim had been continuing a relationship. It wasn't clear what set Watts off.

An NYPD spokesman confirmed the arrest, but declined to comment other than to say more charges were expected to be filed against Watts.

Bond has not been set.

Above the Law, November 20, 2019
Disgraced Attorney Faces Shocking New Charges

We've talked about lawyers behaving badly before, but hold on to your gavels, folks, because this one is a doozy.

Corporate attorney and billion-dollar dealmaker Forest Watts (pictured above) and his wife, Annabelle Watts, face multiple charges including bank fraud, money laundering, and conspiracy.

These shocking charges came just days after Watts was arrested in an unrelated incident for allegedly assaulting his girlfriend in an Upper East Side apartment. In a bizarre twist, Watts's mistress is none other than Cassandra Woodson, the dishonorably discharged associate who was let go from her white-shoe law firm for pummeling a co-worker in a lovers' quarrel turned fight club audition. Dare we say Woodson and Watts sound like they're two of a kind?

The accusations stunned partners at Watts's prestigious firm. "Forest was a rising star here at the firm," a partner who wished to remain anonymous said. "This will kill his legal career."

Ya think? I nominate that for understatement of the year.

Watts is accused of laundering $14 million from a web of offshore companies.

Manhattan District Attorney Heather Buchan explained, "Watts purchased and sold real estate for the express purpose of laundering money for corrupt foreign nationals."

According to the indictment, Watts set up a corporate entity to purchase mutually agreed upon properties using his personal funds. He would then sell the property to an offshore company, the owner of which was veiled behind a labyrinth of corporate entities, for an amount well above fair market value. Upon receipt of the purchase price,

Watts would keep twenty-five percent of the profits and funnel the remaining seventy-five percent back. The oddest part of the detailed indictment is the nearly $2 million Watts evidently funneled back through various purchases of counterfeit artwork. It is alleged these acquisitions were made by his wife, Annabelle.

"The funds Watts was allegedly laundering were the proceeds of bribery and corruption, stolen from the citizens of Colombia," Buchan said.

Financial crimes expert Maureen Tulane points out "only about one percent of the total amount the government says is laundered each year is ever confiscated. When people are caught, it's usually because they made a silly mistake, like using a personal email to set up a company or some other personal identifier."

Makes you wonder what else could be hiding in Watts's email.

If convicted, Forest and Annabelle Watts could each face up to forty-five years in prison.

AMNew York, **November 25, 2019**
Local Crime RoundUp

Police have reopened an investigation into the circumstances surrounding the death of a man whose body was
found on the corner of Himrod Street and Irving Avenue
in Brooklyn earlier this month. A spokesperson for the
NYPD stated new details have emerged.

E p i l o g u e

One year later

I AWAKEN WITH his hand winding around my waist, pulling me closer to his bare chest. I sigh and settle into his warmth, marveling at how transformative it feels to get eight hours of deep, worry-free sleep on a regular basis. Having him in bed next to me might as well be a heavy dose of melatonin the way it relaxes me and quiets any lingering, anxiety-riddled voices in my head.

"Wake up, sleepyhead." His familiar voice rumbles in the darkened room, the sweet sound vibrating through my entire body. "You're going to be late for work."

I let out a soft groan and open one eye, peering out the window. It still looks like nighttime out there, but the red numbers on the clock are saying otherwise. It's November, and the sun doesn't rise in Seattle until after seven A.M. I close my eyes again and run an index finger along the smooth underside of his arm, listening to the sound of the cold drizzle patter against the window. The changing of the seasons is one more reminder how swiftly time has passed. A year ago, I never would have imagined I would be waking up today in a new city, with a new job, beside someone I am falling in love with. I didn't think *any* woman got to be that lucky, let alone me, Cassandra Woodson. But, then again, back then I thought I was tethered to that easily googleable name like an anchor, destined to be forever immobile under its unbearable weight. Who was going to hire me with my name splashed all over the Internet, tied not only to a workplace assault, but now a seemingly seedy affair with a man the press had deemed Al Capone, Esquire? One quick Google search of Cassandra Woodson and I would no doubt be sunk.

The funny thing, though, is it was Google—ever the loyal friend—that ended up throwing me a life raft when I was treading water in despair. A week after Forest's arrest, as I was masochistically searching out and scrolling through the online articles detailing the shocking allegations against Forest, a targeted ad on the right-hand side of the screen caught my eye. It was for a service called DeleteYourself.com, which promised to wipe your entire identity clean from the Internet. *Because your baggage belongs on an airplane, not the Internet,* the ad read beside a picture of a distressed woman looking at a computer screen. It is truly eerie how targeted advertising seems to be able to read your mind these days. Scary, really, when you think about it.

A few clicks, a couple thousand dollars, and a legal name change later, Cassandra Woodson was eliminated and Meghan Smith was born. You can't get more anonymous and untraceable than that.

Having nothing to lose has its upsides, I suppose.

Meghan Smith is nothing like Cassandra Woodson. Cassandra Woodson fell for the lies that men like Forest and Landon told her. Meghan Smith, on the other hand, is much too smart for that. She would never let a man wrong her. Nor would any man ever even try.

I managed to slip out of my old life, like a snake shedding her skin, and began a new one. With my new name, I cleaned out my bank account, cashed in my 401(k), and got as far away from the East Coast as I could manage. For once in my life, I was completely unshackled from my past.

"I'm going to take a shower," Adam said now, dropping a kiss on my shoulder. "You can join me if you want . . ." He trails off, a sly smile tugging at his lips as he traces two fingers down the side of my body.

I bat his hand away playfully. "Then neither of us will make it to work, and you said you have an important meeting today. You take a shower and I'll make some coffee."

He exhales an exaggerated sigh. "It's not exactly a fair replacement, but I'll take it."

"Good, because I don't want to have to find you another job," I tease.

It wasn't hard to land a position as a legal recruiter once I arrived in Seattle. With the amount of research I'd done on my made-up profession for Forest, I was able to proficiently navigate the interview and appear to have every bit of the experience that my fudged résumé claimed I did. You know what they say—lawyers who can, do; lawyers who can't, recruit. It isn't exactly a dream job, but employers at legal staffing agencies are a lot less diligent in checking references than any law firm would be. Turns out, simply putting the phone number of a law firm in New York and a made-up name of a partner is enough to satisfy their criteria.

Serendipity. That's what I like to call it. Because six months after I started my job, Adam, a corporate lawyer with broad shoulders and an easy smile, walked into my office with his résumé and a desire to be placed in the in-house department of a tech firm. I managed to land him the position and acquire enough information about him in the process to slot myself into his life seamlessly.

It was a win-win.

"I brought over some of those Death Wish Coffee pods you like," I call after Adam now as I watch his cute backside disappear into the bathroom.

"You're the best," I hear him say before he closes the door.

Still smiling, I pad into the kitchen and pop a pod into the Keurig, replaying the compliment in my mind. *You're the best.* Nobody has ever said that to me before, and I have to resist the urge to grab a piece of paper and jot it down so I never forget it. I *am* the best, aren't I? While my coffee is spurting into a mug, I lean up against the counter and wonder how long it will be before I officially live here, at Adam's apartment with him. The location is a little close to the train for my taste, but I would listen to that clanging sound all night long if it meant being close to him.

I finally know what it means when people say they're so happy they could die. I could die.

Glancing around, I mentally take stock of the things I'll need to move over from my apartment when the time comes. The bookshelves I picked up at a vintage furniture store on Pine Street would look great on the far wall. And he definitely needs some new dishes so I'll bring my set over. A few of my vases would complete the transition from bachelor pad to a couple's nest. Of course, Adam hasn't asked me to move in with him yet, but I know that's just a formality at this point (I have a toothbrush and pajamas here after all). As my gaze moves around the open kitchen taking inventory, my eyes fix on something sitting on the glass-topped table in the dining nook.

Adam's laptop.

My heart rate ticks up. Adam usually keeps his laptop in a briefcase by the front door, rarely pulling it out when he isn't in the office, but there it is, out in the wild all alone like some kind of wounded gazelle. Without thinking about what I'm doing I take a few steps toward it, eyeballing it as if it might leap up and bite me.

I chew my nail for a second, considering, before I take one more step and let my hand fall and graze the keys gently, as if pressing any harder will detonate a bomb. An itch—raw and physical—begins to tingle across my skin down to my toes. I throw a peek over my shoulder in the direction of the bathroom. The shower is still running. Adam loves long showers. Lately, I find myself timing them. They average around twenty-one minutes. My eyes swing back to the open laptop, as a familiar feeling grows in my chest, like a trapped bird fluttering. Tentatively, I place my finger on the cold, metal trackpad and swirl. My eyes widen in disbelief. It isn't locked. Squinting, I realize I'm looking at his inbox. He must have been doing some work early this morning while I was still sleeping.

My palms grow damp, my fingers begin to twitch as my conscience struggles with my instinct to probe further. *Don't do it. Real relationships are supposed to be built on trust.* Or so I've heard. I nod decisively and begin to turn away before a tiny voice in the back of my head starts up. *But . . . it wouldn't be like I'm breaking in to his email. Adam left it here, open, almost like he WANTS to share it with me. We shouldn't really have any secrets between us, should we?*

I slide my finger along the trackpad, my breath quickening. Who knows when I'll have this opportunity again? Adam will be out of the shower soon, and the chance to do this will be lost. I toss a final look in his direction. Then, as quietly as possible, I raise my index finger and press it down firmly.

Click.

Just one look couldn't hurt.

ACKNOWLEDGMENTS

I AM DEEPLY grateful to my brilliant agent, Alexa Stark, for taking this book under her wing and shepherding me through this exciting process with creativity, patience, and expertise. I couldn't ask for a better advocate and am so fortunate to have you in my corner. Thank you also to Hilary Zaitz Michael at WME for embracing and championing my work.

A big thank you to my talented editor, Anne Speyer. From our first conversation, I could tell that you would enrich this story in ways I'd never thought of, and you have proven me right. Working with you has been an absolute pleasure and a privilege. Huge thanks to the many others at Ballantine for making this all come together —in particular Kara Welsh, Kim Hovey, Jennifer Hershey, Jesse Shuman, Quinne Rogers, Allison Schuster, Jennifer Garza, Jennifer Rodriguez, Diane Hobbing, Scott Biel, Rachel Walker, and Denise Cronin. I'm thrilled to be part of the Ballantine team.

I'm grateful for the support of my family and extended family, who continually encourage me and are generous with their praise. I can hardly express what their vote of confidence means to me. My heartfelt thanks to Mom and Dad, Ellen Montizambert, and the Bohakers, Akerlys, Magrakens, Lamprechts, Camerons, Royales, Brants, Brooks, and all of the Reef Road alums. If you're looking for them, they can be found at their local bookstore ensuring this novel is being prominently displayed.

For their friendship, generosity, levity, and support, thank you to the following fabulous people: Sara and Doug DiPasquale,

Marie-Claude Jones, Jennifer Mermel, Hyewon Miller, Ceylan Yazar, Joanna Rodriguez, Serena Palumbo, Kimberley Hall, Gosia Bawolska, and Michele Murphy. It takes a village and I'm so glad you all are part of mine.

Last but not least, thank you to the loves of my life. Gord, simply put, you make everything possible (including finishing an edit during the first few weeks of a pandemic). We're fifteen years into this party and still keeping the dream alive. Ethan and Elise, any day spent with you is my favorite day. You both fill my heart with pride and light up our world. Keep shining bright.

ABOUT THE AUTHOR

LINDSAY CAMERON worked as a corporate lawyer for many years in Vancouver and New York City before becoming a novelist. *Just One Look* is her suspense debut.

lindsayjcameron.com
Twitter: @LindsayJCameron
Instagram: @lindsayjcameronauthor